MW01257875

# THE WITCH'S ORCHARD

# THE WITCH'S ORCHARD

A Novel

ARCHER SULLIVAN

MINOTAUR BOOKS
NEW YORK

First published in the United States by Minotaur Books, an imprint of St. Martin's Publishing Group

THE WITCH'S ORCHARD. Copyright © 2025 by Affus Gaffus Productions. All rights reserved. Printed in the United States of America. For information, address St. Martin's Publishing Group, 120 Broadway, New York, NY 10271.

www.minotaurbooks.com

Designed by Gabriel Guma

The Library of Congress Cataloging-in-Publication Data is available upon request.

ISBN 978-1-250-33868-6 (hardcover)
ISBN 978-1-250-33869-3 (ebook)

Our books may be purchased in bulk for promotional, educational, or business use. Please contact your local bookseller or the Macmillan Corporate and Premium Sales Department at 1-800-221-7945, extension 5442, or by email at MacmillanSpecialMarkets@macmillan.com.

First Edition: 2025

10  9  8  7  6  5  4  3  2  1

For Scott

# THE WITCH'S ORCHARD

# ONE

ROXANNE'S HAS A SMELL that is somewhere between bacon grease, burnt coffee, and sticky-sweet pecan pie. The linoleum on the floor hasn't been replaced since the fifties but the proprietor changes about every season. A lot of people have tried to keep Roxanne's going, only to realize what bad shape the building's in and how being here all the time means that you also have a smell somewhere between bacon grease, burnt coffee, and sticky-sweet pecan pie.

That smell is part of the reason I'm meeting Max Andrews downstairs in Roxanne's instead of up in my diner-scented office. The other part is that I'm hungry and my client, driving all the way up from North Carolina to meet me, seemed like the kind of client who'd be buying. The kind of client I need now, since I pawned my watch (not for the first time) to pay my bills only a couple days ago. I'm hoping that Max will offer the kind of payday that'll get me out of my current hole.

But, when I see him, that hope evaporates into the greasy air.

"Thanks again for meeting me," he says, reaching out to shake my hand.

He's lanky and fine-boned under the layer of baby fat still clinging to his cheeks, and I realize the kid can't be more than twenty. His face is completely smooth, and his skin has the honey-brown remnants of a summer spent outdoors.

"No problem," I say, as he sits down across from me.

His mouth turns up into a soft smile and there's something quiet around the eyes, sad and sensitive. I think he's probably the kind of guy who always reads while he's eating.

The kind of guy I've always been friends with.

As if proving my point, we've barely ordered and sat down before Max pulls out a tattered old book. He's about to open it when Tonya approaches, carrying his biscuits and fresh fruit. Reluctantly, Max pushes the book aside to make way for the food, and Tonya gives me a half side-eye before sliding the heavy platter of sausage, biscuits and gravy, fried apples, and two over-easy eggs in front of me.

"You came a long way," I say, once Tonya's gone. "What's the drive from down there?"

"Not bad. About six hours."

There's a pause before he says, "I wanted to meet you in person."

I take a big bite of sausage and gravy and watch as the poor kid looks back and forth between the book and his breakfast. He spears an apple slice on his fork and bites half of it off, gives me a weak smile, folds his hands together under the table like he's a little boy waiting to be dismissed from dinner. He stares at me for a few seconds while I guzzle coffee.

"Not what you pictured?" I ask him.

There is no photograph on my website, and I've noticed that I—a short, skinny, freckled woman in her early thirties with no makeup and dishwater blond hair pulled into a ponytail so often it retains the shape when let down—am not what they've expected when they've seen the résumé. The Air Force service, the degrees, the brief stint in private security, the amateur Muay Thai fights.

He gives me an apologetic shrug that I feel pretty sure means, "I thought you'd look older and wiser and not have mustard stains on your shirt." Or, perhaps, "I thought you'd be a man. A big one with a mean scowl and a gun."

The website just says, "A. Gore: Private Investigator."

Though, to my credit, I do have a mean scowl. And a gun.

"Okay," I say, wiping some gravy from my mouth. "Tell me why you're here."

He looks relieved, pushes the plate toward the corner of the table, slides the book in front of him, turns it around so it's oriented for my reading pleasure, and swings it open to a marked page.

This isn't a regular book. It's a scrapbook.

The heavy paper is plastered with an 8-by-10 picture of a little girl. This isn't really what I expected. Guys like Max usually want me to find an ex-girlfriend or maybe find out what an ex-girlfriend did with their savings. Guys like Max don't usually pull out Sears portraits of sweet-looking little girls, and I know, glancing down at the kid and then back up to Max's intense gaze, that this is not a regular job. This is a sad job. Nobody shows a PI a picture of a kid because everything is going just great.

I sigh and study the photo. The girl looks like a little princess with her delicate, Cupid's bow mouth, glossy waves of honey-brown hair, and big hazel eyes. She's wearing a pink dress with a white Peter Pan collar, and though she's smiling straight at the camera, it's a soft, timid smile. Eager to please. The resemblance is clear.

"My sister," Max says. "Molly Andrews."

He turns the page. Now there's another picture and my heart plummets, inexplicably, at the sight.

"An applehead doll," I say.

He lets out a silent laugh and there's a hint of surprise in his eyes. "You know what they are?"

"I'm not from Louisville," I say. "I grew up in a dinky holler in Southern Kentucky. My granny used to make those things."

"A lot of grannies used to," Max says.

We both look down at the photo of the doll, its shriveled apple head resembling an old lady, its black eyes—mere cavities in the apple flesh—seeming deep and endless. It wears a bright red dress with white lace at the neck and a white petticoat underneath. These old-timey dolls are cute or nightmarish depending on who you ask, but considering the context, I'm guessing Max is in the latter category.

Max turns the page again and there's a newspaper article from *The Quartz Creek Herald* that reads, "Third Girl Taken." He points at the spread of black-and-white photos on the front page.

"When I was eight years old, three little girls in my town were kidnapped. The first was Jessica Hoyle." He turns the page to show me a girl who looks about four or five, with pale blond hair and expressive blue eyes. "And the second was Olivia Jacobs." He points at a picture of a girl with porcelain skin, her gaze directed off camera, her chestnut hair curly and free.

"Both times," Max says, "an applehead doll was left in their place."

"Oh . . ." I say. And what I want to say is "Jesus Christ. That's horrible." Which isn't new or helpful information for the brother of one of the girls who was taken and who has clearly been keeping a scrapbook with all the details of the crime ever since.

"After Olivia Jacobs was taken, it was pretty clear something was going on," Max says. "Parents started guarding their kids, not letting them leave the house, no playing in the park without an adult around. But then . . . about two weeks after she was kidnapped, Olivia was brought back."

"Brought *back?*" I lean forward, look closer at Olivia, at the page opposite to Jessica.

"Yeah," Max says. "And then four days after she was returned, my sister was taken. And an applehead doll was left in *her* place."

My heart picks up speed, looking at these kids, these little girls all part of something strange and horrific. I look away from the book and back at Max, and his haunted, intense, birdlike quality makes a lot more sense now.

"I was at home," he volunteers. "I had a piano lesson that day. My mom was out in the garden, weeding. The last time I saw Molly, she was sitting on the couch watching *Snow White*. My mom checked on her before she went out and Molly was asleep. I went outside to play after my lesson and, when I came back inside, she was just . . ."

"Gone," I say, making myself look at the two other girls. "And they never found Jessica?"

"No," he says, shaking his head. "Only Olivia was ever returned."

He flips back to the first photograph, the one of Molly, and says, "Molly was four years old in this picture. It was taken about a week before she was kidnapped. It's the last picture of her we ever got."

"But there must have been an investigation," I say.

"The cops looked. We don't have much in Quartz Creek. Just the county sheriff's station, which consists of the sheriff and five deputies. Fish and wildlife. The FBI came down after Molly disappeared. The search went on for about a year, but . . ."

"Nothing."

I look back at the newspaper article, check the date. The article is ten years old. I think back to my own life, a decade in the past. I grew up only a few hours from Max and his family but I was in the Air Force when the kidnappings occurred. I was half a world away, trying hard to forget all the reasons I'd joined to begin with.

"It's like they vanished," he says breathily. He spreads his hands in front of me like he's offering something. Or begging for something. "I started this . . . casebook, as I thought of it, a couple years later. I was about ten. I just . . . I felt like I needed to do something. I still do."

"Max . . ." I start.

"I know," he says. "I know. I started working when I was fourteen, trying to save up. I did lawn work and I waited tables until the steak house closed down. There's not a lot of work in Quartz Creek. So, I fixed up an old cabin on our property. I've been renting it out as an Airbnb— mostly to fishermen—it's not fancy or anything but I've got money. And I can offer you room and board so—"

"Max . . ." I try, but there's no stopping him at this point. He'd probably practiced this spiel all the way from Western North Carolina.

"My folks hired a PI about a year after my sister disappeared, but they could only get the best one they could afford and that wasn't much. He poked around for a while, never turned up anything."

The gravy on my plate is cold now, congealed and gray. I push the plate aside and pick up my coffee, take a long drink.

"I want to hire you, Miss Gore. I need to do this."

After a moment I say, "Max, after this long, the odds—"

"I know. But that's why I came here. In person. I wanted to meet you. I read about you. I know you're the one who solved the Lehman case."

I let out a sigh.

"The Lehman case was—"

"It was cold for nine years," he says.

"Esther Lehman went missing because she *wanted* to go missing," I say. "The case was cold because she didn't *want* to be found."

"But you found her."

I shrug and say, "The woman had expensive taste in shoes."

"And everyone else missed it. I—listen, I read that you're from Appalachia. You get mountain towns, right? Mountain people? That's why I'm here. That's why I'm trying to hire *you*."

I know, instantly, what he means. Despite cell towers and spreading networks of broadband, mountain towns have retained a certain insular quality, hanging on to old traditions, old ways of speaking, old hierarchies with elders at the top. People in cities—living, working, talking at a fast clip—experience the quiet, slow pace that permeates these communities, and they assume a slowness of mind, a lack of character. Or, worse, they base everything they know about mountain people on the stereotypes in the media. And I should know. Jokes about illiteracy, incest, and shoelessness elicited more than one broken nose while I was in the Air Force.

I look again at the picture of Max's sister, Molly, and sigh.

"Max, I know you know this but . . . little girls, this long . . ."

"Please," he says. "I can give you eight hundred a day plus room and board. My cabin has a five-star rating. There's a brochure in the casebook." He pulls it out and slides it across the table to me and continues, "And the access code is on there. It's keyless entry. The internet isn't great; it's satellite. But the cell coverage is pretty good. The property's nice. It's right next to Quartz Creek."

"Max—"

"My friend Shiloh runs a bakery there. She said you can have anything you want, on the house. She makes great cinnamon rolls. And I can give you the casebook, obviously, and—"

"What about your parents?"

He bites his lips together for a moment, then says, "My mom's not around anymore. My dad's a long-haul trucker so . . . Well, he's not really around much either. I'm pretty much on my own."

The look in his eyes isn't just desperation but conviction, determination. I realize there's something more to Max than his quiet, gentle outer nature. There is something steady underneath, honed to hardness. He could've hired a big-city PI from Charlotte but he's here, after a long road trip, to hire me, a mountain girl whose granny also made applehead dolls.

"Miss Gore," he says. "Just look. That's all I'm asking. I need to do this. Please."

In his voice, I hear an echo of my own. Some hardheaded strength born out of too many years spent in desperation. Something honest and earnest and determined. And I know, already, that I can't say no. I can't tell this kid to drive all the way back to North Carolina, to forget about his sister, to go on with his life.

"I'll give you a week," I say, before I can take it back. "I will come to your town. I will read your casebook. I will poke around and stir shit up and ask a lot of questions that make people uncomfortable. You understand?"

"I . . . yes."

"Cases like this," I say. "With kids involved? They make people edgy, uncomfortable. It dredges up stuff they don't like. They don't like to think their town is the kind of place where little girls are kidnapped, don't like to think it was this neighbor or that one. It's easier to just hope it never happens again, easier to forget it."

"Not for me," Max says, his eyes burning mine, his mouth set.

"This is going to be like poking an old hornet's nest to see if there are any angry hornets still buzzing around inside. You understand?"

"Yeah," Max says. "I understand."

"All right," I say. "I'll come down and I'll see what I can do. But I can't promise I'll find *anything.* It's been a long time."

And I stop myself before I say, "There might not be anything left to find."

"When can you start?"

Tonya steps up to the table, puts down the check, and asks, "You need a box, Annie?"

"Yeah," I say. "And get one for him too."

"Oh, I don't need—" Max starts, sliding a card into the plastic envelope on the check holder.

I shrug. "I'll take it then."

She grabs the payment and leaves. I think about the smell of bacon grease upstairs, the second floor divided into two rooms: my office and my tiny studio apartment. I think about the desk topped with unpaid bills, the little refrigerator I can't keep stocked, and the three loads of dirty jeans and T-shirts I need to haul down to the Laundromat.

"Your rental have a washer/dryer?"

"Um. Yes? They're not new or anything. I got them secondhand so—"

"I'll drive down this evening," I say. "Start first thing tomorrow. That okay with you?"

He nods, so excited he's practically vibrating.

"Max," I say. "You need to know: I probably won't find anything. You might pay me fifty-six hundred dollars just to come down to your town and get people riled up. You understand?"

"Yeah," he says. "I just . . . It's something I have to do. I have to try."

"Okay," I say. "I'll be there."

"Great," he says, standing, brushing nonexistent crumbs off his jeans. "Great." He reaches a hand toward me and I shake it, feel the calluses and taut muscles of hard work, hope I'm not a waste of his money. But all a PI can ever do is the job they're paid to do. I'm being paid to look—as hard as I can—and whatever hidden truths come to the surface is beyond my control.

"Thank you, Ms. Gore."

"Annie," I say. "Call me Annie."

"Okay," he says. "I'll see you later." And then he's gone.

Tonya comes back over to the table with two empty Styrofoam boxes and I start shoveling food in. I figure I'll take it all upstairs, reheat it on my hot plate, eat at my little kitchen counter while I go through Max's notes.

"What's with him?" Tonya asks, watching as Max gets into his old Toyota pickup and pulls out of the lot.

"Tonya, if I told you three little girls were kidnapped a decade ago and never found, what would you think happened to them?"

She sniffs, looks up at the grease-coated ceiling for a moment, taps her maroon acrylic nails against her bottom lip. "Dead," she finally says. "Or maybe sold off to some foreign billionaire."

"Hmm," I say. I scrape Max's fruit and biscuits and the pat of probably-not-butter into the other container.

"Or in some pervert's basement somewhere," she continues.

I throw her a look and she catches it, cocks an eyebrow at me, and says, "What? I listen to a lot of true crime podcasts. Usually it's one of those. If they're ever found at all. And usually they're not. Is that what you've been hired to do? Track down three little girls?"

"No, actually. One of those little girls was returned like they got her from Walmart."

"Returned?"

"Yeah."

"Why?"

"It's weird, right?" I say. "But look at this."

I turn to the page of the applehead dolls and watch as a full-body shiver crawls over Tonya's skin and she makes a noise somewhere between "Gaah" and "Eeeww."

"Applehead dolls," I say. "Or . . . just apple dolls."

"Looks like some hillbilly horseshit," Tonya says. It's harsh, but it's self-defense. No one outside of the mountains has any affection for shriveled-up old-lady dolls and I can't really blame them. "What the hell kind of town is this?"

I close up the boxes and stand, stacking them on top of each other. I grab my bag and the scrapbook and maneuver everything into a configuration I can get up the narrow staircase to my office-partment.

"That's what I'm gonna find out," I say, and point with my freest finger at the nearly empty mug on the table. "Any chance I could get a refill to go?"

# TWO

THE SUN IS SETTING by the time I pull onto the main (and only) drag of Quartz Creek, North Carolina. It's a little run-down mountain town like a lot of other little run-down mountain towns where enterprise and lack of internet have drained away most of the population over eighteen and under forty. There's a couple of boarded-up storefronts on Main Street but there's also a pharmacy, a hair salon, and an apparently flourishing funeral parlor with a sign out front that says to ask inside about specials.

I follow the directions on my phone through the other side of town and onto a gravel road under a canopy of orange, scarlet, and yellow. The brilliant smudge of saffron in the sky beyond the mountains sets the trees alight and I smile at the sight in spite of myself. I'd just about forgotten how beautiful Appalachia is in the fall. Just about gotten far enough away in miles and years from that other, younger Annie in that other run-down, beautiful place to let myself forget.

The engine in my beautiful amber Datsun 260Z rumbles, grumbles, and pops as I roll slowly down the road, passing a row of apple trees— their fruit already fallen—and an old white farmhouse.

"Almost there, Honey," I say, patting Honey's steering wheel.

Honey growls. She's tired. So am I.

Honey is an old lady now and since she came into my life, after I left the Air Force six years before, I've done my best to take care of her, just as she takes care of me.

"Almost there," I say again, reassuring her. Or myself.

I turn in at a wooden sign that says, "Crow Caw Cabin."

The light on the porch of the little A-frame cabin shines bright. The roof is black and a crow is perched at the top. He's so still that, at first, I think he's sculptural. Some kind of interesting weather vane. But then he tilts his head this way and that, staring at me. He flutters his wings and blinks, then takes flight and folds himself into the gathering dark.

I park, turn off the car, listen as Honey's straight six finally sputters and quits. I fight with the trunk for a minute before it lurches open and reveals two Air Force duffels of dirty laundry and a brown paper bag filled with peanut butter, bread, bananas, and beer. The four main food groups.

I load everything inside the cozy cabin and have a look around. The place is a symphony in wood. Wood walls, wood floors, wood-framed sofa. The bedroom at the end of the cabin boasts an antique-looking double bed stacked with quilts. The little utilitarian bathroom features a shower stall that's actually bigger than the teensy closet bathroom in my apartment. Back in the kitchen, I grin when I open the fridge to find yet *more* beer, sandwich supplies, a gallon of whole milk, a carton of eggs, and thick bacon.

"Someone's been shopping," I say, grabbing a dark stout and popping the top with a bottle opener carved in the shape of a fish that sticks to the fridge. I unload half of one of the duffels into the washing machine with plenty of Max's store-brand detergent before heading back into the living room, where I discover a basketful of muffins, cookies, and banana bread with a note on stationery from Shiloh's Sweet Treats that says, *"Thanks for helping out. Call if you need anything—Shiloh Evers."*

Shiloh, I think, is probably the one who did all the shopping in addition to the baking, and I wonder about her relationship to Max as I grab a ginger cookie. I bite into it with a snap, then pick up my old rucksack and plop onto the sofa, pull out Max's casebook, and open it up along with a brand-new gas station–procured spiral-bound notebook and pen. I flip through the pictures and land on a photo of a white farmhouse with a wraparound porch and black shingle roof.

There's a knock at the door. I look toward my rucksack where my gun sits in its locked hard case and remind myself I haven't pissed off anyone in Quartz Creek enough (yet) to dig it out and load it. Instead, I jump up and open the door to find Max Andrews.

"You're a little later than I thought," he says. "Everything okay?"

"Yeah." I push the door all the way open and he comes inside. "When you drive a fifty-year-old car, a six-hour drive sometimes takes eight hours. It's its own kind of time travel."

"Oh. Okay." He glances out at my ancient Datsun, then back to me. I expect him to tell me how beautiful Honey is and what a wonderful machine she must be, a carriage fit for a king.

"I, um . . . I tried to kind of stock the place. Well, Shiloh did most of it. But if you need anything, let me know."

Then again, not everyone can appreciate Honey's unique specialness.

"I think I'm good," I say. "I've got my poking stick all sharpened up."

"Your . . ."

"For the hornet's nest we talked about."

"Oh."

I take a drink of my beer, watch Max put his hands in his pockets and take them back out.

"The house I passed on my way in," I say. "It's the house you grew up in, right? You and your dad still live there?"

His gaze shifts away from me, out the door and east, toward the white farmhouse.

"Yeah," he says. He opens his mouth to say something else but then just says again, "Yeah."

Can't have this conversation all by myself so I say, "Tell me what happened after your sister was taken. You were eight, right?"

"Yeah," he says. Then, there's a long pause before he starts again. "Things got really rocky for my folks after that. My dad used to be a biology teacher at the high school. My mom was a farm girl, I guess. This was her land, originally, her family's land. She rented out some of the fields to local farmers. But she kept the land closest to the house for us. She had a vegetable garden, flower beds. She kept chickens, an old pony, and a couple goats in the barn."

"Oh," I say. "Cool. So . . . your dad wasn't home that day."

"No," Max says. "He was at school. It was summer but he was doing some kind of in-service teacher training thing."

"And you said you had a piano lesson that morning? What was the name of your piano teacher?"

"Oh. It's Mrs. Drake. Deena Drake. She doesn't live too far from here."

"Okay, I need her information if you have it."

"Okay," he says. "I'll text it to you."

"So, you said your dad is a trucker now? But he used to be a teacher?"

"Oh . . . right . . . after Molly—" He stops and takes a deep breath. "Well, after she was taken, he . . . had a hard time being around. He took the trucking job because it paid well and we still got insurance and stuff. He's been doing it ever since."

"And your mom—"

"My mom shot herself three years after Molly was taken. I was eleven."

My mouth snaps shut. I hadn't had time to scour the databases for background before I left. I knew I'd end up stopping at least once to give Honey a drink of oil and then again to let her cool down. I'd just packed up and got on the road. But I should've expected this. I'd seen the damage that befalls a family when they lose a child. And the death of Max's mom correlated only too well with when he started keeping the casebook.

"I'm sorry," I say, and mean it. I get up and get Max a glass of water, if for no other reason than to give him a break.

"Thanks," he says, and takes a long drink.

I feel like he's probably malnourished and some latent mountain woman instinct makes me want to hand him a peanut butter sandwich and watch while he eats it.

"I'm sorry," I say again. As if I can't say it enough.

"It's been a long time," he says eventually. "But that's part of why I had to . . . to look for someone to help me. I could never have solved it on my own."

*And I probably can't either.*

Outside, there's a scream. Long and loud and hoarse.

"The hell was that?" I ask.

He tilts his head toward the door.

"It's the crows," he says.

The noise screeches again. Low at first and then high and strained and throaty. I shudder—can't help myself.

I say, "What? No, that doesn't sound like a crow. Do crows even call at night?"

The scream comes again. Shorter this time. Sharper.

"The ones here do," he says. "Out in the forest there's this big rock formation that's some kind of natural amplifier. The crows found it a long time ago and they go out there and . . ."

"Raise hell?"

He breathes out a half laugh, half sigh, nods.

"There's a story. It's in the book but . . ."

"What?"

"It's just an old legend. And . . . probably illegible. I wrote it down when I was a kid."

"Okay. Tell it to me."

"It's just a story," he says.

"Tell it to me," I repeat, and hold his gaze so he knows I won't be budged.

He takes a deep breath. The door is still cracked and the crows are still screaming and a cool fall wind blows in and rattles a framed print above the TV. I hadn't noticed it before. A monochrome field of corn sways in the breeze and, above it, a swirling spiral of crows fades into the stormy sky. It's masterfully done, and I think briefly that I should know the artist but no name comes to mind.

"There was an ancient witch who lived on the mountain," Max says, pulling my attention back to the moment. "That's what the stories say. An old woman who lived here—in a house in the middle of an enchanted apple grove—when the town was first formed. She had two beautiful daughters and men from the town started coming around, offering to marry the girls."

"And the witch did not approve."

"No. She wanted to protect them. She turned her first daughter into a bluebird and her second into a robin and she put them in a golden cage. Every day she sang to them, and they kept her company just like always. And the witch was happy. But one day, when she opened the door to feed them, they flew away. She turned herself into a crow so that she could catch up with them, fly with them, and keep them. Forever."

Max looks straight ahead, seeming to have forgotten that I'm even there. As if he's just talking to himself, he keeps going.

"But the story goes that the girls *did* get away. That she was too late— she didn't catch her daughters. The witch cried and screamed for them, but they never returned. The story says the other crows learned to scream from her and they scream every night in her memory."

"Oh wow."

"Yeah," he says, finally meeting my eyes. He gives me a bittersweet smile. "The Witch of Quartz Creek. It's an old story. My mom used to tell it to me; she got it from her granny, I think."

"You put the story in the casebook," I say.

"That's right."

"You think they're connected?"

He shrugs. "When I was little I did. I thought the witch had stolen my sister."

"And now?"

He stands, sets his half-full water glass down on the coffee table, wipes the condensation from his hands onto his apron.

"Now, I hired you to find out."

"Fair enough," I say.

"Let me know if you need anything," he says.

We say good night and then he's gone, back up the gravel path that twists through the hedgerow to the white farmhouse. I finish my beer, open my notebook, and sit down with what Max refers to as his casebook but what is, in reality, a little boy's scrapbook.

Flipping through, I find a few drawings of witches and crows and a few Xeroxes of local newspaper articles from the time of his sister's disappearance. There are drawings of applehead dolls and pictures of them printed off the internet along with printed posts from a couple true crime bloggers. I look up the blogs and find them now defunct and, while I'm scrolling through old news articles on my phone, it buzzes and my aunt Tina's face appears on the screen.

I answer the video call and say, "Hey, you get my note?"

"Yeah," Tina says. "North Carolina? That's a hell of a haul. I'm worried about my girl."

"I'm fine."

"I'm talking about Honey," she says, rolling her eyes.

Tina runs a classic-car garage in Louisville and her primary concern where I'm involved mostly runs along Honey's well-being, whether I'm treating her right—whether she needs a tune-up, whether I shouldn't take some time off and give Honey a vacation and spa treatment in her garage. Now I can see Tina's dimly lit kitchen behind her and I know she probably only just got home from work.

"Tina, do you remember about ten years ago when three little girls were kidnapped in the mountains in North Carolina and applehead dolls were left in their place?"

"Sure," Tina says. She's heating up a bowl of something in the microwave. Probably leftovers cooked and saved by her much more domestically inclined partner, Mel. I watch as she puts her big fists on her hips and waits. Tina's a thick woman with extra-large forearms, full-sleeve tattoos, and permanently grease-stained fingernails that suggest she could pull and strip an engine block in under twenty minutes. Which wouldn't be far off.

She looks from the microwave to the phone and says, "There was something weird about it, right? Wasn't one of them brought back the next day?"

"Two weeks," I say. "But yes."

"I always figured it was some religious nutbar," Tina says. "You know, serial killer doing satanic rituals. Something like that."

The microwave dings and Tina uses a pot holder to remove the steaming spaghetti and meatballs.

"Tina, you watch too much *X-Files*."

"And I maintain that you watch too little. It's a modern classic. 'Course, if I had the kind of dreams you—God, what is that noise?"

"On my end?"

"Yeah. It sounds like someone's dragging a sack of cats down a gravel driveway."

"Crows," I say.

"Bullshit."

"It's true. It's a . . . it's a whole thing here."

She pulls a fork from a drawer and a beer from the fridge and sits down at her kitchen counter to eat. She moves the noodles and meat around with a squashy sound and then takes a big bite and says, "All jokes aside, those kids are probably long dead."

"I know."

"Then what are you doing down there? There must be people here who'll pay you to snoop around and be a pain in the ass."

"Yeah," I say. "There are. But I couldn't turn the guy down."

"That hot, huh?"

"That young," I say. "He's just a kid. Looking for his sister. He looks . . . haunted."

"Ah," she says. Like she gets it. Like she remembers helping out another sad, determined, haunted kid.

"Anyway, I said I'd look. So, I'm gonna look."

"Well, I know that tone. No use arguing with you. But you're a long way from home so just watch your ass, all right?"

"I will."

"And Honey's."

"I will."

We hang up and I look back down at Max's casebook, a picture of his sister I'd left it open to. In this photo, she and Max are playing at a park. He's pushing her on a swing and she is slightly blurred, her hair a brown swoosh behind her, her head cocked back in laughter, her mouth wide open. Beside them another little boy pushes another little girl on another swing. It is any old summer day. For this other little boy and girl, a hundred or a thousand of such instances probably lie in a heap of nearly forgotten memories. But, because Molly was taken soon after this picture was snapped, this memory, this moment, becomes important, immortal. Her laugh, frozen forever in a hazy blur, is where she ends.

Unless I find her.

"Okay," I say to myself. "That's enough."

I close the scrapbook, wander into the bedroom, curl up in the quilts, and fall asleep to the screaming song of the crows.

# THREE

THE PHONE BUZZES AGAINST the wood bedside table and I pick it up.

"It's still fucking dark, Leo."

He chuckles on the other end and I grumble, rubbing at the crust in my eyes.

"Yeah, but you're already awake," he says. And he's not wrong. I wake up just before dawn pretty much every day, whether I like it or not. (I don't.)

I grumble and Leo says, "Sleep okay?"

"Sure," I say. And Leo calls, just about every day, whether I like it or not. (I do.)

Despite the crows, my sleep was dreamless and so deep that I woke slowly to a sluggish predawn chill and lay there, bundled in my covers, waiting for the day and, with it, Leo's call. Now, I'm sitting up, tugging my pre-tied running shoes onto my bare feet. This is how I begin every morning.

"Listen, I got an opening over here," he says. "One of my guys up and got the flu. I'm not taking his congested ass anywhere."

"So, get another guy," I say. I stand and wobble into the unfamiliar bathroom, search for the light switch, find it, squint at my reflection in the too-bright glare, and flick the switch back off. I turn on the speaker and put the phone down on the vanity while I pee.

"I don't want another guy," Leo says. His voice is earthy and rich and smooth, like the rest of him. He's a top-shelf product I could never afford.

"Well, I have a job," I say, washing my hands, my face.

"Where are you?"

"North Carolina. The mountains."

"You drive that ancient car all the way down there? Over those hills?"

"If you're talking about Honey, my beautiful and pristine classic 260Z, then yes. I did. We had a wonderful trip, thank you."

He snorts. Leo loves Honey and always dotes on her when he's in town, but he still never misses an opportunity to needle me about using her as my daily driver, arguing that I should get something more dependable for long rides. I always think it sounds like a good idea until I go outside and start up Honey and sink into the familiar purr of her engine.

"I could pay you better," he says. "We got a hell of a contract at the moment."

I take the phone into the kitchen with me, fill a glass of water from the tap.

"I tried that, remember? Two months was as much as I could do. I don't want to work private security for some rich dick who only needs private security because he's constantly screwing people over."

Leo laughs a little. I hear a light spoon clinking against delicate china. Coffee, two sugars, a splash of heavy whipping cream, I remember, smile to myself. The smell of Leo's coffee rushes back to me. The smell of Leo isn't far behind. Faint hints of sandalwood, gunpowder, red wine.

"So you're working for some redneck instead?"

A hint of his South Texas accent comes through. Like me, he's mostly lost his regional dialect but, unlike me, it was intentional. Meeting Leo for the first time, you'd never guess his origins. I'd known him for more than a year before I ever even had a clue.

"Annie," he says. "Just what are you into?"

"Old kidnapping case."

"Stirring up shit," he says, like he's just affirming what he already thought. He's not wrong.

"The kid's probably long gone," I say. "Her big brother hired me. I'm probably getting paid just to go around asking questions that make people feel weird."

"Probably." There's a pause while he takes a sip. "You bring your gun?"

"Yeah."

"Take it with you. Those rednecks are all packing heat. You might as well be too."

"It's an old case, Leo."

"Annie, take your piece."

I roll my eyes. On his end, there's a high *bing* sound, muffled. Maybe an elevator down the hallway. I think he's in a hotel and I picture him somewhere sunny—an open window, a breeze billowing an expensive, sheer curtain. Leo is all low-key luxury. From his tailored T-shirts and designer leather jackets to his three-hundred-dollar haircut that looks exactly as unkempt as he likes, he is the model of unpretentious pretension and, somehow, I've never been able to hate him for it.

"Wheels up tomorrow. Nineteen hundred. You sure you don't want a ride?"

"Positive."

There's another pause where we both just breathe, almost silent. On his side, I hear the bells of a distant church. It's twelve o'clock, wherever he is. Monaco, maybe. Or Madrid, Naples. Beautiful European cities with grand histories and dramatic architecture. Places like that suit Leo.

I look out the window of the cabin, into the predawn gloom, the still-violet light on the cold, dewy grass. My own car in the drive is the nearest sign of human activity. Beyond that, a gravel road, an old farmhouse, a dying town. Places like *this* suit me.

"You know you can call me," Leo says. "You can always call me."

"I know," I say.

"Watch your six, Gore."

"Always," I say. "You too."

We hang up. I glance at the phone. It's not even eight o'clock on Monday morning, the fog not even burned off the ground. It's this quiet, solitary, silvery nature of early morning that, despite my chronic lack of sleep, makes this my favorite time of day. I slide the phone into my pocket, take another drink of water, pull on my light, reflective jacket, and head out the door.

There's a path behind the cabin and I take it. I follow it all the way to the edge of a gorge and down to a fast-running creek. Quartz Creek, I guess. I'm not a fast runner but I'm steady. My heart rate picks up and then beats out a steady rhythm and, as my feet tread over the wet, fallen leaves, I fantasize about a life where I rented this cabin for the sole purpose of standing in this water, waders up to my chest, casting a line over and over and over, hoping for a plump mountain trout. It's a quieter life. Slow and contemplative. The kind of life I've never had. The kind that's better imagined than lived. At least for me.

I cross the creek at a decrepit bridge and then jog up the gentle slope of the opposite bank. There, after maybe ten yards on the trail, I spot what must be the circle of stones Max mentioned. I slow down as I get nearer. My breath and heart rate should be falling but they're not. As I reach a circle of gray boulders, the huge stones embedded with shimmering quartz, my heartbeat quickens. An involuntary shiver races across my shoulder blades. Still, I step into the center and immediately hear what Max was talking about. Every sound is weirdly amplified here. I reach down, pick up a dead twig, snap it in half.

*SNAP. Snap. snap.*

It echoes.

Another shiver.

I snap one of the half twigs in half again.

*SNAP. Snap. snap.*

And then I pause. It's not just the nearness of the stones, the eeriness of the echoes that have pricked my subconscious. I realize, with latent animal instinct, that I am being watched. My heart is hammering now and I'm surprised I can't hear it thumping, echoing off the surface of the rocks. I reach for my gun and remember I didn't bring it. No reason to run with a gun in the middle of the woods, I'd thought.

I turn and lock eyes with an old woman standing just outside the stone circle. Her frizzy, steel gray hair is piled on her head. She wears canvas pants and a long, black threadbare cardigan over a T-shirt that says, "Virginia Is for Lovers." She's carrying two baskets in her red-knuckled hands and her beetle black eyes narrow as she says, "Just who the hell are you?"

"Annie Gore," I say. My voice echoes and comes back to me tight and thin with a sharp tinge of fear. I step outside the stones before I have to listen to it anymore. "I'm a private investigator."

"Why you running around in my goddamned forest?"

"This is *your* forest?"

She gives me a curt nod.

"I thought it was Andrews land," I say. "I'm working for Max."

"This about his sister?" she asks.

"Yeah."

She sniffs and looks down into her basket. The wind catches wild strands of her hair and her oversized sweater billows and flaps like the wings of a crow. I can't help but think of the Witch of Quartz Creek and her two doomed daughters.

"Damn shame," she says. She takes a few steps closer, her old hiking boots crunching over the leaves, and looks me up and down. "You ain't a city girl."

"No," I say.

She looks into my eyes, then follows the line of my cheek, my brow, my nose. I imagine she sees the softness of my features—a face that stays round even when the rest of me is skinny—marred by a couple of thin, white scars, a once-straight nose previously broken and never set quite right.

I give her the same studying. She's a plump lady but not soft. She's strong-boned with broad shoulders and warm olive skin. Deep lines crease her forehead, the space between her eyebrows. Her eyes are sharp and wary as a fox.

"Military," she says, a guess.

I don't reply.

A cold breeze slices the air between us and the sheen of sweat that had accumulated on my body now stings with chill. Goose bumps erupt on my arms and legs.

The woman looks in the direction from which the breeze comes. The wind pushes the hair off her face and she stares into it, her nose reddening, water glistening in her eyes. The wind shimmies around the high stones behind me and whistles as it passes, a high keening.

"Bad things coming," she says, almost a whisper. She looks back at me as the breeze dies down. "You got here just in time, Miss Gore."

"Bad things?"

She doesn't answer, just watches me some more, eyes searching. She frowns.

"I live up the hill a little ways. There's a trail," she says.

She points with a gnarled finger to the north, and I see a slender dirt trail, knobbed with exposed tree roots, winding its way farther up the hill. She says, "I've got to finish my work this morning. You can come by later on, when you want answers."

Then she turns with her basket and walks away.

There's a flap and scrabble behind me and I turn to see a crow landing on the nearest high stone.

"CAAW!" it screams, and the scream bounces around the rocks, echoing madly. I watch the crow for a moment, watch it prune its oil black wings, listen to the *scritch-scratch* of its feet on the rough texture of the stone. I turn back to look for the old woman and find that she is gone.

I look at the crow again.

"Where'd she go?" I ask.

The crow caws, then flaps its wings and flies away.

I look at my phone. It's been half an hour, I realize. Time to head back.

I glance into the forest but, again, I don't see the old woman. I make a mental note to ask Max about her, about the land and who owns it. But I can't ask about the eeriness of her gaze. How it felt like there were insects under my skin while she looked me up and down. Looked into me.

"The Witch of Quartz Creek," I breathe. And then I make myself laugh. And it sounds false. I start jogging back toward the cabin, picking up my pace as I do.

By the time I'm keying my way inside, I've worked up a good sweat and I've got a head full of questions for the townsfolk of Quartz Creek, North Carolina. After another twenty minutes I'm showered and dressed in a black T-shirt, jeans, and a "take me seriously" no-wrinkle charcoal blazer.

I grab my keys from the bedside table, open the drawer. When I'd left the service and got my PI license, I bought a cheap, lightweight .22 revolver at a local gun show.

"What are you trying to do?" Leo said when I told him. He was in a jungle somewhere, a million miles away, and his voice crackled through the line to me. "Gun like that, you shoot someone, you're just gonna piss 'im off."

"Best I could afford."

"Annie, you're little."

"Fuck off," I'd said, though he was right. With a high ponytail and thick-soled boots I barely scrape five-three.

"You get into a mess with anyone big and strong and, like as not, you pull out that twenty-two and they're gonna do one of two things: blow you away with their bigger gun or laugh in your face and *then* blow you away."

"A private eye almost never shoots their gun, Leo."

He chuckled and said, "Annie, you know as well as I do: if you're gonna carry a gun, you'd better be ready to use it."

I received a custom .357 Korth Mongoose two days later. Two-and-three-quarter-inch barrel, all blacked out, in a custom purpleheart wood box with the words "Annie Get Your Gun" engraved on the inside of the lid. A four-thousand-dollar gun, as much a piece of art as a deadly weapon. I never needed to ask where it came from.

Now, I look down at the cool black revolver in its glossy box.

"Annie get your gun," I read out loud. Though it's Leo's voice echoing in my mind.

I pick up the gun, check it, thrust it into the holster that clips into the back of my jeans, and walk out the door.

# FOUR

I T'S NOT EVEN A two-minute drive from Crow Caw Cabin, back down the gravel lane, to Max's family farmhouse. I pull Honey around and into Max's driveway, which winds around the house, and park behind Max's truck. Honey's engine is barely warm and she settles with a grunt.

"Let's get started," I say to myself.

I follow the stone path to the porch and then look around as I climb the steps. The porch is clean and an old porch swing hangs on one end. There are no pots of autumnal mums, no decorations, no water bowl for a dog or cat, no welcome mat. There's also no peeling, no splinters in the wood, no evidence of the quiet, silent damage of time. So, well-maintained but not exactly cheery. I'm about to knock when I see the door is ajar.

I give it a little push and holler, "Max! You home?"

It's a pointless question. I'd seen his truck in the driveway.

I step over the threshold, my hand on the knob, and try again. "Max? It's Annie. I've got some questions before I get started in town."

The house is eerily quiet. I wait. Listen.

Somewhere, farther inside, a clock ticks. And then I hear water whooshing through the pipes. I assume he's in the shower and relax a little. The front door had opened into a living room. An old couch squats against one wall, a flat-screen TV on the other. There's a recliner in the corner, a bookshelf next to it. Beside the door is a table with a bowl for keys and pocket lint and, beside that, a stack of mail.

"Max?" I holler one more time. Wait. Nothing.

I pick up the envelopes and give them a flip-through. The first qualification of a good PI is a lifelong habit of unmitigated snooping. Anyone who tells you different is lying through their teeth. And probably going through your stuff.

"Hmm," I mutter, reading the envelopes. Among the regular bills and junk mail are two letters from prestigious liberal arts colleges. One of them has already been opened and I slide my thumb along the flap, reopening it just enough to peek inside at the header and solicitation.

*Dear Mr. Andrews,*
*It is with great pleasure that I inform you of your . . .*

The water shuts off.

"Max?" I shout again, closing the envelope and putting everything back the way it was. "You home? It's Annie. I need to ask you a few—"

"Miss Gore?" Max says, appearing in the doorway to the side. "Sorry, I didn't hear you come in, I was working on something."

He's wearing an ink-stained apron over an old sweatshirt and jeans with a pair of chunky headphones around his neck.

"I'd like to see the house," I tell him.

"Oh," he says, like the idea that I'd want to see the crime scene had not occurred to him. "Umm . . . I didn't think you'd—I mean, there's nothing here, after all this time."

"Max," I say. "Remember when I said I'd be going around poking at things that "might"? make people uncomfortable?"

He nods. He's holding an old towel, twisting it in his hands.

"This is the first thing," I say.

He twists the towel a little more.

"Max, your sister was taken from this house. I need to see it. This is why I'm here. This is why you *brought me here*."

He lets out a huge breath and his shoulders, which had just about risen to his earlobes when I'd asked to see inside the house, relax.

"Yeah," he says. "Yeah, okay. I can show you around. Sorry."

"It's okay. I know this is tough."

He nods and steps into the living room ahead of me, waves his arm around like a real estate agent showing the place to a potential buyer.

I look around again, this time with him in the picture for context. The house is probably more than a century old, and the architecture feels exactly right. High ceilings, a maze of narrow rooms, hardwood floors.

"Was this the living room ten years ago?" I ask. It's the sideways method of asking if this was the room Molly was kidnapped from, the room where he last saw her, watching *Snow White* on the TV.

"Yes," he says. He points to the sofa. "Everything—all the furniture, I mean—has changed since then. But, yes. This is how it was laid out."

I look at the TV, the sofa, the recliner. They're all only steps to the windows, the front door, the path that leads to the lane.

"Hmm," I say, and gesture for him to continue with the tour.

He leads me through the house, through a middle room that's being used for wall-to-wall built-in bookshelves and into a dining room at the back of the house. There's a matching set of table and chairs that look barely used.

"The piano used to be in here," he says. "There was a table in that corner over there and Molly used to play there sometimes. She had a doll's house set up on it."

He leads me through another hall-room, this one empty. There are still barely visible holes in the white paint where nails once stuck through. From the hall, we come into the kitchen. It's a big, farmhouse kitchen with butcher-block countertops and a white apron sink, tons of cabinets, and a wide island. A kitchen table sits against a window, and I guess that, when Max finds the inclination to eat, he sits right there, alone, a book in one hand and a forgotten fork in the other.

We go out of the kitchen, through another hall, and up a set of stairs. We pause at a bedroom with a full-sized bed covered with quilts, very neatly made up, a pair of tennis shoes at the foot.

"This is my room," he says. There are still two model airplanes hanging from the ceiling near the window. A telescope sits on a tripod under them, pointed at the sky. But there are also bills on Max's desk, a battered laptop, a pad of Post-its, a mostly empty cup of coffee. This is the room of a kid who has raised himself.

"Thanks," I say.

He nods noncommittally and leads me across the hall to a closed door.

"This was her room," he says.

He opens the door.

I'm not sure what I expected. A little girl's room, left just the way it was when she was taken? Stuffed teddy bears and dolls and pink blankets littering the bed? A dresser full of cute little farm girl clothes?

The room is empty.

The walls are white, the floor is bare, there is no furniture. It is an empty room, that's all.

"Where—" I start.

"My dad," Max says with a sigh. "After my mom . . . Well, we sort of cleaned house. My dad donated all of Molly's things along with my mom's. I think it was just too much for him. He called my aunts and they came down and helped him go through everything. It all happened in a weekend."

I look from one side of the room to another.

The emptiness itself tells me something. The room was never filled with anything else. It never became an office or a hobby room or a storage closet or a guest room. It is still Molly's room, just without Molly's things, without Molly.

I scan from the floor, up the wall and over the window, onto the ceiling. There are little plastic stars there, sucking up sunlight. I suppose they do it every day. Just like real stars, they go on shining whether we're here to see them or not.

I thank Max again and he closes the door.

"There's nothing left?" I ask.

"There's a box," he says. He goes back into his room, and I follow him and watch him open a closet and crouch down in the back, pull out a cardboard file box. He puts it on the bed and opens the lid with a heavy sigh.

"It's not much," he says.

He stands there, near the bed but not too near, while I go through the things.

There's a little vintage book of fairy tales with the name "Janice Andrews" written neatly inside.

"My mom's," Max says quietly. His hands are shoved into the barn coat he's still wearing.

There's a white-and-lavender crocheted blanket, sized for a child, and a pair of crocheted angels meant to be hung up as Christmas ornaments. There's a tattered hardback of *Where the Wild Things Are*. I run my fingers over the familiar old drawings, the little boy in the wolf suit.

"Max," I say. It's the name of the boy in the book.

Max nods. "It was mine first, but Molly loved it. I think it sort of tickled her to imagine me in a book. But my mom always teased me that I was never like Max."

"Never wild?"

He shakes his head, looks at the floor.

"Guess I'd rather read books than be in them," he says.

I smile at this kid who still so much—in spite of everything he's been through—resembles the quiet, tender little boy he must have been. Would he have weathered the storm of his childhood more easily if he'd been rowdy, rough, and tough like Max in the book? Or would he have put his frustration, fear, and anger into something more destructive than a scrapbook and an ongoing fund to hire another PI? All of us must do *something* with the formative pain of our early years. And even the Max in the book—at the end of the night—returned to the loving order of his mother's home, something the real-life Max lost years ago. I glance at him and realize this is something we have in common.

I put the book down and go back to the box. I pull out an old mug with pansies dancing around it and a glittery, plastic fairy wand with strips of gauze streaming from its tip. The last thing is a doll with lavender eyes and long shiny blond hair, a lavender dress. I run my fingers over the cheap satin, the rough lace, look into the doll's eyes.

"It's a Lovely Lady Lavender doll," Max says, watching me. "They were made at the factory in town. All the girls in town had one."

"There's a factory in town?"

"Not anymore," he says. "It closed down a long time ago."

I look again at the doll, sweep her backward, let the eyes close automatically before putting it back in the box.

"You collected all this stuff?" I ask. "Your mom's and sister's things?"

He nods. "When my dad and my aunts started going through the house with boxes and trash bags and I realized what they were doing . . . I picked up the things I could find, the things that had been left in my room or the kitchen or wherever, and I put them into a box, just in case. They didn't amount to much in the end. And, honestly, once it was over, I didn't open the box more than once or twice."

"It must've been hard, though," I say. "To lose everything like that, all at once."

"It was. But I guess I understand why my dad did it. After Molly was taken, my mother was the only one who ever went into her room. It became almost like a shrine. She would sit on Molly's bed, take the clothes out of the closet, take the dresses off the hangers, wash them, rehang them. I think that's the biggest reason my dad got rid of everything. I think he thought that obsessing over Molly's memory is what drove my mom to do what she did. Like, the fact that she could come in here every day and pretend her daughter had never been taken kept her from being able to let go? I don't know. Once she was gone, I think he was afraid that having my mom's stuff around . . . Well, I think he didn't really know how to cope."

"I'm sorry," I say.

Max nods.

I step out of the room and back into the hallway. Max continues the tour past a bathroom and a storage closet full of old blankets and puzzles and board games and to the last room, once his parents', now just his dad's. This one is the biggest and a queen-sized bed sits against the far wall. There's a shoe rack, a chair beside it. There's a dresser and a TV on top of it. A closet where a few men's jackets and clothes hang.

"He doesn't sleep here anymore," Max says without any prompting. "When he's home, he sleeps downstairs on the couch."

I nod my understanding and say thanks as we make our way back downstairs.

"Anything you need," Max says. "Just let me know. There's a laundry room to the side of the house; that's usually where I am if I'm not in the main house."

"Laundry?"

"Yeah," he says. And then, as if understanding that most people don't do laundry all day every day and that's why I'm confused, he says, "If I'm not working, I'm usually, um. Well, it's a hobby, I guess. I do printing."

"Like screen printing?"

He shakes his head.

"Woodblocks," he says. "Sometimes linocuts but mostly woodblocks the last couple years. It's just . . . something to do. I like it."

"Okay," I say. And I think about the letter from the liberal arts college sitting open and forgotten next to the door.

"Is that it?" he asks, clearly ready to be done with this invasion of his space.

"Sure."

We walk back through the living room and onto the porch. I go back down the stepping-stone path toward the lane. Max waves goodbye to me as I slide behind Honey's wheel and I watch as he disappears into the house.

"You know what, Honey?" I say as I rev up her engine. "That house was missing something. Besides the obvious, I mean. I couldn't put my finger on it till I got back out here."

I slip the gearshift into reverse, start pulling away, watch the path and the porch and the house recede from my view.

"Not a single family photo. Not one."

# FIVE

I HAVE A LIST OF people to talk to today, and the family of Olivia Jacobs—the second girl taken and the only one returned—is the first on my list since her house, according to the information Max gave me, is closest.

"Good a place as any to start," I say to Honey as we pull onto the girl's street.

The short, tidy ranch house belonging to Kathleen Jacobs, Olivia's mother, is one of many short, tidy ranch houses in a short, tidy subdivision just outside town. There's a tall oak in the front of this one, and its wet leaves litter the lawn in a pretty way.

I walk up the asphalt driveway, still slick with dew, and listen for a moment before knocking. Inside I hear footsteps and the muffled voices of two women, a stereo in another room.

A school bus drives up the road, stops just past the house, and three kids get on. The doors shut and the bus starts off again.

I knock.

A woman opens the door. Probably in her late forties, she has wisps of gray in her otherwise very black hair and deep, vertical lines over her upper lip when she purses her mouth and tries to remember if she's ever seen me before.

"Can I help you?" she finally says. Her Western North Carolina mountain twang is a lot stronger than Max's, and I just barely catch my-self before I smile at the familiar pinched-off syllables not dissimilar from the sounds of my youth.

I ask if she's Kathleen Jacobs. She says yes.

I tell her who I am, why I'm here. I give her my card.

"No," she says.

"I didn't ask anything—"

"You want to talk to Olivia, right?"

"Yes."

"Because that Andrews boy hired you and now you're going to go around asking questions. And that's fine with me. Whatever happened ten years ago ought to come out. It's about goddamned time."

"Okay."

"But Olivia won't talk to you."

"Can I at least—"

"Olivia won't talk to anyone. Olivia *doesn't* talk. I guess Max failed to mention: Olivia is completely nonverbal."

She swings the door open and I see two young women at the kitchen table, finishing up their breakfast, one maybe a little younger than Max, with hair as black as the woman's in front of me, and the other one younger with a cloud of chestnut curls nearly obscuring her face. I recognize the hair, if nothing else. It's the same little girl who was once taken and then, inexplicably, brought back. Olivia Jacobs, now fifteen.

"Olivia doesn't talk to anybody," Kathleen says.

"You done with your cereal, Liv?" the black-haired girl asks.

Olivia doesn't say anything. She's looking off into the distance, clap-ping her hands together under the table in rhythm to the stereo I'd heard playing before. There's a pop song crackling through the speakers and Olivia claps in 4/4 time. The other girl reaches for Olivia's cereal bowl, but Olivia stops clapping and puts her hand on top of the bowl, yanks it back. Milk and bloated rectangles of Cap'n Crunch slosh around and almost spill.

"Fine," the black-haired girl says, completely calm. "No problem, Liv."

Once the other girl retreats, Olivia's hands go back to clapping.

Kathleen looks at her watch. She's wearing teal scrubs with a chunky sweater and black leather clogs.

"I just got home from my shift," she says. "Haven't even taken a shower yet."

"I apologize," I say, but I know I don't sound sorry.

Kathleen sighs, looks back over her shoulder at the two young women finishing their breakfast and says, "Nicole, you about ready for school?"

Nicole, the girl who isn't Olivia, says, "Yeah. Just need to get my bag."

"And you have dance tonight," Kathleen says.

"Oh!" Nicole says. "Yeah. Okay. Yeah, I'll get my stuff."

Nicole runs off, and I hear her rummaging in her room while Kathleen shakes her head, exhausted.

"Look," she says. "Go around and sit on the back porch. You can talk to me once Olivia starts her shows."

"Okay," I say, because it's better than nothing. She shuts the door and I walk around to the back of the house, where I find a little red-stained deck, a porch swing, and a few dewy deck chairs around a glass-topped table. Another oak tree stands just past the railing, so the deck is covered with slick yellow leaves. I notice a cobweb attached to three different points on the porch swing. It wavers a little but I don't see the spider. Dewdrops drip onto the wet wood.

I rattle off the moisture from one of the chairs, then give it a final, in-adequate drying swipe with a hankie from my bag. A few moments later, a voice says, "Bye!" An engine starts and a car rolls away.

A few more moments and Kathleen slides open the back door and comes outside with a cup of coffee that she hands to me. She wipes down her seat with her sweater sleeve and then sits with a bone-weary sigh.

"Gonna be a wet winter," she says.

I nod like I understand weather, take a sip of coffee, put it down in front of me. I wait to see if Kathleen is going to start the conversation. When she doesn't, I say, "Max Andrews hired me because he's desperate to find his sister."

Kathleen is still looking out toward the yard, so I continue, "He's not ready to give up."

"I wouldn't be either," Kathleen says. She reaches into the pocket of her sweater and pulls out a pack of menthols with a pink plastic lighter stuffed in the cellophane. "Mind?"

I shake my head. She lights up.

"When Olivia was taken . . ." she starts, and then stops, takes a long drag, lets it out. "When she was taken, I thought my world had ended. We knew that Jessica Hoyle had gone missing nearly a month before. Same exact thing. An applehead doll and everything. We knew she'd not been found. The whole town knew about it but . . ."

"What?"

"The Hoyles aren't . . . They weren't, um . . . God, it's awful to say. But they're kind of trashy."

I feel my teeth grit together as the familiar slur "trashy" sears through my mind and dredges up old memories. I force myself to take another sip of the coffee, nod encouragingly.

"The Hoyles were . . . Look, they seemed like the kind of people whose kid might have a death by misadventure and they cover it up."

The words are out of her mouth like a train. She's trying to get past them. Past that guilty feeling of suspicion too easily arrived at, another mother's grief too easily brushed aside.

"And, I remember some folks saying that it was all just a big scam. That the family was faking the kidnapping for media attention, donations, whatever. The day after Jessica was taken, Tommy—Jessica's father—started an online donation fund to hire a PI, which, of course, he never did. Anyway, you read stories about things like that, and the Hoyle clan? Well, I hate to say it, but they fit the type."

"Did anyone prove anything?"

"No," Kathleen says. "And even if it had been some kind of Hoyle con, they would've stuck to just having Jessica go missing. But it was only a month later that Olivia was taken, and, just like with Jessica, there was an applehead doll. Of course, once that happened, people started taking

Mandy—that's Jessica's mother—seriously. That's when it became real. For everyone. For me."

"Tell me about the day. Do you remember it?"

"Of course. We were at a church picnic, down at the park. It used to be a yearly thing. We'd just put the food out. I was getting a plate and I was trying to juggle both girls. Nicole was seven at the time and very chatty. We always had to keep an extra eye on Olivia, you know, even then. She's autistic, which we know now, but . . . this is a small town and she was still so young, just barely five years old. You have to understand. It wasn't until later that we took her to a specialist."

I nod and take another drink of coffee, hoping she'll continue.

"Anyway, Nicole was going on and on about what all was on the dessert table and I was listening to her. She asked me a question about the bowl of ambrosia, I remember, and I was answering her and when I turned to look for Olivia, she was gone."

Tears well up in Kathleen's eyes. She blinks them away. Takes another long drag of her smoke. Sharp mint and acrid tobacco fill my nose.

"I just let go of her hand for a *second.* That's all it took. She was gone. I screamed her name but . . . she was never . . . she wouldn't have answered. Some other people asked what was going on. We all spread out and searched for her. I found my husband, Arnold, over by the music stage. He'd been going to play his guitar. We looked everywhere. I took him back to the buffet table where I'd lost her, and there it was."

"The applehead doll," I guess.

"Yes. It was horrible. A little red velvet dress. That awful, shriveled face."

Kathleen shivers and taps her cigarette against the hard plastic arm of the deck chair. Gray ash falls to the planks and turns to thin sludge.

"We thought . . . We *knew* we'd lost her for good. Search parties went out that night. And the next day. And the next. Everyone came back empty-handed. The news came. And then the FBI. There was nothing. *Nothing.* I felt so, so hopeless. I remember wishing I could just . . . go back. God, it was awful. But then, two weeks later, I came outside one night for a smoke. And there she was."

Kathleen's eyes stare across the porch at the empty, weathered swing and farther. Into a decade ago.

"I thought . . . God, at first I thought she was dead. She was lying there on her side in the swing. Asleep. And when I touched her . . . she was so cold. It was summer but it had been a chilly week. Cloudy. And . . . I don't know how long she'd been out there. Just . . . asleep like that."

"You woke her up, took her inside," I say.

She nods, puts out the butt of her cigarette. Lights another one.

"She was covered in scratches and bruises. All over her arms and legs. We begged her to talk to us. But she . . . she never would. Never, never could. And then, two weeks later."

"Max's sister," I say. "Molly Andrews was taken."

She nods. The cigarette shakes. She sniffs and wipes her eyes with the sleeve of her sweater.

"Does Olivia communicate? Does she type or draw or . . ."

Kathleen shakes her head.

"She draws pictures if she has chubby crayons. And, when she's inclined, she'll use her iPad and a program with picture cards to tell us things she wants or needs. She's not mute—her voice box works just fine. Sometimes, in her sleep, she moans. Sometimes she screams at us, wordless." Kathleen looks back at me, a hint of a challenge in her eyes now. "I'm a nurse. I've taken her to all kinds of therapy. When Arnold was still around, he took her everywhere he could. All the specialists in the state. We're all just doing the best we can, Ms. Gore."

"I know."

"Arnold left when Olivia was in middle school. He stuck around that long. He tried."

"Where is he now?"

"He's a contractor. He went to another town. Got another job there. Another life. He pays his child support, though. On time. Every month. When she feels up to it, Olivia goes to school, but usually it's just too overwhelming for her. So, at most, it's a couple half days a week. She has a homebound tutor who's very good with her. Lord, we're lucky for that.

I work nights so I can be here in the day and Nicole stays with her in the evenings."

"I'm not DSS, Mrs. Jacobs. I'm not here to check up on you or look into Olivia's living situation," I say. "I'm just trying to find out what happened to Molly, what happened to all of them."

She chews on her bottom lip for a while and then lets out a sigh.

"I know," she says. "I just . . . I feel guilty. I feel sick every time I think of that Andrews girl. It makes me want to puke."

She pauses, swallows hard, takes another drag. Smoke billows out of her mouth as she says, "Because I know that she took my daughter's place."

Tiny taps of rain begin to spit around the porch, hit the deck, the table, me. Kathleen stubs the cigarette out and stands up. I stand with her. This meeting is over.

"If I wanted to talk to Olivia—"

"You can't."

"But if she could—"

"She won't. Listen, you think this is the first time someone's come around, trying to talk to her? You think the cops didn't try to talk to her after she was brought back? The FBI? No, she didn't talk to them. And she won't talk to you. I've been more than generous, and that's because I feel for poor Max. I really do. He's a good kid and he deserves a better lot than life handed him. But I've got nothing more to say to you. I'm tired. I'm going to bed. Please leave or I will call the sheriff."

She turns and stomps back inside the house, slides the door shut. I move off the deck and back toward the road. Around the front, through the living room window, I see Olivia Jacobs sitting on the sofa, watching a British gardening show. Two women in neat cardigans prune roses in front of a stone Cotswold cottage. The blooms fall to the pristine green grass. Music plays. Olivia watches, rapt.

I slide my hands into my damp back pockets and head to the car.

# SIX

NEXT ON THE LIST is Jessica Hoyle's residence, and between the now-driving rain and the remoteness of the address, it's not exactly a quick jaunt. Rain hammers Honey's roof as I pull off the side of the switchback road and find the pink stuffed pig in the passenger seat floorboard. It was left over from a case I'd worked when I first got my PI license, almost five years ago. A mom and little boy trying to get away from a bad situation. The boy had left the pig in the car when I drove them to the airport and they'd never called to get it back. I suppose I could've donated it or given it to a neighborhood kid, but the pig had made itself an instant reminder of what success in this job can mean for the people who hire me.

I look down at the pig. The Fog Hog, Leo had called it when we sat together in my car the last time, using the back of the soft pig to mop the windshield on a cold, misty night.

I mop up the windshield now, smack the dash where the vents are. Seems like sometimes that helps. Seems like sometimes maybe I just need to smack something.

Nothing happens. I smack the dash again, right in the middle.

Lo and behold, the vents sputter to life and warm air breezes onto the windshield and the fog begins to clear.

"Presto!" I say. The Fog Hog makes no reply. The rain falls in heavy drops.

"You just need to wake up, Honey?" I ask the car. She rumbles. The heat vents blow.

I look back at my phone and check that I'm on the right track. This old mountain road is nothing but trees and deadly drop-offs and I'm lucky I found this shoulder at all. I pull back onto the road, go three more miles, then turn down Garbler Lane.

Honey sloshes in and out of the underfilled divots in the road. This place hasn't been re-graveled in years, I think, and it's been washed out by rains like this one over and over. Scraggly apple trees grow, higgledy-piggledy, along the lane, their twisted gray branches bare of fruit.

"Jesus," I spit as we skid across a particularly bad dip.

I pass two run-down houses and a couple old single-wides before I come to the last house on the lane. It's like a shabby, ugly older brother of Max's family farmhouse, and the old adage "Too proud to whitewash, too poor to paint" comes to mind. The siding is dirty and gray, or stained green on the side nearest some huge old conifers. The roof slumps a little toward the chimney. The columns that support the porch are crumbling. A chain-link fence surrounds the house and, just inside, there's a muddy patch where a dog sleeps with his nose poking outside a red doghouse. It's a black nose on a white muzzle. Just like Snoopy.

I pull up and park beside a relatively new Chevy pickup and an old, battered Civic—mostly red but with a blue trunk lid. I reach into the backseat for my leather jacket, maneuver it on over the blazer, get out of the car.

The dog hears the car door and jolts out of his little house like it's on fire. He's an unneutered pit, and he lurches against the length of his chain, scrabbling his powerful paws into the wet mud and snapping his maw at me, snarling and barking and growling.

If anyone's in there, they'll hear Snoopy and come check things out.

I stand at the fence and wait.

Sure enough, there's a waver in the curtains and then the door opens. A man steps outside. He's tall and lanky and he's wearing a tight T-shirt under an open flannel along with about three days of rust-colored scruff. This, I think, must be Tommy Hoyle, father of the first girl taken, Jessica.

"Who the hell are you?"

I tell him who I am, who hired me, what I'm doing there.

He shakes his head.

"Go away," he hollers. Then, "Shut the fuck up!" at Snoopy.

He turns and goes back in the house. The dog settles down for a minute and looks at me. I look back at him. We both wait for something else to happen.

After a few more moments, it does. The door opens again and the guy comes back out, walks down the steps and across the old concrete stepping stones and through the gate.

"Mister Hoyle?" I ask. But he doesn't pay any attention. Just keeps going. Once he's past me, he says to the air in front of him, "She wants to talk to some fucking detective, who the fuck am I to say no?" He smells like mouthwash and grilled cheese.

He steps up into his pickup and starts it and backs up, just barely missing Honey (practically a shooting offense, in my book) before he wheels it around and kicks up mud and gravel as he revs away.

I'm still glaring after him when the door opens again, and a woman comes outside in an old green rain jacket.

She points her finger at Snoopy, snaps, says, "Dozer. Shut it. Go sit down." The dog obeys. She tosses him what looks like a chunk of Velveeta and the dog catches it and disappears into his house.

She comes to the gate, opens it, lets me in.

"I'm Mandy Hoyle. Come on in."

Jessica's mother. Immediately, I see the resemblance. The pale blue eyes, light blond hair, and milk-white skin. Something else, too. Some quality I can't quite put my finger on.

"Okay," I say, and follow her.

Inside, the house is old and worn and chilly. It's cluttered with knickknacks and shoes of all sizes and hoodies cast over the backs of chairs, but there are no dust balls on the floor or empty cans and unopened mail sitting around. The house is cluttered but clean. I follow Mandy into the kitchen, where she takes off the rain jacket and slips it over the back of a white kitchen chair before picking up a plastic scrub brush. She's been doing the breakfast dishes, I see. The sink is full of sudsy water and Corning plates from thirty or forty years ago. Yellow flowers and butterflies adorn the rim of the cream-colored plates.

"I'll rinse," I say.

"Sure," Mandy says.

As she scrubs, I tell her that I was hired by Max Andrews to look for his sister.

"We tried to hire a PI once," she says. "Well, I wanted to. We couldn't afford it. Tommy was out of work at the time. He'd been up at the toy factory but it closed down right before . . . right before she was taken. It was bought out. They sent the plant to Mexico."

"Was that Tommy who just left?"

She nods, hands me a plate. There's a green bruise, almost healed, ringing her right wrist. I take the plate. I rinse it carefully and slide it into the plastic strainer. The kitchen's been cleaned with vinegar and the smell still lingers. Everything in here is old or dollar store and I smile at a little pink flower in a jelly jar on the windowsill. A weed, I think, pretty and cheerful, its petals open and hoping for sun.

"What do you want to know?" Mandy says.

I ask her to tell me about the day Jessica was taken. She takes a long, shuddering breath, then nods, more at the soapy sink than me.

"I was at this playground; I needed to get out of the house for a while. There's a Baptist church up on Laurel and they have a sweet little playground. Just some swings and a slide but it's the real nice kind with the wood and dark green plastic? I'd taken Jessica up there to play for a while. She was swinging on the swings and . . . then she wasn't."

"What do you mean?"

"I mean, I was watching her. I looked away for a second. And then she was gone."

She pulls her hands out of the suds, wipes them on a threadbare kitchen towel, and says, "Let me show you something."

She walks out of the kitchen and I follow her into a living room, where there's a bricked-up fireplace and a space heater that's not been turned on. There's a red velour sofa and a gorgeous old rocking chair and a TV sitting on a plain pine table with a stack of DVDs next to it. But none of that is what Mandy wants to show me. She walks over to the wall behind the couch and points at the pictures hanging in a straight line the length of the wall.

There are a few children here, one girl and three boys. The oldest boy, with curly auburn hair, has pictures all the way through high school. His senior picture hangs last in the line. He's got Mandy's soft expression but everything else about him is like a copy-paste of Tommy. Same chiseled bones, same wavy auburn hair. The other two boys' photos stop at football pictures somewhere in late elementary or early middle school. And then there's the girl with the fine, straight, corn-silk blond hair. The only girl.

"Jessica," I say.

"That's right," Mandy says. The kitchen towel is still in her hand, and she uses it to wipe some invisible dust from the top edge of the picture frame.

Jessica's huge eyes stare through the lens of the camera. Ice blue, I think. There's a pink bow in her hair and she wears a black-and-pink dress and her hands are placed delicately on her lap as no child sits in real life and all children sit in professional photographs.

"That's just about the last one we got," Mandy says. "Before."

I nod my understanding.

She sighs and points at the oldest boy and says, "This is Tam. Tommy Junior is his real name but we've always called him Tam and that's what he prefers. He graduates this year. Not even a year older than Jessica. Irish twins, they say. Then Jeffrey and James."

"Mrs. Hoyle, when you saw that Jessica was missing, you found a doll. Is that right?"

She nods, closing her eyes tight. She's still got on heavy black eyeliner and mascara from last night, and it doesn't budge when she scrapes tears from one eye with the side of her thumb.

"An applehead doll," she says. "An applehead doll in a sky blue dress."

"And you showed it to the police?"

She nods again.

"Yes. And I told them someone had taken my baby girl. They . . ." She pauses, her mouth twisting into a bitter frown before she continues. "The cops came. Asked me questions, looked around. They checked the cars of all the people at the church that day. But it's not like they really made an effort or anything. No dogs, no hunt in the woods up behind the church. They think us Hoyles are trash. Always have. The cops accused me of 'misplacing' my child."

She laughs bitterly, hugs her arms tight to her body. She's a small woman, shorter than me and waif-thin, her nearly white-blond hair and uncanny blue eyes and upturned nose making her look like a tragic fairy who wandered out of a storybook and never found her way back.

"How do you 'misplace' a child?" she asks. "Jessica was a good girl. She wouldn't run off. She was sitting right there, swinging. Pumping her little legs. She was wearing pink tennis shoes. And then she was gone."

"I'm sorry," I say. And I am. I'm sorry for the way she was treated. Sorry for all the grief she's endured. Sorry for this last photograph of Jessica beaming out at Mandy every day, a reminder of what she has lost. But I'm not here to get caught up in the maelstrom of Mandy Hoyle's pain. I shift my weight as if I can shrug off the heaviness of the emotion that's just been laid on me.

"What time of day was it?" I ask. "When Jessica was taken?"

"Morning," Mandy says. "It was morning. I was pregnant at the time with James and I'd been having powerful bad morning sickness. And Jeffrey was in the backseat asleep in his car seat. That boy never once slept through the night. Bad dreams and howling like you wouldn't believe. But he always drifted off in the mornings so I just let him sleep."

"Did you notice anything strange before Jessica was taken? Anyone hanging around?"

Mandy shakes her head.

"She'd been just about to start kindergarten, though she was already reading a bit. I'd been helping her with books I got from the library. I'd taken her up to the school, got her registered; I was so excited for her. And a little worried too. She was small for her age. Almost six when she was taken."

"What happened between the time Jessica was taken and the time Olivia Jacobs went missing?" I ask. "I heard something about a donation fund."

Mandy's cheeks redden and her mouth pulls together in an angry frown before she lets out a puff of air and says, "Tommy started an online donation fund basically the day after Jessica was taken, which I didn't even know about. He said later on, when I asked him about it, that we couldn't trust the cops and that's why he did it. But I never saw a single cent of that money and we never did hire a PI. Still, I can't say he was wrong about trusting the cops. I was shouting the whole time that they should've called in the FBI right from the start but nobody listened to me. Not until after Olivia Jacobs was taken did anyone pay a single bit of attention. Before that, plenty of people were going around town whispering about how Tommy and Dwight—that's Tommy's cousin—had cooked up the whole thing to get rich and betting Jessica would turn up in our backyard like nothing ever happened."

"Were they questioned?"

"Of course," she says. "But it didn't come to anything. And then Olivia Jacobs went missing and suddenly everyone realized it was real. That someone was taking our babies."

"Why did they suspect Dwight?" I ask.

"I just told you—"

"Right, but why him specifically? Were he and Tommy close?"

She hesitates. I wait. Outside, the rain lets up a little.

Eventually, she says, "Well, it turned out the donation campaign *had* been Dwight's idea, at least according to Tommy. And, well, he'd done something similar before. Kidnapped his own little girl."

"Kidnapped her?"

"Well, you know what I mean, not like a *real* kidnapping. Not like what happened to Jessica. The common kind. Dwight and his wife split up. She took the daughter, moved back in with her mama, and got a lawyer to handle the court stuff. Then, one day he picked the girl up from school to stay with him for the weekend and he just didn't bother bringing her back. His ex-wife called him and asked what was going on and he said if she wanted her daughter back, she'd have to take *him* back too. Well, she wasn't having it for a second. She went straight to the sheriff's office, and they went over there and explained he'd have to go sit in jail if he didn't hand over the kid."

I nod. Mandy is right. This kind of kidnapping is depressingly common. The sort of thing ex-spouses do to hurt each other when, mostly, it only really hurts the kid.

"So, what happened?" I ask.

"Well, she got her daughter back, took full custody, and moved out of state. She lives all the way up in New Hampshire, if you can believe it. But this was years ago. Dwight is older than Tommy by seven years. He'd already gone and got remarried to Elaine Davis by the time Jessica was taken. But everyone knew about what happened. Still remembered it. You can't keep something like that quiet in a town this small and nobody was shy with their accusations."

She sighs, looks back at the photo of Jessica, and says, "Then, later on, I remember Dwight had something to do with the last kidnapping."

"What do you mean?"

"Something about the day Molly was taken," Mandy says. "He was at the Andrewses' farm that day fixing a pipe. When they went around interviewing people, I remember Elaine being worried they'd try to pin it on him and the rumors would start all over again, but it never came to that. All Dwight had to do was give a statement. He'd been called over there to fix a pipe and that was the end of it. But after that, I think they'd sort of had their fill of small-town gossip. They moved to Charlotte not long after."

"Can I get their number?" I ask. I'm not sure what help they can be, but if Dwight was a witness on the day Molly was kidnapped, I can't ignore it.

"He's not there anymore," Mandy says. "He and Elaine moved back."

"When?"

"Oh, a couple months ago, I guess. Beginning of summer."

"Why'd they come back?"

"Elaine's mama passed. Left them the house. I guess they figured taking over her old place was cheaper than paying city rent."

"You don't talk to them?"

"I don't hardly have the time. Besides, gone this long, I barely know them. They come into Ellerd's—the diner where I work—but I don't much get to speak to them since they always come during the dinner rush. They didn't bother to keep in touch—even to ask how the search for Jessica was going—and I suppose I understand. But I never felt the need to reach out, if you know what I mean."

"Can I get their address?"

She gives it to me and I fish inside my bag for a moment and pull out a card, hand it to her. She looks at it.

"If you think of anything else . . ." I say.

She stands there, staring at me a moment, my card in her hand.

"Hold on," she says. She turns and jogs out of the room. I hear her going up some stairs and then I hear her walking around above me. While I wait, I look at the old picture of Jessica. Of all Mandy's children, Jessica is the one who most resembles her. It's the same fair skin, the same pale blond hair, the same tiny nose. There's an intelligence too, I think. A daring bright spark that shines through Jessica's eyes the same way it shines through Mandy's. That's what I saw when I met her at the door, I realize. That keenness.

Jessica is the kind of kid who draws media attention. Maybe she would have. Maybe if she'd grown up in a neighborhood of cute brick ranch houses instead of this old, run-down holler. Maybe if her family hadn't been broke and rowdy. Maybe if her daddy hadn't been out of work, her mom exhausted, abused, and poverty-stricken, a sense of ruinous resilience permeating from her hungry blue eyes, the kind of woman who makes people uneasy, puts them off guard with her earnest need.

I turn my gaze to another set of photos and find what must be Mandy's and Tommy's relatives. In a wedding photo from fifty years back, a lanky red-haired man grips the waist of his plump, dark-eyed wife. There's a framed photo of Mandy, Tommy, Jessica, and Tommy Junior—*Tam*, I think. Mandy's hair is ten-years-ago stylish and Tommy looks less haggard and restless, almost happy. Then there's another senior photo, this one of a young woman I don't recognize. She has bright eyes and her pale, strawberry-blond hair hangs in long, shimmery waves around her bare shoulders.

"Odette," Mandy says as she reenters the room.

"Who?"

"Odette. Tommy's little sister. She died. Eleven years ago now." Mandy smiles wistfully at the photo. "She was a good girl. So sweet. She used to keep Tam and Jessica for us. But, she had a real sad streak. She drank too often and too much. Never around the kids, of course. But she'd have spells, you know. Anyway, she had a spell, drank too much. Passed out and didn't wake up. Poor thing. What a waste."

I find myself frowning at the photo. At the tragedy heaped on tragedy around me.

I don't have the time or inclination to dwell on it, though, and I'm about to leave when Mandy holds her fist out toward me and says, "I want you to have this."

She opens her hand like a flower. There's a wad of tightly rolled bills inside.

"I've been saving up," she says. "Wherever I can."

"Mrs. Hoyle—"

"I want you to find Jessica too," she says. "Please."

"Mrs. Hoyle, I'm already looking for Jessica. Because I'm looking for Molly. Max Andrews is paying me to look for a week. You don't need to pay me." I close her hand around the money and gently push it back toward her. She bites her lips together and tears come to her eyes again. Her eye makeup still stays put. It's got a lot of practice, I think with a sad, sick feeling in my stomach.

"I will look for Jessica too," I say around the lump in my throat. "While I'm looking for Molly, I will look for Jessica."

"You promise?" she asks, barely a whisper.

"Yes," I say. "I'll be here for a week. I will look all day, every day. I promise I will look, but I can't promise I will find her."

She nods, sniffs, closes her fist tight around the money.

"I've been . . . I've been hoping to leave," she says, waving her arm to take in the room, the house, the holler, this whole life. "I could never afford it. Not with the kids. This is Tommy's house, Tommy's family's house and land and everything. I'd like to take the kids to my cousin's in Virginia. Start over. She could get me a job at the place where she works, I think. There're benefits. Good pay. But I always thought"—her voice goes tight and tremulous—"what if she came back?"

The sick sadness spreads out of my belly and up through my chest. My heart is hot and angry inside my ribs and I feel my cheeks flush. It's a familiar feeling. An aching pity mixed with rage and helplessness. Something I haven't felt since I was a kid. Since I was home, standing in front of my own mother, the waves of her throbbing need crashing over me.

"Jessica," I say. My voice, higher and thinner than it should be, surprises me. I clear my throat but it still feels thick.

Mandy nods. She says, "What if Jessica came back and she couldn't find me?"

"I'll look," I say. And then again, "I will look."

A few seconds later I'm back in my car. The rain thrums the roof and I take long, slow breaths with my hands tight on the wheel as I watch Mandy Hoyle carry some scraps out to the dog and wave at me.

"Oh, Honey," I breathe, turning the key. "I'm in over my head here."

Honey rumbles sympathetically. I pull out. Roll back up the hill and out of this holler. I tell myself to think about something else. Anything else. But everything in sight reminds me of my home, my old life, and all those old memories are stirred to life.

# SEVEN

Y OU GOTTA TALK TO the cops, Annie," Dr. Horton had said.
This was years ago.

I can't help thinking about it. Driving out of that muddy holler and back toward Quartz Creek, there is a sick heat in my belly at the remembered scene, and I can't stop it from coming.

I was sixteen at the time. I had my license but no car. Still, I'd been able to drive my mom's ancient Escort, my mom moaning in the passenger seat, to Leila Horton's place, Happy Paws Veterinary Clinic.

Leila was an old friend of my mom's. They'd grown up together—the same rough neighborhood, the same rough parties. But Leila got a scholarship to Eastern Kentucky University and my mom got married and pregnant, not in that order.

"I can't," I told her.

"She's got three cracked ribs," Leila said.

My mom was resting in another room. It was Sunday and the clinic was closed except for emergencies. We were standing in Leila's office. It was nice, with pictures of her kids on the desk. Her kids were younger than me. A little girl and a little boy wearing nice sweaters, playing in the leaves with a golden retriever. I'd never had a pet. Never had a cat or dog to bring to Leila's. I always just brought my mom, even before I could legally drive.

"Annie, he's gonna kill her," Leila said. "I know he's your daddy but—"

"I can't make her press charges," I said. "I can't make her do anything."

"Oh, Annie . . ." Leila said. She crossed her arms and sighed through her nose. "You still mostly staying with your granny?"

"Yeah," I said. "I can't stay with them."

"All I can do is give her some Tylenol, wrap her up in elastic bandages," Leila said. "You know I can't prescribe anything."

"That's okay," I said. "I just wanted to make sure she wasn't bleeding inside."

"Jesus, Annie," Leila said, and then looked chagrined, like she hadn't meant to reveal her horror. "Is there anything I can do? Anything you need?"

I'd shrugged and said, "What I need is the ability to get around, Leila. I need wheels."

She'd pressed her lips together, looked out the little window.

"How about a job?" she said.

That was how I was able to get my first car, a 1993 Pontiac LeMans. I cleaned the Happy Paws Veterinary Clinic after school every other day. I only quit when I joined JROTC. I took my mom to the clinic four more times before I graduated. The day before I left for the Air Force, I sold the car for what I could and took the money to Leila, told her to put it in the charity vet care fund.

I didn't own another car until I got out of the service.

"Okay, Honey," I say now, my voice a little strangled as I pull onto Main Street. "Let's get something to eat."

I need to take my mind off my own hard case, I think, and put it onto the one I'm actually getting paid for. And I might as well get some lunch while I'm at it.

Honey purrs at me, and I look for a spot. Parallel parking with Honey is its own kind of adventure, and if you're not careful you'll wind up with Honey's ass sticking out for any old car to come by and smack. I take a deep breath and keep an eye out, eventually maneuvering into a tight space just a few yards down from Shiloh's Sweet Treats.

"See," I say. "I had it all along."

I get out and lock her up, my belly already grumbling.

Like the rest of Quartz Creek's Main Street, Shiloh's is a two-story red-brick rectangle with a glass storefront. Unlike the rest of Main Street, it's busy. A woman comes out and gives me a quick "Howdy!" before going past me. I take the brief pause in traffic to make my way inside, where I'm nearly bowled over by the intensity of the warm, sugary air. I work my way around the crowd to a long glass counter filled with breads and cookies, cupcakes, and pastries. A few other customers peer into the glass and some sit at little café tables jammed into the corner of the store.

"Morning!" a woman says. She's young and smiling and she wears a red apron.

"Shiloh?" I ask.

She shakes her head. "In the back. You need to talk to her?"

I say that I do.

"Shiloh!" she yells through a set of double doors. "Somebody here for you!"

Another woman comes out a moment later, wiping flour from her hands. She's broad-shouldered and she'd probably be six feet tall if she weren't wearing chunky platform heels. But she is. So, she's more like six-three.

"Hi!" she says. "You must be Annie. I'm Shiloh." She thrusts her hand toward me. Big open smile, big curly brown hair, big strong hand. I get the idea everything about this woman is outsized. Like she's too grand for this small, normal world but she's making the best of it. I like her immediately. I take her firm hand and shake and feel flour dust in her palm.

"I've got some bread going in the back. Did you need to talk or were you just coming in for brunch?"

"Both, actually."

"Okay!" she says. "Just follow me."

She heads behind the counter and through the double doors and I follow her into the kitchen while she says, "I just took the pumpkin bread out." She cuts a slice off the orange loaf on the cooling rack and puts it on a little white plate with a pat of butter and a silver spreading knife. She sets both down on the butcher-block work surface, where a wad of pale dough sits, puffy, in a sea of flour. "You want some milk?"

"Sure."

She pours a glass of whole milk. "Good?"

"Yeah. Thanks." I smear butter over the warm bread, my mouth watering. I almost forget that I didn't just come here for lunch. Shiloh was Max and Molly's babysitter the summer Molly was taken, so she's the closest thing I can get to being able to speak to a parent in person. And it's always possible she knows more than she thinks she does.

"How's it going so far?" she asks before plunging her knuckles into the ball of dough.

I shrug. "About like I expected. Asking questions that have mostly already been answered in Max's notes or by Max himself or, at least, in old news articles."

"So why ask them?"

"Well, sometimes asking those same questions stirs people into some kind of action. Sometimes, if someone's been sitting around . . . maybe knowing something they should've said and didn't or maybe they didn't do something when they should have, even remembered something that didn't seem meaningful at the time but does now . . . you come back around and ask them again, without a badge on your chest, and they get stirred up. Think maybe they have a second chance."

"That makes sense."

"So today I go around asking questions. Tomorrow, I see if anyone wants to do anything about it. I did meet someone I didn't expect, though."

"Oh yeah?"

"An old woman in the woods out past the creek."

"Ohhh," Shiloh says. She pauses kneading for a moment and sighs. "That would be Susan McKinney. She's, um, sort of a psychic? Did she offer to read your cards or anything?"

"No, but she did say I could come by later, if I wanted answers."

Shiloh goes back to kneading. "Well, that's cryptic."

"Have you ever been to visit her?" I ask.

Shiloh snorts. "When I was in high school one of my friends—Amy— wanted to go. It was her sixteenth birthday and she'd been fighting with her boyfriend . . . something about . . . Gosh, it seemed so important at the time; I can't believe I can't remember now. Anyway, me and her and a few of our other friends crammed into Susan's cabin and she read Amy's fortune and told her that Bradley was cheating."

"And?"

"Well, wouldn't you know it? The very next day Amy found him down at the parking lot with Kacey Bazler. Anyway, Susan McKinney is harmless, as far as I know. A lot of women in town visit her and give her a little cash or whatever they happen to be able to trade for whatever it is she provides. Maybe it's just peace of mind, you know?"

"Yeah."

I watch her knead the dough for a while and then ask, "You were the Andrewses' babysitter, right? It was in the book Max gave me."

Shiloh nods.

"Yes," she says. "Just that one summer. Before Molly was taken."

"Not after?"

She shakes her head. Her hair and eyes are the same shade of deep coffee brown. She sighs, sad and reminiscent, as she pushes her fists into the dough. I take a bite of the pumpkin bread and have to keep myself from groaning at the spicy-sweet warmth of it. The bread is otherworldly. Magical. Or maybe I'm just cold and wet and frustrated. Either way, I'm grateful for the unexpected treat.

"No," she says. "After Molly was taken, the Andrews family didn't use a babysitter anymore. Mrs. Andrews didn't . . . go out. She never left Max alone after that. She took him to school. She picked him up. If he had band or sports or whatever, she went along and watched."

"What were they like? Max and Molly?"

"Max was quiet," Shiloh says. "Like he still is."

She frowns, looks away from me and down at the dough and says, "Molly was rambunctious. Good-natured, though, super sweet. She had a ton of energy but she was very eager to please. I remember she drew me a picture one day and, when I got there, she was running with it to show me. She was so excited. She tripped over a toy in the living room and smashed her face against the leg of a chair. She had to get stitches where she'd split her chin open, and I felt *so* bad. But the family was really good-natured about it. Mrs. Andrews just iced it right up and I watched Max while Mr. and Mrs. Andrews took Molly to the doctor instead of going out to dinner."

"You weren't there the day the kidnapping happened, right?"

"No, I mostly only babysat when Mrs. Andrews went to PTA or church meetings or when she and Mr. Andrews went out. She didn't really need a babysitter that often. Honestly, Max could've been left alone. He was eight and never got into trouble but, like I said, Molly was a bundle of energy and had a touch of wanderlust. A scary combination in a four-year-old. Anyway, I knew them from church and I'd just turned sixteen and I wanted spending money so it worked out."

"And the day Molly was taken they were . . ."

"Mrs. Andrews was working in the garden, as far as I know. That's what Max said. And he was in a piano lesson."

"With"—I roll through my memory—"a . . . Deena Drake?"

"That's right. Have you talked to her yet?"

"No, but she's on my list."

I take another bite.

"How is it?" Shiloh asks.

"This is the best pumpkin bread I've ever had in my life. I could eat it every day forever."

She giggles. It's a bubbly laugh for such a big woman, and I can't help but smile at the sound of it.

"I went to culinary school," she says. "I actually worked in an upscale bakery down in Asheville for a couple years, but I always wanted to come back home. You know?"

I shrug. I *don't* know. I never wanted to go home. And my visit to the Hoyles reminded me why. I shove another warm hunk of bread in my mouth, try to forget about the cold in my bones.

"When my grandmother died, she left me some money. Not a ton but, combined with what I'd managed to save, I came back home and started up the business."

"Looks like it's going well," I say.

"So far, so good," she says, and then flops the dough into a wooden bowl, covers it with a towel, wipes her hands and the work surface before pulling an iced cake from a rack behind her. I watch as she fills a bag with orange buttercream and then twists it closed.

I ask, "Did you notice anything strange in the days or weeks leading up to when Molly was taken?"

"I've thought about that a lot over the years," Shiloh says. She kneels over the cake, turns it on its stand, and begins piping orange roses onto the top. Bright orange petals swirl outward from their center, their sugary smell wafting toward me.

"But things just seemed so normal at the time. Max and Molly were the same as ever. I didn't see Mr. Andrews much, except at school."

"Max said he was the biology teacher."

"Yeah. I had him junior and then senior year, which was the last year before he quit and started trucking. He was pretty haunted after Molly disappeared, but not like Mrs. Andrews."

I think about Max's mom. The picture of her in his casebook was actually one of the whole family, everyone dressed up, standing in front of the farmhouse. In this picture, Janice Andrews is wearing a blue floral A-line dress with her long ponytail pulled over her shoulder. She'd been a sporty-looking woman with a golden-brown tan, wide-set hazel eyes above freckled cheeks, and a straight-toothed smile. Hard to imagine that kind of woman doing what she did.

I catch myself, pause, ask myself what kind of woman it's easy to picture locking the bedroom door behind her and sitting down on the bed to end her life. I stop before I go too far down that road.

Instead, I ask Shiloh, "Did you notice anything about her beforehand?"

Shiloh shrugs. "Mrs. Andrews seemed kind of stressed out that summer. She was doing a lot of community work. The toy plant closed down that year, and it put most of the town out of work. She was involved with fundraising and food bank stuff with the church."

"The church?"

"Yeah. First Baptist out on Laurel. We went there too. Mrs. Andrews was on some . . . committee? She did outreach work, organized bake sales, Vacation Bible School, that kind of thing."

"Do you remember when the first girl was taken? Jessica?"

"Vaguely," Shiloh says. "I was sixteen, you know? So busy with stuff that seemed so important at the time. I remember there being talk about a little girl going missing, but that's all."

"Right," I say. "But then Olivia Jacobs was taken."

"Exactly," Shiloh says with a meaningful nod. "Once that happened, I think everyone sat up and paid attention. Worried there was some kind of crazy serial killer or pedophile lurking around. I mean, the applehead doll thing *did* feel sinister. God, it still does."

She shivers, and I admit to myself that I was thinking the same thing. Serial killers leave trophies, tokens, evidence of their presence. No bodies were ever found, but most of the bodies of serial killer victims are still hidden, likely never to be uncovered.

"And then Olivia was returned," I say, reminding myself that at least one girl escaped whatever dark fate someone had planned for her.

"That's right," Shiloh says. "The strangest thing, isn't it? Olivia Jacobs taken away and then just . . . poof. Brought back. To be honest, once I got older, I suspected some kind of trafficking ring, but . . . the dolls? And what kind of trafficker actually returns a kid unharmed?"

"I saw Olivia this morning," I say.

"Really?" Shiloh says, pausing for a moment. "I'm surprised Kathleen let you in the door."

"She didn't. Kathleen talked to me on the back porch."

Shiloh snorts.

"Kathleen's good people," she says. "But she's protective of Olivia. You can understand why. I don't think I ever really understood what real fear was until Lucy came along. Children change you in ways you just don't expect."

She finishes one rose, pauses to turn the cake and give it another look, then starts on another rose.

"Mama?" a little voice croaks from a doorway on the other side of the room, as if on cue. She's carrying a stuffed pony with a purple-yarn mane and her hair is a mess of frizzy dark curls. She looks like she just got up from a nap.

"Hey there, Cupcake!" Shiloh says. "You finish *Peppa?*"

Lucy nods.

"You want some pumpkin bread?"

Lucy nods again, then seems to see me for the first time. Shiloh prepares a plate with pumpkin bread and butter and a glass of milk identical to mine and says, "This is one of Mister Max's friends. She came to help him find something. Her name is Miss Annie. Can you say hello?"

"Hello, Miss Annie," Lucy says. Like her mom, she's tall, all arms and legs and big brown eyes.

"Can you tell Miss Annie how old you are?"

Lucy holds up four fingers with one hand while she uses a kid-sized fork in the other to hack into the orange bread.

My mouth stretches into a broad grin at the sight of this unkempt, hungry little girl, and I say, "Nice to meet you, Lucy. And you can call me Annie."

"Annie," Lucy repeats, and throws her full focus back onto the pumpkin bread.

"Anyway," Shiloh says, piping another rose. "I think it's really good you're helping him out."

"Well, he's paying me."

"I know. But I think it's good for him to put this to rest. Max needs to have . . . He needs some kind of closure, I think."

"I'm not sure I can help him there," I say. "Like I told him, it's unlikely I'll turn up anything after all this time."

Shiloh finishes the last rose and sets down the piping bag. She turns the cake again and again, then pushes it aside and rests her big fists on her hips.

"He saved up for this attempt you're making. It's all he's wanted for years. And I think that he knows it's all he can do. I think he just needs to know he did the best he could. I don't think he can go on with his life until he's tried. Finding his sister is all he wants. . . . He's an amazing artist. Did you know that?"

"He told me he does prints."

She nods.

"He's so good. He needs to be out there—in the world—becoming the guy he deserves to be. But . . . he can't. Not until he can get past the grief and guilt he's saddled with."

"You think he blames himself?" I ask. It seems crazy, but I've seen crazier.

"I think so."

"He was only eight when she was taken," I say.

She shrugs and says, "I know. But he was right in the other room. And he was her big brother. He always will be."

The double doors open, and the woman who'd been working out front sticks her head in the room. "Hey, some cops here to see you."

"Oh?" Shiloh says.

"No," the woman says, "Her." She points at me.

"Ah," I say. I toss back the last of my milk. "It's about that time."

# EIGHT

THE COPS ARE WAITING out front, beside Honey. Both men are wearing brown Marley County Sheriff's Department uniforms. The taller one is probably mid-fifties, narrow-waisted and broad-shouldered with a grim mouth and a hard gaze underscored by dark circles. He looks like he stays up late, wakes up early, has been getting by on three hours' sleep for most of his life and is just now feeling the effects.

"Annie Gore," he says, more a barked statement than a question.

Dealing with cops in this job is usually smooth. They want a case solved, but they don't have the time or the manpower to work it once all the leads have been exhausted and all the obvious pieces have been put together. Mostly, in those times, they're happy to let you go about your business as long as you aren't shooting up the place and causing problems. Sometimes, though, cops get aggressive about their turf. And cases like this one? Cases with kids involved? They stir emotions.

I run my eyes over his set jaw and the subtle splotches of angry red in his cheeks and figure this isn't a situation where I can smooth-talk my way into an easy investigation.

"That's right," I say.

"I understand you're a PI. I need to see your license."

I take out my wallet and hand him my driver's and private investigator's licenses and my concealed-carry permit.

"You armed?"

"Yes."

He squints at my various forms of ID and then hands them back to me with a low grunt. I get the feeling he was hoping I wasn't on the level. Hoping I was just some chick waltzing around with a four-thousand-dollar gun strapped to my belt for shits and giggles and he could tell me to get out of town with a warning. That course of action having failed, he changes tack.

"Need to have a word with you."

I look him up and down and then shift my gaze to the other guy. The shorter one—too young to be sheriff so probably a deputy—with warm pecan skin and bright brown eyes is stocky in the way college athletes gone to seed often are. I remember Leo calling it "hard fat," and the corner of my mouth ticks up at the memory.

"That right there, Gore," Leo had said, pointing at a Security Forces staff sergeant trudging across a base on the edge of a sweltering jungle, sweating like crazy and not complaining for a second. "That's hard fat. Man's been hitting the cafeteria extra hard, but he's got some power in him. Like a bull."

"A bull?" I snorted.

"Sure," Leo said.

"Okay, so what are you?" I asked.

He grinned.

"Me? Hell, Annie, I'm a hawk. I go where I want, hunt what I want, do what I want."

"And what am I?"

"Don't you know?" Leo said, a deep laugh escaping his throat.

I shook my head.

"Girl, you're a crow."

A laugh, instinctive and raw, had escaped my throat. I felt myself smiling, matching Leo's grin, but inside I felt some powerful truth in the label. Almost like holding a real, living, oil black crow in my hands, the notion felt both familiar and dangerous. Soft and sharp at once.

"A crow?" I said, nudging him with my shoulder to get more of an explanation.

"Damn straight," he said. "Always sticking your beak into the messes others shy away from. Raising a ruckus no one wants heard. Digging out truths no one wants seen."

Now, on the street, I look back at Night Owl Cop, clearly in charge, probably the sheriff. He's got the attitude of a guy who looks at my height and weight and thinks I can be pushed around. But, like Leo said, I'm a crow. And crows are wily.

I puff up my invisible feathers, spin my keys in my hand, and say, "I'm a little pressed for time."

Night Owl steps in front of me, arms crossed, and says, "We can do it now. Or we can do it down at the station."

"Okay," I say. "What's the word?"

"Excuse me?"

"You said you need to have a word with me. What is it?"

Behind Night Owl, I see Hard Fat press his mouth into a tight line. The color in his cheeks deepens. He's got a pair of very defined dimples when he smiles. They make him look too sweet to be a cop.

"You've been going around town asking questions," Night Owl says.

"Correct."

He takes a step closer to me, says, "About a ten-year-old case."

I match his move. Then, hands on hips, I stare up at him and say, "I've been asking questions about three little girls who disappeared one summer ten years ago, two of whom were never seen again and one of whom—"

"One of whom is my *niece*." The word comes out like a hiss.

"Oh," I say. I finally get around to reading the name tag on his chest.

Sheriff Jacobs. So, obviously related to Kathleen and her daughter, the once-missing Olivia Jacobs. *Great.*

"My niece is a vulnerable young woman," he says. "Whatever she went through—"

"Which she won't talk about."

"She *can't*—" Jacobs growls.

"Either way. Max Andrews hired me to look for his sister. That's what I'm doing."

"You think we haven't looked?"

Hard Fat steps up, puts a hand on Sheriff Jacobs's shoulder.

"Sheriff, she's just doing her job."

I'm still matching Jacobs's glare but, in my peripheral, I see Hard Fat shift his attention to me. "Ms. Gore, did you actually question Olivia?"

"No," I answer, still looking at Jacobs. "I just talked to Kathleen."

"Well, there ya go," Hard Fat says.

Jacobs narrows his eyes at me.

I hate to break up this fifth-grade staring contest with Jacobs but someone's got to do it. I blink, shift a step back, lean against Honey's front fender, cross my arms over my chest.

I take a deep breath and say, "I told Max Andrews that by now, all this time later, it's unlikely I'll turn up any new leads, that the only thing I might find is a lot of frustrated, angry people with hurt feelings and old suspicions about those kidnappings."

Sheriff Jacobs opens his mouth to say something else, but I keep on going. "I told him all that but he didn't care. People can get pretty emotional when it comes to family, can't they?"

Jacobs lets out a breath. He says, "Kathleen told you all she's gonna say. You got no right to talk to Olivia without her say-so and she says no. That girl's been through enough."

"Sure," I say.

He narrows his eyes at me and then turns to Hard Fat and says, "Keep an eye on her, AJ."

Then he stalks off, swings open the door to Shiloh's, goes inside. It's hard to make waltzing into a bakery look edgy and badass, but Jacobs just about manages it. Hard Fat, actually apparently AJ, shrugs his great big shoulders and says, "Where you staying, ma'am?"

His voice is smooth, gentle, very country. I suppress a sneaky grin.

I've always had a soft spot for corn-fed country boys who call every woman over the age of twenty "ma'am."

"Max Andrews's cabin."

He nods.

"I live right down the lane from there. I've known Max since he was little."

"Oh yeah?"

"Back before everything happened, I was his scout troop mentor," AJ says.

I bark out a laugh, "That tracks. You look like you've been in uniform your whole life."

"Can't deny it," he says with a chuckle. He has a soft smile and a gentle laugh and I feel like being the Sheriff's Deputy of Quartz Creek, North Carolina, is both the best and the worst possible job for him.

"I've tried to keep an eye on him through the years. He mentioned a few months back he was finally going to hire a PI. I'm glad you're here."

"Even though I'm already stepping on your toes?"

"Sheriff Jacobs can be protective of Kathleen and her daughters. You understand."

"Yep."

"Look, Max may only be eighteen, and eighteen-year-olds can be pretty difficult, but he's a good kid. And I consider him a friend."

He pulls out a genuine cop notebook, just like in the movies, and writes down his number, rips out the page, hands it to me. I slip it into my pocket.

"If you need anything," he says, "let me know. I want to help if I can."

"Sure."

"And try to steer clear of Sheriff Jacobs."

# NINE

MY NEXT STOP IS the church Jessica Hoyle was taken from. Quartz Creek First Baptist is a mostly brick building with a white roof and steeple. The wet, gravel parking lot looks like it would fit more than fifty cars but there's only one sitting there when I pull in, a late-model gray Buick Regal.

"All right, Honey," I say. "Let's see what the local holy rollers have to say about these girls."

I turn the key, get out, and walk toward the church, passing a tasteful cream and burgundy sign advertising the annual First Baptist Fall Festival in a couple of days.

I head up the front steps, through the huge front door, and into the hunter green–carpeted foyer. Padding into the sanctuary, I look past the pews toward the empty pulpit. The ceilings are high but not beamed and the windows are plain glass that look out to the parking lot and empty playground on one side and a tree-dotted meadow—mostly apples, oaks, and elms—on the other. Nothing to distract from the Lord's word, I guess. Certainly not interesting architecture.

"Hello?" I call. I hear some rustling of papers and then a woman comes out of a door in the foyer. She's reed-thin with a white fluff of short, full curls that sweep away from her face. She is dressed in a skirt suit that, while simple, looks perfectly tailored from soft, gray wool. Probably a pattern from McCall's, I think.

"May I help you?" she asks.

I tell her who I am, what I'm doing there.

"I'd like to speak to the preacher, if he's around," I say.

"Oh, I'm sorry. He's not in at the moment. He'll be here tonight for Bible study."

She takes a pamphlet from a plastic rack on the wall and hands it to me. It's the church schedule, and, sure enough, there's Bible study with Brother Bob Ziegler, right there on the events for Monday night.

"He was in this morning to take care of some paperwork and then he left to do some visiting."

"And you are?"

"Oh, I'm Rebecca Ziegler. I'm the church secretary, and Brother Bob's wife."

I look back at the pamphlet, read the schedule. "It looks like he'll be in again tomorrow morning? For this . . . Promise Keepers thing? Could I come by then?"

"Promise Keepers is men only. But the meeting should be over around eight o'clock. It's early but—" She looks me up and down, no doubt a little dubious about whether or not I'm capable of being awake before noon.

"I'll be here," I say. "Can you let him know?"

"I will. Do you have a card?"

She pulls on a pair of gold-rimmed glasses attached to a thin gold chain around her neck. While she's reading my name and job title and phone number, I ask, "Can you tell me anything you remember about the disappearances of those three little girls?"

"Heavens," she says, still looking at the card. "It was an awful thing, wasn't it? Of course, the Andrews family attended here."

That was confirmation, at least, that Max and his family were familiar with this place, the scene of the first crime, where Jessica went missing from the swing set.

"The Jacobses too?" I ask, wondering about Olivia's family.

She nods.

"And the Hoyles?"

"No. They never have. Mandy's come around a few times, requesting food from the food bank. Formula when her youngest two were still in diapers. We sent them Christmas dinner a couple times, but I got the feeling Tommy didn't appreciate that so we stopped."

"Jessica Hoyle was taken from here."

She nods and says, "That's right. Out on the playground in broad daylight."

"Were you here?"

"Yes. There was a committee meeting that day. Quite a few of us were here to plan that year's Vacation Bible School. I remember Mandy coming into the church, screaming that something had happened to her girl. We all started looking, trying to help. I think most of us figured the girl had wandered off or was maybe hiding somewhere. But we found no sign of her."

"Can I get a list of everyone?"

She sighs, "Well, it's been . . ."

"Ten years," I say.

"Mercy," she says, letting out a breath. "Has it really? We still keep those girls and their families on the prayer list." She appears lost in thought for a while, like maybe she's wondering whether, after all this time, those prayers are being wasted.

"About the planning committee list . . ." I nudge.

"Oh yes. If you're coming by tomorrow, I could get you a list. But it might not be the most accurate. I'd just be guessing at who all was there. A lot of us are still on those committees but, you know, it's been a while, like I said."

"That's all right," I say. "I'll take any list I can get. I understand that Olivia Jacobs was taken from a church picnic. Would that have been a First Baptist event?"

"Yes," Rebecca says. "It was awful."

"What do you remember about it?"

She breathes out heavily through her nose and then says, "I was at another table, helping some of the women organize the drinks. I heard a scream. It was Kathleen. She was searching for Olivia. I remember thinking, at first, that Olivia must have just wandered off. She was always an obstinate girl. But then there was the doll."

"Where was it found?"

"Lying against a tree," she says, bringing her fingertips up to touch the small gold cross at the hollow of her neck. "Near the tables where Olivia went missing. The whole congregation split up to search for her but . . ."

"You found nothing."

"No," she says. "Nothing."

"Did the police question you at the time?"

"Of course," she says, her voice going shaky. "They questioned everyone. Anyone who'd been around either of the kidnappings. But we didn't know anything. All we could do to help those girls was pray to the Lord for their safe return. Which we still do."

"Okay," I say. "Well, I appreciate your help. And if you can get me that list, I'd really appreciate it."

"Yes," she says. "All right."

"Thank you," I say. And because sometimes you catch more flies with honey, "I really appreciate it, ma'am."

I leave and walk back down the steps and across the empty parking lot. I slide behind Honey's wheel and rev the engine, but I don't move. Instead, I sit there for a minute, thinking. Jessica was taken from this church. Olivia was taken from a picnic hosted by this church. But what about Molly? Shiloh said Max and Molly's parents attended this church, but was that the only connection?

Instead of backing out and leaving, I pull to the rear of the parking lot, to a little playground sitting under the edge of a tree line. Just like Mandy said, there's a dark wood swing set and slide with one of those square towers at one end. A little sun-bleached now, but still plenty usable. The chains on the swings have been oiled or replaced over the years since Jessica was taken from one of them.

I sit in the driver's seat in the cool, damp air and watch the swing. "She must've been exhausted," I say to Honey.

Honey purrs.

I think about Mandy. Tired and hungry and probably feeling hopeless and sad. A baby in her belly, another one in the backseat, another one on the swing.

Jessica had been there, I think, picturing the little blond fairy of a girl. She had been there pumping her legs. And then what?

I rest my hands in my lap instead of on the wheel and watch the swing and think about those dolls with their little bright dresses and their empty black eyes and think about the witch who turned herself into a crow and taught the other crows to cry and I think about Susan Mc-Kinney seeming to look at me and right through me at the same time. The heater runs, blowing hot air over my feet and hands. The top blower isn't working. The windshield fogs.

*Watch the swing,* I think.

*Watch the swing. Watch the swing. Watch the swing.*

It's almost hypnotic. A little girl, swinging. Mandy so tired. A toddler snoozing in the backseat, the rhythmic sound of his breath lulling and calm.

My eyelids begin to droop.

A crow caws. Startles me awake. The crow is standing on the top of the swing set's tower, looking down at me, his feathers a wet, glossy black, his eyes like polished glass. He caws again.

I hear Leo's voice from so many years ago, the first time I met him.

"You always gotta go after shit. That's what they tell me," he'd said, slapping a file down on the table in front of me. "Can't leave nothing alone."

I'd shrugged. I'd been looking into a suspicious money trail on my own time. I was still in Security Forces then, but the unofficial case had fallen well outside of my purview. Still, I'd refused to let it drop, and my searching had led to the discovery of a first lieutenant's paying off a local girl to keep quiet about some of his boys getting rough with the strippers at the club in town, part of a larger, disturbing pattern I couldn't keep quiet about.

I'd thought I was going to catch hell from Leo, the way I was digging around. I figured the moment I stepped foot in his office, I'd be booted out of the Air Force for all my meddling. Instead, he recruited me to his unit within the Office of Special Investigations. I'd be operating both within and apart from the Air Force. Much of the time, I'd be investigating our own airmen.

"Now you can find shit out for a job," Leo had said. "Seems like you got the stones for it, and maybe, working for me, you won't get yourself killed."

My mouth had dropped open in surprise, and he'd laughed. The first time I ever heard his laugh.

The crow caws again.

I stare up at the crow, watch him stretch his wings in slow, rhythmic motions. Watch him lift into the air with a *thwip-thwip-thwip* and disappear into the trees.

"Okay, Honey," I say. "Time to get back to work."

# TEN

Back in town, I stop at a gas station and buy myself a Coke from the back of the fridge before heading to the pump and pushing the button for premium gas. I stand against Honey's fender, watching the cost tick up while both of us take long, thirsty drinks.

When we're done, I look at the address Mandy gave me for Dwight and Elaine Hoyle and, realizing it's not too far, start in that direction. A few minutes later I arrive at a little blue house on a twisty lane crammed with other houses. There's no vehicle in the drive but I get out anyway and try my luck at the door. I bang a few times but there's no answer, and when I start trying to peer into the window, I'm interrupted by the sound of throat clearing behind me.

Turning, I find a woman in her sixties with arms as big as a bear's crossed over her chest.

"You here to buy soap?" she asks.

"What?"

"Elaine's damn soap business. She said she's gonna sell at the farmers market, but I've yet to see her down there."

"She's making soap?" I ask.

"Oh sure," the woman says with an exaggerated eye roll. "Says she's making holiday soaps for the Christmas season, but if you ask me the whole place smells like a reindeer fart. If you're not here to buy soap then who the hell are you?"

I tell her who I am, what I'm doing there.

"Well, it's pretty clear they ain't home," she says, taking my card. "So maybe you can take this ruckus elsewhere."

"You know when they'll be back?"

"Not one idea," she says. "They ain't hardly ever here since they come back. Except for soap-making time. That's every Sunday so far, right when I'm trying to get ready for church."

"Well, if they turn up, would you give them my card? Or call me?"

She gives me a long look, her lips pursed to the side, then clicks her teeth and nods.

"Thanks," I say. And then she stands there and waits for me to get in my car and leave. I'd forgotten how territorial people are here. How much neighbors look out for one another, even if they don't care much for them.

We pull away from Dwight and Elaine's place and back toward the highway. I'm already exhausted, but, I think, it's worth it to talk to everyone on my list before word of my activity spreads all the way around town and people start getting their hackles up. It's always better to catch people off guard.

"Come on, Honey," I say as I rev her engine. "One more and then we'll pack it in."

Deena Drake, Max's former piano teacher, lives up a road named Lilac Overlook Lane. It's paved and the asphalt runs like a gray ribbon up and up and up under arched branches colored gold and red. After several minutes of twists and turns, between thick clusters of mountain laurel, I finally break into open land on a cleared mountaintop with a two-story, glass-fronted luxury log cabin at the center of a still-green lawn.

I park beside an older but still solid-looking Range Rover, get out, and wander up the cedar steps to the front door. But just as I'm about to knock, there's a voice beside me.

"Hello," a woman says. I turn and the woman's standing in the grass next to the porch. In spite of the gardening hat, apron, and gloves, she is—in every way—prim. Her blond bob, brushed with silver, is sleek and perfectly straight and grazes her sharp chin. Her dark blue eyes—almost lavender in the half-light—look at me with open curiosity from under the sun hat.

"Deena Drake?" I guess.

"That's right."

I tell her who I am.

"Max Andrews hired me," I say, coming down the steps and around the porch to close the distance. "I'm looking for the girls who disappeared ten years ago."

She eyes me for a long moment, reading something in my face. I look back at her and try to appear as amiable as possible.

"May I see some identification?" she says.

I take my wallet from my back pocket, pass her the cards. She reads the IDs carefully, one at a time, then hands them back. Again, she gives me a long look, as if deciding whether to talk to me.

"A'right," she says finally. "You'll have to come around back, I'm very nearly finished and I want to get these bulbs in before dark."

I follow her around the house to a sprawling flower garden. Seasonal blooms of pansies and mums fill the space nearest the house, paths of white gravel running between them. The space beyond the house is filled with rosebushes, likely numbering more than a hundred. Most of their blossoms have dropped but I spot several still-vibrant red, orange, yellow, and pink blooms among the rows. Beyond them, the whole mountain-top is bordered by evergreen mountain laurel bushes, their pale pink and white flowers already dropped but their waxy leaves unmistakable.

"Wow," I breathe, staring at the garden. "This is beautiful."

"Thank you," Deena says.

I've always been envious of the green-thumbed. My granny was one of those people who could make anything grow, and clearly this woman has the same talent.

She leads me to one of the nearest beds and kneels beside it, where a bag of bulbs waits next to churned-up black soil.

"So," she says. "The Andrews boy has hired you?"

"Yes."

"It's been a while," she says. She digs in the soil with a spade and drops a tulip bulb in, covers it over.

"Yes," I say. "Ten years. I wanted to talk to you because—"

"Because I was there that day. The day Molly was taken."

"Yes."

She nods. "Unfortunately, I doubt I'll remember anything more about it now than I did then. But I'm happy to tell you what I know."

"Okay. You were Max's piano teacher. Let's start there."

"Yes. Max had just started lessons a few months before. It was his mother's idea, I believe."

"Was he good?"

"He wasn't a prodigy, if that's what you're asking. But more patient than the average little boy, I'd say. Less wiggly."

"And Molly?"

"Goodness, I barely saw her. She was a pretty little girl."

"Tell me what you remember. About Molly, the family, that day."

"It was the end of summer," Deena says. "Unbearably hot. And they had no air-conditioning. They lived in an old farmhouse, you know. Lots of small rooms. It was like a maze. Their piano was in an old dining room at the back of the house, and I believe Molly had been playing in the front of the house, the living room."

"And their father was at school," I say.

She digs another hole, plants another bulb.

"As I learned later, yes."

"And their mother was working in the garden, to the side of the house."

"Yes."

"So what happened?" I ask. "When Max came out and found his sister gone."

"Well, that's the thing, actually. I'd already left by then," Deena says. She takes one gardening glove off and pulls a wisp of silvery blond hair back behind her ear. Her fingers are long and elegant and her manicured nails are the color of the inside of a conch shell. "I'd gone out the kitchen door, which was on the side of the house. My car was parked around the side, in their driveway, so it just made the most sense. I always came and went that way. As far as I know, everyone did. Anyway, Max finished his practice and I left. I felt very guilty about it later."

"Guilty?"

"Yes," she says. She closes her eyes briefly and puts her bare fingertips to her forehead as if the guilt is a sharp pain above her eyebrows.

When she opens her eyes, she says, "I didn't check to see that Janice Andrews was still in the house. She usually was, you see. Or, if she went out, she took the children with her. I didn't understand that she'd gone to the garden alone. I had another appointment almost immediately after, so, when the lesson was complete, I gathered my things, shouted goodbye to Janice—whom I thought was still in the house somewhere—and then went on my way. I ran into a man on the way out. A plumber, I think."

"Do you remember his name?" I ask.

"No," she says. "But it must be in a file somewhere at the station because of course they questioned me later. Anyway, the plumber had come to the house after me and parked behind me and I remember thinking I'd have to ask him to move, but he was leaving as well." She pauses to let out a long sigh and then says, "It wasn't until the next day that I heard about it."

"And what did you hear?"

"That little Molly had been taken, just like the other girls."

"Jessica and Olivia."

"Yes."

"And that an applehead doll was left in her place," I say.

"Yes. I did hear about that. Ghastly looking things. I'd never heard of them before that summer."

"Where are you from?" I ask. Deena's accent lacks the hard twang of her neighbors, and her open, genteel bearing is a lot more Deep South than high holler.

"Georgia, originally," Deena says. "Savannah."

"Oh," I say. "Pretty."

She nods and puts her glove back on, and I watch her carefully bury another bulb.

"What brought you here?" I ask.

"My husband. He was from here originally and he owned a couple of mills and factories in the region, including one in town."

"The one that closed the year the girls were kidnapped," I say.

"Yes. That's actually . . . Well, that's a bit my fault."

"How so?"

"My husband passed earlier in the year. Harvey had already been having trouble keeping the business afloat, and once he died I simply had no idea what to do with it. I sold it off as soon as I could, and the new owners moved operations out of town."

"Hmm," I say. I watch her pull another bulb from the bag, then ask, "Do you attend First Baptist?"

The change in direction doesn't seem to faze her. She smiles at the bulb as she buries it and says, "Yes. Brother Bob performed Harvey and my wedding ceremony. He and Rebecca were a great comfort when Harvey passed."

She stands and faces me. She looks like the kind of woman who's had a nine-step nightly skin-care routine from birth and has never missed a day.

"What did you think of the Andrews family?" I ask.

She sighs and takes off her sun hat for the first time.

"They seemed a very nice couple. The wife was quiet. The husband was intelligent. I was very sad to hear of Janice Andrews's passing."

The word "passing," I think, isn't right. It's too quiet. Too soft. Too nice a word to describe the way Janice Andrews left this world.

We turn back toward the house and as we pass it, with the sun setting to the west, I look out from the high vantage of Lilac Overlook. Quartz Creek and all its lower hills and valleys spread out below. From here, I can see the little Main Street. Closer, there are acres and acres of hilly farmland. It's a lovely patchwork of autumnal color spread out like a quilt, prepared for the coming winter.

"It's beautiful up here," I say.

"Isn't it?"

"I guess I'd better head down before it gets dark."

I give her my card. She takes it and slips it into her gardening apron pocket, and I feel fairly certain it'll go straight in the trash as soon as she gets inside. "Let me know if you think of anything else. I know it's been a while, but I've promised Max I would look and, you never know, sometimes people remember things a long time after."

She squints at the card, biting her lips together for a moment, obviously mulling something over before she finally meets my eyes again and says, "I believe I've told you all I know. I went over this many times with the police ten years ago."

"Yes but—"

"Please don't come back here," Deena interrupts. She takes a sharp inhale of breath, pausing. Her inborn politeness is fighting what she wants to say, but she carries on anyway, "The year Harvey died was the hardest of my life. And these questions only remind me of that time. Of his absence. I may have been in the Andrewses' house that morning, but I have no knowledge of where those girls went. Please, I only wish to be left alone."

"I can't promise that," I say. "I may need to talk to you again."

"And I may need to call the sheriff if you step on my land again." It sounds less like a threat and more like a calm statement of fact. I nod in response, and she gives me a brief smile as if all this is just a small misunderstanding.

She follows me to Honey, and I turn back before I open the door. I look up at the elegant, A-frame, glass-fronted cabin.

"It's a beautiful house," I say.

"Thank you," she says. "Take care."

"Sure," I say. "Have a good night."

She waves me off and I swing into the driver's seat and rev the straight six. After a very long day, I'm down the switchback road twice as fast as I climbed it.

# ELEVEN

'M AT MY LAPTOP—sitting behind the narrow strip of butcher-block countertop in Max's cabin taking notes—when I hear whispers and footsteps outside, see shadows pass through the warm, orange light of the porch bulb. There's a knock on my door and the sound of a little kid giggling. I slip my gun back into the holster I never got around to taking off, and answer.

"Hi!" says Shiloh, exactly as cheerful as I'd seen her earlier that day. Max, Shiloh, and Shiloh's little girl—Lucy—are all there. Shiloh is holding a basket and Lucy a tiny pumpkin with a long, curly stem.

"Sorry to disturb you," Max says, his cheeks flushed from the night air. In the company of Shiloh and Lucy, he is smiling—a real smile—and I realize it's the first time I've seen it.

"We're looking for a good carving pumpkin," Shiloh says. "Lucy liked this one but it's a bit too small. We thought it might look nice in the cabin and I was bringing this by anyway."

She hands me the basket, and my belly grumbles at the scent of pumpkin bread and fresh cinnamon rolls.

"You're amazing," I say, staring down at the treats. "Marry me."

"I've got enough on my hands as it is," Shiloh says with a chuckle, "without hitching myself to a woman of action."

I take the basket and she says, "Oh, I put some savory hand pies in there too. Sausage from my daddy's farm. I'm told people can't live on sugar alone."

I offer my heartfelt thanks, and then Lucy tugs at the hem of Max's barn coat and says, "Can we look at the creek?"

Max glances at Shiloh, who nods, and then he leads Lucy down the steps and onto the path.

"You take good care of him," I say, watching Max and Lucy.

"I've tried to watch out for him, that's all."

"Can't have been easy. You were just a kid yourself, weren't you?"

"Sixteen when Molly was taken, yes. But it was the right thing to do," she says. "He lost his sister, his father, and his mother all within a couple of years. He was left alone to carry the burden of what had happened. I kept in touch when I went to culinary school. Then, when I came back, he helped me refurbish the building for the bakery. He's been saving for a PI since he was a kid. I think he needs to do it. Needs to know he did what he could do. He could have a big future, I think, but . . ."

She looks past my shoulder, and I turn, following her gaze to the woodblock print above the fireplace.

"Did he tell you about that?" she asks.

"No. I was actually going to ask where he got it."

"He *made* it," she says.

"That's his?" I ask, staring at the print with fresh eyes. The depth of the line, the gradation in value, the balance of the composition. The way the crows seem *alive* as they melt into the sky. He'd said that he did woodblock prints, but this was way beyond the capability of a teenager.

"Max is such a talented kid," Shiloh says, reading the look on my face. "He's completely self-taught. He was offered scholarships to five different schools and even an internship in Japan to study with one of his heroes, which, I confess, I applied to for him because I knew he wouldn't."

"Wow."

"But he won't go," she says. "Not until he's done what he needs to do. And he needed to hire a PI."

"Even if the PI doesn't turn up anything new?"

"Do you think that's what'll happen?"

"It's likely, I think. But I understand why he has to try."

We watch Max and Molly in the distance. He picks something up from the ground and waves his hand like he's performing a simple magic trick. She laughs and jumps up and down.

I look back at Shiloh and ask, "What can you tell me about First Baptist and Brother Bob?"

"You think they're connected to the kidnappings?"

"Do you?"

"When I was a teenager, I remember there being questions. Later, when I saw Max's notes and everything . . . Oh, I don't know. I did wonder. All the girls taken had some kind of connection there. But as far as personal knowledge about the place? My family went to that church and so I went to that church but, aside from a couple family funerals, I haven't been in years. Brother Bob must be in his, what, late sixties, at least? And what would he or anyone else from the church have done with a couple of little girls?"

"What's Brother Bob like?" I ask. "He wasn't there today."

Shiloh's lips purse to the side for a moment before she says, "He's sort of like . . . Santa Claus in a glen plaid suit and loafers. He always struck me as harmless."

"He never talked to you?"

"In passing, sure. But, he ministered from the pulpit. We had a couple youth ministers over the years, for the teenage crowd, but none of them really stand out."

"And you don't go now?"

Shiloh barks out a laugh.

"No. They're pretty traditional, and I'm a single mom. I didn't marry Lucy's dad because, well, I just plain didn't want to. He's a nice guy but we barely knew each other. My folks *love* Lucy, and they take her to some of the church's more benign functions. Festivals and picnics and Easter egg hunts. Stuff like that. Somehow my mom conned me into making a bunch of stuff for this year's festival. Though I still don't intend to go."

"What can you tell me about Deena Drake?"

"She used to teach piano," Shiloh says. "But my sisters and I didn't take lessons. My daddy was much more interested in making sure we were all crack shots." She pauses while we watch Max and Lucy stand at the edge of the gorge, looking down at the creek. "I was shooting clay pigeons out on the farm by the time I was eight."

She shakes her head at the memory and then sighs and says, "But, aside from Deena being Max's piano teacher, I know she came to town about twenty years ago and married Harvey Drake, the factory owner. Then he died and she stayed up in the house on the hill."

"It's a beautiful house. I was up there today."

"Oh really?" Shiloh says. "I've heard the view is gorgeous. She has Christmas parties up there whenever the weather permits, and my parents usually go, but I've never seen it in person."

We watch as Max and Lucy start back toward the house, Lucy still clutching Max's fingers.

"You mentioned the church's 'more benign functions.' Are there some that are less benign?"

She half shrugs. "Well, just revivals and that sort of thing. They have guest preachers in sometimes who are more or less fanatical about God's word and the literalness of it. They occasionally have big prayer meetings where they get together to pray over someone who's sick or suffering, sort of low-key faith healing. It's fine for my parents but just not really for me."

She turns toward Lucy and Max as they step onto the porch. "We'd better get home if we want to carve that pumpkin before bedtime."

They all take off and I watch them go before I close the door. Back in the cabin, I make coffee and dig into background checks. What I expected is pretty much what I get. Drunk and disorderlies for Tommy Hoyle. I look up his cousins, Dwight and Elaine Hoyle. They both have records—misdemeanors for possession and DUIs—but nothing in the last year. I find their last known address and then look at the street view online. It's a big apartment complex with a ton of tiny balconies, cheek by jowl, overlooking a parking lot.

I shift my focus to the local constabulary. There's a long record of service in the department for Sheriff Cole Jacobs. And there's AJ Barnes, former running back for Appalachian State, a deputy for the last two years with an Instagram account showing off food from his mom and dad's barbecues, sun-dappled shots of him working on a cabin up in the woods, him in a tux at his sister's wedding.

I find some old pictures from an archived Savannah society magazine of Deena as a fresh-faced debutante. I don't find much about Brother Bob Ziegler. Just a lot of old newsletters from First Baptist, usually penned by Mrs. Ziegler.

I look up Susan McKinney but, while I find a few other women with her name, I can't find anything about the woman who'd startled me in the woods during my run. I remind myself that not everyone has an online presence and that for older people in this region that's probably even more accurate.

I look back and forth between photos of all these people and photos of the applehead dolls from Max's scrapbook. I remember my granny sitting on the porch and peeling an apple. I remember being little, watching the long spiral of skin falling away from the pale flesh, dropping to the floor with a dull plop. I remember sitting there into the night, my mom working late, my dad off doing God-knows-what. And my granny telling me to come on in, no use waiting up; they weren't coming to get me.

I look back at the little shriveled faces of the black-eyed dolls and think of the witch who turned her daughters into a bluebird and a robin so they might sing for her forevermore.

I'm still lost in thought when my phone rings, and I answer.

"How's the hoedown?" Leo asks. His voice is like velvet, wrapping around me. Instantly, I feel myself relax.

"Just getting started. You know what an applehead doll is?"

"Nope. Why don't you enlighten me."

"Don't you have other things to do? Cleaning guns or counting money or doing rounds through your secret under-a-volcano base?"

Leo laughs, and I smile at the sound.

I update him on the case.

"It's unlikely they're still there," Leo says. "After ten years?"

"I know." I look again at the photos of the dolls, shake my head. "Most likely, someone took them away and they're long gone. Or they were murdered, and their bodies are buried somewhere in these hills."

"That sounds about right. How's the law down there? They giving you much trouble?"

"You know me."

"I know you like to stir up shit. Things get thick, I'm always a phone call away."

"I thought you were wheels up tomorrow. Won't you be in Singapore or Dubai or somewhere?"

"I'm always a phone call away, Annie."

"Okay," I say, smiling in spite of myself.

We hang up and I eat some of what's in the fridge while I jot down a few more notes, take a shower, watch reruns of *Andy Griffith* on the little TV in the bedroom.

I fall asleep to the heavy drumbeat of Barney Fife's theme song and an under-chorus of screaming crows in my ears.

The next morning I'm awake just before dawn. I sit up, put my shoes on, splash water on my face, slip into my jacket. I hesitate before I'm all the way out the door, go back inside and tuck my holster and gun against the back of my leggings. It's not a great feeling to run with a gun, but it's not like I didn't do it for years—with a much heavier gun—before I veered off my old path and onto this one. I leave the cabin and make sure it's locked. I jog the length of the gravel road, head down by the gorge, across the bridge, up the other side.

I'm working up a good sweat as I close in on the ring of boulders.

And then I stop.

There's more than one crow today. There's a swarm. It's a dense, wavering cloud of black feathers and a screaming, echoing chorus of hoarse cries. They're circling a dead animal. Fighting over it. Laughing and crying and shrieking at each other.

I almost turn and jog away. Seeing a deer being dismantled isn't my idea of a good morning.

But it's the color. A redder red than blood and, attached to it, an intricate, snow white froth of lace.

Shivers run up my spine, catch in my throat.

"Oh no," I breathe. I pull my gun on instinct, hold it at the ready. Check my surroundings. The forest is quiet. There's nothing here but crows. I reholster as a sick, ugly feeling grows in my stomach.

I take a step closer, pull my jacket off, wave it at the crows. They flap and caw and finally settle on the stones, their talons scrabbling against the rough surface.

There, in the center, is a young woman. Her honey brown hair is wavy and shiny and princess-long, streaming over the fallen leaves. She wears a soft-looking red dress and she is, unquestionably, dead. The scene is like a Waterhouse painting, all bright colors and fair skin and tragedy.

Except for the ring of red around her neck, the speckles of blood in her eyes. This young woman has been strangled and left here, exposed.

Finding a corpse is never a pleasant experience.

But the corpse of a murder victim? It is something else altogether. It's a fist closing around your heart. Oxygen burning your lungs. Blood pounding in your ears. All reminders that you are still alive while the person in front of you is dead. A sudden certainty that you continue to exist while this person remains only as a body. A memory. A victim.

Years of training have stripped whatever instinct I might once have had to scream, run, cry, vomit, call for help.

I clench my jaw shut. And I force myself to look.

The crows have been at her. Nips have been taken from her cheeks and hands, revealing red flesh within. Her eyes, though, are mercifully untouched, her delicate lids pale and thin, half shut over hazel irises and whites dotted with burst blood vessels, the evidence of her body's desperate fight for air. A ragged ring of red encircles her pale neck. The cause of her death.

I move a little closer, careful where I put my feet.

Her Cupid's bow mouth is slightly open above a bright white, inch-long scar on her chin. Exactly as Shiloh had described. The little girl. The excitement. The fall. The trip to get stitches.

I swallow the lump in my throat and force myself to stare at that scar.

No longer a child, then. No tiny, unmarked grave full of small, fragile bones.

A girl, very nearly a woman.

"Molly," I breathe. "I found you."

And my voice reverberates off the rocks and rises into the air around me.

"I found you . . . found you . . . found you . . ."

# TWELVE

DEPUTY AJ BARNES'S HANDS quiver as he slides them from his pockets. "Jesus," he says, just a whisper. I almost don't hear it.

I called the sheriff's station first, told them there was a body in the woods. Then I called Shiloh, told her what had happened, that Max would need someone with him. I couldn't leave the body. Max deserved to be told about this in person, but I didn't want him coming down and finding this scene.

I took a few pictures while I waited for the cops to show up. I walked around the area, touching nothing, looking for anything that might help. I found nothing. The windy mountain night had blown leaves all over the place and I didn't want to walk more than five feet away from her with all the crows standing sentinel on the stones, looking down at her with hungry eyes and sharp mouths.

And then Sheriff Jacobs and Deputy Barnes and an older man in a suit and a female deputy with a bag full of camera gear all tromped down the Andrews side of the gorge, crossed the creek, and made their way up to the stones.

I watched them. And I waited.

And now they were here.

"Jesus," Barnes says again.

"Is it her?" I whisper.

We are all trying to ignore the echoing of our words, all of us talking so low it's as if we don't want the forest to hear us and repeat what we've said.

"Barnes?" I whisper again. "Is it Molly?"

He shakes his head, says, "I don't know. She was just a tiny little kid when I saw her last. Hell, *I* was just a kid."

"It's her," Jacobs says. "It's her. I've stared at those pictures long enough."

He's talking to himself, I realize. Not to me. His skin, which had been ruddy yesterday when he confronted me outside the bakery, is a sick gray color, and I think for a minute he might step away to vomit in the bushes.

He sighs instead, scrapes a rough palm over the stubble on his cheeks and chin, and then he turns to me and bears down with a hard stare. But before he can open his mouth the little old man in the suit clears his throat and leads us all out of the stone circle, then says, "Strangulation. With, perhaps, a fabric belt or scarf. There are claw marks on her throat and blood under her nails. I'd guess she scratched at her own neck, trying to get whatever it was off." He pauses and sighs and then says, "I've still got Molly's records on file. Her dental will have changed but . . . I treated her when she sliced open her chin. Six stitches. You can still see the suture marks."

He holds the tip of his index finger just over the scar.

"Ah, hell," Deputy Barnes says. We turn and there's another deputy and a pair of EMTs with a stretcher coming down the hill. Behind them, standing with his eyes screwed shut and his hand over his mouth, is Max Andrews.

I watch as Barnes takes off across the creek and scrambles up the side of the gorge toward Max. Beside me, Sheriff Jacobs is seething. His voice is all bitter bile as he bites out, "This is *your* doing."

I don't turn to look at him. I just watch as Barnes puts his hand on Max's shoulder.

I say, "How is that?" I keep my tone soft, calm.

"You just had to ride into town with questions. Getting people riled up."

"Max hired me to find his sister," I say.

"Well, you sure as hell did."

He moves away and directs the deputies. The female deputy opens up her bag and takes out a big DSLR camera and the flash goes off and off and off, and I watch as Shiloh emerges from the field and runs up to Max and puts her arms around him and he buries his face on her shoulder and cries.

"Yeah," I say to myself. "I sure as hell did."

# THIRTEEN

AT THE SHERIFF'S STATION I sign a statement and initial page after page of everything I'd done that morning and everyone I'd spoken to, everywhere I'd gone the day before. The process takes hours, and the whole time all I can think about is Molly's pale face, Max crying on the hill, the sound of screaming crows.

When I finally get back to Honey, I am exhausted and it's afternoon. My stomach groans for food, but I feel a weird, sickening guilt about even being hungry.

"Hey," a voice says.

"Deputy Barnes," I say, turning to him.

"AJ," he says, "Please call me AJ."

I nod and lean against Honey's door, let her hold my weight.

"Hey," I say. "How's Max?"

"I'm not sure," AJ says, crossing his arms over his chest. He shakes his head and looks down at the cracked asphalt between his black boots. "I left him with Shiloh."

"Okay," I say. I open the driver's-side door.

"What will you do now?" AJ asks.

I say, "I don't know. Max hired me to look for Molly. I did. And now she's been found. This is a case for the police now. A case for you."

My voice is hoarse and strangled, and my belly writhes with angry guilt. I slide into Honey's driver seat and roll down the window enough to say, "Good luck." And then he gives me a short wave and I pull out of the station parking lot and head back to Crow Caw Cabin.

When I get there, the door is hanging open.

"Damn it," I breathe. I get out of the car and pull my gun.

It's probably just Max or a cleaner he never mentioned, but I did spend an entire day poking the hornet's nest and now Molly is lying in the morgue. As tired as I am, my old reflexes surge to life and adrenaline sharpens my senses.

I sweep into the cabin, alert and ready. I take stock. In the living room, my rucksack is open and its contents litter the floor. A change of clothes, some pens and an old notebook, chewing gum and a package of crackers, crushed to crumbs and bursting from the plastic. My laptop is gone.

Pushing into the kitchen, slowly, head on a swivel, I see that the drawers and cabinets have all been interfered with, but nothing seems obviously missing. The bedroom is next, and my duffels have been emptied of my clothes, which lay in heaps on the floor. The nightstand sits open and the case for my gun is gone. I push into the bathroom, swish back the shower curtain, throw open the tiny linen closet. Nothing.

I pull out my phone and call AJ's number.

It's about fifteen minutes before his car rolls up and, as it does, I go out on the porch only to see Shiloh and Max approaching as well. For a moment, I'm surprised I don't see Lucy with them, and then I realize Shiloh must have left the little girl with her family. How painful would it be for Max to see the child right now, I think.

"What's going on?" Shiloh asks.

"The cabin was raided while I was at the station," I say to her. I come down the steps and face Max, finally, and for the first time since I'd discovered Molly. "Max, I am so, so sorry."

He looks at me, eyes glistening. No longer could he tell himself that maybe Molly was safe. No longer could he hope for her return. All of that was gone now. And heaped on top of it was the ugly reminder that not even his own land was safe.

"What did they take?" he asks, barely audible.

AJ parks and gets out of his cruiser and approaches us.

"I've got Flora on her way with the fingerprint kit," he says. "You sure they're gone?"

"Yeah, it's clear. They were long gone when I got here."

"What'd they take?"

I tell him about my laptop, my gun case.

"The case?"

"It's a really nice case," I explain. "And it was shut when I left. It locks automatically, so I'm guessing whoever it was thought there would be something valuable inside."

"Anything else?" he asks. He walks past me and into the cabin and I follow, with Max and Shiloh in my wake. We all look around at the turned-over living room, my clothes on the floor.

"The TV," Max says. "The TV's gone."

I see now that the little flat-screen that had sat in the corner on a wooden end table is gone, and then I groan inwardly as I realize the other thing that is missing.

"Damn it," I hiss.

I meet his eyes.

"Max, they took your casebook," I say.

I watch as all the tension, the raw energy of fresh grief holding him together, drains out. He sinks down into the chair beside the front door and puts his head in his hands. Shiloh sits on the arm of the chair next to him and lays her hand on his shoulder. AJ, Shiloh, and I all stand there for a while, looking at each other and at the cabin and at the things that aren't there and at the boy who brought me here. He breathes heavily through his hands.

"Max, I—"

"I want you to find them," he says.

Max looks up at me now. His eyes are red-rimmed, and it seems as though he's aged a decade since this morning.

"Max—"

He holds up a hand, and I stop. His voice is stony when he speaks. "I hired you to find Molly, and you did. Now, I want you to find who killed her. I want you to find out where she was. I want you to make sure this *never* happens again."

"I—"

"Will you do that?" he asks. His teeth are gritted, and they gleam.

The bewildered boy is gone, and in his place is a man pushed to his limit by grief and anger.

"Yes," I answer. "Yes. I will try."

# FOURTEEN

I STAND ON THE PORCH with AJ, leaning against the railing while Deputy Flora goes around the cabin looking for prints that likely aren't there.

"You don't risk the trouble of burgling a PI unless you have at least some sense of what you're doing," I say. "It's a dangerous business, stealing from someone whose job it is to track."

AJ nods and says, "I've been telling Max to put cameras out here, but he said the fishermen who usually come like it rustic and don't care for the intrusion on their privacy. He needed the money."

"So he could hire a PI."

He nods.

Max and Shiloh have returned to Max's farmhouse, where, undoubtedly, Shiloh is whipping up some kind of warm, healing homemade bread. My belly growls, and I remember again that I haven't eaten since last night.

"You got anything sensitive on that laptop?"

I snort. "You mean like naked selfies?"

I'm basically whistling past the graveyard but, at this point, it's all I can do. If I let myself dwell in the misery and misfortune of every case I worked, I'd surely be lost for good. Instead, I watch as an almost imperceptible blush creeps up AJ's thick neck and deepens the color in his cheeks. I bump him with my shoulder and he shakes his head, a sheepish grin stretching his mouth.

"I just meant—"

"No, I know. There's a lot of sensitive casework on there. I wiped it remotely when I saw it'd been taken. It's backed up on a drive back at my office."

"That's good," he says.

"The worst thing is Max's casebook," I say. "He's had it for years."

"I know," AJ says. "He showed it to me when I became a cop. But it's more of a scrapbook than a case file."

"It's got no value to anyone but him," I say.

"You think somebody came looking for it?" he asks.

"I doubt it. I think someone figured I'd have some expensive spy shit laying around. Little did they know the extent of my gear is a six-year-old laptop and a car that's older than I am."

We both look out at Honey, and I smile at the beautiful amber hue of her paint and the sleek, elegant line of her body and send up a silent prayer of thanks that she, at least, wasn't harmed today. Lucky for me, most folks don't see the beauty in rusty 1970s Japanese imports.

"Don't forget about that piece," AJ says. "Think I haven't noticed the dang designer gun you're toting?"

"Been looking at my ass?"

He blushes again, and I laugh. I feel glad for the company, glad for his closeness. I'm not generally a lonely person, but the day has worn on me and AJ's warmth is an unexpected comfort.

We watch the field for a few moments, watch the long brown grass waver in the breeze, watch as a crow swoops through the sky and disappears down into the gorge.

"AJ, you know Molly went missing from this town. And she was found again, this morning, in this town, not even a mile from where she was taken."

"Yeah," he says with a sigh.

"So, either someone took her and then brought her back . . ."

"Which—"

"Could be because someone heard about Max hiring a PI," I say. "Some kind of perversion, returning to the scene of the crime when attention falls on it. Out for some kind of thrill?"

We look at the field some more, the faraway trees, and I consider that option for a while.

He says, "You know, we're not that far past the ten-year anniversary of when they were taken. If they took the girls away, then maybe the kidnapper brought them back as a kind of reunion."

I nod.

"It's that or she was here the whole time," I say. "I don't know what's more unlikely. But either way—"

"Makes you sick, don't it?" AJ says, finally turning toward me.

"Yeah," I say. "It does."

It's all I can manage. I watch the wind in the field, try not to think about it.

"If she *were* here," I say, "who would have the means to hide a girl for that long?"

AJ says, "About anyone with a little bit of land. Even anyone with an extra room. Two young girls, I guess all you'd need is a sturdy setup. Everyone around here values their privacy, and we respect it until there's a reason not to. So, as long as Molly and Jessica were kept somewhere out of sight, somewhere they couldn't make too much noise . . ."

"She could've been just about anywhere," I say. "Some kind of *Flowers in the Attic* situation."

"Right," AJ says.

Deputy Flora comes out of the house with her case snapped up.

"All done," she says. "You're free to go on back inside."

"Find anything exciting?" I ask.

"Looks like he came in through the bathroom window. The lock on that side was jimmied off. I found what was left of it on the floor."

I nod, and she heads down the steps, gets in her cruiser, and drives away.

"Your sheriff isn't gonna like me staying around this town," I say.

"That's okay," he says, watching the cruiser disappear down the lane. "*I* want you to stay."

"You don't trust Jacobs?"

He shakes his head. "It's not that. Jacobs is a good man, but he's short-sighted and underfunded. Ten years ago, the cops looked for the girls. Fish and Wildlife looked for the girls. Hunters with bloodhounds looked for the girls. The FBI came down and looked for the girls. Hell, even my scout troop pitched in, combing the woods. Nobody found anything, and after that, officially, it was over."

"But unofficially?"

"Unofficially, off the record, Cole Jacobs has a whole board of evidence still standing in his home office. I saw it once. When I became a deputy, he and his wife had me over for dinner. I don't think I was supposed to see it. I took a wrong turn looking for the toilet. "Anyway, he's never been able to find anything. And I don't think it's for want of looking."

"So, what's the problem?"

"The problem is him and me and Max and all the rest of us were born here. We have our own suspicions and we have our own biases."

I think about Mandy Hoyle and the way Kathleen Jacobs had called the Hoyles "trashy." I think about how the FBI didn't show up until Cole Jacobs's niece was kidnapped. I think about how she's the only one that was ever brought back.

Until now.

"You want fresh eyes," I say.

"We *need* fresh eyes. My kin went to school with Max's kin who went to school with Sheriff Jacobs and all their kin went to school with each other and married each other and whatever. We *know* each other."

"Or you think you do."

"That's the problem," he admits.

"What can you tell me about Susan McKinney?" I ask. "The old woman who lives in the woods across the creek."

"Susan? You run into her?"

I tell him about my encounter with the old woman the day before, standing in the very spot I found Molly this morning. I leave out the fact that she'd given me actual, full-on heebie-jeebies.

"Local psychic," he says.

"Dangerous?"

"Not as far as I know. She lives in a little shack in the woods and mostly keeps to herself."

"Was she questioned the first time around?"

"Yes," he says. "I was only fifteen when it happened, but even I remember hearing about her being taken in, questioned. Both the cops and the FBI. They may have even held her overnight, but I don't remember for sure. I'd have to check the records."

"Speaking of the records . . ."

"I'll get you copies."

"And the coroner's report for Molly's body?"

He nods.

"You could lose your job," I say.

AJ shrugs. "It's not important."

"You sure?"

He meets my eyes.

"Molly Andrews was murdered," he says. "*That's* what's important. And Jessica Hoyle is probably still out there. *That's* what's important."

I nod.

"Okay, then," I say. "Get me those case files and the coroner's report."

"What are you gonna do?"

"I poked the hornet's nest yesterday," I say. "This evening, I'm gonna go out and see who's buzzing around."

# FIFTEEN

THERE ARE ABOUT TEN other cars when I pull into the lot of First Baptist again. I get out, go up the stairs and inside, and then follow the sound of shouting and the loud *thwap* of fists and shins against pads downstairs into the church basement.

The pamphlet had advertised Good Works Mission Karate, and there are maybe twenty kids here. They have a variety of belt colors and they're all sweating with exertion, their hair plastered to their faces.

Over to the side stands a man exactly like Shiloh had described: Santa Claus in a glen plaid suit and loafers. Only, this man doesn't look at all as roly-poly as I'd pictured. He's easily a foot taller than I am, with meaty arms and a neck so thick the pale yellow oxford shirt barely contains it. Up top, he's got a horseshoe of snow white hair, and while his cheeks are slightly flushed, I wouldn't call them rosy.

"Hello," I say when I approach. I tell him who I am and he holds his hand out for a shake. His palm is smooth, strong, and warm.

"Nice to meet you," Brother Bob says, extra friendly.

Something about the guy is familiar. Something deep down under all the outsized gregarious handshaking and smiling. I almost get my finger on what I'm sensing when he directs me into a little alcove by an old water fountain and says, "I heard about what happened this morning. How is young Max holding up?"

"About as well as you could expect."

He shakes his head, clasps his big paws behind his back.

Again, I'm struck by a strange sense of familiarity, and then he shifts his weight from foot to foot and the bee buzzing around in my brain finally stops and stings and I know what it is. Military. The guy's a vet. I don't know how I know. I just know. Like I know a Charger from a Shelby Cobra by the sound of the engine, I know this guy served.

"And you're . . . still on the case?" Brother Bob asks.

"Yes," I say.

He opens his mouth to say something, then stops and shuts it, sighs through his nose.

"I wanted to ask you about that time. I understand the Andrews family attended services here."

"That's right. Janice Andrews was raised in this church."

"You knew her that long?"

"I came along in '81. She was a child at the time. Her family were dedicated parishioners."

"And her husband?"

He gives a noncommittal shrug and we both watch the proceedings in the basement for a minute. A gangly man with a big smile and a threadbare gi instructs the kids, showing them the movements for a new kata. The kids follow along, stepping when he steps and arranging their arms like his.

"Greg was a biology teacher," Bob says, still watching the class.

"Does that preclude a person from spiritual belief?" I ask.

"No," he says. "Not at all."

And that's the end of that.

We watch as the karate teacher swipes his hand and forearm through the air like a sword. The kids follow.

"How well do you know Mandy and Tommy Hoyle?"

"Not well at all. I've seen them around, that's about it. I believe Mrs. Hoyle has used our food bank before, perhaps the Christmas present fund."

"And Kathleen Jacobs and her husband, Olivia's family?"

He sighs through his nose again. Longer this time. He's still looking in the direction of the karate kids, but that's not where his brain is. His eyes take on a defensive sadness.

"Yes," he says. "Kathleen and Arnie both attended until a few years ago."

There's a long pause while he chews on the inside of his cheek. I wait it out.

Eventually he says, "Olivia's uncle is the sheriff, you know."

"I do."

"We tried to help Olivia."

"How so?"

"We laid on hands. The whole church, when she was little. Her parents brought her in and asked us to pray for her and so we did. We sent up our prayers to the Lord but . . ."

"No change," I say.

He shakes his head.

"Were you expecting one?"

His eyes swivel down to me now, and they go narrow like he's trying to read a map but the print's too small. Eventually he gives up, looks away again. Doesn't bother answering my question.

"Jessica Hoyle was taken from this church," I say, hoping to catch him off guard.

"From the playground by the parking lot," he corrects, without missing a beat. "She's still in our prayers."

"Do you recall who was here that day?" I ask.

He shakes his head. "It was a long time ago."

"A decade," I say. "She's been gone ten years."

We say nothing for a moment. The gangly guy tells the kids to pair up and assists them when necessary. I watch as a little girl and her big brother face off.

"You know," Brother Bob says, almost absently. Again, he's looking toward the kids but not looking at them. "After a while, I really hoped they would just find, I don't know, something. Some little old bones? Give the families and this whole town some place to lay their grief, something to bury, something to pray over and send to heaven."

His jaw trembles a little and he shuts his mouth. I look away and watch as the big brother jabs and the little girl dips, plants her front foot, and whips a kick up to the brother's side. He laughs and so does she.

Brother Bob continues, "But . . . finding Molly like this."

"She was alive," I say. "All this time."

He nods his head, curt and quick. His eyes are watery, but I can't tell if it's emotion or just high blood pressure.

"Do you remember anything about that summer?" I ask. "Anything stand out to you at all?"

"It was a hot summer," he says. "Hotter than usual, I recall. We had a lot of our usual activities outside because we didn't have air-conditioning yet and it was just too hot indoors. And . . . that's the year the plant closed, wasn't it?"

He's not really asking me. He's talking to himself and he answers himself, "Yes. Because that's the year Harvey Drake died."

"Did you know Mister Drake well?"

"He was a Gideon. He came to the group meetings. He sang in the choir. He took me down to Junaluska a few times for golf."

"How did he die?" I ask, thinking of that beautiful house and the small, southern, stylish woman who still inhabits it.

"Massive stroke," Brother Bob says. "It was awful. He lingered for days."

"Must've been tough for Mrs. Drake."

"Rebecca'd know more than I would," he says, pointing to his slender wife across the basement. She's wearing yet another hand-tailored skirt suit and her white hair looks—curl for curl—exactly as it did the day before. She's talking to one of the parents, both casually watching the kids.

"I counseled him," he says. "In his final days and hours. He struggled. He was not ready to meet his Lord and Savior."

"Are any of us?" I ask.

He shrugs. At the front of the room, the gangly man claps his hands twice and the children form themselves into two lines before him. He bows to them. They bow more deeply back. Then the class breaks up and the kids start scurrying around the room like beetles. One of the parents begins making his way toward us, and I dig a card out of my bag and put it into Brother Bob's hand.

"If you think of anything," I say. "Anything at all. Call me."

He smiles benevolently at me and slips the card into an interior pocket before moving away to shake hands with one of his flock.

I make my way around the edge of the basement and walk up the stairs, where I find Rebecca Ziegler again. She's opening the heavy front doors, pulling down the stopper with the toe of a tan pump.

"Did you happen to get that list for me?" I ask.

Her mouth purses a little to the side as if what she'd like to do is tell me it's none of my business, but instead she nods her head and says, "Yes. Right this way."

I follow her into a small office with an outdated computer and neat stacks of paper in labeled drawers. Several different Bibles line the shelves. They all look basically the same to me, somber and thick. But I suspect Rebecca could tell me the subtle differences.

She opens a drawer and plucks out a sheet full of names.

"Again," she says. "I'm really not sure about most of those. Several women here that day were on that committee going back ten or twenty years, but we no longer have the meeting minutes."

"Shame," I say.

"Indeed. We simply don't have the space."

She passes the paper to me.

"Thank you," I say, and fold the paper in half, slip it into my bag. "I appreciate it. Can you tell me what you remember about the day Jessica was taken?"

After a short hesitation she says, "It's not much. It seemed like a regular day. It's not until so much later that you realize . . . any small thing could've been something. I know I unlocked the church that morning.

Elva Stringer came right after me. I remember because she offered to make coffee for the meeting. Others were coming in and talking and we were all setting up for the meeting and then Mandy Hoyle burst in, screaming, saying that her little girl was gone."

"What happened next?"

"Well, someone offered to call the sheriff's office. I don't remember who. And one of the other ladies volunteered to help her look. Soon, we were all searching. When the sheriff came, we looked through all the cars. We all thought she'd just wandered off."

"Even with the doll?"

She shakes her head.

"The doll wasn't found until later," she says. "Sitting at the bottom of the slide. No one thought much of it. We'd all seen applehead dolls before. We figured another child held left it behind the day before. It wasn't until Olivia Jacobs that . . ."

She looks down at the desk for a moment and then says, "I hope that you find her. The Hoyle girl. It breaks my heart what happened to Molly. The whole family . . . It breaks my heart. Bob and I have prayed for them ever since."

It's a small statement. But a big one for her. Where her husband is seemingly affable and open, Rebecca is tightly wound, drawn, inward-looking. And yet there is something, if not honest, then at least earnest about this small, clear-eyed woman.

"How long have you and Brother Bob been married?" I ask.

"Oh," she says, straightening, as if she had expected a different question. "Since '78."

"So, after he left the Army?"

"That's right," she says, confirming my assumption. She starts to say more but then eases off, shifts her weight, clasps her hands in front of her. I know I won't be getting anything else out of her. Not here, not today.

"Okay," I say. "Call if you think of anything. I'm going to be sticking around town for a while."

She nods, silently, and I leave the room and maneuver past a couple of sweaty kids and out to the parking lot. When I get to the car, I take out my phone and call Leo's number. As I expected, I get his voicemail.

"Hey," I say. "I don't know if you've still got contacts in the Army these days or what, but if you do, could you help me find out about a Bob or . . . maybe Robert Ziegler? Probably served in the seventies. Thanks."

I open the list of names and go down them, calling every number Rebecca's provided. Beside a few of them, she's written "Deceased," so I don't call those. It's a reminder that it's been ten years and people pass away or leave town.

For most of them, I get a woman who politely answers my call and then politely tells me she remembers very little about the day Jessica was taken. Their recollections are very similar to Rebecca's. They arrived at the church to plan activities for Vacation Bible School and then Mandy burst in, screaming. They all recall looking for the girl. Some remember the sheriff checking their cars.

I ask about the church picnic from which Olivia Jacobs was taken, if they were there, what they remember. Those who were there remember Olivia's mom, Kathleen, screaming. They remember looking under all the tables, in all the cars, in the park bathrooms. One remembers how good Mrs. Lawrence's potato salad was and how sad it is that she's dead now. One tries to turn the tables and pump me for information about Molly's death.

"Was she really half eaten by crows?" she asks. "The whole town's talking about it."

I hang up.

I leave a few voicemails, a message with a granddaughter.

Toward the bottom of the list is Deena Drake's name and the word "Piano" beside it. I call her and she answers on the second ring, a violin sonata playing in the background, which she turns off. I ask her about whether she was at the church the day Jessica was taken.

"Yes," she says. "I wanted to practice my piece for the following Sunday—the piano at First Baptist is a little different from my own and I always like to hear the pieces on the instrument beforehand."

"Were you there when Mandy realized Jessica was gone?"

"Yes," she says. "We all looked for her. I helped the sheriff look through the cars. We checked everyone's."

"Even yours?" I ask.

"Yes," she says. "Of course."

"Do you remember anything else from that day?"

"I remember feeling very bad for Mandy Hoyle. But that's all. When it seemed clear there was no more use searching, I went home. I think we all thought she'd turn up within a few hours, probably wandered into some corner of the church we couldn't get to and fell asleep. That's what we thought. Things like that happen all the time, don't they?"

It's not really a question and so I don't answer. Instead I say, "Were you at the church picnic the day Olivia was taken?"

"Yes," she says. "But only to drop off some hors d'oeuvres."

My mouth breaks into a smile and I barely suppress a snort. I've never in my life heard of someone bringing grub to a church picnic and having the audacity to refer to it as "hors d'oeuvres."

I manage to recover enough to say, "So you weren't there long?"

"Probably not more than twenty minutes. I wasn't there when Olivia was taken or else I'd have helped look for her. I didn't hear about it until the next day."

"Thank you," I say. And I draw a line through her name the same as everyone else's.

Janice Andrews's name is on this list. Kathleen Jacobs's is not.

I call one more name.

A very elderly woman answers and talks to me for fifteen minutes about the church and the committees in general and how lovely Rebecca and Bob were when her Earl passed and how she wishes she could get her grandkids to go but you know how young people are, think they have all the time in the world.

As she talks, I watch the descending fog swirl around the playground and picture Jessica sitting there on the swing set. There one minute. Gone the next. I think, for a moment, that I can hear the chains on the swing creak and squeak, but no, it's only a crow, perched on top of the slide. His head tilts as he watches me, the setting sun casting an orange hue on the tips of his wings.

"Are you saved?" the woman asks.

"I'm sorry," I say. "But that's between me and Jesus."

I hang up, let my head fall back against the headrest, and groan as the mess of information I've just received sorts itself into piles inside my head. After a while, I sit forward and grip Honey's steering wheel.

"I think it's time to pay another visit to Olivia's mom," I say to Honey. "She's gonna be thrilled to see me again."

# SIXTEEN

OLIVIA'S NOT GOING TO talk to you," Kathleen says when she opens the door. She's packing up her purse, putting on a sweater. She has a Marley County Hospital name tag clipped to her scrubs and her hair is pulled back into a cute little ponytail with the ends all curled together. "And I have to go to work."

"Okay," I say. "That's okay. I can come back tomorrow."

"You shouldn't come back at all."

"You heard about Molly," I say. "You must've."

She pushes her way through the door now, shooing me in front of her like a goose. She says in a whisper, "Yes. Yes, of course I did. Yes. I feel awful. Jesus. Jesus Christ, of course, I do. But I've already told you everything I can."

She huffs and then opens the kitchen door again, leans her head in, and shouts, "Bye, girls! Be good, okay?"

I hear, "Bye, Mom!"

"Jessica Hoyle is still out there," I whisper. "She could be next. She could turn up just like Molly if we don't find her."

She shuts the door again, then pauses with her handful of keys halfway to her purse and blinks at me.

"Please," she says. "I can't help you."

"Well, your brother-in-law tried to make that clear, but—"

"Cole? Did he talk to you?"

"I assume you sicced him on me."

She rolls her eyes and walks toward the driver side of her little worn-out Kia.

"No," she says. "He must've heard me telling Emily—the dispatch over there, and a friend of mine—about you. Cole tends to take things personal. Ever since Arnie left, I think . . . he's just trying to protect us."

"Sure," I say. "Listen, what if I talked to Nicole?"

"Nicole?" she says. "Why would you want to talk to Nicole?"

I shrug. "Nicole's Olivia's sister. Obviously, you would be there when I spoke to her."

"Nicole was *seven* when Olivia was taken. She was just a kid."

"They're sisters. You think your siblings don't know stuff about you that nobody else does? Even if you never told them?"

"Miss Gore," she starts. "I don't have time for this. Please do not bother my children or I *will* have Cole speak to you. Good night."

She gets in the car and hauls ass out of the driveway and down the street and I watch her thinking I wish I'd had a field medic with that kind of get-up-and-go when I really needed one.

For a moment, the wind doesn't blow cool and damp from the mountains. It's another wind grazing my face. Another wind. Another time. The scent of my own blood fills my nose. Not the real scent, I remind myself.

The memory of the scent.

The ringing in my ears, the throbbing in my head, the confusion, the shouting, the fire. The hot sticky wetness on my own side. I had put my hand there and been surprised at the oily gush, the grit of debris.

I'd been upside down. Buckled in and watching as the Security Forces airman across from me—also belted in and hanging like me—breathed his last breath, blood dripping from his mouth and running up his cheek and over his forehead, into his hair.

I'd held my hand to my side and unbuckled my belt, dropping to the vehicle's ceiling with a thud, the wind knocking out of my lungs, the distant *whump-whump-whump.* Dust-off inbound. The taste of blood is fresh in my mouth.

"RAAWWWW!" a crow screeches.

I turn toward the noise, jolted out of my memory. At the edge of the driveway, a crow bounces on the knotted branch of an apple tree. There is no fruit and the leaves—thin on the branches and thickly piled around the trunk—are a deep, blood red.

"Raww! Rawww!" the crow screeches again.

I turn again and walk back toward Honey, but pause when I realize my hand is pressed tight to my side.

# SEVENTEEN

ON THE WAY BACK from the Jacobses' neighborhood I pass a strip mall boasting a Taco Bell, a Laundromat, a boarded-up ice cream shop, and a little local diner with an unlit sign above the place that says "Ellerd's" in old-fashioned spaghetti Western–style letters. I tell myself I should just go back to the cabin and make a peanut butter sandwich to save money, but then I spot a familiar, beat-up, mostly red Civic on the far side of the lot.

"Perfect," I say. I pull in and park. It's nearly seven o'clock and I figure this is as good a place as any to get some chow.

Inside, Ellerd's looks like it's had a few iterations over the years, with remnants of each preceding generation's remodel left behind. There's the fifties black and white tile floor and the seventies Formica tables along with the Western-themed wood bar and nineties mauve seat cushions. The whole place is an exercise in transitory properties, like low-rent, small-town eateries.

I sit down at the bar and pick up a laminated menu and am trying to decide between the chicken fried chicken and the chicken fried steak when Mandy Hoyle emerges from the double kitchen doors. She almost drops a plate of pork chops when she sees me but recovers and keeps going toward a table with a couple of farmer types in battered boots and Carhartts.

A young woman who's probably fresh out of high school steps up on the other side of the bar and asks if I'm ready to order. I tell her I'd like the chicken fried chicken with tater tots, extra gravy, a side of fried apples, and a large coffee. She nods and leaves.

And then Mandy Hoyle is there. She puts a red plastic cup of ice water down in front of me and then looks from side to side, her huge blue eyes watery and scared.

"I heard what happened," she whispers. "About . . . about Molly."

"Yeah," I say.

"Are you leaving?"

I shake my head.

"You're going to keep looking?"

"Yes," I say. "I am."

Her pale blond eyebrows draw up and together and her eyes fill with tears but she bites down hard on her bottom lip and sniffs.

"I need to talk to you," I say. And I say it more because I feel it's what she wants to say. Like this is a play and she forgot her line and I'm just cuing her to keep things rolling.

She nods her head, then turns and looks at the big black and white clock above the doors to the kitchen.

"I get a break in about thirty minutes."

"Okay," I say.

"Can you meet me out back?"

"Sure."

Mandy sniffs again and then heads into the kitchen. Soon enough, the young waitress returns with my plate of food. I knew I was hungry, but I hadn't realized just how famished I was until that salty, greasy goodness appears on the bar before me. My eyes fill with honest-to-God grateful tears, and if I weren't so wholeheartedly focused on stuffing my face, I'd get down right there in the middle of Ellerd's and thank this angel for bringing it to me.

Instead, I wolf down every single bite of the crispy chicken and peppery white gravy. The tots are, each of them, explosions of salty, oily starch and the apples slip around in my mouth, slick and cinnamony and perfectly tender.

"Mmm . . ." I can't help but moan. I chase the whole thing with coffee and check the clock. Ten minutes left.

The eighteen-year-old comes back and picks up my plate.

"Can I ask you a question?" I say before she can disappear.

"You that PI?"

"I guess."

"This about those girls?"

"Yeah."

"Okay," she says, and puts my plate back down.

"What do you think happened to them?" I ask.

She looks side to side, then crouches closer to me and says, "You know one was found dead this morning, right?"

"I do. I was the one who found her."

Her eyes widen, but then she takes on a skeptical look and says, "So why ask me about it?"

I shrug. "You work in here. You hear stuff. You live in this town. You hear stuff."

"Okay," she says.

"So, what do you think happened?"

"Well." She pauses. Squeezes her lips together. Glances around. Leans even closer. "I always heard they probably were kidnapped by some pervert who put them in a basement."

"A basement?"

"Yeah, or like . . . a hole in the ground somewhere. Or, you know, my friend Jada always said they probably were sold to some billionaire to use as sex slaves. Nasty."

She shivers and then says, "But now with Molly Andrews turning up dead . . . Pretty creepy. Makes you wonder what happened to the other one."

"The other one," I repeat, encouragingly.

She leans in and whispers, "Mandy's daughter, Jessica. Makes you wonder if he's going to kill her the same way. Leave her right in Mandy's backyard just like he left Molly out behind the Andrews place. Poor Max. I always liked him. You know my cousin asked him to prom? He said no. Didn't even go."

Trying to get her back on track, I ask, "Has Mandy ever said anything to you about Jessica?"

"No," the girl says. "But I had homeroom with Tam, Mandy's oldest kid. He never wanted to talk about it. But once I remember he said they were probably killed a long time ago. Some serial killer, he thought. But I don't know what he thinks now. I graduated in May."

"Congratulations."

"Thanks. I'm going to the community college over in Mason."

"Congratulations," I say again.

"Whatever. I want to be an X-ray tech. They make good money."

"What does Tam want to do?"

She snorts.

"Dumbass wants to be a cop," she says. "You believe that?"

"Yeah," I say. "I do."

I get up and say thanks, leave behind a tip and pay at the register before heading back out into the cool night. I let out a sigh and then get behind the wheel, pull around to the back of the shopping center, and park. I get out and lean against the fender to wait. I check my phone. Five minutes.

Soon enough, Mandy Hoyle comes out the rear door with a black trash bag. She throws it in the dumpster and comes over to me. She doesn't have a sweater or jacket so she stands there shivering, her white arms crossed in front of her, her hands brushing up and down her skinny biceps.

"Shit," I breathe. I reach into my car and pull out the nearest fabric thing I can find, an old hoodie. I hold it toward her and she takes it but doesn't put it on, just drapes it around her shoulders.

"You found Molly," she says.

"Yeah."

I feel like this is going to be an exact repeat of our earlier conversation and I know Mandy probably has only a five-minute break so I short-circuit the whole process and say, "Mandy, the day Jessica was taken, did you fall asleep in your car?"

She gives me a wide-eyed, terrified stare. And then she bursts into tears.

They're hard, racking, ugly sobs. She holds her thin fingers up in front of her face, mashing them into her skin like that can make the tears or the pain or the needing stop.

"It's okay," I say.

She shakes her head.

"No," I say. "It's understandable. It just . . . it helps me know how things happened. You didn't look away and she vanished."

"No," Mandy says. It comes out jittery and thick.

"You were exhausted and pregnant. You had a toddler asleep in the backseat."

"She was *right there*," Mandy heaves. "She was right in front of me. She was a smart girl. She knew not to run off."

"I know," she says.

She sniffs, wipes her nose on the back of her arm.

"I was so confused. I fell asleep. I wasn't asleep long. I swear. I'd been listening to the radio, really low, and . . . I know I was still awake when Dottie did the weather at ten after. I remember her saying the time. Then, I opened my eyes and Jessica was gone. I remember I looked at the clock and it was almost twenty after and she . . . she was gone. My baby. My baby girl."

The last word draws out in a long sob.

"I lost her," she moans. "It's my fault."

"No," I say. I take a step toward her and squeeze her shoulder. "You thought you were safe."

She nods.

"The church," she says. "I thought, well, hardly anyone was there but . . ."

"Do you remember anyone? Remember seeing anyone?"

"No," she breathes. "No, I've tried so hard. But it was just cars. And I don't go to that church. I didn't know any of their cars except the Zieglers' Buick. And I remember thinking that if we wanted to pee we'd have to drive on into town and use the bathroom at McDonald's because . . . because I didn't go there. And maybe if we'd gone there . . . maybe someone would've hel-hel—" Her word disappears into hiccups, which she swallows before she tries again and finally gets out, "Helped us."

I tug Mandy's shoulder, and she comes without any resistance. Falling into my arms, she's just as small and thin and light as I thought she'd be. She cries into my jacket for a while and then, when she's finally all cried out, she backs away.

She pulls a phone out of her pocket and looks at the cracked screen.

"Oh," she says. "I have to go back in."

She turns on her phone and holds the camera view up to her face, checks her makeup. It's still there. Amazing; drugstore mascara is truly a marvel of modern science. She scrapes at the redness under her eyes like that will help and then adjusts the strands of hair that have gone frizzy with her wallowing on my shoulder.

"I'm sorry," she murmurs.

"Don't be."

"You're going to keep looking?" she says.

"Yeah," I say. "Yeah. I'm going to keep looking."

She meets my eyes and nods. Then, she turns and walks back into the diner.

I get in my car and drive back toward the cabin.

"Not long now, Honey," I say. I am exhausted, I realize. I began this day before dawn, finding Molly's body in the forest in the wan early light and now, in the dark, I slow down as I pass the Andrewses' farmhouse. Max's truck is there, solitary in the driveway, but there are no lights on inside.

I keep going and pull down the lane and into the driveway in front of the cabin.

There's a sheriff's department cruiser waiting for me.

I breathe out a long sigh. My night is not over yet.

# EIGHTEEN

"YOU'RE GONNA WANT TO see these," AJ says as I get out of the car. He's holding up a manila envelope and looking very serious.

"Have you seen Max?" I ask.

"Not since this morning; I've been at work all day. Shiloh's been over there, though, and I think that's all the company he wants right now. She texted me earlier, said Greg Andrews is on his way home."

"Max's dad?"

"Yeah."

I let us both inside and, making my way toward the kitchen, I pause to shove my still-scattered belongings into piles.

"I don't suppose you've ever been burgled?" I muse, scooping up my errant pens and notebooks and tossing them back into my rucksack. I double-check as I go to see whether anything else is missing, but as far as I can tell it's only the casebook that's gone.

"Can't say that I have. This your first time?"

"No," I say. "It happened once when I was in college, after the Air Force and before I was a PI. And it happened again when I first moved into the office I have now."

I pause in the kitchen, flicking the coffee maker on.

"You catch the guy?" he asks.

"No on the first one. I always suspected it was my roommate's ex, on account of how it was mostly her lingerie that went missing. The second one I did get him. It was the guy who'd had the office before me. Left some coke under a floorboard and came back to get it."

"What an exciting life you do lead."

"Never a dull moment," I say, and remember with disgust that all my clothes have been rifled through. I move into the bedroom, grab a big armload of clothes, stuff them into the washer and set it going. Then, finally, I trudge back into the kitchen.

I pour both of us a cup of coffee, then sit before him at the butcher-block countertop, where he has put down a manila folder.

"It's the autopsy photos," he says, a warning.

"Okay," I say, and let out a long breath.

He opens the folder and reveals the pictures. In them, Molly Andrews is lying on a silver table. There are close-ups of her slender throat, encircled by thin, regular bruises and erratic, vertical claw marks. Close-ups of her eyes, spotted red with dots of blood. Close-ups of her fingers, bloody with her own flesh under her nails.

"She probably clawed at whoever was attacking, too," AJ says. "The doc's sending off DNA to check. But that'll take weeks, months. Who knows?"

"Okay," I say. "So, good for the courtroom but not helpful immediately."

He shakes his head.

"No sign of sexual assault," AJ says as we look over the photos. "No sign of bruises elsewhere or physical abuse, but . . ,"

"What?"

"Well, Doc Jenkins isn't sure. He's putting in a call to another coroner he knows. But it looks like there was damage to her esophagus, her heart, her liver. Evidence of stress. But it's subtle. He's not sure what could've caused it. The esophagus, he said, looked like a bulimia victim, but very mild."

"Poison?" I ask. "Some kind of . . . food torture? What had she been eating?"

"He said her last meal was simple. Biscuits, he said. And tea with honey. But he's sending off all kinds of samples. We don't have the kind of lab here to process this stuff. He sent everything to Raleigh and told them to rush it."

I look down at the photos of Molly's face.

"She has a few freckles," I say.

"What are you thinking?"

"I'm just wondering about the condition in which she was kept. Her hair is long, combed. Her dress is clean aside from the mud along the trim. There are cases of girls kept as young wives, ultimately found, usually with Stockholm syndrome. And there are cases of girls kept in horrifying dark basements . . ."

"But you think it's the former."

"I wish it were neither. But if wishes were horses . . ."

He drinks the last of his coffee and I take the mug, rinse it out, set it in the sink.

"You want anything else?" I open the fridge and look inside. "Max and Shiloh left some milk, sweet tea, and Cokes in here."

"I'll take a glass of milk," he says.

I grin into the fridge, involuntarily. I've long believed there's nothing like a glass of cold milk at the end of a long day. And today has been the longest day.

I pour two tall glasses, set them on the counter.

AJ thanks me, and I watch him take a drink. The muscle in his forearm is thick and ropy and he drinks noisy gulps, his Adam's apple bobbing. Something about him, sitting there at that counter, drinking that cold milk, helps distract me—however briefly—from the grief and the guilt I feel about Molly Andrews.

"You doing okay?" he asks when he's finished half the glass.

"Yeah," I say. "It's just . . . I just got here the night before last. Now, I'm sitting at the kitchen counter looking at autopsy photos of a girl I found only this morning, a girl I never expected to find at all."

"Okay," he says, closing the file. "Look, let's take a break. Talk about something else."

I snort, "Like what?"

"Tell me about yourself."

"Not a lot to tell."

He gives me a sly smile.

"Now we both know that's not true."

"Not sure where to start."

I take a drink, set the glass down, look into the pure white opacity of the milk's surface.

"What are your folks like?" he asks after a moment.

"They were . . . my folks. I guess. They've never got along."

"Like oil and water?"

"More like a lit match and kerosene."

His eyebrows raise in a mix of humor and pity I've seen before. It's a look I hate, so I just start explaining my way through it. It's an old story. Common enough.

"My dad could never hold down a job and he drank too much," I say. "My mom worked third shift cleaning a nursing home. Neither of them were doing what they wanted to do in life and their favorite hobby was fighting over whose fault it was. An activity that usually turned violent, almost always ending with my mom on the losing end, in the hospital if they could afford it, which they never could."

I pause, then add, "But they stayed together, so I mostly stayed with relatives. Usually my granny. Sometimes my great-uncle, Jovial."

"How'd you end up in law enforcement?"

I laugh. "My granny said I should pick up an extracurricular activity so I wasn't underfoot all the time. My uncle had been a SEAL in Vietnam—"

I put a hand, unconsciously, to my wrist and then remember that the watch Jovial had given me—the Rolex Submariner he bought on the cheap during his service—was sitting in a pawnshop back in Louisville. I'd gotten behind on my bills and the watch was the only thing of value that wasn't an absolute necessity in my day-to-day life. I remember that it was one more reason I took this case. Spend a week on a lost cause, turn up nothing, get paid, get my watch back. But now I look at my naked

wrist and think I never should have come. That my being here has only
made things worse.

"A Navy SEAL?" AJ asks, snapping me back. "Wow."

"Yeah," I say. "But you'd never know it. He hates talking about it.
You'd think I'd have learned some kind of lesson from that, but no. I
joined JROTC, tested high on the ASVAB—then went straight into the
Air Force. I was in the service for six years. When I got out, I spent three
years in college getting art history and English degrees, just for fun. Before I graduated, I got my PI license and started my business."

"Why a private eye?"

"I just sort of knew how to do this. Look for things, find stuff out. I did
enough in the Air Force to know I liked it."

I don't tell AJ that I was a special investigator. That I was recruited
by Leo. That, even when I was in the Air Force, I couldn't talk about my
position or my rank or any of the cases that I worked. That I spent a lot of
time being hated by my fellow airmen and that having virtually no social
life was all right with me because I just wanted more time to read books.

"Why not a cop?" AJ asks.

I shrug. "I've had more than my fill of the command structure," I say.
"Now, I report to myself. That's enough for me."

"And the car?" he asks, grinning.

"What about the car?"

"It's a weird car," AJ says, pointing toward the front of the house
where Honey is parked, oblivious to his rudeness. "I mean, it's cool, but
it's weird. I had to google what the hell it was."

"Honey was my aunt Tina's," I say. "Well, she's not really my aunt.
She was on her way out of the Air Force when I was going in. We were
from the same general part of Kentucky, and she sort of took me under
her wing. When she left, we stayed in touch, and she was always there for
me. She understood, better than most, how hard being away from home
can be. And how necessary. When I left the Air Force, I moved to Louisville, where she'd opened her own garage. She was fixing up Honey at the
time, as a side project, and I helped her out. It was good for me. Pouring a

lot of my frustration into an engine block. When we were done, she gave Honey to me."

I finish my milk, rinse out the glass, put it in the sink, realize I'd rather talk about a murdered girl than my own past.

I reopen the folder, go back to the pictures, studying the shots from the morgue. I get out my notebook and read over everything I'd written down. AJ waits patiently for my next question, takes another drink of his milk.

"What I need are the files from ten years ago."

He nods. "I started getting into them today. The system was a complete mess ten years ago, so it'll take some time to track everything down, but hopefully tomorrow."

"Okay," I breathe. "In the meantime, what can you tell me about Jessica's father? Tommy Hoyle?"

I think about the man I'd seen leaving that run-down house in that run-down holler the day before. The way he'd screamed at his dog, at me, kicked up mud as he sped away.

"Local lowlife," AJ says. "Beats up on Mandy."

"I got that far. He was laid off from the toy plant around the time the girls were kidnapped, right?" I ask.

"That's right. My dad worked the same plant."

"What's your dad do now?"

"He went over to the community college after he got canned. He does HVAC repair now."

"Well," I say. "Tommy seems to have had no such aspirations. Mandy said he drives a digger or something, over in another town, but it didn't really ring true."

"Could be, I guess," AJ says. "But mostly I just see him hanging around at Yellow Dog."

"Local bar?"

"Wow, it's like you're a professional or something."

I snicker, and AJ smiles as he watches me.

"He do a lot of day drinking?" I ask.

"Enough we've had to pull him out of there a few times. We take him back to the cells, let him sober up so we don't send him home to Mandy like that."

"So if he doesn't work, how does he pay the mortgage?"

"Well, they don't have a mortgage," AJ says. "That house belonged to Tommy's folks and he was the oldest so it's his now. But everything else? How they put food on the table and keep their kids in clothes and sports uniforms? Mandy waits tables at Ellerd's, and I'd guess that's all the money they've got."

"What about Dwight Hoyle and Elaine, the cousins? I heard from Mandy that they just moved back from Charlotte. I went by their house, but they didn't seem to be home."

"If they're back," he says, "I haven't seen them. But I can ask around."

"Mandy told me that Dwight was questioned after Jessica disappeared," I say. "But that it didn't come to anything."

"I'll have to look back at the files, but I wouldn't be surprised."

I nod.

"Do you think he had something to do with all this?"

"I don't know," I say. "Anyone in town with the guts and the drive to do it—anyone with enough space to keep two little girls, though as we've said they don't take up *that* much space—could have taken them. I just have to poke around and see what turns up. But this is what being a PI is. It's just following every road and seeing where it leads. Most of the time, you get to a dead end."

"What do you do then?" he asks.

"Turn my ass around," I say. "Go back to the start. Try a new road."

"And what happens if all the roads are dead ends?"

"Then I go back to where I started—make sure the client hasn't run out of money, and start over again, looking for new roads."

"Sounds like police work," he says.

"It's more hyper-focused," I say. "I spend all my time on one thing. Don't have to pause what I'm doing to direct traffic or respond to a 911 call. And I set my own hours."

"Speaking of which . . ." AJ says, glancing at his watch. "I'd better head out. Early start tomorrow."

"Okay," I say. "Thank you, AJ."

We both grow quiet, pondering, I guess, everything we've put together so far—which is, admittedly, not very much. Some mild evidence of abuse, a regional history of poverty and desperation, a possible connection to a local church.

"It's possible that Jessica's still out there," I mutter, closing my eyes. "I realize that Molly was the last girl taken and that maybe Jessica was dead before Olivia was ever nabbed at the church picnic but . . . I can't stop now. I need to find out what happened. If Molly was alive this whole time, then maybe Jessica's still out there and . . ."

"Yeah," AJ says, his voice soft and deep. "We'll find her."

I feel his warm palm against the back of my free hand.

The air in the room feels too hot, suddenly. AJ is exactly the kind of man I could seek comfort with. More than comfort. But not tonight. Tonight, I need to lie awake while the crows scream outside and remind me that, until sometime early this morning, Molly Andrews was still alive.

And that now she is lying on a slab in the morgue, her beautiful hair wound into a coil beside her.

"I need some sleep," I say, finally.

He nods, squeezes my hand, lets go.

"I'll round up the old case files," he says. "Bring 'em by tomorrow. Soon as I can."

"Yeah," I say. "Thanks, AJ. Thanks, again."

"Just doing the right thing," he says. "Night, Annie."

"Good night."

I watch as he goes out the door. As the headlights on his cruiser shine through the curtains. As he pulls away.

# NINETEEN

I AM STANDING ON MY granny's porch.

It's raining and the raindrops splatter and drum on the tin roof overhead. My skin is cold and wet and my hair drips.

My granny is beside me, but I can't turn my head. I only know that she's there.

She's peeling an apple. I hear the *scrape scrape scrape* of her knife, sliding under the skin, separating shiny peel from tender sweet flesh.

The rain splatters and drums.

She has potted plants all over the porch. There is no gutter and the rain slides off the corrugated tin and into the pots. The plants glisten and their leaves bounce and the heavy heads of the flowers bow under the pressure of the steady, relentless, cold, thrumming rain.

"Here," my granny says beside me. I still don't see her but I hear the chair creak as she gets up. She puts the peeled apple in my hand and I feel its mealy flesh against my palm.

I hold it up.

There is a face in the apple: two black eyes and a carved-out mouth.

The rain splatters and drums and the eyes in front of me blink and the mouth twists into movement. It says, "Annie. You killed her."

I throw the apple into the rain and a crow sweeps down from a scraggly, twisted apple tree and catches the apple by the stem. The crow makes a circle and perches on the porch railing and drops the apple, and the face goes rolling off the edge of the porch and into the sodden ground below.

"Annie," the crow says. "Annie, will you kill the other one too?"

And then the crow opens its mouth and a hard buzzing comes out. Like a thousand bees, it vibrates through my teeth and into my brain and, finally, I open my eyes.

"Dream," I whisper, groggy. "Just a dream."

And yet the buzzing continues. I look to my left.

My phone is vibrating, wiggling itself to the edge of the nightstand.

I pick up, answer, put it on speaker.

"Annie," Leo says. "You okay? I've been calling you the last twenty minutes."

"It's . . ." I look at the window.

It's already past dawn. I rub my eyes and sit up in bed and say, "I was dreaming. I . . . I guess I was dreaming."

"You gotta get out of that hick-ass town, Annie. That shit is crazy. I saw they found your girl."

"Yeah," I say. I don't remember telling him the name of the town I was in but I'm not surprised he knows, not surprised he checked the news. "I found her yesterday morning."

I sit up and discover that I'm wobbly, still tired, still half in the dream. Outside, it's raining. It's a cold, foggy, pelting rain. I yank on my tennis shoes regardless.

"You okay?" Leo asks again. The worry in his voice startles me, and I realize I must sound as bad as I feel.

"Yeah," I say. Carrying my phone, I stumble into the bathroom, where I splash my face, pee, wash my hands, hold my mouth under the spigot. "Yeah. I'm okay. But . . . Leo, that girl was probably here the whole time."

"Yeah," Leo says. "Or else someone went to a whole lot of trouble to bring her out there just for someone to find."

"Yeah," I say. "Me."

I pull on my leggings and try to focus on the feel of the fabric against my skin, the tight laces of my shoes, the too-bright light of the phone.

"Are you still in . . . wherever you are?" I ask.

"Yeah," Leo says. "Just about done. We've got some loose ends to tie up—I've got to track down some stuff, get things . . ."

"Tied up," I say. My eyes are closed.

I sit on the edge of the bed and listen to the rustle of the breath in my chest and think about how much I just want to crawl back under the covers and how much I have to get up and get moving.

"Tell me what you ate for breakfast," I say. It's an old trick. Something Leo started and neither of us ever put into words. It was, like so many things between us, simply understood. A place to steer a conversation when you want to admit you're a raw nerve but not in a place—either physical or emotional—that you can have a soul-bearing discussion.

Translation: I am in a bad way, but there's nothing I can do about it and I need to hear the sound of your voice.

"I had these chicken coconut noodles," Leo answers, no hesitation. "They came in this yellow fish sauce. I think turmeric, probably. Lots of garlic. Two boiled eggs in there, nice and soft. They were small eggs, too. Not like you get back in the States. Velvety." There's a pause and then, "Hey, you ever had Velveeta?"

"Yeah," I say.

"I should think it's nasty but I don't," Leo says. "Always have a special place in my heart for Velveeta."

My mouth breaks into a smile. In the end, it's the sound of Leo's voice that brings me back to reality, brings me back to myself. I pad into the kitchen, get a glass of water, take a few sips.

"Hey, listen," Leo says. "I've got a guy looking into your Bob Ziegler."

"Okay."

"Should know something later."

"All right. Let me know."

"I will."

I slip my jacket on and then pull a rain shell over it.

"Have a good run," Leo says.

"Sure."

"And take your gun."

I tuck the Mongoose into the usual place, slip my phone into an inside shell pocket, check all the locks on the windows, check Honey's locks and windows, and leave. After my late start, the sun is already up over the far ridge, but hidden behind deep gray clouds and sheets of rain, so it's still mostly dark.

I step off the porch, walk a few steps, break into a slow trot, and then find my stride.

Even in the rain, even when it's cold, even when I'm haunted by bizarre dreams of talking appleheads and crows, it feels good to run. It feels good to let my mind slip from the frenzied minutiae of the case and let it flow as I flow, one step at a time, in a thumping, steady rhythm.

It's no time before I find myself at the stone circle again. I stop outside it. The whole area is cordoned off with police tape. Little flags are stuck in the ground where items of interest were found. A piece of hair maybe, a footprint that's been washed away in this rain. I can't help myself: I stare at the ground picturing Molly Andrews's body, so peacefully laid to rest that she almost looked asleep.

I think about that summer, ten years ago, when first Jessica, then Olivia, then Molly were kidnapped. Think about the desperation in a town whose primary source of employment had just closed. I think about Molly's long hair and pale skin and subtly abused insides.

"Where were you . . ." I whisper.

"You standing around out here feeling bad for yourself, or what?"

I snap to attention at the rattly voice and look up to find Susan McKinney, this time in a long black mackintosh and high green rubber boots. Most of her gray hair is hidden under a wide-brimmed hat, but wisps of it stick out, curling like corkscrews in the damp.

"I—"

She jerks her chin back up the trail and says, "Why don't you come up."

It's not a question. And I don't answer.

I just follow her and watch the clear water stream over her oiled black shoulders and splash onto the muddy trail under my feet.

# TWENTY

SUSAN MCKINNEY'S KITCHEN IS small and close and it smells like green things. The room is hot and smoky, thanks, in part, to the wood cook stove in a corner of what seems to be a three-room cabin. I'm sitting in the kitchen/living area beside a floor-to-ceiling bookshelf. Beyond an open doorway, I can make out the pattern of a quilt on a bed. Another door, painted bright green, leads to what I assume is the washroom, though the lights are off and no outside light illuminates the room. Area rugs of all ages, sizes, and styles cover the hardwood floors.

"How long have you lived here?" I ask.

"All my life."

She puts a cup of tea in my hands. I look at it dubiously.

"Elderberry," she says. I take a sip and she adds, "And arsenic."

I almost spit, and she starts cackling.

"Nah," she says. "I wouldn't even give arsenic to a rat. If I wanted to kill you, I'd just shoot you. Grind you up into fertilizer."

"Good to know," I say.

She puts a jar of honey on the countertop and hands me a spoon.

"The tea is astringent," she says. "You might want some of that."

I add a spoonful of honey to the tea and take a small sip. I haven't had elderberry anything in years, and my mouth puckers at the forgotten taste. I try another sip and then put the cup down and watch her as she rattles around at the countertop, emptying her basket of greens onto the counter.

"Chickweed," she says. "Comes in the spring, flowers in the summer, and then disappears. But . . . usually after some rain, it returns in the fall. Everything in its season, so they say." She pats the greens dry, then cuts the tops off and discards the lower portions into a wooden bowl on the far side of the counter. "Take that out to the chickens later," she mutters to herself.

She has a thin bandage on her wrist, gauze under a linen wrapping.

"What happened to your arm?" I ask.

She pauses, looks down at the bandage as if she'd forgotten it was there. She pulls her sleeve down over it and says, "Rooster. Damn things get ornery sometimes."

I've just opened my mouth to ask another question when she mutters, "He keeps acting up, I'll have to put him down."

Then she turns to me and says, "We're going to get some decent food in you."

I watch as she adds butter to a cast-iron skillet, already hot on the woodstove, whips up three eggs and then goes back to chopping. I'm mesmerized by her actions in the dim light of an overhead incandescent, and I watch as an omelet comes together before me. Susan adds a handful of the topped greens and some homemade red sauce from a little bottle on an overhead shelf, and then folds the omelet in half. She cuts it with her wood spatula and slides the halves onto two heavy ceramic plates. She puts one in front of me.

"What you been eating?" she asks.

I shrug, take the fork she hands me. She sits down across from me and slices into her own omelet half, takes a big bite. I watch her chew and swallow and decide I'm hungrier than I am afraid of her. I cut off a bite.

"I had dinner at Ellerd's last night," I say around a mouthful of egg. The omelet is soft and buttery and the greens sharp.

She laughs, wet and croaky. When she settles down again, she sniffs and looks into my eyes, searching like she did before.

"You feeling bad about Molly," she says. She takes a few bites while I shrug and stare at my eggs. "But you're not the type to blame yourself. Not usually."

I shrug again.

"But, in this case, you think you stirred someone into action."

"Yeah," I finally say. I look up at her and find that she is watching me. Her dark eyes shine like jet in the low light.

"You likely did," she says after a few long seconds. It's a statement of fact more than an accusation, and it feels like a gift. It takes something off me. A weight and a dread and an ugliness. The acknowledgment that, yes, I came here and poked around and now Molly Andrews is dead when she was not dead before.

"What do you know that you aren't saying?" I ask. I put down my fork. Both our plates are clean, and the scent of cooking and herbs and woodsmoke hangs between us. "I heard in town that you call yourself a psychic."

She places her hands on the table and looks at them, and I follow her gaze to the gnarled fingers, swollen red knuckles, short choppy fingernails.

"I don't call myself nothing. What other folks wanna call me is their business," she says. "But, I do have dreams. And, sometimes, I read some cards."

I look back to her eyes and hold her gaze.

"I heard you were brought in for questioning after Olivia Jacobs went missing, that you were held."

Her eyes narrow, and she shifts.

"Of course you heard that. They say I'm a witch, don't they? And they say a witch took those girls. So how long do you really think it was before everybody and their dog was pointing at me?" She rolls her eyes and then lets out a tired-sounding breath and says, mockingly, "Ol' Susan McKinney lives up on the mountain, probably up to no good. Probably running around taking little girls and replacing them with poppets."

"They must have had more than a suspicion. If they brought you in after Molly was taken and not at the very beginning with Jessica?"

She smirks at me.

"Quick one, you are." She looks down at her hands, but I keep my eyes on her face and see pain there. When she speaks again, a lot of the bite is gone from her voice. "It was because of Sheriff Kerridge."

"Kerridge?" I ask, confused. "Not Jacobs?"

"No," she says. "Nobody told you?"

"Told me what?"

"Jacobs was just a deputy then. Donald Kerridge was the sheriff when Jessica was taken, but we were close. Nothing romantic—get your head out of the gutter. We'd always been good friends, you understand? Since we were kids. And he knew I had nothing to do with any of it. Of course, he came around and talked to me after Jessica was taken *and again* after Olivia went missing. But . . . look at this place. Look around and tell me where I could keep two little girls, first of all."

I admit to myself that the cabin is tiny. Still, it's not outside the realm of possibility that she could have a root cellar somewhere.

"But the practicality of it was beside the point," Susan says. "I *wouldn't* go around kidnapping little girls, and Donald Kerridge knew that."

"So, what happened?"

She frowns, clicks her teeth against her tongue.

"Donald died. It was just after Olivia Jacobs was taken. I remember because there was some question about whether Cole Jacobs should really take his place, what with his own niece missing. But what other choice did we have? He was the most senior deputy and everyone in town knew him."

"How did Sheriff Kerridge die?"

"He'd had heart problems for years, just like his daddy. He was running himself ragged with the case. People want to say the cops didn't listen to Mandy when she reported Jessica missing, but I know for a fact that Donald Kerridge was at his wit's end worried about it. Eaten up with it. And then after Olivia was taken? I think it pushed him right over the edge. He had a heart attack right on his kitchen floor. I found him the next morning. It was an awful blow. For the town. For me."

"I'm sorry," I say.

Plowing forward as if she didn't hear me, she says, "Next thing I knew, Olivia was returned, fine as you please. It got quiet for a couple weeks and then, Molly Andrews went missing just like Olivia and Jessica. And it was right after that, early one morning, the FBI were beating down my door, wanting to see inside my house."

"Did they say why?"

"Anonymous tip is all I ever heard."

"Why did they hold you?"

"The applehead dolls," she says. "They found a couple of old applehead dolls in my bedroom on the shelf. Had 'em for years. A lot of folks around here used to, but I guess they figured mine must have special witch powers or something."

"What happened?"

"I told them to charge me or let me go. But I knew there wasn't enough evidence to arrest me. I'd never had a one of those girls in this house. Well, except Jessica once. Her mama brought her in tow when she was just a tot, and she nearly got her finger bit off by one of my chickens. I told Mandy if she was going to bring the girl, she'd have to train her better."

"Did Mandy visit you often?"

"Well, yes, she came to me," Susan says. "More than once."

"Before or after the girls were taken?"

"Both."

"Recently?"

"Oh, it's been a couple years back now, I'd say. I think it's awful painful for her."

"You tell her fortune?"

She shakes her head and says, "I read her cards, that's all. I told her what I saw in them. I told her that, if she saved, she would—someday—take a long journey. That she would prosper. I told her she would be reunited with someone she loved but . . . that might've been a mistake."

"Why's that?"

She sighs, and her gaze drifts toward the small window to her left.

Outside, I see a few hens in a pen, pecking at the muddy earth, grubbing for worms.

"Because," Susan says, "if I'd left off that last part, she might've left town a long time ago. I hate to see a woman beat up like that. A girl sharp as her, too. She could've gone to college."

"How long have you known her?"

"She came here as a teenager. They often do. She and her friends showed up at my door one night asking about silly things that young people pay heed to. Mandy was poor, she said, couldn't pay me. She was saving her money for college books. Odette said she was going to school on a big scholarship and Mandy blushed pink as a petunia. They were kinda poking fun, but good-natured. I told her nothing comes for free and she said okay. But then, you know what she did? She came back the next day and said she'd noticed my house needed dusting and, if she cleaned it, would I do her cards."

"Did you?"

"Sure enough."

"You said Odette was there? You mean Odette Hoyle? Tommy's little sister?'

"That's right," she says. "The very same. Odette came often enough, poor thing, before she died. And she's the one who first brought Mandy."

Susan looks away from me for a moment and then back, a deep sadness in her eyes. Sadness, I assume, that follows Mandy around.

"Did Mandy come a lot?" I ask.

"Not regular or anything but, a lot of times, when she was at the end of her tether. That happens a lot. No therapists around here, you know. No psychologist to sit you down on a sofa and listen to your woes, write you a prescription for Xanax. They come to me, tell me about their worst day, and ask when it's gonna get better. But, for some of them, it never does. Never will. All I can do is advise the best I can. Help where I can."

"Sounds like it's as hard on you as it is on them."

She shrugs.

"Did Kathleen Jacobs ever visit? Olivia's mother?"

Susan rolls her eyes and says, "Hell, no. Those Jacobses are too churchy for all this." She waves her hands to acknowledge the interior of the small, shabby cabin and all that it contains, including us.

"I'm guessing Bob and Rebecca Ziegler would also be considered 'too churchy'?"

"Well, almost," she says, giving me a knowing eye. "I opened my door one morning stunned as anything to see Rebecca Ziegler standing there. Good Lord, you could've knocked me over with a feather."

"What did she want?"

"Well, that's the thing. I invited her in and offered her some tea and sat her down. Same as anyone—I'm never going to turn away a woman in need, am I? And then I waited for her to say something—which I could tell she wanted to do—you know, ask me for a reading or for advice or for medicine. Some women come up here wanting birth control, off the record. And some want the opposite. Well, I waited and waited, but then suddenly Rebecca just stood up and said coming here was a mistake and she turned around and walked out."

"And that was it?"

"Yes, ma'am."

"You never found out what she wanted?"

"No, and I wish like anything I had. I've seen her around town over the years and she's never spoken to me once."

"What about Deena Drake? Do you know her?"

"Up on the mountain? Sure. I pay her for the rose hips I collect on her land."

"Rose hips?"

"I make tea and oil, sell it at farmers markets. *Rosa Rugosa* is my favorite to use but it won't grow down here. Too dark under the canopy and too cluttered up with mountain laurel. Deena Drake grows some of the best roses in the state, and she knows it. Every year, I hoof it up the mountain after the first soft frost and take those rose hips."

"And she knows about it?"

"She better. I pay her a decent enough wad of cash for it. Don't let that miss-priss attitude fool you. The woman knows her plants *and* she knows how to drive a bargain. But is this really what you want to know about? Herbal remedies and where to procure them? Ain't you here for some more pressing reason?"

"Molly Andrews," I say.

"That's right," she says. "Poor little lamb. You know her brother came to me."

"Max? He wanted his fortune told?"

"Yes. About one year back."

"And what did you tell him?"

"I told him what I saw. That he would find help. A warrior from another mountain would put his heart to rest, put an end to his suffering."

I snort at the hokeyness, the vague imagery.

"Well, you're here, ain't ya?"

My mouth opens and then snaps shut again, and Susan gives me a sardonic look.

She gets up, goes into the other room. I hear the opening and closing of a drawer and then she comes back. She puts a battered tin box on the table between us and clears away the plates. The box has the imprint of a queen of hearts on the lid.

Susan opens the box and takes out a set of grungy playing cards. The backs feature art nouveau daffodils, the green and white set against a deep red field, all made darker by years of use.

"My daddy served in World War Two. Brought these back," she says, shuffling the cards. "From England."

"They're very pretty," I say.

She nods, puts the cards down in front of me, taps them with the hard end of her first finger, says, "Shuffle 'em."

I laugh.

Susan clears her throat once and says, "You came here. You asked me questions. You ate my food. Now I offer you a reading for free, you know what you do? You do the polite thing. You shuffle the cards and you get your reading and you say, 'Thank you, Miss Susan.'"

I let out a long breath through my nose and take the cards. I shuffle them in a low bridge, but they're so fragile-feeling that I change to overhand instead and just mix up choppy piles. I look across the table and find Susan watching my hands.

"Where did you learn to read cards?" I ask.

"Don't really know. I don't read 'em like you're supposed to, probably. They just help me focus. That's enough."

I set the cards in the middle of the table and Susan picks them up and then deals four cards, face down, in a line between us.

"This," she says, tapping the card on her farthest left and moving right, "is where you came from. This is where you are now. This one is where you are going, and this"—she taps the last card, set a little aside—"is *who* you are."

"Okay," I say.

She flips the first card, my past. It's the five of diamonds, and she nods at the card like it's the one she was expecting. "You came out of hardship. A darkness and a struggle. You still carry the weight of it."

She flips the next card, my present. It's the five of hearts. She makes a *Hhm* sound, deep in her throat, and says, "You are grieving. You played a game and you lost and now you are injured. It's . . . This is because of Molly. This is Molly's card."

She runs a thumb over the grimy red heart in the center and shakes her head. "You lost Molly and now your heart is angry, you want to fight, but there is nothing to fight. Not yet."

She glances up at me, and I meet her eyes and realize my face is set, hard, tense. I'm frowning at what she's saying, the hard thump of my heart, the sweat on my palms.

"Go on," I say.

She flips the next card, my future. It's the five of clubs. Now Susan tilts her head to the side, staring at it. She laughs silently, her shoulders bouncing once and then settling.

"It will not get easier," she says. "Forces are working against you. You will struggle. You will struggle and you will fight. There is darkness."

She closes her eyes and raises one hand to touch the crown of her head. Her eyelids flutter and she says, "A betrayal. And . . . anger. Sadness. Deep sadness."

She takes her hand from her head and opens her eyes as if waking from a dream. I've seen psychics on street corners all over the world. I know how it works. I know that they trade in vagaries and happenstance. I know that we remember what we want to remember, that we all just want to believe we're being watched over, that we want a shortcut to answers and so, when all is said and done, we recollect the hits and forget the misses.

I know all this. And yet I can't stop my heart from pounding as she puts her finger on the last card. Turns it. It's the jack of spades. A blond man, looking to the right, holds a curly staff, maybe a halberd. It's too smudged to tell.

"As I told Max," she says. "The warrior. You are governed by what you feel is right in your heart and you use your sharp tongue like a weapon though it opens no doors for you. You are not big or strong and, sometimes, you are reckless. But you will fight like a dog for the truth."

She taps the card and says, "But, listen now, one day this fighting may get you killed."

I meet her eyes, so dark and shiny I can't tell pupil from iris, and I ask, "Susan, where do you think Jessica Hoyle is?"

"Not dead," she says. "I feel certain of it."

"Who do you think took those girls? Why leave an applehead doll in their place?"

"I don't know," Susan answers. "I wish I did. Only thing I have is a feeling. A feeling of desperate, desperate longing."

"Whose longing?" I ask.

She shakes her head and says, "I wish I knew, I really do. All I know is, when I think about those girls—now just Jessica—what I feel is desperation."

I sit back in my chair, hands folded in my lap, and watch as Susan gathers the cards, shuffles them, stacks them, and slides them back into the box. The rain hammers the cabin and the chickens peck outside and somewhere, likely in this town, Jessica Hoyle is waiting for me. And, because of this woman and her little spread of cards, I feel more like I can find her.

I let out a deep breath and say, "Thank you, Miss Susan."

# TWENTY-ONE

WHEN I GET BACK to the field that leads to Crow Caw Cabin, I am soggy and cold and irritated. I look at my phone and find that it's nearly ten o'clock; apparently, a visit to the local psychic can really eat up a person's morning. I think about Susan and her story, her tiny shack in the forest where she makes herbal remedies, her applehead dolls. I wonder if a transcript of Susan's questioning is in the sheriff's department files or whether the FBI had sole control at that point.

I'm so absorbed in my thoughts that I jump when I see a man sitting on the cabin's front porch. Instinctively, I swing my hand around to my lower back, get my palm on cold metal, then realize who it is I'm looking at.

Hunched forward in the wooden chair, palms flat together, thin and lanky and birdlike but with deep lines around his mouth and wavy hair that's more salt and pepper than chestnut now, is Greg Andrews, Max and Molly's father.

"Hello," I say as I step toward the porch.

He stands, and his hands hang awkwardly at his sides. He's wearing Dickies and a button-up chambray shirt under a sun-washed barn coat.

"Hello," he says. "Greg Andrews. I'm Max's dad."

"I'm so sorry about your daughter," I say. "Truly."

"Can we talk?" Greg says.

"Sure." I unlock the door and lead the way into the cabin. I fill the coffeepot and flick the switch and the machine hums to life.

"When did you get in?" I ask.

"This morning," he says. "As soon as Max called I found someone to finish my drive and flew back to Knoxville."

I take two mugs from the hooks hanging above the back counter.

"I understand that Max hired you to find out what happened to Molly," Greg says.

"Yes," I say. "He hired me to look for her and then . . ."

Greg sits on the same barstool that AJ used the night before, and I remember the manila folder of autopsy photos, still sitting on the edge of the countertop. I pick it up, slip it into a drawer.

"And now you're searching for her killer?" Greg says, watching me.

"Yes."

He sighs.

"Well," he says, "I'd like you to stop."

"Excuse me?"

"It's police business," he says, directing his eyes toward the wood grain on the counter instead of me. "It's—look, it doesn't matter."

"It . . . What? What the hell does *that* mean?"

"It doesn't matter," Greg says. His voice is cool and emotionless. "Look, Miss Gore, you've been here, what, three days? And already you've turned my son's life inside out. I've already lost almost everything to this . . . this applehead doll person. Whoever they are. I lost my little girl and I thought it would kill me. Then, it *did* kill my wife. I thought losing Janice would kill me—finding her like that—and, instead, I only wished it had."

He pauses, his jaws clamped together, and exhales through his nose before he starts again. "I cleaned out all their things. I didn't want us to be ruled by their memory. I don't know if, if that was right. But I did my best. I got my sister to look in on Max, make sure he was doing okay. He was always a quiet kid but . . . I thought he'd finish high school, go to college, get out of here, leave it all behind. Instead, he became obsessed. Wouldn't spend his money on anything besides what would help him hire a PI. And now you're here. And Molly's gone. Forever."

I sigh and sit down opposite him, make him meet my eyes. Like Max's, they are a green-brown hazel like fall leaves, framed by long lashes and, in Greg's case, deeply etched crow's-feet. For all their beauty, though, they feel blank. Like someone tipped him over and drained all the juice out.

"Mister Andrews, I don't think it would have helped. I don't think a change in scenery would've done anything to sway Max from looking for answers. I don't think he could have left it behind. Finding out what happened to his little sister has been his purpose in life, if not since Molly was taken, then at least since—"

I bite my tongue before I say, "Since you abandoned him. Since his mother did."

He stares at me, cold and hard. Then nods and looks away, back toward the farmhouse he left behind years ago.

"Please stop," he says. "Now that Molly's been found, maybe I can convince him to leave this place."

"Mister Andrews—"

He holds up a hand, stands.

"Please stop," he says. "I'll pay you to stop. Whatever he's paying you, I'll pay you double. Whatever it takes."

I shake my head. He stares at me, eyes watering, and he says, "Think about it. Think about what this is doing to him. If I lose him too . . ."

It's less of a threat and more a moment of quiet anguish, frustration born of powerlessness.

"Please," he says. He opens his mouth to say more, but then turns and leaves, shutting the door quietly behind him.

"Shit," I breathe. Then again, "Shit."

I march off into the bedroom and then the bathroom and strip down. I leave my damp clothes in a heap on the floor and my gun on the top of the toilet tank while I take a steaming-hot shower, running the honeysuckle-scented soap through my hair and over my skin. It smells like summer, I think.

And I think about that hot, desperate summer when three little girls were taken and one was brought back. I think about the plant that closed and the jobs that were lost and the empty swing set at the church. I think about the carved faces of the applehead dolls and their empty, black eyes and their lace-lined dresses.

"Shit . . ." I say out loud. I slam off the water, grab a towel, and wrap it around me. I pit-pat into the kitchen and yank the drawer open, take out the manila envelope, open it, slide the pictures onto the cabinet.

Yes, here is Molly clean and naked as a baby on the slab in the morgue and here, clothed in the forest, just like I found her. Her hair is arranged in beautiful waves around her, like a halo, and her skin is ashen gray except for the white scar on her chin.

And her dress. Red velvet. White lace.

"Red velvet, white lace," I say. "Red velvet, white lace."

I close my eyes and try to focus. I open them and call AJ.

"Hey," I say. "Any luck on those original case files? I need to see something."

"Working on it," he says. "There are a lot of files. A lot of stuff is from the FBI and a lot of it is incomplete. Plus, here in good ol' Quartz Creek, everything was still on paper ten years ago. The files were all scanned into the system a couple years back but nothing was labeled the same or tagged like we do now so . . ."

"I need the picture of the applehead doll that was left in Molly's place."

"Okay," AJ says. "Let me see . . . I remember running across all that stuff when I came in. But then, there was a break-in at the pawnshop this morning and I've been caught up with—oh, okay, here it is."

"Describe it to me," I say.

"It's red. Uh . . . with white around the . . . oh."

"Red velvet. With white lace, right?"

"Yeah," he says. "Damn. She's dressed like . . ."

"A doll," I say. "And not just any doll. She's dressed like the doll that was left in her place."

"And now she's been returned," he says.

My phone buzzes in my hand and I look at the screen.

"Hey," I say. "I've got a call coming in. Come by tonight if you can, with the files."

"Sure," he says. "I'll be there after work. Around seven."

"See you then."

I hang up and switch to the other call.

"Is this Annie Gore?" the voice says. It's female and young. For a brief, heart-thudding moment, I think maybe it's Jessica. A fantasy blooms in my mind that maybe she's somehow found out that I'm looking for her, maybe she's escaped—however briefly—found a way to get ahold of me.

"Yes?" I answer. "Jessica?"

"What? No, I . . . look, meet me at Starling Point," the voice says. "Twenty minutes. I have information for you."

"Wait, what—"

But the line is dead. I look at the phone in my hand, grab my keys, and go out the door.

# TWENTY-TWO

A QUICK SEARCH ON MY phone and I find directions to Starling Point. After a few near misses and slow crawls, I turn onto a little upward-tilted gravel road and follow it up the side of a high hill. Mountain laurel bushes, still green and dense, whoosh by both sides of the car; their flowers have dropped and a few half-rotten blooms lie on the ground below. Beyond the bushes, deeper into the forest, all I can see is mist.

I'm relieved when the greenery opens up at the top of a hill and I find a little hatchback parked against a guardrail and two teenagers standing together against the passenger-side door. I roll up slowly, watching them, and realize these are the older siblings of Jessica and Olivia: Tam Hoyle and Nicole Jacobs.

"Hey," Nicole says when I get out of the car.

"Shouldn't you be in school?"

Nicole shrugs and says, "Yearbook staff." Like that explains everything.

"Cool car," Tam says. Obviously a guy of impeccable taste.

"Thanks," I say, giving Honey a little pat. "What's up?"

They trade a glance and then Nicole says, "We want to help."

"Okay," I say. "But . . . how?"

Nicole bites down on her bottom lip, and Tam nudges her shoulder.

"Come on," Tam says. He's tall with broad shoulders, built a lot more like Tommy than Mandy Hoyle. But Tam's voice is soft and thoughtful, with an undercurrent of kindness that I could never picture coming from his father.

"We can trust you, right?" he says.

"Sure."

Nicole leans back, dipping her hand into the car's passenger seat. She comes back out with a little stack of folded-up papers. She hands them to me and I open them.

It's all drawings, in crayon. Spirals litter page after page after page. Red, yellow, orange, and pink, they run corner to corner.

"What is this?"

Nicole crosses her arms tight in front of her, hunching her shoulders together protectively the same way Kathleen does.

"My sister's drawings," Nicole says. "Olivia made those when they brought her back."

"You mean after she was kidnapped?"

She nods.

"For how long?"

She shrugs and says, "I don't know. A while. She still does them sometimes, but she hides them or tears them up after. She doesn't show them to Mom."

"Okay," I say, my eyes moving over the spirals. The crayon is thick and heavy, indenting the paper even after all these years. I look back up at the two of them.

"You two are friends?"

They glance at each other, and then Nicole nods and Tam says, "We've been on debate team together since freshman year."

Illuminating.

"And you heard about Molly," I say.

"We went to school with Max," Tam says. "I always thought hiring a PI was sort of hopeless. Probably a waste of money. But you show up in town and, two days later, Molly is back. I want you to find Jessica. We have to find her, before it's too late. I want to help."

"Well, I don't know how much you *can* help," I say. "But this is good. Thank you for this."

They don't say anything and my gaze drifts from them, down to the crayon drawings, and back up to them. I say, "You two were pretty young when your sisters were taken."

"Yeah," Tam says.

I say, "Nicole, why do you think Olivia was returned?"

She lets out a breath I hadn't realized she was holding; maybe she hadn't either. She says, "I sort of . . . God, don't tell my mom. Look, I love Olivia. She's my sister and I love her more than anyone. *Anyone.* And I think Olivia is perfect the way she is. But if you didn't know her? I know what people think. What they say."

She bites her lip again and her cheeks go pink as she looks off into the distance, beyond the overlook and across the valley. Tam moves his hand, subtly, just barely touching Nicole's between them.

Nicole is still looking away when she says, "They think she was returned because she was defective. Because she wasn't normal. And . . ." She glances at Tam, whose face is set and hard while Nicole's eyes fill with tears.

Tam says, "And if you take a little girl and bring her back because she's not normal then what would you have been using her for? I mean, why did they bring back Molly Andrews? Why *now*? Is it because you showed up here? Started asking questions? Or is it because it's been ten years? Like it's some kind of . . . anniversary?"

"You sound like you have a theory," I say.

Tam glares at me for a few long seconds and then looks at Honey instead.

"Tell me," I say.

"What if someone took Olivia all those years ago and brought her back because they realized she wasn't suited for whatever *purpose* they had."

Nicole bites her bottom lip, looks from the horizon to Tam to me.

She says, "Everyone always underestimates Olivia. They see that she doesn't talk and that she's not like regular people and they assume she's an idiot. But she's not. She's smart and she's brave and she's sneaky. People assume that Olivia was brought back intentionally, but I've always wondered . . ."

"You think maybe she escaped?"

She shrugs and looks back across the hills.

"Maybe," she says, quietly. "Maybe he never meant to let her go."

I look away, down toward town. Quartz Creek lies in a low valley, and I can follow the line of Main Street from here. I'm on the opposite side of town from Max's farm, the woods beyond it, Susan's cabin.

"You two ever been to visit Susan McKinney?"

Tam snorts and Nicole looks down at her shoes.

"So, that's a 'yes,'" I say.

Nicole nods.

"What'd she tell you?"

Nicole groans and says, "She told me to be brave."

"Be brave?" I ask.

She nods.

"Just generally or . . . ?"

"She just said to be brave."

"Okay. What about you, Tam?"

"Shit," Tam says, his voice edgier now. "My mom's wasted enough time up at that witch's house. I don't need to clean some old lady's cabin to know I've got to get my ass out of this town."

"I get that," I say.

"Oh yeah?" Tam cocks a dubious eyebrow at me.

"Yeah," I say.

"I looked you up, you know," Tam says. "You were in the military, right?"

"Yeah, Air Force."

"You recommend it?"

"Not particularly."

He laughs, and I say, "But if you're set on it, let me know. I might be able to get you a leg up with recruiting."

He looks at me for a good long while and then nods his head once and looks away, toward the horizon. I let out a breath and think about Tam, so much like I was at that age only better-looking and cooler and more grown-up, and I think about the military and what it did for me, *to* me.

I follow his gaze and see a tall, brown-brick building off in the distance.

"What is that?" I ask, pointing.

"That's the old factory," Tam says.

"Yeah," Nicole says. "DrakeCo. Everyone used to work there when we were little."

"Okay," I say. "It's not being used for anything now?"

Tam frowns, bites his bottom lip. Nicole looks up at him, her eyebrows raised as if prompting him to come clean about something.

"What is it?" I ask.

"My dad," Tam says.

"What about him?"

"Couple guys at school," Nicole says when Tam fails to answer. "They saw him over there the other day. Him and Tam's uncle."

"Dwight?" I ask. "Dwight Hoyle?"

Tam nods.

"I thought the building was closed."

"It is," Tam says. "It's . . ."

"Haunted," Nicole says. "People say it's haunted. But nobody goes there unless . . ."

"Unless they're doing something they shouldn't be doing. Kids don't even park there. Not anymore. It's like only the hard-core tweakers go."

"And your dad's going?"

Tam shrugs.

Nicole pulls a buzzing phone out of her back pocket and checks it.

"Hey," she says. "We need to head back. I can't be late for calc again."

"Yeah," Tam says. "Okay."

"I hope those help," Nicole says, looking toward the drawings in my hand. They're on old paper, faded and fragile, but they feel impossibly heavy in my grasp. I look at these kids and I feel that same heaviness. A mix of fear and worry and a gnawing, sick feeling.

Nicole starts around to the driver side of the car but pauses when I ask, "Whose number did you call me from?"

"Mine," Tam says. "Nicole's mom watches her phone like a hawk."

"Okay. Well, call me again if you think of anything else."

"Okay," Tam says, but he almost seems like he's not listening.

"You two aren't going to go investigating, right?"

They glance at each other.

"Please don't," I say. "Please just call me. Call me, okay? Anything comes up, call me."

Nicole looks at Tam, who finally says, "Okay."

They get in the car and drive away. I stay there a while longer, looking down at the papers, the endless spirals all joined together, hundreds of them, filling every page.

"What did you see?" I ask the spirals and the mind that they came from, the young woman who does not speak but whose head might hold the key to all of this. "Where were you taken?"

I lean against Honey and stare at the spirals until I'm dizzy with their spinning color. I close my eyes, then look again at the waving horizon and the DrakeCo Toy Factory on the distant hilltop. I wonder whether Tommy and Dwight Hoyle are there now. What they might be up to in an abandoned factory that even local teenagers shy away from.

"Seems like something worth checking out," I mutter. I climb back behind the wheel and put Honey in gear.

# TWENTY-THREE

U P CLOSE, THE DRAKECO Toy Factory is even more dismal than it was from the hilltop. Two stories of brown brick with big, rusting double doors on the front and most of the windows broken. Ivy—brown now with the fall weather—clings to the side and roof. The old lot, almost completely overgrown, is littered with soda bottles, beer cans, condom wrappers, and actual condoms. Otherwise, it's empty. I'm the only one here.

"Lovely," I say as I sit there taking it all in. It's the very picture of rural dilapidation, the symbol of a failed local economy and all the poverty that comes with it.

"Is there anything sadder than a defunct toy company?" I muse aloud. There's no particular reason the girls might have been kept in a place like this, but I can't help wondering what Tommy and Dwight Hoyle are up to, now that Dwight's back in town. And I can't help wondering if it—whatever it is—is somehow connected to Molly and Jessica. The factory did make dolls, didn't it? And the girls were traded for dolls, they were dressed like dolls, and both Tommy and Dwight used to work here.

My phone buzzes, startling me.

"Hey, AJ," I answer. "What's up?"

"Wanted to let you know I've just about collected all these case files. You still available at seven?"

"Sure thing," I say.

"Want me to bring dinner?"

There's a moment of silence while I catch myself smiling, feel a flush of heat in my cheeks.

"Yeah," I say. "Yeah, that'd be nice."

Nothing can be awful all the time. Otherwise, we'd all go crazy.

"You wanna hear the choices?" AJ asks. "There are many fine dining options in beautiful Quartz Creek."

"Nah," I say, laughing. "Surprise me."

He chuckles, and I'm about to hang up when I see a glint in one of the upper windows. The window itself is mostly gone, a few shards of glass clinging to the frame. I think maybe I'm just seeing things. Maybe just a shift of light and shadow. Maybe a reflection caused by the way the sunlight cuts through the fog on the mountains. Maybe there are swallows nesting inside. Maybe bats.

"AJ," I say.

"Yeah?"

"The DrakeCo factory . . ."

"What about it?"

"What happened after the factory shut down?"

He sighs heavily and says, "You mean like socioeconomically or—"

"No, was the building ever bought by anyone else?"

"No," he answers. "No one wanted to set up shop in Quartz Creek. The factory sat defunct most of the time I was a kid. It was up for sale for a few years but, after a while, it was in such bad shape that it was abandoned and condemned. Then it was just . . . You know how much it costs to demolish a building?"

"And now it's mostly used by stoners and stuff?"

"Uh, yeah?" I hear him shuffling papers around at a desk, the sounds of the sheriff's department going on around him, a phone ringing, people talking.

"Was it not locked up?"

"No, it was. Mostly kids hang out outside, but it's not a fortress. Lately it's been a rougher crowd around there. Fewer stoner kids, more serious addict types. Someone could've got in. What's going on?"

I see the flicker of light in the glass again and I get out of the car, phone still in hand.

"Well—"

I pause, freeze in place, at the sound of shattering glass. A yelp.

*BANG!*

A gunshot.

My heart leaps and all my old reflexes come alive, firing, ready. I duck beside Honey, pull my gun with a whispered, "Shit!"

*BANG!*

Another gunshot.

Into the phone I hiss, "Gunshots in the factory. I'm going in."

"Annie—" AJ says.

I hang up, slide the phone into my back pocket.

There's another pop and boom. Another high, yelping scream. It's a woman's voice, I think, but I can't be sure. The quality is thin and hoarse. There's a frantic, pained quality to it, and, before I can reconsider, I'm running.

I slam into the front doors, yank against their old handles. They're locked. Chained from the inside. I run around the east side of the building, searching for an entryway. Nothing. All the windows here are boarded up. I push against each one, but they don't budge. I round the corner. There's a loading bay in the back. Locked. A small door up a set of stairs. Locked. There's a nearly new Chevy pickup parked on the crumbling concrete, but it's empty. On the other side of it is a little multicolored Honda. Mandy Hoyle's car.

There's another bang. Vibrating with energy and adrenaline, my heart thumping against my ribs, my lungs burning, I run around the west side. Smoke streams out of an upper window.

"Shit," I breathe.

I try the windows again, giving each slab of plywood a hard shove as I run along. Finally, toward the middle of the building, one gives. Almost like it's hinged. I push it again. It gives some more.

Up above, the screaming starts again. Wordless and horrified. Again, a woman's voice.

"Mandy?" I call. But there's no real answer, just more frantic screaming.

I push the plywood all the way in and find a tattered blanket lying folded over the rusting sill and old glass. I ease myself into the window and look back at the plywood.

If this place is burning down, I need to be able to find a way out. I yank at the wood, but it doesn't come off. I look around. Find a couple old bricks, prop the plywood open so at least I can see the sunlight through the cracks.

Inside, the place is damp, dusty, and dark. Huge pieces of rusty machinery take up the entire ground floor. Here and there, pieces of dolls litter the equipment, the cement floor. They're even nailed to the plywood over the windows. Some of the pieces, mostly heads, are defaced with markers or bullet holes. Some of the dolls' plastic eyes have been plucked out.

Pretty much exactly what you'd expect in a defunct toy factory.

*BANG!*

I keep my gun ready, run to where I hope the staircase is. With all the dust and the dingy light and the smoke billowing down from upstairs, it's hard to see.

I find a set of creaky metal stairs and hope they're not rusted through.

It's been only ten years since this place closed, but it's humid in these mountains and this place isn't exactly hermetically sealed.

I start to climb the steps, let my hip rub along the stair rail, guiding me up.

"Mandy?" I call.

A wave of acrid gray-black smoke crashes into me. I cough and sputter against the burning in my throat and pull the collar of my T-shirt up over my nose and mouth.

I hear yelling, screaming. A man's voice shouting. Shouting that he needs help. And still the woman's voice, screaming in terror.

I hit the top of the stairs and find that, unlike the open bottom floor, the top is split into several big rooms. I work my way through them as best I can. Up here the smoke is worse, but at least the windows aren't boarded up, so some light comes in. I use what little of it I can to find my way around the maze of rooms, ducking under the smoke.

I follow the sound of the screams.

"Help me, goddamnit!" the deeper voice screams again.

I round one more corner and finally find the source of the fire.

Smoke billows out of a room that's too small for production, that maybe was once used for storage or as an office. A man lies on the floor in front of me, half his face melted off, his clothes charred black, still smoldering, no longer moving. I recognize him from the picture in the criminal records I'd pulled up my first night in Quartz Creek.

It's Dwight Hoyle.

"Shit," I hiss again.

Another scream behind me. I turn and see a smaller figure crouched in the corner across the room, just barely in my field of vision. It's Elaine Hoyle. Staring at her husband, her mouth open to let out a prolonged, horrified scream.

"Elaine," I say. "Elaine—"

But she doesn't seem to hear me. Her hair, stained black from soot, is plastered to her face. She holds her fists so near her mouth, I'm surprised she hasn't bitten her fingers off.

"Elaine!"

Across the room, the other, deeper shouting starts again.

"Help me! Goddamnit! Help me!"

I duck under the smoke and try to locate the source of the scream. On the other side of the room, his leg caught under a fallen wood beam, is Tommy Hoyle.

Bottles of chemicals are stacked on an old table, and they're burning. Fire belches out of the bottles, streams across the table and down the other side, where another bottle has spilled. The bottles are everywhere, overturned and discarded, piled up in a pitifully undersized plastic trash can and stacked on makeshift shelves against the back wall. There are two large, smashed windows back in the main portion of this floor, and a big squishy tube leads to one of them. Smoke billows out everywhere it can go, but the room is still foul-smelling and hazy.

This is the cause of the fire and the smell and the screams. This is the source of the bang, I realize with sudden awareness. Not a gunshot. Worse.

This is a meth lab. It is melting down. This whole place is about to blow.

Coughing, I wrench my phone out of my back pocket and dial 911. I can't hear anything. If someone is there or not, I don't know. I shout, clear as I can, that there's a fire at an exploding meth lab at the old DrakeCo factory, then cram my phone back into my pocket. I duck down, as far under the smoke as I can, and look around.

Lying in a folding camp chair against the nearest wall are a couple of full-face respirator masks. Made of soft green rubber with a big black canister at the end, they look like they came from an Army surplus store. I grab the nearest one and slide it over my head, hoping the filter's still half decent. I grab the other one and crouch-run over to Elaine.

Questions of her being high or armed or both flit through my mind, but as I approach her all she can seem to do is stare, wide-eyed and more than half crazed, at Dwight Hoyle and scream.

I grab her by the shoulders and shake her.

"Elaine!" I shout, my voice coming out muffled through the mask. "Elaine! Can you walk?"

I grip Elaine hard, pull her to her feet, and drag her out of the room. Her legs are jelly, all but useless. Still, she's thin and light and fragile-feeling, so I drag her all the way around the corner and prop her against the wall nearest the stairs. She slumps down, still screaming, eyes wide open in addled terror.

Another bang. Dust falls from the ceiling.

"Damn it!" I shout.

I fight against her wriggling, panicked form and squish the mask down over her head so the respirator covers her screaming mouth. I'd rather have her suck rubber than go on scream-inhaling the toxic fumes.

"Get out!" I shout through my own mask. "Get out of here! Go!"

Elaine doesn't move. She only continues her screaming.

"Help me! Help me! Please!" Tommy shouts from the other room.

I leave Elaine and run back the way we'd come. The smoke is worse now. Black and awful. I duck under it and find Tommy. The beam is on fire and flames lick at Tommy's pant leg. Another beam has fallen from the ceiling and smashed the table. The chemicals leak all over the floor, catching flame.

"Is Mandy here?" I shout as I make my way back to him. The question sounds absurd. Like I'm just knocking on his front door again.

"What?"

"Mandy? Where is your wife, Mandy?"

"She's not here!"

"Her car is—"

"She's not here! Fucking help me!"

"Damn you, Tommy Hoyle!"

I grit my teeth and grab Tommy's hand. He grips back. I pull. He doesn't budge. I sit back on my butt, brace myself on my elbows, and kick the old fallen, flaming timber. Once. Again. The sound of my steel-toed boot on the wood is like the crack of a bat, but it still doesn't shift. I breathe through the respirator and tense my body. Brace. All my strength. Again. Finally, a single point shatters into flaming splinters and Tommy pulls free.

"Come on," I yell.

He does. He crawls out after me. We rush around the corner and I look for Elaine. I shout her name but she is gone. All I can do is hope she found her way out.

I lead Tommy down the rickety staircase, through the smoke.

*BANG! BANG!*

The whole building rattles, shakes. The windows vibrate. The plywood clatters against the windows. We both duck instinctively, covering our heads with our arms. Tommy screams again, and I resist the urge to punch him in the face for putting me through this to begin with.

I squint through the smoke and dust and see the tiniest sliver of sun-light. I yank Tommy's arm and lead him toward it, and just as I'm about to reach for the plywood, it flies open and there's AJ.

"Annie!" he hollers, reaching for me.

*BANG! BANG! BANG BANG BANG!*

And everything goes dark.

# TWENTY-FOUR

I AM FALLING. THROUGH DARKNESS. Through space.

I hear my name and open my eyes and see Jessica Hoyle reaching out for me, her little-girl hands raking the air between us as she tries to grasp mine. I reach toward her, but she slips through my fingers like vapor. I crash to the ground. The wind is knocked out of me in a bone-jarring thump.

I cough, my ribs aching.

I open my eyes. Fight my way back through the fog to reality.

I blink as the world comes into focus.

Taking stock, I find that I am sitting on the ground, propped against AJ's cruiser. He's holding an oxygen mask to my face while an EMT does something to my leg. The lower half of my right jeans leg has been cut away, and I groan inwardly. These were good jeans.

I try to find Honey but I can't.

"Is Honey okay?" My voice is raspy, weak.

AJ laughs, nods.

"She's parked on the other side of the cruiser," he says. "She's fine."

"Oh, thank God."

Another EMT brings me a silver-foil blanket, a bottle of water. I hold my hand out for it and AJ pulls the mask away long enough for me to drain half the bottle. The plastic crunches in my hand.

"Tommy?" I ask.

"We got him. He's in the ambulance. Under arrest."

"A meth lab?" I ask.

He nods.

I sigh, and the sigh turns into a cough. I manage to get another drink from the bottle, make the coughing stop.

"It's a good thing you found that mask," he says.

"Yeah," I say. "It's too bad they didn't. Oh! Elaine Hoyle. She was in there. And Dwight Hoyle. Did you find them?"

"Annie, you and Tommy are the only ones who came out."

We look back toward the burning factory. Ugly black smoke rolls out of the wreckage and what's left of the top floor is aflame. A fire engine stands nearby, tapped into a hydrant I'm surprised still works. They're hosing the building down, but it doesn't seem to be doing any good. I hear a shouted conversation about HAZMAT, about suits, about other firefighters coming in from another county, but all the words seem jumbled, far away.

The EMT gives my leg a gentle tap, and I look down, first at the bandage, then at the EMT's hands, and then at her face. She's a full-figured lady with rosy cheeks and a choppy gray pixie cut.

"You're gonna live," she says.

"But my jeans tragically could not be saved?"

I can barely hear my own voice over the ringing in my ears, and I begin to wonder if I actually said anything, especially since the EMT completely ignored my attempt at humor.

Instead she says, "Easier to cut the pant leg than pull the whole pair off. 'Specially with these big-ass clodhoppers you've got." She taps my half-calf-high tactical boots, and I'm suddenly overcome with gratitude that she decided to cut my jeans instead of my boot strings. They're broken in just right. And, like my gun, they were a gift from Leo.

"Girl who kicks up as much shit as you do ought to have some reliable boots," he'd said. I smile at the memory, and my face feels tight and hot. I try instead, to relax and watch the EMT's hands at work on my leg.

"Thanks," I say to her.

"No problem," she says. "Looks like you grazed something in there."

I figure it must've been that beam I kicked but who knows. I grimace at the gauze on my shin, just above my boot. I look closer and see a long scrape up the black leather and offer a silent thanks for well-made shoes.

"I cleaned it out," she says. "Your boots absorbed the worst of it. Didn't even break the leather. You don't need stitches or anything, so that's good. We'll get you to the hospital and—"

"Nope," I say. "Nope. I'm . . . I'm okay. I'm fine. Nothing's broken, right? Not bleeding from anywhere?"

"Well, I can't make you go. Just keep it clean," she says, hands on her hips. "Keep fresh gauze on it. And you're going to want to report to the hospital in the morning. Get you a tetanus booster."

"Oh," I say. "I'm good."

She gives me a practiced side-eye.

"Military," I say.

She nods like that explains everything.

"Chest X-ray wouldn't hurt either. But you got lucky."

"I know."

"Promise you'll go to the hospital if you start to feel worse."

"Scout's honor."

She rolls her eyes and walks off.

"Most of the second floor collapsed," AJ says. "Right after we pulled you out."

I put the water bottle to my mouth. Drain it.

"Yeah. You sure you don't wanna go to the hospital, Annie?"

"Don't like 'em. Can't afford 'em. And, right now, I don't need one. I'll be fine. I just need a shower and some food."

"Okay," he says. "I can help with some of that, at least."

I smile at him, exhausted, and lay my head back against the cruiser and close my eyes. Almost instantly, I hear the sound of another car crunching over the gravel and into the lot. A door slams and boots hit gravel.

"Somebody tell me what the hell happened here," Sheriff Jacobs barks to the general crowd from the other side of the car.

I open my eyes and find AJ looking not at his boss but at me.

"Oh, come on," I say to the sky, pleading. "Just a shower. That's all."

"You!" Jacobs says, rounding the corner. "Just what the hell are *you* doing here?"

"I only—"

"I swear to Christ, it's like you're a walking bad-luck charm!" His cheeks are red with some blood-pressure-raising mix of frustration, surprise, and anger as he points at the smoldering factory and shouts at me. "Does chaos just happen to follow you around or do you invite it along for rides in that ugly clunker of yours?"

A growl works its way from my belly, up through my chest, and into the back of my mouth before I realize I'm too tired to fight and, anyway, there's no getting out of this. The growl turns into an exhausted sigh.

It's an hour and a half at the station, for the second time in two days, making a statement and signing all the paperwork. I'm sitting, filthy and exhausted, in the same little room as before initialing everything with a Bic ballpoint, barely even reading it, when AJ comes to get me.

"You okay?" he asks.

"Shower," I say, getting up with a groan and almost plowing into him. "Food."

Thirty minutes later, I pull up outside the cabin. AJ, who traded his cruiser for his personal truck, pulls in right behind me. I go straight around the side of the cabin, where I'd seen a little garden hose the day before. AJ starts to follow me, then turns around when I strip naked and toss my filthy clothes in a heap.

"Please," I shout to him. "Dinner."

Then, I take a bracing deep breath and turn the cold water on my body, not wanting to breathe any of the steam that might come off me in a hot shower. Once the water running onto my feet is mostly clear, I shut off the hose and walk, stark naked, back around to the front of the cabin. There, AJ is waiting with a towel, his eyes averted and a deep blush in his cheeks.

"Feel better?" he asks.

"Almost." I take the towel, wipe my feet on the mat, pad into the cabin, and head straight for the bathroom.

I turn the shower on and step in. In spite of my best efforts with the hose, streaks of black and gray still spiral around my feet and disappear down the drain.

"Gross," I mutter. "This is disgusting."

"Are you sure you don't want to go to the hospital?" AJ hollers through the bathroom door.

"Yeah," I shout. The cut on my shin opens under the scalding water. Bright blood mixes with the streaks of gray. "I've had worse."

There's no reply, and after a few minutes I ask. "You order that dinner yet?"

I wash everything three times, scrubbing with one of Max's nice pale blue washcloths and honeysuckle body wash and wishing I'd asked AJ to just hand me the bottle of dish soap from the kitchen.

After the third scrub, I toss the washcloth toward the trash can, but miss. It hits the wall with a wet slap and leaves a dark streak as it slurps down to the floor. I pull another one from the little hutch above the toilet and start over.

When I get out, I wrap a clean towel around my middle and give my hair a good tousle with another one, run a comb through it. I pull the bag out of the trash can and tie it off, replace it. I look in the mirror and find that I am pink and shiny. Satisfied, I let out what could almost be called a contented sigh.

I go into the kitchen, towel still wrapped around me, hair dripping down my shoulders. AJ's got a fire going in the fireplace and the cabin is toasty and nice and I realize I've probably been in low-level shock since I woke up next to AJ's cruiser.

"Oh," AJ says when he sees me. "You're bleeding."

I look down and find that the cut on my shin is open again. A streak of red runs onto my foot.

"Come on," he says. He holds out a cold beer as a lure and leads me to the kitchen chair.

"Max has a first aid kit in here," AJ says as I sit and take the bottle and have a good, long drink.

AJ opens a cabinet over the stove and pulls out a little red hard-shell case and then kneels down on the floor in front of me and opens it up. He cleans the wound with an alcohol pad. I grit my teeth, but I don't hiss or shiver.

"What were you doing in there?" he asks.

"Shower," I say.

He gives me a "You know what I meant, smart-ass" look and says, "DrakeCo Toy Factory."

"Tam Hoyle told me that someone saw his dad and Dwight Hoyle over there. I thought . . . what if it had something to do with Jessica and Molly?"

"Well, it was searched after the girls were kidnapped. The FBI did an entire investigation around it; I saw the files today. Ever since, it's hosted a few unsavory types and we have to run them off, but, as far as I know, you stumbled into the first meth lab."

"Lucky me," I say.

He holds the back of my calf in one hand, cradling the muscle like a bird, while he applies antibiotic ointment with a swab. His touch is so light, I barely feel it.

"Deputy Flora questioned Tommy at the hospital. He *says* he was just visiting his cousins."

"At their meth lab?"

"Yeah," AJ says.

"Jesus," I breathe.

AJ keeps his eyes on the wound. His hands are warm and firm and strong. His voice is even and smooth. I feel myself melting into his care, feel the tension beginning to drain away from me, feel the shock of my day receding.

I realize that, even after he finishes dressing my wound, even after we eat dinner, even after we spend the evening discussing the case, I am going to want him to stay the night. I am going to need his big, warm, easy bearing close to me.

"How's this?" he asks, blowing a cool stream of air across my exposed flesh. "Does it hurt?"

"No," I say. "It's okay. You're doing a good job."

He lets go of my calf, tears open a sterile package of gauze, and applies it carefully to my shin. He picks up the roll of tape.

"Did Tommy say what happened?" I ask.

He pulls a strip of tape from the roll and attaches the gauze, pressing it down gently.

"Well, of course, Tommy says he had no idea his cousins were cooking."

"Of course."

"He says he was just taking them some lunch."

"What a nice guy."

"And he says when he got up today, his truck was broken down. So, he got a ride to Ellerd's, grabbed some food, then took Mandy's car. He went up to the factory and they were—according to him—arguing because he was telling them what a bad idea it was to be cooking meth."

"Sure."

"And then Elaine went to the window on the other side of the building for a smoke. She saw you pull up, saw you on the phone. She was stoned—ran back into the lab to tell them they were being watched and forgot she was holding a lit cigarette in her hand."

"And it all went downhill from there."

"Yeah."

He tapes the other end of the gauze down, and I watch him in silence.

"I didn't know they were there," I say. "Not until—"

"I know." He lets go of my calf but he's still kneeling on the floor in front me. He raises both hands, lays them on my bare knees, looks up at me. And he could say things like, "It wasn't your fault." Which I know. And "You saved Tommy's life." Which I know. And "They shouldn't have been in there cooking meth in the first place." Which I know.

But he doesn't.

I'm no closer to finding Molly's killer. At least two more people are dead. Tommy Hoyle is in the hospital. And Jessica may still be out there, awaiting the same fate as Molly. That's how I balance my ledger at the end of this day. That's where I am in this moment.

And AJ could tell me that I'm lucky to be alive, which I know. Lucky I'm not lying in the hospital room right next to Tommy, hacking out toxic muck, which I know. Lucky that after I faced an explosion and a fire and a crumbling building, I'm still here. And I'm not alone.

I know it. AJ knows it.

Neither of us says it.

I lean forward and kiss AJ's forehead, the bridge of his nose, the dip above his lip.

He runs his palms up, over my knees, and onto my thighs.

The towel drops away.

I don't say anything. And neither does AJ.

Neither of us has to.

# TWENTY-FIVE

LATER, TWO MOSTLY EMPTY boxes of pizza lie conquered on the coffee table in front of us. AJ sips a beer while he consolidates the leftovers into a single box.

"What do you think of this?" I ask, holding up one of the papers Nicole gave me.

He considers the picture in my hand. I've just found them, folded up in my bag, not having looked at them since I left Starling Point.

He shuts the empty boxes and licks some orange grease from his thumb.

"Where'd that come from?" he asks.

"An interested party. Tell me what you see."

"Is this like an inkblot test?"

"Yeah," I say. "Just like that."

"Spirals. Hmm. They're like . . . seashells."

"Huh," I say.

"Seashells, or maybe snail shells. That's what it makes me think of."

AJ's out of uniform now, wearing a pair of sweatpants and a plain beige T-shirt of mine. Most of my loungewear is men's and oversized, but I get the feeling AJ wouldn't be bothered by a pair of cute terry cloth shorts either, long as he gets out of his brown polyester. His big body is solid but not stiff as he leans forward on his knees and studies the picture.

"Where'd it really come from?"

"Olivia Jacobs. She drew them after she was brought back and, according to her sister, she's been drawing them ever since."

"All crayon."

"Yeah. And she hides them from her mom."

"Interesting."

"I mean, she was questioned when she was brought back, right?"

"As far as anyone *could* question her, yeah. But they didn't get anything from her."

"She was still so little," I say. "How much of what happened would she have even understood, let alone been able to convey to a bunch of people in uniforms?"

He shrugs and stands and takes the pizza stuff into the kitchen. Folds the empty boxes in half and slides them into the trash, puts the box of leftovers in the fridge. He comes back and opens a worn backpack that he probably carried around at college and pulls out a laptop. From a little pocket, he takes out a USB drive and plugs it in.

"The files?" I ask, as he opens the folder on the drive and reveals tons of scanned documents and photos.

"Yeah," he says. "Witness statements, newspaper articles, photos, police reports. And the stuff I could find from the FBI, too. Reports they wrote up, photographs they took. Some forensics."

"Did you have time to look at any of it?"

"Well, no, not really. I scanned some of the initial reports and glanced at a few pictures. It's mostly just the applehead dolls, though. Besides that, there wasn't much of anything to take a picture of. Just empty places where those girls had been. The park and church were too heavily trafficked to get clean prints of any kind and no other evidence was found on the scene. There were no prints besides the Andrewses' and a few other family members and guests at the Andrews place."

He pulls the photos up and we look through them. The empty swing set. The empty park grounds. The empty living room.

We look through the police reports.

The sun is long gone now, and the crows are beginning to scream.

"This is a weird place," I say with a dark, breathy laugh.

AJ shrugs.

"Did you think about going anywhere else after college?" I ask.

"Nah," he says. "I like it here. I came back every weekend even when I was in school."

"You like being a cop?"

He nods. We sit together for a little while and think about our sameness, our differentness, as we listen to the crows.

Eventually I say, "I need to refresh my brain on all of this. It's getting too twisted up in my head. So . . . let me lay it out for you. Pretend you've never heard any of this before."

"Sure," he says. "Tabula rasa."

I go to the fridge and pour two glasses of milk, bring them back, get situated.

I take a long drink, then put the milk on the table, lean my head back against the couch, and close my eyes.

"Jessica Hoyle," I say. "Taken in May. Olivia Jacobs, taken in July, brought back two weeks later. Molly Andrews, taken just after, early August. The kidnapper must've been local, right?"

"Why do you say that?"

"Because the kidnappings took place over three months, with awareness and paranoia ramping up all the time. If there'd been a suspicious stranger in town, anywhere near where the girls were taken, people would've noticed."

"Okay."

"Also, the applehead dolls. Only mountain people know about those dolls. People from Appalachia, so most likely here. A local. But where did he take them?"

AJ shakes his head. No idea.

"What about the clothes?" I ask. "That dress Molly was wearing? Where did it come from?"

AJ clicks around on his laptop, looking at the case file, I assume.

"Hmm. No brand. Looks like it was all custom-tailored, I guess. Special-ordered?"

"Or homemade," I say. "Like the doll clothes my granny used to make for me when I was little."

"Hard to imagine you playing with dolls," AJ says with a smile.

"Only child," I say. As if that explains it all. As if that tells the story of how I didn't mother my dolls but befriended them, treated them like siblings. I think about Honey in the driveway and decide to push the topic elsewhere.

"Molly was a replacement," I say. "She was replacing Olivia. Nicole—Olivia's big sister—said that everyone believes Olivia was brought back because she was 'defective,' but it's not impossible that Olivia could've got away on her own and that afterward she was too difficult to snatch again. Easier to pick a new target."

"But to take a kid from her own home?" AJ says, his hand on his chin while he rubs his lower lip in thought.

"Are we sure she was taken from her home, though?" I say.

"Yeah," AJ says. "Of course she was. Max—"

"Was in another room, sitting next to his teacher, banging away on a piano. His mom was out back in the garden. Max said he went outside to play after his piano lesson, so Molly was alone in the house for who knows how long."

I picture the house on that day. The back dining room where the piano sat. The little front room where Molly was watching *Snow White*. The maze of hallways between them. I can almost hear the clunky playing of *Moonlight Sonata* drifting through the house. Picture the front door swinging open, picture the shadow of the person standing there, blocking the sunshine.

"Who might've been in the neighborhood that day?" I ask. "You said you live down the lane, right?"

"You caught me," AJ says with a broad grin. "It was me all along."

I nudge him with my shoulder, and he laughs.

"Impressive work for a fifteen-year-old," I say. "What was your alibi?"

"Pretty sure I was running wind sprints until I puked just about every day that summer. I was determined to get a football scholarship and Coach told me I should start early."

"Okay, I'll mark you down as improbable."

He rolls his eyes dramatically and I ask, "How many other houses are down the lane?"

"Six down around me, but more farther on." He rubs a hand over his stubble, thinking, his gaze traveling up to the ceiling. "The road forks, with one side going up the mountain and another going down into a woodsy holler."

"Anyone of note?"

"Now that you mention it . . ." he says.

"Who?"

"The Zieglers. Pastor Bob and Rebecca. They live out a piece in a split-level they built when they moved here."

"Is it a big house?"

"Big enough for what you're thinking, yeah," he says, his eyes scanning the report from the day Molly was taken as he talks. "It's not a palace or anything, but maybe three thousand square feet? I think Rebecca inherited a bunch of land and money from her father or someone and—oh—"

He stops mid-sentence, and I watch him, hopeful for some big break.

"What is it?" I ask.

"The Zieglers were there that day," he says, looking up at me.

"Does it say why?"

"No, and I can't find their statement. I'll have to look again tomorrow. God, I can't believe what a mess these files are. All I have is a list of those interviewed concerning Molly's disappearance. Bob and Rebecca are on the list."

"Jessica was taken from the church parking lot," I say. "Olivia was taken from a church picnic."

"But not Molly," he says.

"No, but the Andrews family went to First Baptist. And it doesn't say why they were visiting that day?"

He shakes his head.

"I'll have to talk to them," I mutter. I go back to my own thoughts, letting my mind wander, hoping some connection will suddenly spring up, but the only one I can find is fairly weak.

"You know who else goes to First Baptist?" I say.

"About half the town?"

"Deena Drake. She plays piano there. She said she gave a statement on the day of Molly's disappearance, and she was at the picnic and the church the day Jessica was taken. Is there anything from her on that day?"

He flicks through until he finds an old scan of a handwritten list.

"It's not a lot to go on. A list of people in attendance when Jessica went missing, and all the cars they went through—make and model—with the names crossed off once they were searched. Deena's car is on here, that old Range Rover she drives. It's the only one in town, pretty distinctive."

"Who checked it?" I ask.

"Donald Kerridge," he says. "The sheriff. That's his initials by the car's check. At the bottom is a note about how they called in Fish and Wildlife to help look in the woods."

"Did you know him?"

"Who?"

"Sheriff Kerridge."

"No, not really. I remember him because I was a teenager at the time and teenage boys tend to harbor a healthy fear of law enforcement, but my memory is that everyone respected him. Loved him, even."

"That's what Susan McKinney said," I tell him. "Apparently they were pretty close."

We sit in silence for a while as he goes back to the file.

"There was a plumber here that day too," he says eventually. "The day Molly was taken. There's a note scanned in here from the FBI with the business card stapled to it obstructing the name on the paperwork."

I remember what Deena had said about talking to a plumber on her way out.

"Dwight Hoyle," I say. And I relay what Mandy had told me. That he'd been sent there to fix a pipe and that he had to give a statement about what he saw that day.

I put my hands to my face and recall what I'd seen only hours before. Dwight Hoyle's half-melted face. His wife screaming. The flames and black smoke engulfing me.

"Annie—"

I shake my head, my hands still mashed into my cheeks.

"I tried to talk to them. I went to their house the first day I was here. I'd hoped to get him to tell me anything he hadn't mentioned to the police, but now we don't even have his damn statement. God . . . I was *at their house.*"

"I know. I'm sorry—"

"It's not your fault. It's just this whole case is like one big knot. Normally, I don't mind taking my time to untangle things, but with Jessica still missing and Molly dead, I'm . . . I'm at a loss. I'm out of my depth, AJ."

I rub my eyes. They're gritty with lack of sleep, and I wince at the sensation of sand rolling over my eyeballs.

"Annie—" AJ says softly, squeezing my shoulder. "You're doing everything you can."

I let out a long breath, and some of the tension drops away.

His hand runs up to the back of my neck and I sigh as the side of his thumb caresses the base of my scalp. "You can't solve this case in one night."

I grumble.

"Not even with help from an expert sheriff's deputy like myself."

I grumble some more but I'm smiling now.

I turn toward him and lean into him like a cat, rest my head against his warm palm.

"Time for bed," AJ says.

"Would you like to come?" I ask him.

"Oh yes."

# TWENTY-SIX

THE NEXT MORNING, I'M already in the kitchen, drinking a glass of water, when Leo calls a little before dawn. I pick up the phone before it has much time to buzz.

"Hey, Leo," I say softly.

"What's with the whisper—you got someone over?" he asks, chuckling in that deep, velvety way he has. "You manage to find the one person in that hick town worth a good lay?"

I snort.

"I'm glad you have such a high opinion of my standards."

"Oh, I know you have high standards," he says. I hear a train station speaker in the background rattling off information in Japanese. "Listen, I'm about to have to go. Everything okay?"

"Yeah," I say. "You?"

"Always. I got that information for you. Who says Army intelligence is an oxymoron?"

"All right, spill." I get a pen and my notebook ready.

"There's no record of a Bob Ziegler matching your man, but there *is* a Brian Robert Ziegler the third."

"The third, huh?"

"Yeah, but don't be getting ideas about him having airs. He's a nobody.

That was part of his problem, actually. He hooked up with some chick he met at a hippie party back in '69. He was eighteen. She was fourteen. They were stoned. Bottom line, they got caught. And her daddy—some bigwig councilman—had him arrested. Ol' Bob got railroaded. The judge said he could go on to jail and serve down at the state pen or . . ."

"Or join up with Uncle Sam and wage war on Charlie?"

"Bingo."

"So he joined the Army to avoid a stat rape charge," I say, writing down what I can. "Then, while he was in there, he found Jesus or whatever and became a preacher?"

"Sounds like."

The light, bright female voice chimes out more information over the speakers. It's followed by a jazzy jingle and then I hear the *clicka-whoosh* of a train pulling into the station.

"That's me."

"Okay," I say. "Thanks."

"I'll be back stateside soon," he says.

"Okay."

"When you get done, I'll take you out for a drink."

"I think I'm gonna need one."

"Thought you might."

We hang up. I finish my water, stretch out, inspect the gauze on my shin.

"You run every morning?"

I look up and see AJ standing in the doorway, his eyes sleepy and a soft smile on his mouth. It's almost enough to make a woman want to go back to bed.

"Pretty much," I say. "When I'm away from home. It's more practical."

"More practical than what?"

"Hauling around a heavy bag. I live about two doors away from my aunt Tina's garage and she lets me keep my gym stuff there, including the bag I work."

"Boxing?"

"Muay Thai. I picked it up."

He scratches his bare chest as he yawns, looks at the clock above the stove. I tell him the news about Bob Ziegler's history and AJ lets out a whistle, shakes his head.

"Not what you want to find out about the shepherd of your faith."

"No," I say. "But it was a long time ago."

"You gonna talk to him about it?"

"Yeah, I'm going to go by first thing this morning."

"I'd better start getting ready for work," he says.

I'm still watching him scratch his chest when he smiles at me again and says, "Something on your mind?"

"Just thinking there are other ways to get a workout in besides running."

He chuckles, his big shoulders bouncing, says, "Don't even have to leave the house."

"That's right," I say. I kick off my shoes.

An hour later I'm in the shower and AJ's gone. I give my hair a quick blow-dry and then slide it up into a ponytail, still damp. I find a clean pair of jeans and look them over with vague distaste, mourning the pair I lost yesterday. I eat some of Shiloh's leftover pastries and some bacon that AJ left for me and drink two cups of coffee. Then I lace up my boots and head out the door.

I drive to First Baptist but only Rebecca is there. I interrupt as she and a flock of ladies who look like her fill grab bags for the coming festivities.

"Bob is visiting a parishioner of ours," she says, pulling me aside. "In the hospital."

"I'll come back later," I tell her. "I need to talk to him about something."

She nods and goes back to bag stuffing.

Back in the parking lot, I run Honey's heater and look through the files AJ brought on my phone. I find the report from the day of Molly's disappearance and, while the witness statements are missing, there is a record of Dwight Hoyle's being there, along with the name of his employer.

"Mack's Pipe and Plumbing . . ." I mutter. "Maybe Dwight told this guy something." And I find the address and put Honey in gear.

Mack's Pipe and Plumbing is housed in an old brick building on the backside of Main Street. When I go in, there's an old man sitting behind a desk doing a crossword puzzle in a book. He wears Coke bottle glasses and his black hair has gone mostly white and mostly away.

I tell him who I am, what I'm doing there. He tells me that he is, in fact, the eponymous Mack.

"Heard about you," he says.

"What'd you hear?"

"That you're looking into those missing little girls."

"That's right."

"And that you found Molly Andrews dead in a ditch after all these years."

"Not a ditch."

He shrugs.

"I'd like to ask you a few questions," I say.

"That's fine, but I've got to get to a call at ten."

I look at my phone.

"It's ten after ten."

He shrugs.

"You had a call at the Andrews house on the day Molly was kidnapped."

"Sort of."

"What do you mean, sort of?"

"Well, I had a call. But I couldn't go. There was a backup at the high school—you should've seen the turds. Anyway, no, I couldn't go. They were having a problem with the drain in an old outbuilding, I believe. I figured it probably just needed to be snaked."

"Pretty good memory," I say.

He taps a thick first finger to his temple. "It's like a vault, I tell you. Wanna know the secret?"

"Crosswords?"

"Damn," he says, and whistles through his teeth. "You really are a big-city PI, huh?"

"That's right. So you sent Dwight Hoyle," I say. "Is that correct?"

"Lord, they should put you on TV," Mack says, standing and putting things in his pockets, closing his toolbox. "Anyhow, that's right. The very same Dwight Hoyle died in that explosion yesterday. Jesus Christ, you know I could hear it from here? 'Course, I have a top-of-the-line aid." He taps the huge chunk of plastic in his ear. "Turns up and down, you know. Amazing. I ordered it online."

He leads me back to the front of the shop and out onto the sidewalk.

"He made a statement with the cops," I tell him. "But it seems no one can find it. Do you have any idea what he said? Did he ever talk to you about it?"

"Well, not much," he says. "He said something about a lady being there."

"A lady—you mean Deena Drake? The piano teacher, the woman who married the factory owner?"

He shakes his head. "I don't recall. But I don't think it was her. I thought it was someone else. Someone he saw out in the field. That's what he told me. Said it nearly scared him half to death."

"Why?"

"Said he thought she was a scarecrow at first," he says, his voice low.

"A scarecrow? Why?"

"Don't know. He was pretty shook up. The cops were on him, and he and Elaine were nervous as all get-out. They left town right after."

He rattles the handle of the shop door to make sure it's locked, then turns to face me.

"You want my opinion," he says. "It wasn't no ordinary human."

"What do you mean?"

"Like a haint, weren't they? How does one person even do what they did? Move like they were never there and leaving a doll behind? I think it was something supernatural, a spirit or a demon or . . ."

He stares at me, eyes pinched to slits.

"A witch," I say.

He winks, taps the side of his nose with a gnarled first finger.

"Now you're thinking right. Some kind of satanic ritual."

"Satanic ritual?"

"Three little girls go missing except one's brought back, probably 'cause she's touched in the head—you can't go making satanic offerings with damaged goods, can you? So anyway, two little girls go missing and then one's found—all of ten years later—down in that ditch."

"Not a ditch."

"Well, it's a ravine, ain't it? And what's a ravine but a big ditch carved out by water? Anyway, that stone circle down there's probably cursed. That's what the stories say."

"You mean about the witch and the crows?"

"That's right. She killed her very own daughters."

"What?"

"Yeah. The old witch. She killed her own daughters because they could sing prettier than her. She turned them into songbirds and then she ate them and took their voices and their youth."

"What?"

"You know, I could tell you where I got this hearing aid."

I narrow my eyes at him, and he laughs. It's a rolling cackle, wet and self-satisfied.

When he's done, I ask, "So what happened? This isn't the version of the story that I heard."

He gives me a look like he's about to take pity on me since I'm the village idiot and then graciously proceeds with the story.

"The witch had two daughters who were prettier than her and could sing better than her. She climbed up on this powerful big horse she had and rode to the stone circle and asked the Devil for power over them and every year he gave it to her. But, eventually, he turned his eyes on the daughters. Gave them power instead."

He looks down at the open palms of his hands, rough and ragged, and continues.

"Oh, powerful jealous she got. So jealous she couldn't hardly stand it. So, one night, she killed and ate them up and in so doing took all their gifts. Now she had their youth and their beauty and their singing voices. She married a woodcutter who was deep in love with her, but one night, when he raised the candle up to look at his beautiful wife, he saw her for what she was."

"Okay."

"Well, I guess she was pretty dang ugly. He came after her with an ax, but she turned herself into a crow and flew away. And he hunted her down. He hunted all the crows down until he found her in that stone circle. And that's where he killed her. And she turned back into an old witch and her blood soaked the stones and the Devil drank it up and that's why they make that echoing sound. That's the Devil laughing."

"Because . . . of blood?"

"Yeah," he says with a shrug. He opens the big box in the back of his pickup and stows his tool kit, then slams it shut. "Magic blood."

I watch him get in the truck and drive off and I stand there thinking about stories. The way mythology twists around on itself and throws out new branches every now and then. How the key ingredients are the same in both stories. *A witch. Two daughters.*

My phone rings, and I answer.

"Hey, AJ," I say.

"Hey, I wanted to let you know I opened up Dwight and Elaine Hoyle's house. An investigation hasn't officially been opened just yet, but I need to check the premises for risks of another explosion."

"Find anything?"

"Nothing nefarious. There's a bunch of soap-making stuff laying around. Aside from that, looks like they did most of their science experiments in the old factory," he says. "Also, no sign of Jessica or Molly. It was a long shot, but . . ."

"It's better to check," I say. "But nothing?"

"No. And this place is pretty small. Two bedrooms, one bath. There's a crawl space but no basement. No attic. Anyway, I've only been here about half an hour and I've got to head back out. There's a bunch of goats loose out on Cooper's Cross."

I can't help but laugh.

"I feel like when I watch those suspenseful TV cop shows, they usually omit the nail-biting goatherd scenes."

"The life of a public servant is a never-ending roller coaster. I did want to let you know one thing before I leave."

"What's that?"

"Like I said, I haven't been here long, but I did do a quick sweep. From what I understand, neither of them worked. Dwight took disability from a forklift operating injury about six years back and Elaine had the occasional side hustle—"

"Like soap and meth."

"Exactly. That's the thing. They drove a pretty new truck and they have a recent-model TV in here. A new laptop. Not brand-new but all within the last couple years or so. I found a bank statement. All their deposits were made in cash."

"Sounds like typical drug dealer behavior to me."

"The thing is, County Fire pulled both bodies out last night and they've been going through the wreckage today. Far as they can tell, neither of them were armed."

"Huh," I say.

"Yeah. Like I said, I've only been here about thirty minutes but, still. When's the last time you met a drug dealer who didn't pack heat?"

"Huh," I say again. "Maybe they were just getting started, didn't want to risk racking up more charges in case things went wrong."

"Maybe."

I let him rush off to the great goat escape and check my phone for the time. Right on cue, my belly grumbles. I start up Honey and we roll around to the other side of Main Street and park in front of Shiloh's Sweet Treats. I follow my nose inside.

I look past the small crowd to the door behind the counter. The girl in the apron gives me a nod of recognition and I walk into the back. Pushing my way into the kitchen, I find Shiloh in a cloud of sugar-scented air, stacks of cakes and lavender cake boxes on the counters and tables around her. She hugs me as a matter of course and then ushers me to her big stainless-steel counter and pours me a glass of milk. Before I can even thank her, she pushes a plate of pumpkin streusel in front of me.

"I—"

"Just eat," she says. "You look famished, Annie. You're pushing yourself too hard."

"Me? What about you?" I gesture toward the huge tower of cake boxes beside her.

She throws back her head and lets out a long, loud groan.

"They're all for the Fall Festival's cakewalk. My mom talked me into it. Heaven help me, I don't know why I agreed to it in the first place. Even under normal circumstances it would be tough to get all these done around our regular business, but with Molly being found and . . ."

She sighs.

"I heard Greg Andrews is back," she says. "Has he spoken to you?"

"Yeah. Max's dad is a real prize. He wants me to quit the investigation."

"Wow," she says. "He never wanted Max to hire a PI. He and Janice tried it once, when Max was little, and they didn't find a single thing. I think he feels like PIs are some kind of con. No offense."

"None taken."

"You're not going to quit, are you?" she asks.

"No," I say. "I'm going to do what I said I would."

"Then, eat. You've got to keep up your energy."

I sigh and dig in. And we stay that way for a few minutes, Shiloh bustling around the kitchen while I take long drinks of milk and eat progressively bigger bites of streusel. Eventually, I get around to the real reason for my visit. I want to hear the witch story, from her this time.

"The witch story?" Shiloh asks from behind several boxes of cakes.

"Yeah," I say. "The Witch of Quartz Creek, right? The one with the daughters?"

"Yeah," she says, writing "White Chocolate Raspberry" on a label and sticking it on the outside of a box. "Only, the way I heard it, they weren't *her* daughters."

I'm too busy letting the pumpkin and cinnamon tastes roll around on my tongue to make real words so I say, "Hmmm?"

"No," Shiloh says. She opens another box and writes "German Chocolate" on the label, sticks it to the thin pink cardboard. "No. You know my family settled here eight generations ago?"

"Mmm?"

"Of course, a lot of other families did too. Anyway, my mamaw told me the story when I was little. She was sort of our family historian. She knew all the old legends from this region. She said that one winter, long ago, it was colder than it had ever been, and snow turned to ice and froze everything. Everything. People couldn't keep fires lit—that's how cold it was. And their food stores ran dry because the winter lasted so long."

She opens another box and looks inside, then closes it and writes "Tiramisu" on the label.

"But, amidst all of this cold, there was a witch who lived in the woods up above Quartz Creek. She had an apple orchard full of bright green apples that never took a chill and grew all winter long."

Picturing the apples, bright green, in a landscape of ice and snow, I can't help but shiver. I take another fortifying bite of streusel.

"One day a young mother took her six starving children up the high climb to the witch's home. She told the witch that they were starving. That she would do anything to keep them fed."

She opens another box and inside I see a round white cake topped with beautifully delicate buttercream roses. Shiloh smiles down at the cake and then closes the box and writes on the label: "Rosewater Vanilla."

"The mother pleaded with the witch," she says, sticking the label on the outside of the box. "And the witch said that if the mother gave her her two oldest daughters, she and the rest of her children could take all the apples they could carry and that the apples would not wither or rot but would stay bright and fresh until eaten. And the girls would be fed and educated and taught to sing and dance like fairy princesses."

"She couldn't refuse," I say.

Shiloh shakes her head, her eyes downcast and full of emotion.

"It never hit me," she said. "How awful the story was. I guess it's different when you're a mom, what you'd do for your kids." She lets out a long breath, her hands flat on the countertop. She blinks, shakes her head.

"Anyway," she says, clearing her throat. "The girls grew into beautiful young women, with the most delicate singing voices in all the mountains. But the witch became jealous of their voices, the attention they received, their radiance."

She opens another box then closes it, writes, "Sugar Free Chocolate."

"So she turned them into birds—a robin and a bluebird—and put them into a silver cage. And their songs made her joyous. Until they made her bitter." Shiloh sticks the label on and then surveys the next cake. "She killed the birds and ate their hearts and took the beauty and youth and songs of her daughters. She married a young huntsman who was taken with her stolen gifts, but, eventually, he discovered her true identity. He tried to kill her, but she turned herself into a crow."

"Did he ever find her?"

Shiloh shakes her head.

"No," she says. "She flew into the forest, where every night she tried to sing the very songs she had taught her daughters, only to hear the sound of her ugly crow voice forever and evermore."

"Wow."

"Yeah, I know."

We both look into the next cake box. A mouthwatering orange buttercream rose sits in the middle of a field of white icing and caramel drizzle.

"You haven't seen Max, have you?" she asks.

"Not since he asked me to find Molly's killer," I tell her.

She nods, then sighs and says, "I'll check in with him tomorrow. After all this festival stuff is done."

She looks over the boxes, all labeled, and crosses her arms on her chest.

"This is all for First Baptist's festival?" I ask.

"Yeah. The festival raises money for the church's food bank, which, whatever I might think of First Baptist's politics, I can't argue about feeding hungry people. Now, I just need to load them into the van."

"You want a hand?"

"You sure you're finished with all your important PI stuff?"

"Who says I'm done asking questions?"

I help her move the cakes onto a rolling rack and then, as we're wheeling it out to the van, I ask, "You said you went to First Baptist when you were a kid, right? What was your impression of Rebecca Ziegler?"

"Hmm . . . She always just . . . seemed like someone's strict grandma. The sort of woman who handed out little stockings at Christmas with toothbrushes and mini New Testaments inside."

"Was she a grandma? Did she have grandkids?"

"Huh," Shiloh says, loading the cakes into the van. "You know what? No, I don't think so. I don't think her and Brother Bob ever had kids." She puts the last cake in and then shuts the door and looks at me with her head tilted, her hands on her hips. "Do you think they had something to do with the kidnappings?"

I take a deep breath, the story about the witch and the birds still spinning in my mind. "This whole thing feels very ritualistic," I say, and realize I'm echoing an old coot who intentionally makes people wait for his plumbing services. Maybe I'm grasping at straws, but I don't think so. All he'd done was give voice to a feeling I'd already had and been afraid to say.

"The dolls, the velvet dress, the stone circle, the crows . . ."

"Which is why you're asking about the witch," Shiloh says.

"Yeah."

"And you're wondering who, among the old women of Quartz Creek, might be a witch."

"Do I sound crazy?"

She laughs.

"No," she says. "You're just starting to sound like someone from around here. When I was a kid, it was practically common knowledge that the Witch of Quartz Creek took those girls. I remember it made Max's dad furious."

"Why?"

"Because I guess . . . in his mind, you'll never find the truth if you go around trying to catch someone who doesn't exist."

I open my mouth and then close it, but an uneasy feeling flutters around my heart.

*Are you so sure the witch doesn't exist?*

She climbs into the van, starts it up, and opens the window. "You coming to this shindig tonight?"

"Yeah," I say. "I want to talk to Bob and Rebecca. I'll be around."

"Okay," she says. "See you there."

I watch as she pulls out and drives away, and I think about the mother who traded her little girls for all the apples she could carry.

# TWENTY-SEVEN

THE PARKING LOT OF First Baptist is so full, I have to circle twice before I find a spot. The doors to the church are open and a few adults linger there, talking. But the festival proper is going full swing in the big side yard. The field is interspersed with tall, old oaks, and between them children run from booth to booth in costume.

"Wow," I say as a kid scoots past me in a squishy-muscled Batman suit. Far across the crowd, I spot Brother Bob standing beside the grab bag table talking to a group of older adults all wrapped up in sweaters and nice coats like this is just another church service.

"Hey!" Shiloh shouts, waving me over from the cakewalk booth. Reluctantly, I push my way through a throng of families and kids with buckets and pillowcases full of candy and make my way to her booth.

"Hey," I say. "I didn't realize you were actually working this thing too. I thought you were just baking cakes."

She rolls her eyes, hands on her hips, "Yeah, I know. But Betsy Hopewell's kid got into the candy early. She's been hurling Reese's cups into the bushes for the last half hour so my mom took over Betsy's booth. I wouldn't trade her. It's a DIY candied apple booth. God, so many apples are going to be stuck in so much hair tomorrow."

I laugh, and she hands me a cupcake and I feel like this is her superpower—handing people delicious baked goods that seem to appear from nowhere. I eat the magic cupcake and ask, around a mouthful of rich chocolate cake and caramel buttercream, "You haven't seen Rebecca, have you?"

Shiloh squints out at the crowd and says, "Well, I thought she was here but . . . gosh, I don't see her."

"Oh well," I say. "It's Bob I really need to talk to anyway."

I turn and push through the crowd to the grab bag table and approach Bob.

"Good evening," Bob says, breaking away from his parishioners to face me.

A kid approaches with his mom and they both take a grab bag from a nearby table, wave at Bob, and walk away.

"Where's Mrs. Ziegler tonight?" I ask, seeing the empty chair behind the table and assuming that it should belong to her.

He glances around, searching, and then an answer seems to dawn on him.

"Oh, that's right," he says. "We needed an extension cord for one of the heaters. We thought it was here, but I think she ran home to get it. She'll be back soon."

"I'd like to ask you a couple of questions in the meantime."

"All right."

"You visited the Andrews house on the morning of Molly's disappearance."

"I suppose so."

"Do you remember why?"

"Rebecca and I both went, I believe. But the matter was private."

"Private? It's been ten years."

"Miss Gore, counseling sessions are always private."

"Counseling? Were the Andrewses having trouble?"

He looks down, and I follow his gaze. He's wearing knit gloves and rubbing his hands together. When he catches me looking, he says, "Arthritis. I'm afraid I'm not as immune to the cold as I once was. What were you asking?"

"The Andrews—" I start. But my phone starts buzzing in my pocket. I check it and see AJ's number.

"Hey, what's up?"

"I just got off duty. Wanted to see if you'd like me to come by tonight?"

"You're all done with the goats?"

"We can only hope. Sheriff took off early tonight and I decided to stick around the station to see if I can find any more of the old files. My God, you'd think this entire place burned down after Sheriff Kerridge died. The whole system from that time is a wreck. Between that and the stuff that was cross-filed with the FBI, I'm still not sure I've got everything. But I'm happy to bring by whatever I can. Have you eaten? There's a place in town that does some great fried catfish."

"You really know the way to my heart. How about—"

I'm interrupted by the sound of shouting.

Shiloh, I realize. *It's Shiloh's voice.*

"Gotta go."

I turn and, amid the crowd of festivalgoers, I see her shouting at someone.

There is a heavy, sick feeling in the bottom of my gut, and I feel myself being pulled to the sound of Shiloh's voice. I push through the throng of princesses and superheroes and cowboys and ponies and the sugar-scented air and the vibrating murmur of questioning while Shiloh's voice booms out above the rest.

"Lucy!" she shouts. She draws the word out so it's long and it carries and only barely wavers at the end.

"Shiloh, what's going on?"

She's standing beside two people who can only be her parents. The woman on her left is slightly shorter than Shiloh with the same good looks. The dad is a beanpole with salt-and-pepper hair and his hands shoved into the pockets of his thick barn coat.

"Lucy," she breathes. "Lucy is gone. We can't find her. She was with my mom."

I look to the woman beside her.

"What happened?"

Big, thick tears roll down Shiloh's mother's cheeks as she blubbers something about turning away for a minute and then Lucy being gone.

"Keep looking," I tell Shiloh. Shiloh takes her dad and they grab other members from the church, who begin to spread out and search.

"Lucy," they shout. "Lucy!"

The name rings out like disparate, off-tempo bells as word spreads that a little girl is missing.

"Where?" I say to Shiloh's mom. "Where? Show me the booth."

The woman leads me to her booth. Close to the church and situated right under a huge oak, her table is littered with apples and a vintage fondue pot full of melted caramel. There are a couple bowls of nuts and chocolate sprinkles and marshmallows and a big tray of apples, already driven through with sticks. On the back of her plastic folding chair is her coat, and behind that a little blanket strewn with toys.

"This is where she was?"

Shiloh's mom nods and I watch as she pulls herself together enough to talk to me.

"She was *right there*," she says. "I told her that as soon as her pepaw came back from running the hayride he'd take her around the festival. She said okay. She was playing with her toys. I gave her some marshmallows and then I got up to talk to my friend Lisa. I only stepped away for a *minute*. She was *right there*."

"Okay," I say. I kneel down before the blanket and stare at the scene. There's a plush little dog and a couple of storybooks and a heavily rubberized tablet with a game still playing. There's a doll, too, lying face down.

It's an old doll.

The doll's delicate arms and legs hang out from its fancy lavender dress, trimmed with ruffles and lace. I reach for the doll, then hesitate, suddenly very aware that this is likely a crime scene. Still, I have to know. We all have to know. And it has to be now. I pull a pen out of my pocket and use the base of it to gently turn the doll onto its back.

Its head is an applehead. The shriveled flesh is wrinkled and grainy, and the hair fastened to the top of it with glue and pins is exactly the same hue and texture as that of Molly Andrews.

"Oh . . ." I breathe. "Oh no."

# TWENTY-EIGHT

I T GOES LIKE YOU'D expect.

The festival breaks into groups looking for Lucy. The cops arrive. AJ comes in uniform. Sheriff Jacobs is a few minutes behind him, looking freshly showered and dressed for a steak dinner. A deputy with the camera equipment comes. A deputy with a dog comes.

Soon, some of Shiloh's dad's friends with hunting dogs come. The dogs all follow the same trail behind the church and around the little playground on the other side and into the still mostly full parking lot. And then there's nothing. The deputies take statements. Rebecca Ziegler returns with an extension cord, and then she and Bob lead the cops around the property once again, calling Lucy's name.

Max comes. He gives Shiloh his heavy barn coat and stands beside her, pale and gray and cold as a stone. She wraps her arms around him. I don't know whether she's comforting Max or herself. He begins to shake, and I realize he's crying.

"It'll be okay," I hear her whisper, like a mother to her child. "We'll find her. We'll find her. We'll find her."

A mantra. A litany. A prayer.

We all look.

We look in the field and we look in the trees behind the field. We look in the playground and we look in the church and the church basement and all of the Sunday school rooms and all of the cars. We look under the booths and in the apple bobbing tub and up and down Laurel Road and then, again, in all the same places we looked before.

We don't find her.

We all call Lucy's name into the night and the air grows cold and it hurts our lungs and still we call her name and, eventually, the stars fade and the night goes from black to gray to a velvety violet and a fog lies on the land.

There is no answer.

I put a cup of coffee in Shiloh's hand.

We sit on the steps in front of First Baptist. The sun is rising, hidden behind a wool gray mist. Max is out with Shiloh's dad's friends, the deputies, the dogs.

There is a blanket around Shiloh's shoulders. I don't know where it came from. I don't know how long she's been sitting here.

In the field beside us, men and women from the church clear away the booths, the candy, the toys, the cakes.

The coffee grows cold in Shiloh's hands.

Shiloh's parents approach and look at us. Shiloh's dad's hands are still shoved deep in his coat pockets and Shiloh's mom holds her purse tight to her body.

"Come on, Shiloh," her dad says. "It's up to the police now."

She blinks, slowly, and swallows whatever thoughts her dad's words have conjured.

She stands and turns back toward me and her voice is hoarse from screaming her daughter's name as she grips my shoulder tight and says, "Find her, Annie."

# TWENTY-NINE

I LOOK AT THE PHOTO of the doll on my phone. I'd snapped it before the sheriff's department showed up, and now I'm zoomed in on the doll's shriveled apple face while I sit at the counter in the cabin's kitchen after about three hours of restless sleep. It's Friday morning, the fifth morning of this investigation, and all I can feel is a dismal unease. I pour another cup of coffee, try like hell to think of anything I could've missed, anything I can do. Eventually I just go back to staring at the doll face.

I swipe the photo around, looking at a close-up of the hair. It was gathered together in little bunches and then joined with a rubber band, which was then glued to the apple, and, the glue failing, the clumps of hair were stuck in with straight pins.

I call AJ.

"How's Shiloh?" I ask.

"Not great," he says. "We've got a deputy with her back at the bakery. She didn't want to stay at home."

"What else have you got?"

"We took more dogs out this morning. Nothing. We're sending the doll down to Raleigh for analysis."

"Make sure they test her hair," I say.

"Her hair?"

"It looks just like Molly's."

"You think maybe it *is* Molly's?" AJ asks.

"Maybe."

I look at the doll's dress. It's not the same as the others. It's not the same kind of simple, home-sewn garb made with velvet scraps and bits of cast-off lace. This is a store-bought doll dress, all cheap shiny fabric and scratchy lace.

"This body . . ." I say. "This is a Lovely Lady Lavender doll."

"Jesus," AJ breathes. "My sisters had those. Everyone had them. They were made—"

"Yeah," I say. "I know. They were made here in town."

In the very factory I'd barely escaped two days before.

"Find anything else at the scene?" I ask.

"No," he says. "Just like the others. It's like they vanished into thin air."

"Except for the dolls."

"Sheriff Jacobs has been on the phone with the FBI all morning. He's trying to get a team down here."

"It's about time," I say.

"I think he's realized that what happened ten years ago isn't really over," AJ says.

"Yes," I say. "I don't think it ever was."

There's a knock at the door and, hand on my gun, I yell for whoever it is to come in.

It's Greg Andrews, Max's dad. He's looking the absolute opposite of combative, holding a sealed bottle of whiskey, his mouth pulled into an aggrieved frown.

I tell AJ I'll talk to him later and we hang up.

I hold the door open for Greg and he walks across the room and sets the bottle of whiskey on the counter.

"What's this?" I ask.

"An apology," he says.

I look at him and his bottle and his red, haggard eyes.

"I accept."

I pull two short tumblers from the cabinet and fill them halfway with the amber liquid. We both drink.

"I take it you want me back on the case?"

"Were you ever off the case?"

I shake my head.

"This is going to kill my son," Greg says.

I nod.

"I think he's worried that his friendship with Shiloh got Lucy kidnapped."

"It's more likely that my meddling did it," I say. But, in truth, I'd already considered whether someone was targeting Max. Taking his surrogate little sister the same way they took Molly. But who would do such a thing? It's not like the introverted, artistic eighteen-year-old had spent his whole life going around making enemies.

I take another sip of the whiskey. It's not great but it's good. It burns appropriately for eleven o'clock in the morning the day after one was present at a little girl's kidnapping.

I put my glass down and look back up at him and ask, "So why do you want me looking into it now? What's changed?"

"Like I said the other day, the cops couldn't do it ten years ago. I don't trust them to do it now. I just . . . I thought it was over. But it's not. And this isn't right. It's not right. I like Shiloh. She's a good kid. She doesn't—no one does—no one deserves to go through what Janice and I did."

"Fair enough."

"I can pay you," he says.

"I'm already being paid."

"Okay."

I tilt my glass and watch the liquid slide. I tilt it the other way.

"Were you and Max's mother having marriage problems before Molly was kidnapped?" I ask.

The question takes him for a wild ride. His eyes widen and then darken, and his cheeks go red like he might be about to shout, but in the end he just slumps down where he sits.

"Yes," he says. "Did Max say something?"

"No. If Max remembers it or ever knew it at all, he's never mentioned it. Were you getting counseling from Bob and Rebecca Ziegler?"

He half sighs, half groans.

"Of a sort."

"What's that mean?"

"It means I sort of didn't want to do it."

I look at him. He looks at his drink.

He says, "Janice wanted more kids."

"Okay."

"I didn't. She grew up with four brothers and two sisters."

"Big family. Where are they all now?"

"Brothers all joined the military, moved away. One sister stayed here. She used to look in on Max. But she died—cancer—a couple years ago. The other one went with her husband—Navy guy. They're in San Diego now."

"Janice wasn't satisfied with two kids."

He shakes his head.

"And you were?"

"I didn't think we could afford any more kids. Didn't think it was a good idea."

"So, she wanted counseling."

"Yes."

"From two people who didn't have any children."

He shrugs and drains the rest of his drink and then says, "Yeah. She said the flock were the Zieglers' children. The congregation. It sounded like a line straight from Bob."

"You were never very religious, though, were you?"

Headshake.

"And it—the argument about kids—did it get worse after Molly was taken?"

Nod.

"Mister Andrews, who did you think took your daughter, back then?"

He looks at the bottle like he's thinking about pouring himself another drink but then rests both his hands on the wooden countertop instead.

"Someone from the church," he says. "I was sure of it."

"Why?"

"It all went back there, didn't it? The little Hoyle girl was taken from there. The Jacobs girl was taken from a church picnic."

"But Molly wasn't."

"No," he says. "No, but the Zieglers were here that day. They were in our home. Bob and Rebecca sat right there at our kitchen table and told us all about prayer and listening to God's voice and whatever, and a couple hours later my little girl was gone."

"Dwight Hoyle was also in your home."

"Yes," he said. "Apparently, he was. But—"

His brows draw together in agitation, and he looks down into his glass.

"What?"

"I went to school with Dwight. He smoked pot and I always had the idea that he sold it, but a lot of kids did. He could be enterprising, but he wasn't a criminal mastermind or anything."

"Enterprising?"

"Senior year, he started this racket where he broke into teachers' desks after hours. He was working part-time on the janitorial staff, you know? So, it was easy. Anyway, he would take our test or quiz answers, copy them, put them right back where he got them, and then sell them. Never classes he was in, though, so I don't think he ever got caught."

"How'd you know about it?"

Greg winces, and then a pained smile crosses his face.

"How do you think I passed my AP Geometry midterm that year?"

"So, you never suspected that Dwight took the girls? Even though he was here the day Molly was taken?"

"But he and Deena saw each other, didn't they?" he asks.

"Yeah," I say. "I haven't seen their statements but, from what I hear, they saw each other leave."

"I remember a pipe was leaking out in the barn," he says, his gaze distant. "I called Mack's after Bob and Rebecca left and before I had to go to school for some teacher training on a new STEM initiative. I asked if he could get someone out to the house. I remember Janice saying that she would take all the extra water in buckets and pour it on the garden. It was a hot summer. We couldn't afford to waste the water. I remember saying that sounded like a good idea but not really thinking about it. Not really thinking about her or Max. Or Molly. I couldn't find my keys. I was distracted. I was in such a hurry to leave that morning . . ."

I watch him, waiting as he gets lost in the memory of the day Molly was taken and then blindly gropes his way back to the present.

"I had no idea," he says. "How can anyone . . ."

He shakes his head, and we sit in the quiet for a little while before he says, "How do you do this? How do you get involved in stuff like this? It all feels so . . . nebulous. Like fog."

"I don't know," I admit. "I'm just following every lead I have. Most of what PIs do is go around gathering information until they get ahold of something with substance. Then they follow that thing until it either turns up results or doesn't. If it doesn't, we go back to gathering."

He nods understanding.

"That year—you hear people in town talk about that year like it was cursed," he says. "The hottest year we'd had for decades. And the factory closed. The whole town went out of work. That spring, I remember seeing the look on these kids' faces. Kids who always just assumed they'd go work at the same factory their moms and dads worked at."

"And that was no longer possible. What did they do instead?" I ask. But I already know the answer.

"Army, mostly. Recruiters swooped in. It was a poverty draft."

I feel myself smile. It's the same draft that got me. The same one that got so many other kids in Appalachia. The only path to education through a war zone.

"And then you left as well."

"I didn't leave," he says, defensive.

"You took a long-haul trucking job."

"I thought losing my daughter was the worst thing that could happen to me. I . . . Yes, I ran away. I just couldn't stay in that house. I'm not proud of it. I didn't know what else to do. I just couldn't stay in that house. Janice had the church."

"But not you."

"No. I just . . . I never liked the Zieglers. I never trusted them."

"And you brought this up at the time?"

"Yeah."

"To Sheriff Jacobs?"

"Yeah."

"Did he check them out?"

"Sure, but, you know, he was still new to the job. I never felt like he was up for it . . . not like that. Not the way the job was handed to him in the middle of his own niece's disappearance. I always thought the church . . . the Zieglers . . . I just never got a good feeling from them. Jacobs told me he investigated but . . ."

"Well," I say. "I think I'll do some extra investigating. Just to be sure."

# THIRTY

I TIME MY NEXT VISIT to First Baptist for when the Friday afternoon prayer meeting should be letting out, and I'm not disappointed when I pull up and see several older men shaking hands with Bob Ziegler before heading down the steps. They all look somber and sad, and I recognize a couple of them as some of Shiloh's dad's friends who brought their tracking dogs last night.

They nod to me as I approach the church. I nod back.

"Any news?" one says. I tell him no.

"Afternoon," I say to Bob Ziegler. He's changed his suit since last night. "I've got some questions for you."

"Miss Gore—" he starts.

"About your time in the Army," I say, and I watch as most of the color drains out of Bob's face and disappears behind the collar of his crisp navy blue shirt.

He recovers fast, offers the men around him a polite goodbye, and waves me into the church, across the foyer, and into the same office with the big desk Rebecca had taken me to. He shuts the heavy door behind us.

He walks behind the desk, but he doesn't sit. He also doesn't invite me to sit.

Instead, we stand on opposite sides of the desk from each other and, as is in both our natures after years of practice, we fall in, spines straight, shoulders squared, hands at our sides.

The look in his eyes is intense and defiant but not squirrelly, not angry.

I cut to the chase.

"You were in the Army before you were a pastor."

"Yes."

"You were in the Army because you were given a choice between the military and jail."

He grinds his teeth by way of answer, so I keep going.

"You committed statutory rape and were told that you could go to jail or join the Army. Is that right?"

He grinds his teeth some more. I wait.

Behind him, on a bookshelf, is an array of framed photographs. Bob and Rebecca in front of the church. Bob and Rebecca at a fundraiser twenty or thirty years before. Bob and a man I vaguely recognize as Harvey Drake standing in front of a cabin made with huge, waxy-looking timbers, the sunshine illuminating Bob's white hair and Harvey's straight white teeth. Rebecca at a Christmas parade with Bob dressed as Santa. Rebecca receiving an award of some kind from a man in a suit.

Bob looks at me looking at the pictures. Then he looks toward the window. Then the ceiling. Then back to me.

Finally, out of things to stare at, he says, "That's right. That's what happened but—look, I had no idea about the girl. I was at a party. It was a big party, and my friend took me. I didn't know anyone. There were a lot of drugs, a lot of drinking. I had sex with a girl I didn't know."

"She was fourteen."

"I didn't know."

"And after?"

"After?"

"Have you ever had sex with another underage girl?"

"Certainly not."

I shrug.

"Maybe you didn't know."

His eyes narrow, and the color comes back.

"I did my time. Maybe not behind bars but I did my time. I made a mistake and I did my time, you understand? And when I got out, I went to seminary and I met Rebecca and—"

"Where did you meet?"

"She was the daughter of one of my teachers at seminary."

"Hmm."

He ignores that, keeps going, "I met her and I married her and I finished school."

"And you moved here."

"Yes. I preached at a small church in Georgia for a few months and then this position became vacant and it was closer to where Rebecca grew up—"

"Which was where?"

"Just over in Hardstone County, few miles down the road."

"So you met Rebecca and you got married and you moved here and started preaching for First Baptist."

"Yes."

"And you never had kids . . ."

He looks away. His big shoulders slump.

"It's odd," I say, pressing it.

"It's not your business. That's between a husband and a wife. You wanted to know about my time in the Army, the mistake I made to put me there, you got it. If I can help you find that missing little girl, then I will. But my history and mine and Rebecca's private life have nothing—and I mean nothing—to do with it."

"Okay," I say. "Where were you last night?"

"Here. I was here, you saw me."

"And Rebecca? She went to get an extension cord, is that right?"

"Yes."

"That's all? Nothing else?"

He nods.

I'd timed my drive from Max's to First Baptist on the way here. I knew it didn't take more than fifteen minutes, but I wasn't sure how long Rebecca had been gone or exactly how much farther Bob and Rebecca's house was.

"She helped search," Bob says. "When she got back. We both did. We searched all night. You saw us."

"Did you notice anyone strange in the crowd? Anyone who shouldn't have been there?"

His eyes search the cottage-cheese ceiling for answers and then he finally shrugs.

"No. Like I already told Sheriff Jacobs. I don't know. It's a public function. The whole purpose of the festival is to get the community to visit the church. There were scores of people I didn't know. You were there."

"Can I see your hands?" I ask.

"My—"

"Your hands. May I look at them?"

He grits his teeth and blows a huff of air out through his nose like a bull. But he does finally put his hands out over the desk.

"What's this about?" he asks as I inspect his thick fingers and the tops of his hands, his white-haired wrists.

The skin is unmarked. Clean. His nails are clipped short, the edges neat. There are no scrapes or scratches.

"Nothing," I say.

I get up to leave, turn toward the door, then turn back and ask, "Does Rebecca know about your mistake with the fourteen-year-old?"

"Of course," he says.

"Okay," I say.

I go back through the church and out to Honey and start her up. As I pull out, I see a news van from Asheville roll by. It won't be the last. Lucy's disappearance has resurrected a tantalizing story, and I know that before long national news teams will be flowing into town. It's the job of the press to report the news, but it irks me that the rest of the world only ever sees towns like Quartz Creek when they're at their worst.

I drive back toward Max's farm but turn off early onto Lilac Overlook Lane, thinking about Deena Drake. Of everyone I've spoken to, she's the one who knows the Zieglers the best. The one who would know if there were any leads I might be able to follow.

Honey putters and sputters on the climb so I take it slow, and I have plenty of time to keep an eye on the forest around me, on the near silence of the fog-laden trees, almost bare, and the carpet of scarlet and gold and plain, almost colorless brown. It's early afternoon and not nearly time for the sun to be setting, and yet the dull dimness—not darkness but absence of sunshine—is almost palpable. No shafts of light seem to cut through the cloud cover today. No beams of illumination scatter the fog before me.

I take a huge inhalation of air as I break through the trees into the cleared mountaintop, unaware I'd been breathing so shallowly. The oppressive dimness is gone, replaced by a plain, flat autumn sun. There is no Range Rover in the drive.

I pull up, park, and get out. The property is quiet. A breeze rustles the trees and red leaves swirl around my feet. The scent of roses and mountain laurels fills my nose.

"Where is she?" I ask myself, and walk up the steps and onto the porch. I knock on the door and it swings open.

"Mrs. Drake?" I shout into the house. The large, open living room is empty, and the only sound I hear is the ticking of what must be a huge grandfather clock.

I look back at Honey, sitting alone in the driveway. I think about what I told Greg Andrews only an hour ago. How all I can do is follow every possible lead until I run out or someone makes me stop. How it has occurred to me, more than once, that Deena Drake was at every crime scene and lives alone on this mountaintop. How if I don't take an opportunity to unravel a knot when it's presented to me, then why am I even here, what good am I.

"Mrs. Drake? Are you in?" I shout once more.

I look around the porch again for cameras.

"Nothing," I say to myself. I poke my head into the living room and see expensive furniture and rugs, but, again, no cameras and no sign of Deena Drake.

"Who leaves their front door unlocked these days?" I mutter. "Anyone could just walk right in . . ."

And then I push the door fully open and walk over the threshold.

# THIRTY-ONE

FROM THE OUTSIDE THIS house had looked huge, and yet, once I'm standing in the great room, I realize that this is a partial illusion created by its position on a mountaintop and the two-story bank of windows on its front. The windows had reflected the sunlight, the mountain atmosphere, the rolling horizon. They had made the house seem immense but, inside, I realize the great room alone probably takes up a third of the home's square footage.

Standing still, I feel eyes upon me and look around to find a variety of exotic animal heads mounted on the wall. Elk, ibex, some kind of toothy cat I don't know the name of. Their glass eyes are polished to a high shine, and they watch me as I take another step into the room.

One more time, just in case, I shout, "Deena! Mrs. Drake, are you here?"

No answer. I commence to snooping.

I breathe in the scent of the house, like dewy flowers and woodsmoke, and walk past the vintage sofa and chairs, the glossy grand piano that sits on a mini stage nearest the bank of windows. I walk into the kitchen, where all the appliances are top-of-the-line. They don't look new, but they look like they were bought to last a lifetime. There's a plate of cookies on the counter, a jar of honey alongside antique cream and sugar containers, a bowl of fruit, half full.

Off the kitchen is a little office space with a computer and printer and old-fashioned ledger on top of an old cherry desk. I tap the computer's space bar and the monitor comes on, prompting me to put in a password. I leave it, nudge open the ledger. Deena has been using it as a household accounting book, and I take a brief look through it to find bills for groceries, utilities, insurance. Every month, there is a cash withdrawal. Always one thousand dollars, always at the start of the month. Deena's spending budget, I'd guess. And it probably goes back to Harvey Drake's handing her a grand of pin money every month and, even before that, to her likely sizable allowance as a Savannah debutante.

There's an old filing cabinet, but forensic sleuthing takes weeks or months of combing through numbers; it's not the kind of thing one can accomplish with a quick rummage around. I leave the office and continue down the hall, where I find a guest room, made up and smelling a little stale. It looks clean but completely unused.

I pop into the bathroom, but there is nothing more exciting in it than the fact that Deena refills her fancy glass hand soap dispenser with a store brand. The floor, mirror, and even toilet shine. I try to picture Deena in here on her hands and knees with a scrub brush and decide she obviously has a maid.

Across the hall is a small library with a huge old grandfather clock and wall-to-wall bookshelves, another desk, and two armchairs. Scanning the spines, I find mostly hard copies of war histories and Walt Whitman, along with a few books on business theory and some gardening books with titles like *Growing Champion Roses* and *Practical Hedge Paths*, which looks very well worn, and a newer paperback of *Wildflowers of Appalachia: A Botanical Guide*. There are several classic novels with the spines more or less intact. I notice that *Bleak House* seems pristine while *Wuthering Heights* looks to have been well-thumbed.

I could spend hours in here, I realize. But, as with the filing cabinet and the ledger, it would take more time than I have to go through them all. I pull myself from the library and pad back down the hallway toward the great room where I peek outside for any sign of Deena Drake—still nothing—and then head upstairs.

Because half of this floor is open to the great room, there's less square footage to cover. The walls here feature yet more dead animals and a few decommissioned, antique rifles, mounted on glossy plaques. One of them, a vintage Remington, would make even Leo drool. There's a bedroom that has been converted into storage, with a few trunks lining the wall and old clothing packed into the closet. Another guest bedroom that looks completely unused. Another bathroom, this one with an impeccable little shower stall. And then, finally, at the end of the hall, the primary bedroom.

"Wow," I breathe, taking in the room.

The walls are all Tudor-style with white wattle-and-daub panels between what looks like old-growth beams. A ceiling fan hangs down from the high ceiling, but the room is illuminated with skylights. A gigantic four-poster bed dressed in actual linen linens rests against the far wall between two medieval-style tapestries depicting deer hunts. The bed looks like it could fit about six people, and I imagine the petite, slender Deena Drake curled up in it, alone. The idea makes me slightly sad, and I move away from the bed toward what I assume is the closet door.

Inside is a carpeted walk-in closet that, by itself, is probably half the size of my whole apartment. With the help of a skylight, I find a dressing table with a small jewelry box—containing a few vintage rings and one modern locket, all tasteful—and a wall of Deena's dresses. The other wall is, I'm surprised to find, all men's suits and shoes. About half are in old-looking dry-cleaning bags but many hang free. I open the lapel of one of them and find the words "Made Especially for Harvey Drake" and then the logo of a fancy tailor I've never heard of.

"Geez," I whisper. It's hard to imagine the prim and fastidious Deena Drake as a pack rat, and so I can only assume she's kept all of this out of sentimentality, grief. I feel just a little bit bad being in this room. This house. Uninvited. Unwelcome.

I think, as I walk into the bathroom and over to the window that overlooks the mountainside, that I'm likely just wasting my time. I admit to myself, standing there among her private things, that if Deena had taken those girls she would have left with them, years ago. She had the means to leave, to start over. Yes, she was at the church and the picnic and even Molly's house. Yes, she was connected to the church. But now that I've gone through nearly all of her house, I have to admit to myself that there's nothing here but evidence of a sad, lonely widow. That my prejudices about pampered women with money might have clouded my judgment.

"You gotta watch that blind spot, Annie."

That's what Leo told me. It was the first case I worked for him in the OSI. We'd been looking into possible skimming from certain Air Force accounts. I'd ignored evidence pointing to an airwoman I'd sympathized with—a single mom from a poor background—and spent hours digging up dirt on a bad-tempered officer from a wealthy family who turned out to be completely innocent. Leo pulled me into his office after the airwoman shot her friend and fellow airman when the guy found and confronted her about the same evidence I'd ignored. The airman was in the hospital in critical condition and Leo had spent the whole morning dealing with the fallout.

"I don't have a blind spot," I said defensively.

He shook his head and sighed.

"It's about a mile wide," he said, then crossed his arms over his chest and looked at me long and hard and said, "And one of these days, if you're not careful, something's gonna crawl out of it and bite you in the ass."

Now, as I stand in Deena's quiet bedroom, I feel the same flush of embarrassment I felt that day in Leo's office when I'd willfully overlooked evidence and spent valuable time investigating the wrong person and nearly got a man killed.

I let out a long breath and look out the window, thinking. I see the valley and the town, several farms, and even Max's farmhouse. Little cabins dot the hillsides and hide among the trees. Larger houses are tucked back from wider lanes. And leading to me is Lilac Overlook Lane, which empties out into Deena's driveway.

I watch the trees waver in the breeze, the rustle of the mountain laurels, and Honey sitting quietly in the driveway, and it occurs to me, like a gentle tapping at the base of my skull, that something about this view is off. Something is wrong. From this vista, I study the horizon. I look again at the little train set of a town, the patchwork of farms, the ribbons of asphalt that connect everyone. Again, I have the same thought. Something is off.

"What is it?" I ask myself. "What is missing?"

And then I squint at the road, because on it, the sparse sun glinting off the red body, is Deena Drake's Range Rover, making its way home.

"Shit," I hiss. And break into a jog.

# THIRTY-TWO

I'M ONLY A LITTLE out of breath when Deena pulls into the driveway and finds me leaning against Honey like I'd been there all along. There's a rustle in my chest and I cough, hard, before she approaches me, annoyance and frustration rolling off her.

"Miss Gore, I told you—"

"That if I came back, you'd call the sheriff. And I'm sure he'd love only too well to have a reason to escort me off the premises, but a little girl has been taken. She wasn't taken ten years ago. She was taken last night. I need your help."

I give her my "I'm not going away" stare and, finally, she sighs and nods toward the front door. When she gets there, she seems unsurprised to find the door unlocked, and so I guess this must be a habit with her.

"Oh wow," I say, as I enter the great room behind her. Trying, possibly harder than I need to, to sell that I've never been inside. "What a lovely house."

"Thank you," she says, and drops her keys into a little bowl on the table next to the door.

"Would you like some coffee? Tea?" Deena asks, her southern lilt and slow, easy demeanor have been unadulterated by over twenty years of mountain life.

"No, thank you," I say.

"It's tragic what's happened," she says. "Absolutely awful."

"Do you know Shiloh?"

"I used to see her at church, when she was younger. But, no. Really, I only know her from the bakery. She is truly an excellent pastry chef. I can't imagine a bakery like that will last very long in a town like this but . . . Well, as I said. It's a tragedy."

"Yes," I say.

I'm sitting on the very edge of the well-worn, overstuffed sofa. If I sat any farther back, I'd sink in and be too dangerously comfortable for cogent questioning.

Deena settles onto a high-backed antique armchair. Her slender form fits well within the confines of the beautifully carved wooden arms. Her feet rest flat on the floor and her posture is impeccable.

"I heard about the accident at the old factory," she says. "I've been saying for years they should tear that place down. Are you unharmed?"

"Yes," I say. "I'm all right. Thank you."

She tilts her head to acknowledge her own graciousness in asking after my welfare. Her hands are folded in her lap. Her long, supple fingers seem almost weightless, neither tense nor fully at ease.

"Did you attend the festival last night?"

"No, I'm afraid not."

"Do you usually attend the church festivals?"

If she'd had worse manners she'd have shrugged. Instead, the corner of her mouth just barely twitches.

"Christmas," she says. "I attend the Christmas Eve service. And, of course, I play the piano for all of the holiday services."

"Why don't you attend the other festivals?" I ask.

"They are somewhat . . . garish."

"They're for kids," I say. "Kids are sort of garish."

"I suppose."

"You don't like kids?"

"I do not have much experience in the area."

"You didn't have kids?"

"No. Do you?"

"No," I say, automatically.

"Do you want them?" she asks.

It catches me off guard.

"I . . ." I start. "No. I do not. At one time—but no."

"It happens," she says. I do not know what, precisely, "it" is. And yet I can feel it. Can feel the shape of it. The heaviness. "It," whatever "it" is, is a thing that women know of. A thing we all carry. A decision. A gift. A burden. A chance. A mistake. A choice.

"Yes," I agree. "It happens. Not all of us are destined for motherhood."

I'm desperate, suddenly, to pull the focus away from childbearing, and I glance around the room. The river-stone fireplace, the raw-edge coffee table, the elegant drapes. Every surface is perfect, clean, dust-free.

"Do you have a maid?"

"Of course," she says, the unspoken and sarcastic "Don't you?" omitted but implied.

"Does she live in?" I ask.

"No," she says. "She lives in town. She comes two days a week, or sometimes more if I need her an extra day."

"Like when you throw the Christmas party?"

"Yes."

I look around the room. The head of a water buffalo hangs over one wall, its brown glass eyes and gentle mouth so lifelike as to be disarming.

"Ten years ago," I say. "You visited the Andrewses' home to teach Max piano."

"Yes."

"And, while you were there, you saw a plumber? What do you remember about him?"

"Not very much."

"Try," I say. "The thing is, he's dead now. He died in the factory explosion and so I can't interview *him*."

"I see," she says, looking down at her hands. "All right. I suppose . . ."

She closes her eyes and I watch her, even admire her. Her composure. Her posture. Her easy grace. I feel my suspicion creeping back up and remember, again, what Leo had said about blind spots.

"He was very tall," she says. "Sort of scruffy but strong-looking. He was carrying a very large toolbox, I remember. Larger than the usual kind. And he had a piece of pipe slung over his shoulder."

"Did he speak to you?"

She opens her eyes and meets my gaze.

"Only to say what a hot day it was. And to say that he was leaving. His truck had been blocking my car, you see."

"And then you both left?"

"Yes."

"Anyone else?"

"No, I . . ." She stops herself, abruptly, her hands knotting together on her lap.

"What is it?" I ask.

"It's nothing—" she says.

"Anything might help," I say. "Anything at all."

"It's only that . . . well, I remember I thought I saw someone in the field."

"The field behind the Andrews farmhouse?"

"Yes. As I was coming out. I was standing on the back porch and I thought I saw someone in the field, but I was wrong. It was only a scarecrow."

"A scarecrow?"

"Yes," she says.

"But you didn't get a good look at it?"

"No, I was worried about making it to my next appointment. I was in a hurry to leave. I remember being a little startled—thinking someone was in the field watching me—and then I realized it was only a scarecrow. It was quite far away and I'd never noticed it before, that's all. But, as I say, I realized it was only a scarecrow and I went down the steps and toward my car. And that's when I saw the plumber."

I think back to what Mack had said. That Dwight had also seen what he'd taken to be a scarecrow that had turned out to be a person. But for some reason, it had spooked him. I think, again, that I need to get those witness statements from AJ. See exactly what was said on that day. What was seen. Now, though, I need to get back on track and back on the road.

"Did you know that the Zieglers also visited the Andrews family on the day Molly was kidnapped?"

"Did they?"

"What is your opinion of the Zieglers?" I ask.

"They're friends of mine," she says.

I'm surprised to hear Deena identify any of the residents of Quartz Creek as friends. "Are they?"

"Yes."

"Do you think they're good people?" I ask.

She blinks at me, her head tilted in mild confusion. "I'm not sure I understand what you mean."

"Are they decent?"

"Decent?"

"Do you have a high opinion of them?"

"They would not be my friends if I did not."

"Did they ever offer counseling to you and Mister Drake?"

Her lips purse into a near smile but she turns it off almost before I see it. "I'm not sure how that's relevant to your investigation, Miss Gore."

"I'm not sure either," I say.

"Excuse me?"

"Well, I'm asking questions for the explicit reason that I do not know their answers. It's only when I have answers that I begin to understand their relevance and am able to form a larger picture."

"Like a puzzle," she says.

"More like a map," I tell her. "A map that I'm trying to fill in."

"The Zieglers offered Mister Drake and me the same gracious service they would offer to any member of First Baptist's congregation."

"Was your husband close with them?"

A small hesitation. And then, "Yes. Bob and Harvey were as close as two men of that generation ever are. They played golf together. A few times, Bob went with Harvey on hunting expeditions. Bob and Rebecca occasionally had us over for dinner."

"Not anymore?"

"Not since Harvey passed. It reminds me too much of the time before. We fell out of practice and then, well, it simply never came up again."

"You sound like you miss it."

"I miss everything about the time before Harvey passed."

"I'm sorry," I say.

We sit and look at each other.

The grandfather clock down the hall ticks. The animals stare.

"Have you ever visited Susan McKinney?" I ask.

There's a hesitation. She looks down, away from me, and then at her fingernails.

"She buys my rose hips from me."

"That's not what I asked," I say. "Have you ever visited her, in her cabin."

"I—yes. Several years ago, after Harvey died. I was grieving. I needed . . . I don't know. I needed someone to talk to, I suppose. I'd heard about her in town."

"Did she tell your fortune?"

"Yes. It was all just hokum. Platitudes," she says, letting out a frustrated exhalation. "I should never have gone. Susan McKinney knows the plants of these mountains better than anyone and her teas are second to none but, when it comes to any sort of . . . *ability*, she's no less a fraud than the psychics you see on television."

I feel certain there's something else there. Something she isn't saying. I wait awhile longer. Let the grandfather clock tick by. But she offers nothing else.

Eventually, I ask, "Do you know the story of the Quartz Creek Witch?"

"Yes. Harvey told me the story several years ago."

"There are a few different versions," I say. "Could you tell me the one you heard?"

"I'm not sure if I remember it."

"Just tell me what you remember," I say.

"There was a witch, long ago, who lived deep in the forest amid a grove of enchanted apple trees," she says. She begins slowly, but, as the story goes on, her voice picks up a melodic lilt.

"The apples shone with the brilliance of emeralds and rubies, even in winter. Even in the coldest winter. The worst winter. One night, a poor widow woman knocked on the witch's door, begging for apples from the witch's grove. She said that her husband had been a woodcutter. That he had died in the forest and now she and her children were starving. The witch saw the woman's two beautiful daughters, their eyes hollow with hunger and grief, and she offered the woman a trade. She promised the woman that if she handed over her daughters, then the woman would never want for apples. Would never be hungry or cold or sad again. The woman agreed to the deal."

Deena pauses to take a breath and her chin wobbles almost imperceptibly before she continues.

"But the witch was cunning. She turned the woman into one of her apple trees. And the woman bore fruit forever after, and stood silently by as her daughters grew into beautiful young women who sang like the dawn chorus. Eventually, the girls forgot about their mother, forgot even that it was the witch who had given them their power. The witch turned them into birds, fearing to lose them. But the daughters, in their fury, only plucked out her eyes. Then, they took her eyes and threw them into Quartz Creek, where the witch's eyes could see only the sky through glassy water."

I feel my jaw open at this section of the story but stay silent as Deena finishes.

"The witch, blinded and grieving, mourned them desperately, and in her mourning she became a crow. Destined to wear black forevermore. She flew blindly from the house, crying for them. Hoping for their return. She searches still, even to this day, Harvey used to say. That is why you hear the crows here screaming each night. They are screaming the names of those girls, lost forever to the hills."

Deena's eyes glisten, and she dabs at their corners with the knuckle of one finger.

"I'm sorry," she says. "It's a silly old folk story. It's just the last time I heard it, I was sitting where you are now. And Harvey was telling it to me. It was only a few weeks before he passed."

"No need to apologize," I tell her. "Grief has a way of sneaking up on us, reminding us how powerful it is, even after a very long time."

She nods.

I stand, and Deena does too.

"I doubt I'll be the last one to come around asking questions," I tell her. "The FBI is on their way, because of Lucy. I imagine they'll want to talk to anyone who was a witness the last time."

"Again," she says, with a sad sort of exhaustion. "It's happening again."

"Yes," I say.

I give her one last look. With her silvering blond hair and her keen blue eyes and impeccable makeup and clothing. As before, I see the fragility of her. The glassiness of her eyes when she looks toward the wall of windows and says with a soft whisper, "Those poor girls."

I walk with her to the front door and pause at a small, stylish end table next to it. Her keys rest in a hand-lathed bowl, and beside it is a framed photograph.

From perhaps twenty years before, it is the Drakes' wedding photo. Deena was in her early thirties, I remind myself, though she looks nearly the same age in the photo as she does now. The photo is a crisp black-and-white, perfectly balanced, and the couple stands together, under a bower, in a beautiful rose garden. Deena wears a pale, flawlessly tailored dress that just skims the short grass at her feet. Harvey wears a well-made suit. Her hair is cut in a twenty-years-ago version of the bob she wears now and her makeup is natural and timeless, just as now. Deena's light coloring is nicely contrasted by Harvey's dark features. Dark hair, dark brown eyes, tanned skin. They smile serenely in the face of this evanescent moment.

"This is lovely," I say, gesturing toward the photo.

"Thank you," she says, quietly, genuinely.

"You must miss him very much," I say.

"Yes," she says, a whisper.

"I'm sorry," I say. "But you must have family in Georgia. Why not move back?"

She smiles again and waves with that pretty, weightless hand to the high walls and towering windows and massive fireplace and her ever-present company of dead beasts, and says, "I simply couldn't. Leaving this place . . . I would lose him forever."

We walk out onto the porch.

"I'd better head down the mountain," I say. "I've got more people to bother."

"All right," she says, as if she does not care whether I stay or go.

I stop on the steps, with her standing in the doorway behind me, and look again at the view of the mountains and the valley below. In the distance, I see the charred remains of the factory that Deena's husband once owned, the factory that she sold off, the factory that I barely escaped and two others perished in. I see Max's family farm and his empty fields and the little white farmhouse where he has grown to adulthood, waiting for Molly, waiting for me. And I see Main Street and the little bakery in which Shiloh Evers sits and waits and can do nothing more.

# THIRTY-THREE

I T'S DUSK WHEN I finally get back to my little rental cabin and AJ is there with a six-pack and two Styrofoam containers of food from King's Garden, Quartz Creek's one and only Chinese restaurant.

"Marry me," I say, taking the six-pack and leading him up the porch.

He chuckles and says, "Now here I was thinking you weren't the marrying type."

"Oh, yeah," I say, shrugging. "I forgot."

"We could settle down right here," he says. "Couple of kids, a big ol' farmhouse, church on Sundays."

I get us both in the door and set my keys on the counter, stash the six-pack in the fridge, get out two cold ones.

"I rescind my offer," I say.

He winks at me and says, "Thought you might."

He puts the Chinese food down and opens the containers to reveal lo mein, sweet and sour pork, black pepper chicken, egg rolls, crispy crab Rangoon, and plenty of fried rice. It's a veritable smorgasbord that only barely resembles food from actual China but is *everything* Chinese food is to this southern mountain girl.

"I wasn't sure what you liked so I got two buffets to go."

"Amazing," I say, taking a pair of paper-wrapped chopsticks from him. "Maybe I could become the churchgoing motherly type after all."

He laughs, and we dig in.

"Nothing on Lucy?" I ask. I know if he had anything he'd tell me, but I can't help checking, hoping there's some new thread to follow.

He shakes his head.

"State troopers are pitching in, doing what they can. They canvassed the mountain behind the church today. Dogs and everything. No trace yet. Reporters are starting to get into town. It's going to be a circus before too much longer."

"What about the FBI?" I say. "Are they coming?"

"Yep. They're sending a task force. Should be here tomorrow," AJ says. "A few other towns have sent deputies already to help comb the area but . . . nothing so far. Everyone who's not working to track Lucy is working with the fire department to collect evidence at the explosion site."

We mull things over while splashing soy sauce out of packets and into the already oversalted food.

AJ says, "So you saw Bob Ziegler today?"

"Yes."

"Did he admit to seducing a fourteen-year-old?"

"He did."

"And he was how old?"

"Eighteen."

"Hmm."

"It's not the same, though. Right?" I say. "That's what I keep telling myself. A teenager having sex with a younger girl at a party in the sixties where he maybe didn't even know her age isn't the same thing as kidnapping three little girls. Jessica was the oldest. She was almost six. But she looked younger."

He nods.

"I don't know, Annie. I don't think we can rule anyone out."

He tells me the cops paid a visit to Lucy's dad today and checked up on him. He was at his home, in Asheville, with his wife and her little boy and their dogs when they got there. Last night, they were all at a birthday party together.

"So, it wasn't him," I say.

"No."

"But we knew it wasn't."

"Had to check," he says.

We both eat some crab Rangoon, dipping the deep-fried cream cheese wonton into the sweet tangy red sauce.

"Have you ever been out to Susan McKinney's cabin?" I ask.

"Once," he says. "Sort of a creepy place. But not big enough to hide a couple kids, is it?"

"No," I say. "And the FBI searched her cabin after she was brought in for questioning. She told me herself they found a bunch of applehead dolls in her bedroom. But, hell, my own granny had some of those sitting on a shelf in her room. I'd love to know what was said when they questioned her, though."

"Oh," AJ says. "That I can actually help you with."

He hops off his stool, opens the backpack he'd left lying on the floor, and pulls out a manila folder. I'd been hoping for a thick stack of reports and witness statements but, instead, what I see is maybe ten or twenty pages.

"I still don't think I have all of it. I spent most of the day out combing the woods, but I did manage to find these."

He slides the folder across to me and I open it up. Here, again, is the list of cars checked the day Jessica was taken. And a small stack of pages of statements from the church picnic. Finally, I discover Deena's statement from the day Molly was taken, and I read over it while eating, never bothering to look at what I'm putting in my mouth.

"It's just like she said," I mumble after reading through it. She came at her usual time. When she was finished, she shouted goodbye. She ran into a plumber on the way out and was afraid she'd lose time trying to get him to move his truck. He was leaving. They exchanged pleasantries. She had no idea Molly had been taken until the next day.

"She told me today about a scarecrow," I tell him. "But she doesn't mention anything about it in the statement."

"Probably didn't think it was relevant," he says. "If she was sure it was a scarecrow."

I find the same version of events from Dwight Hoyle's point of view. Came to fix a pipe. Heard piano music. Finished up. Saw Janice in the garden, later heard her talking to someone. Saw Deena. Left.

"Someone else was there," I say.

"What?"

"Someone else was there. Dwight says he heard Janice talking to someone in the garden."

"It must have been Deena," AJ says.

I shake my head.

"No," I say. "No, Deena didn't know Janice was in the garden. She told me when I first questioned her that if she'd known Janice wasn't in the house, she'd never have left without letting her know."

"So it wasn't Deena talking to Janice?"

I look back at Dwight Hoyle's statement.

*I saw Janice Andrews working in the garden when I got to the house. She was taking water from the burst pipe and pouring it over the garden. After I finished, I left the barn and heard her talking to someone. She was saying something about the weather. Something about the heat killing her zucchini. As I left, I waved to her, but whoever she was talking to was around the other side of the barn. I didn't see them. I went back into the barn to get the pipe so I could take it for scrap. It took me a while to get it and my toolbox situated. Once I did, I went to my truck and saw that piano teacher woman. We talked for a minute, just saying hello. And then I left. I didn't see anyone else.*

"Someone else was there," I say again. "But who?"

"And he doesn't mention any scarecrow," he says.

"No," I say. "But he told Mack. Mack said something about it creeped out Dwight. Picture a scarecrow. Tell me what you see."

He swallows a big bite of pepper chicken and then closes his eyes.

"Burlap face. Like a sack. Maybe painted. An old hat. Overalls, usually. But sometimes just old worn-out clothes. A flannel shirt and jeans. Stuffed with straw."

"Yeah," I say. "That's what I picture too."

I poke at my food for a few moments and then say, "Molly's kidnapping is an outlier. Jessica was taken from what is essentially a public place. The playground outside of a church. Olivia was taken from a church picnic in the park. But Molly was taken from her own house. In broad daylight. Who else could've been there?"

AJ shakes his head.

"I don't know," he says. "Everyone around here leaves their doors unlocked. Even now. Even after everything this town has been through. And Molly was sitting right there in the front room."

I groan and mash one palm into my forehead, as if that will make my thoughts form some kind of cohesive solution. "Uggh. I don't know. I feel like I'm not any closer to figuring this out than when Max hired me. And all I've done is stir up trouble and probably get Molly killed when she was *apparently* just fine all this time."

"Annie . . ." he says. "She wasn't fine."

"No, I know," I breathe. "Whoever took Molly and Jessica left those applehead dolls in their place. It's not the work of someone in their right mind and—"

I stop and look toward the door, alert. There's a car outside. Voices. It's not Max. It's female. There's a low moaning. A *shushing* sound. I look at the clock. It's just after eight.

AJ and I are both off our stools and across the room by the time there's a knock at the door.

"Who is it?" I ask, hand on my gun.

"Annie? It's Nicole Jacobs. Can you please open up?"

I open the door.

Nicole is standing there wrapped up in her coat and scarf. Leaning on her, looking disheveled and pissed, is Nicole's sister, Olivia Jacobs.

# THIRTY-FOUR

AJ AND I TRADE a look and then I step backward and let the girls inside.

"Please tell me you did not kidnap your sister," I say, closing the door behind them.

Nicole rolls her eyes before helping Olivia out of her heavy coat.

"She's stronger than I am," Nicole says, taking off her coat and flopping it and Olivia's across the arm of the nearest chair. "I can't make her do anything she doesn't want to do. Come on, Liv."

She leads Olivia to the sofa. Olivia glares at Nicole but then, finally, sits. She looks around the room, wide-eyed, and begins to rock back and forth.

"I heard moaning," I say.

"Yeah," Nicole says. "She hates car rides, but once she gets inside she's usually fine. Let me just put on some music."

I breathe out a sigh but say okay.

"Look," Nicole says as she rummages through her bag. "My mom and Uncle Cole are, like, intense. They want to protect Olivia and they're so sure she can't or won't help you but—"

"But you think she can?"

I look at the young woman rocking back and forth on my sofa.

"My mom's at work," Nicole says. She takes a phone and a little portable speaker out of her bag and sets the speaker on the table. A few seconds later, Top 40 starts drifting out of it. Olivia's rocking pace changes and she taps gently on the tops of her thighs in 4/4 time.

Nicole lets out a relieved breath and says, "This is my time to sit with Olivia. I figure we can sit somewhere besides our own living room."

I take out my phone.

"Jesus, please don't call my mom!" Nicole shrills.

"I'm not going to," I say. "I don't have a laptop anymore. I need to bring up the case notes and this is all I have."

"I should . . . probably not be here," AJ says, grabbing his coat. "If Olivia's mom does happen to come home and find her girls aren't there, I'm sort of up the creek if Jacobs finds out."

"I'll make sure not to rough them up too much," I say.

He rolls his eyes and heads out.

"Are you guys, like, dating?" Nicole asks once AJ's gone. She's making herself comfortable in the armchair on the other side of the sofa.

"We're helping each other," I say. Nicole tries to stifle a mischievous grin but doesn't succeed. I ignore her, sit down in the one other chair, face Olivia, take a deep breath.

"Okay, Olivia. Do you know who I am?"

Olivia rocks back and forth, taps her thighs. If she hears and understands me, there's no sign of it.

"My name is Annie Gore. I'm a private investigator. I've been hired to find answers about something that happened here ten years ago, when you were a little girl."

*Rock, rock. Tap, tap.*

"Is it okay if I show you some pictures?"

*Rock, rock. Tap, tap.*

I glance at Nicole. She shrugs.

"Okay," I say. "Is it okay if I come a little closer?"

*Rock, rock. Tap, tap.*

I glance again at Nicole. She says, "If she hates it, you'll know."

"Great."

I get up and sit near enough to Olivia that she can see my phone screen if I set it on the coffee table but not so near as to be threatening, I hope.

"Okay," I say, wishing like hell I had Max's casebook with all his pictures and notes. Instead, I bring up a photo of Olivia when she was a little girl.

"This was you," I say. "When you were little."

Olivia's mouth twitches a little, almost a half smile. She looks like Nicole when she smiles.

I have another picture of her and Nicole together when they were little. It's Christmas and Nicole is playing with a set of light-up plastic blocks. Olivia is watching, wide-eyed. I show it to Olivia.

Olivia's mouth twitches again but otherwise she just keeps rocking. The song changes but the meter stays the same and she rocks and taps.

"When you were little, someone took you away and then, a few days later, they brought you back. Do you remember any of that?"

She jerks her head. I glance at Nicole. She's biting her lips together, looking a little nervous.

I reach over, fish in my bag, and get out the pictures Nicole gave to me the day before. I open them and spread them on the table.

Olivia's eyes dart from page to page, spiral to spiral. Her rocking goes off time. Her tapping stutters.

"Can you help me understand what these are?"

*Rock. Rock, rock. Tap tap tap tap.*

I get my notebook and pens from the bag. I open the notebook to a fresh page.

"She won't use a pen," Nicole says.

"Okay," I say. I look through the bag and find a fat yellow highlighter. I uncap it and hold it out to Olivia.

"Can you draw for me anything that you saw when you were taken away?"

Olivia holds the highlighter. She sniffs it. She scrunches up her nose.

*Rock. Rock, rock, rock.*

Her taps come one-handed. *Tap. Tap.*

"Okay," I say. "How about I show you some pictures?"

I open my phone and scroll through the files I've saved. Olivia rocks faster.

"She um . . ." Nicole starts.

"What?"

"I've seen Uncle Cole try this with her. Twice before. She um . . . did not react well. But—"

"What?" I say, holding my phone close to me, away from Olivia.

"I think you should try it anyway."

"Are you sure?"

"Everyone's always trying to protect her. But Olivia is strong. Aren't you, Liv? And you want to help Miss Annie find Shiloh's little girl, right? Remember when Shiloh made you that pretty cake and brought it to the house with her little girl? You want to help find little Lucy, right? Remember how cute she is? Remember how she sang 'Twinkle, Twinkle' for you?"

Olivia gives her sister an irritated growl, and Nicole laughs.

"Okay, maybe I'm laying it on a little thick, but you do want to help, right, Liv?"

Oliva breathes out a huff of air through her nose and her rocking slows a little.

I look at both of them and ask again, "Are you sure?"

Nicole looks at Olivia and then back at me and nods.

"Just go slow," she says. And then, to Olivia, "You can stop if you want to, okay? We can go home whenever you want. Just wave at me, okay?"

*Rock. Rock. Rock. Tap. Tap. Tap.*

Deep breath. I open a picture of Cole Jacobs from a news article. Hold it toward Olivia.

"This is your uncle, Cole. Do you recognize him?"

Her rocking continues. She holds the highlighter tight in her left hand, taps with the other.

"And this is Bob and Rebecca Ziegler. They work at your church."

She looks at them and then immediately looks away, a low growl in her throat.

"She doesn't like them," Nicole says.

"Oh?"

She shakes her head.

"Do you know why?"

"When we were younger, my parents tried to have Olivia prayed over and baptized . . . I don't know. Anyway, Olivia *hated it*."'

"Did she have a problem with Brother Bob or Rebecca before that?"

Nicole shakes her head. "I don't remember. I was little."

"Do you remember the service?"

"I remember my mom took Olivia up to the front of the church and everyone put their hands on Olivia's head and shoulders. You didn't like it, did you, Liv?"

Olivia rocks faster now. Bangs her hand—balled into a fist—against her thigh.

"No," Nicole says. "She was not a fan. I wouldn't be either."

"It's okay," I say to Olivia. "We're not going to do that. We're not going to touch you."

Top 40 plays. There's a chorus about love and listening to a heartbeat and Olivia rocks along and I wait until she steadies.

"I'm going to show you another picture. Okay?"

*Rock, rock.*

She's still holding the highlighter as I scroll through my phone.

*Rock, rock. Tap. Tap.*

I decide to introduce a control. I switch over to my browser and search for stock photos. I show her a picture of a woman in a pretty dress.

*Rock, rock. Tap. Tap.*

I show her a picture of a man making bread.

*Rock, rock. Tap. Tap.*

I show her a picture of a couple sitting on a sofa together.

*Rock, rock. Tap. Tap.*

Just in case, I show her an old mug shot of Dwight Hoyle.

*Rock, rock. Tap. Tap.*

And Elaine Hoyle.

Still nothing.

"Okay," I say. "How about this person?"

I pull up a picture of Deena Drake. The photo is one from the records AJ had, a picture of Deena and Harvey from before he died. It's a studio portrait and the couple is sitting in front of a teal-painted backdrop looking serenely happy. Deena's blond hair shimmers in the bright light and her smile is soft and elegant. I show the photo to Olivia.

Olivia pauses her rocking, stares at the photo.

Then goes back to nothing.

*Rock, rock. Tap. Tap.*

The music plays. The song turns over.

This one's more downbeat. Olivia adjusts her rhythm.

*Rock, rock. Tap. Tap.*

I pull up some more stock photos. A woman in a bright red dress. A man drinking coffee. I bring up a picture of Tommy and Mandy Hoyle and put it down on the coffee table. There is no change. She rocks along to the song. A woman sings about her heart.

"Okay, just a couple more."

I show her a picture of Molly Andrews when she was little.

"Do you know this little girl?"

She rocks and taps. Rocks and taps.

"Okay. Let's try this one."

I try to find one of Susan McKinney but then remember that I was never able to find any presence for her online. I go back to the file AJ brought and page through it. But Susan was never booked. There was no mug shot.

"Does the name 'Susan' mean anything to you, Olivia?" I ask.

*Rock, rock. Tap. Tap.*

No change. It's all I can do. At least for now.

I reopen my phone and decide to start fresh, look for stock photos of kids for a clean slate. I find a little boy in a dinosaur T-shirt and show it to her. No change. I find a little girl with long brown braids eating ice cream. No change. The song carries on. The woman sings about her pain.

I find pictures of scarecrows. One in an old shirt and jeans. One in overalls. One from *The Wizard of Oz*. I show them all to her.

*Rock, rock. Tap. Tap.*

Nothing.

I tab over to the case pictures and flick through the images until I get to the last known photograph of Jessica Hoyle. Her ice blue eyes shine out of the picture and she grins, her front two teeth missing. I put it down on the table in front of Olivia.

A low, grating moan grows in Olivia's chest and crawls up her throat. She doesn't open her mouth. She stares at the picture and moans and rocks, her eyes wide.

"Okay," I say. "You've seen this little girl?"

She moans and rocks.

"Did you see her when you were taken away?"

She moans and rocks and smacks her leg, growls at me.

My brain buzzes. I feel like I'm vibrating.

*Olivia saw Jessica Hoyle when she was taken away.* But I already knew that, right? I just didn't expect the certainty of it to hit so hard, and I wonder, like everyone has wondered, what else Olivia saw, what else she experienced. How to get the information from her. How to help her and Nicole and Max and Mandy and Shiloh and this whole town get past this darkness and through to the other side. And is that my job now? No longer an investigator but a shepherd?

A knight? A warrior from another mountain?

I get my breath under control and lean as close to Olivia as I dare.

"All right, Olivia, I know this is really hard. But, if you can, could you please . . . draw something . . . anything that you saw when you saw this little girl. Can you remember anything?"

She moans and rocks and her body contorts as she comes closer to the paper and presses the highlighter hard against it. I think for a moment that the tip might disappear into the plastic but it doesn't. Instead, she begins to draw.

Her hand, crabbed around the marker, travels in a circle and then squeezes in and in and in. A spiral. She lifts the marker again, hovers over the paper a moment, then presses the tip close to the outside of the first spiral. She draws another, same as the first. Another. Another. Another. She turns the page. Starts again. *One spiral. Two. Three. Four.*

"What is it?" Nicole asks.

"I don't know," I say. "More spirals."

The song changes. A man sings about how he's sorry about his love, his pain.

Olivia draws another spiral. Another. Another.

"Olivia?" Nicole asks, leaning closer to her sister. "What are they? Can you show me what they are?"

I pull up a picture of snails, a picture of seashells, a picture of water going down a drain. Anything spiral-shaped I can find. I try to show them to Olivia—as I'm sure others have done before me—but she ignores my phone now. Ignores me.

She draws another spiral. Another. Faster. Harder.

"Liv?" Nicole asks again, very soft. "Can you show us? Can you show us what they are? For Lucy?"

Olivia pauses long enough to glare at Nicole, then lowers herself even farther, until her face is just inches above the paper. She takes a deep breath through her nose. And again. And then the moan grows in her chest and travels up her throat.

"Okay," Nicole says, calming. "It's okay."

Olivia taps the paper with the marker.

"Okay," Nicole says.

Olivia moans again. Longer this time. Louder. She still doesn't open her mouth. The moan never turns into a scream. It's a guttural noise like growling, urgent and necessary.

I watch her and listen to the song and look at the paper and the spirals and decide to take a wild stab in the dark.

"Olivia, do you know the story of the Witch of Quartz Creek?"

Olivia turns to me, stares, her dark eyes boring into mine, glassy with fresh tears. And the moan becomes a scream now. She rocks and nods and flaps her hands.

"It's okay," Nicole says, moving next to her sister on the sofa, wrapping an arm around Olivia's shoulders.

I realize that everything I'd seen till now was born of frustration at my inability to communicate with her, but this is different. This is pure terror.

"Are you afraid of the witch?" I ask, my voice calm and quiet.

Another scream, and then Olivia melts into tears.

"I'm sorry," I say to both of them. "I'm sorry. I had to ask."

Nicole nods, and Olivia waves her hands wildly.

"It's okay," Nicole says to her sister again. "You're safe now."

But there's nothing for it. Olivia can't stop sobbing now that she's started. Can't stop howling with terror, like it's all happening again.

Because it is.

"I think it's time to go," Nicole says. "You want to go, Olivia?"

Olivia waves. Her tears are slowing. Her screams are quieting. But her face is still an angry red, her lip still quivering.

"Thank you," I say, getting to my knees in front of her. "Thank you for coming here, Olivia. For helping me."

"Come on, Liv," Nicole says softly. She stands and Olivia stands with her. They move toward their coats. Nicole helps Olivia into hers and then hands Olivia a tissue.

When they're both bundled up, Nicole faces me and says, "What's happening? Who is taking these little girls? Who would do something so awful? Is there really a witch?"

All I can do is shake my head and tell her the truth.

"I don't know. I'm sorry. I don't know."

# THIRTY-FIVE

I'M SITTING ON MY granny's porch. It is autumn and the air smells like sweet rot.

"Did you see her?" my granny's voice asks.

I am dreaming.

"Who?" I ask. I'm still looking straight ahead. Sitting on the porch, I'm waiting. For my father? My mother? Someone. My face is propped on the heels of my hands and my elbows dig into my thighs. I am small. Bony. Everyone has always thought I am younger than I am. Little.

"The woman," my granny says. "The witch."

"I saw a witch," I tell her.

There is a flapping sound and a crow lands in the dirt in front of my feet. I hold out my hand to it. It drops an apple core into my palm. The flesh is wet and brown. What's left of the skin is a green so bright it hurts my eyes.

"Those seeds are toxic," my granny says.

I pull the apple closer to my face, close enough now that I can smell the way rot is taking it, the way it takes us all. Inside the core, there are two black seeds.

"Every apple—" my granny says. And her voice is a crow's voice. It rustles through the air behind me, and I shiver to hear it.

"Every apple has a little poison in it."

I wake up.

Groggy, I glance at the window. Dawn is breaking.

I scrunch the sheets in my fists, anxious to feel something tactile and real. Something to tell me that, finally, I am awake. Alive. Present.

I breathe, and my breathing comes in grating rasps, and I try, briefly, to deny to myself that I'm sick, but I feel feverish. Chilled and hot. Shaky.

I sit up and the file full of papers slides off my chest and tumbles onto the floor. I'd fallen asleep reading ten-year-old witness statements, and now I blink at what seems impossibly small text.

"God," I mutter. "What day is it?"

I look at the phone on the nightstand, find myself wishing it would buzz. Wishing to hear Leo's familiar deep voice while he laughs and drinks and exists—so easily—in the world in which I struggle.

When the phone does vibrate, my heart lurches. But it isn't Leo. Tina's picture and number show up on the screen instead.

I answer with a question: "What are you doing up, Tina?"

"Figure the ass crack of dawn is just about the only time to catch you."

"Mmhmm," I mumble. My voice rustles in my chest. I suppress a cough.

"I mean, rest of the time you're running all over hell and half of Georgia blowing up meth labs, finding dead girls. Good night, Annie, you know that town you're in is all over the news?"

"I'm not surprised," I say.

"And another little girl is missing?"

"Yes," I say.

I put her on speaker, sit up, and cough as I tug my shoes on.

"You sound like hell. I'm telling you that country air isn't good for you. You need to bring Honey back home. It's safer here."

I snort, and the snort turns into a cough.

"Seriously," Tina says when the coughing dies down. "Are you okay?"

"Yeah," I say. "Just working. I don't even know if I'll be able to stick around. The FBI is rolling in."

"Well, it's probably for the best," she says. "But until they boot you out of there, will you be careful?"

"Of course," I say. "I'm always careful."

"Annie, sweetheart, you've got a lot of excellent qualities, but 'careful' cannot be named among them. Watch your ass."

"Okay," I say.

"And Honey's."

"Okay."

"Bring her back safe."

I finally manage to get off the phone and stumble into the bathroom. I try to remember what day it is, and it takes longer than it should to figure out that this is Saturday. I've been here since Sunday night. Almost a week, which is all I promised Max. And yet, in spite of how awful I feel, and the fact that the FBI are on their way, and that all I've managed to do so far is probably make things worse, I know I can't and won't stop looking until someone makes me.

Washing my hands, I hazard a glance at my reflection, and grimace at the sight. I look like nine miles of bad road, but I force myself back into the bedroom, where I pull on leggings and a T-shirt and a threadbare Cincinnati Reds sweatshirt. I clip on my holster and my gun and stutter-step out the door.

There is an almost imperceptible rain. It is almost only fog. Almost only water suspended in the air. And yet, when I run, it splatters against my cheeks and slides down, over my jaw, onto my neck, and into my clothes.

I ignore the rain, or try to ignore the rain, and think.

Ten years ago, someone took Jessica Hoyle from a church playground while her mother slept in the car not fifteen feet away.

Weeks later, someone took Olivia Jacobs from a picnic in the park while her mother was distracted by Olivia's big sister.

Days later, they brought her back.

Weeks later, someone took Molly Andrews from her house in broad daylight.

Five days ago, after I arrived in Quartz Creek and began asking questions, someone brought Molly back. She had been strangled with a length of soft fabric and left for the crows wearing a handmade red velvet dress, her insides damaged by some unknown catalyst.

Two days ago, someone took Lucy Evers from a Fall Festival at her grandparents' church while her mother ran a cakewalk booth.

In every instance, an applehead doll was left behind.

I think of my granny's words in my dream.

*Every apple has a little poison in it.*

I listen to the sound of my feet pitter-patter over the trail and grass and mud.

*Pit-pat. Pit-pat. Pit-pat.*

So much of investigating is just walking around in the dark, shaking trees, hoping you don't get plonked in the head by whatever falls out. I wonder, as I run and my breath comes out in rasping gasps, whether I've shaken enough trees. Whether I've shaken the right ones.

*Pit-pat. Pit-pat.*

And I wonder whether I got Molly killed. And I think I must have. And I hope I'm not just out here spinning my wheels and—

*BANG!*

"Shit!" I hiss, as a shot whizzes past me. There's a sudden, scalding heat in my side.

It didn't just go by me. I'm hit.

I'm on the edge of the gorge and I drop to my butt and go skidding down the bank, in the mud.

*BANG! BANG!*

The shots zip over my head. One chunks into the bank and sends mud and hard-packed dirt flying. It's a high-caliber hunting rifle being shot from some distance. Even if I could stand still long enough to spot the shooter, my two-and-three-quarter-inch barrel isn't going to do a thing against it. I scramble to my feet and sprint farther into the gorge, following the line of the creek. I scan the mountainside as I run but see no sign of the shooter within the fall trees. It's all just brown and red and gold sheathed in silver fog.

*BANG!*

This one's far over my head, and I think the shooter's lost me. Still, I bound over the creek and up the opposite bank and into the circle of stones, holding my side with my hand as I go.

*BANG!*

The noise rattles around me in a weird, distorted way. Crows fly up from the forest and flap, calling and crying and screaming into the sky.

I cough, and my cough echoes and I know I have to move. The stones might provide some level of cover, but the echoing amplification of the circle will only give away my position.

I dart out of the circle and, quiet as I can, I run up the mountainside, following the trail to Susan McKinney's cabin. If she's the one behind everything, I guess I'm screwed, but out in the open, I'm as good as dead.

# THIRTY-SIX

T HE DOOR TO SUSAN'S cabin is unlocked, and I throw myself inside.

"Susan?" I call. But there's no answer. "Susan?"

Holding a hand to my side, I lay my gun on the table, pull out my cell phone with the other, and dial 911. But I get nothing. This deep in the woods, there's no signal.

"Shit."

"Susan!" I shout. But she isn't here. The house is empty.

I go to her sink and find a clean cloth, press it to my side.

"Shit," I breathe. I look around the house. Does she have a landline? She must, I think. The shots have stopped, but it doesn't mean the shooter isn't just following me, waiting until I step outside to try again.

My breath comes in hot, rasping gasps. I cough. And the pressure from coughing makes the blood from my side come faster. I hold the cloth tight.

And then there are steps on the porch.

I drop my phone, pick up my gun, and aim straight at the door.

"What the hell's going on out here?" Susan shouts as she swings the door open. She's wrapped up in her thick black sweater and wide-brimmed hat. Her black eyes stare at me in alarm. Her hands go up beside her, empty.

"Shooter," I say. "Shooter on the mountainside. Where were you?"

"On my way up the mountain. We had a soft frost, so I was going to pick the rose hips and—good God, have you been shot?"

"Yes. I need to call the police. Don't stand near the windows."

"I'm not an idiot," she says. "And your cell won't work here. This whole mountain's a dead zone. I keep a satellite phone for emergencies."

She gets the phone down from a high shelf and calls 911, tells them what's going on. Then she goes to a cabinet and opens a drawer, gets out a fresh washcloth, goes to her line of jars on the back shelf, takes one down, and opens it.

"Do you think they're done?" she asks. "I haven't heard anything since I was on my way back."

"I don't know," I say. "They might just be waiting for me to go back up the hill toward the cabin but . . . if they see the cops, they'll probably split."

Susan uses a spoon to dab some yellow-green ointment onto the cloth and then, before I can react, she tugs up my sweatshirt and T-shirt. There's an angry line of red right above my hip bone. She presses the cloth to it and then grabs my hand and mashes it onto the rag. The rag is damp and smells like weeds.

"Grazed," she says. "It ain't pretty, but I'd say you got lucky. Hold it there."

I watch as Susan goes around the house closing her shutters. She flicks on the lights and adds another hunk of wood to the woodstove in the middle of the house, then goes to the battered old couch and pulls an orange and burgundy afghan from it. She comes back to me and wraps it around my shoulders.

"You're in shock," she says.

"No," I say. "No, I'm not. I've . . . I've been under fire before and this isn't—"

But I can barely get the words out. It's as if I'm hypothermic. My teeth chatter. I shiver. The blanket begins to fall, and Susan squeezes it tight again. She pulls a pin from her scarf and sticks it through the afghan, and now it holds as tight as she does.

"I've been shot at—" I say as much to myself as her. A reminder of who I am. What I can do. What I can recover from.

"Don't matter," she says, rubbing her rough palms over my shoulders. "Don't matter. You burn yourself on the stove, you're always wary of that stove. Days or weeks or months pass. You'll never forget the stove—the pain it caused, the scar it left."

She leaves me and puts a kettle on and picks a mortar and pestle up from the counter and brings it back. She pulls sprigs of dried things out of different jars and then sits at the table in front of me and begins grinding.

"You've got a fever," she says. "Did you know you're sick?"

"I was sort of trying to ignore it," I say, my voice raspy.

"Running yourself ragged, I'd say."

I cough. It's an ugly, wet sound.

"I told you to take better care of yourself. But no. You ran off and blew up a meth lab instead. You go scampering around in the fog in the most ungodly hours with no socks on. You don't take care of yourself, Miss Gore. It's almost like you don't care what happens to you."

I cough some more. Susan pours the crushed herbs into a ceramic mug.

"Did you get a look at them?" she asks.

I shake my head.

"Sounded like a rifle," she says.

The kettle whistles. She gets up and pours a stream of steaming water into the mug. A green, herby smell rises in a cloud. She pulls a jar of honey, the comb within, down from another shelf and sets it on the table, dips in a big spoon. She adds it to the tea, stirs for a while, sets it in front of me.

"What—"

"Just drink it," she says. "Just drink it and feel better."

I'm too tired to argue. The tea tastes like summer. Like a meadow and like sunshine and flowers.

"You were going to get rose hips?" I ask. The question comes unbidden, as if from the ether of my brain. I'm almost surprised to hear myself ask it.

"Yes," she says.

"Deena told me that she visited you," I say. "That she came to get her fortune told."

"Yes," she says. "Right after Harvey died."

"What did she want?" I ask.

"You know I can't tell you that."

"Can you give me a hint?"

She snorts and looks away from me and toward the windows.

"She was grieving," Susan says. "She wanted help. A potion or some such. But I told her there is no shortcut through grief. There is only one road, and it is a long one. I offered to read her some cards. Make her some tea, that's all."

"Did it help?"

"In the end, we found we had more in common with gardening than anything else. That's how I started picking the rose hips. Now hush up and drink the rest of your tea."

I take a few more slow sips. It seems to warm me from the inside out.

I close my eyes and, for a few seconds or minutes, I fall asleep. When I wake, Susan is at the windows, peeking out the side of the shades. I watch her, the black cardigan puffy with the humidity of the cabin interior, her dark eyes keen and searching.

"Do you know the story of the Quartz Creek Witch?" I ask her, my voice bleary.

"Of course," she says without looking at me.

"Will you tell it to me?"

"Will you drink another cup of tea?"

I nod.

"Okay."

She sighs and pours more tea into my cup. I hadn't even remembered putting it down. I watch as steam wafts off the surface, and I inhale the aroma and cough.

"There was a witch woman," she says, sitting down in front of me again, watching me as I pick up the cup. "She lived within an orchard of apples that, as long as she tended them, would never rot. Always, they would grow bright and green, as long as she sang to the trees each morning. She loved her apples more than anything, but, as all women do, she grew old. Her voice began to turn and sour. She knew that she would have to teach another voice the song if her apples were to go on."

I drink my tea and listen. The taste of grassy green meadows and tangy apples and sweet honey swirls on my tongue.

"As it happened, that winter was the coldest she had ever seen. All the land lay frozen under many feet of snow. Every day the folk of this valley prayed for sun, but only more and more snow fell. Nothing could grow. Nothing could survive. Except for the witch woman's apples."

Susan pauses and lets out a sigh. Her shoulders under the black scarf and sweater heave as if she might take flight. She settles, instead, into her chair. The wood creaks. She goes on.

"It was deep into this winter that a beggar woman came calling. She had nothing but two beautiful daughters. They were, all three of them, terrible hungry. The beggar woman pleaded with the witch woman to take her daughters and feed them. The witch woman said that she would, on the condition that they would be *her* daughters from that day forward. They would belong to her and her alone and she would grow them as proud and bright and beautiful as she had grown her apple trees."

I hold the mug close to my body, let its warmth sink into my skin and deeper, into my bones and the soft places, hidden away.

"The beggar woman agreed. She traded her daughters for all the apples she could carry. The witch woman raised the girls as her own, just as she promised. The girls grew bright and proud and beautiful. And that was its own curse. The girls did not sing to the apples. They were too curious about the outside world, too entranced by their own beauty, too taken with the wonders which beguile the young. The witch woman's voice faltered and the apples began to sour and, in a last gasp of her magic, the witch turned both girls into songbirds—a robin and a bluebird—so that they would be forced to sing each and every morning with the dawn."

I realize, distantly, that I have closed my eyes while I listened. That I was picturing the green apples and the beautiful daughters and the orchard. It was only the witch woman I could not picture. Only her that I could not see or hear. I open my eyes and watch as Susan toys with a loose string on her sweater. The piece of gauze that was on her wrist is gone. In its place is a red line, still puffy, but healing.

"They were beautiful birds," Susan says. "The most beautiful. But, one morning, they escaped their cage and flew away. The witch woman was devastated. She turned herself into a crow and flew after them. She cried for them, night after night, while her apples withered and died. And, to this very day, she cries for them still."

"Still," I repeat.

"Yes," Susan says. "Because a mother's grief is everlasting. That is the sound the crows scream at night. They learned it from her. It is the witch woman's cries. Her mistakes made manifest."

"My question," I say, drinking the last of the tea and feeling more like myself, "is what happened to the beggar woman who traded her daughters for food?"

Susan smiles. And then there's a knock at the door.

"Miss Gore? You in there? It's Sheriff Jacobs."

Susan opens up and he steps inside, takes his hat off, looks around.

"We're clearing the hillside now," he says. His cheeks are red from the cold air and exertion and, probably, the constant low-level aggravation he feels. "When you're ready, I'll walk you back to the Andrewses' place."

I look up at him and smile blithely.

"My hero."

He rolls his eyes.

# THIRTY-SEVEN

IT'S JUST SHERIFF JACOBS and me and an EMT back in Crow Caw Cabin on Max's farm. This is the same EMT who worked on my leg at the factory. She's opening up a kit of medical supplies. She also found and made coffee and put a blanket around me, wrapped it tight, just as Susan had only a couple of hours before. I didn't think that was strictly part of the EMT service, but who was I to argue?

"You couldn't see anyone?" Sheriff Jacobs asks.

"No," I say. "I couldn't see anyone."

All of his deputies had paused their search for Lucy to look for my shooter, and I feel guilty for having taken up their time, in spite of the fact that someone was out there trying to kill me.

Now, apparently safe, I'm sitting on the cabin's little couch, staring at the woodblock print over the fireplace, watching the ink black crows as if they might fly away.

Jacobs is talking but it's a while before I understand what's going on. I'm still in shock, the EMT has said. My brain is still lagging. Despite Susan's tea, I still feel sluggish and worn and my thoughts are swirling in a fog. The EMT is taking my temperature, my blood pressure.

"—found these shell casings up on a deer stand."

Jacobs holds up a baggie of rifle brass and then adds, "Of course, it could be a hunter's."

"Prints?" I ask.

"We'll see. But doesn't look like it. Brass smells fresh, though. Doubt they've been up there long."

"Hon, you're running a fever," the EMT says. "The scrape on your shin is healing pretty good and I've got butterflies on this new one here. Any deeper and I'd have made you go to the hospital for big-girl stitches. Lord have mercy, though, that cough of yours is sounding—in my medical opinion—gross. You sure you don't want to go in for a chest X-ray?"

"I'm sure," I say. "I don't have time."

She shakes her head.

"Were you wearing a high-visibility vest?" Jacobs asks.

"It wasn't some old coot mistaking me for a deer," I say. "They shot the bank right over my head and then followed me down the gorge. They could see me just fine."

"I told you, you should've left town," Jacobs says.

"I have a job to do."

"Well, so do I," he says. "And I can't do it if I'm spending my whole morning trying to keep your ass out of the morgue."

I can tell I'm getting pulled into a staring contest with Jacobs and I feel, suddenly, what years of searching for the answers I've been searching for can do to a person. What they've done to him. I think about the picture I saw of him only ten years ago, when he was just a deputy, just an uncle, just a man without the whole weight of Quartz Creek on his shoulders. I look at his hollow cheeks and dark circles and I realize I saw the very same thing this morning in the mirror.

The EMT rips open my blood pressure cuff with a loud *scccrriicchh.*

"You sure I can't give you a ride to the hospital?" the EMT says.

"I'm sure."

"Well, get some of Susan McKinney's cough tincture," she says. "Some elderberry wine wouldn't hurt either. And lots of rest."

"Sure," I say.

"I mean it," she says.

"Okay," I say.

She shakes her head again, then snaps up her EMT kit and leaves.

Once she's gone, Sheriff Jacobs takes a seat in the chair nearest the door. His arms are wiry and taut and covered in freckles. I'd not noticed the freckles before, and I feel strangely amused by them now. I really do need a nap.

"Are the FBI agents coming?" I ask, looking out the window past his head.

"They should be here in a couple hours. Takes a while over the mountain roads."

I nod.

"You could've been killed," he says.

I nod.

"And you're just going to keep at it, aren't you?"

I meet his eyes.

"Yes."

Jacobs rasps his hands together, sighs, looks at the floor. We sit like this for a while, with me watching him and him watching the floor.

"It's all happening again," he says, echoing the words I've heard over and over since Lucy was kidnapped. I wait for him to continue, too exhausted to ask questions.

"The year those girls were taken," he says eventually. "A lot of rumors flew around. You know how many fights I broke up? How many people—lifelong friends—started pointing fingers at each other? It was ugly. An ugly you hate to see."

He sucks in another big breath like this story is using up all his oxygen and it's the only way he can keep going.

"When Olivia was taken, the FBI sent a team. Big-city types. They looked around here—looked at us—like we were scum. Like we weren't nothing to them. Just a waste of their time. They found out Kathleen worked at the hospital and they started questioning her about methamphetamines, opiates. Whether she was part of some racket. Whether she and Arnold were in over their heads to some drug runner. Whether they themselves were users."

Jacobs clicks his tongue against his teeth, shakes his head.

"And I didn't even know how to tell the FBI to stop. I'd just taken over—in the middle of everything—because the sheriff before me, Donald Kerridge, had a heart attack and died after Olivia went missing. I was just doing the best I could, trying to handle everything at once, and the FBI walked all over me. There was nothing I could do about it. I'd never wanted to be sheriff. I was happy as I was."

I watch him as he struggles with these admissions, this airing of grief and grievances, and stay silent.

"They went out and took one look at the Hoyles—their home, Tommy's record, Mandy's bruises—and decided Tommy must be involved somehow. They pulled up Dwight's and Elaine's rap sheets and decided they were probably in on it. They were working up some hillbilly mafia tale like you wouldn't believe. And the whole time, these little girls are gone who knows where. The main one. The team leader? Agent Rachel James. She had her eye on some big bust. Wanted to make a name for herself. They brought dogs. They walked the church grounds and the picnic area. They questioned everyone's families. Dug out any dirt they could find. And then, one night, Olivia turns up right there on Kathleen and Arnold's back porch. Safe and sound."

My shock is starting to wear off, I realize. My palms are sweating. My heart is thudding. I'm beginning to feel alive again.

"God, it was such a relief. Such a relief to have her back. But . . ."

Jacobs goes on looking at the floorboards and not at me. His voice has been getting thinner, and he clears his throat like the problem is just allergies and not his heart swelling up with feeling.

"Olivia's barely been home half an hour when Agent James corners her. Rushes the whole family to the station for evidence collection. Separates them. Kathleen and Arnold are so relieved that Olivia's back, so stunned by everything moving so fast, that they don't even think to question it. They just obey Agent James. Olivia's the only person who knows who the kidnapper is. The only person who can say . . . But she *can't* say."

He clears his throat again. Takes another big breath. Keeps going.

"We didn't know, at the time, exactly what Olivia's situation was. We understood that there were developmental delays. Understood that there were hurdles. But my Aunt Betty had been delayed. And she ended up living a pretty normal life, just slow to start. Always quiet. What's the word they say now? 'Introverted.' Different. But she carved out a life for herself. At the time, I don't think it occurred to us that Olivia—just turned five years old—would *never* speak. Would *never* communicate like other children."

"What happened?"

He shrugs.

"I wasn't there. I was out on a call across town. The place still had to be policed. I was breaking up a fight between Tommy Hoyle and another man after the man accused Tommy of taking the girls for a kidnapping ransom scheme, saying Tommy's donation campaign was all a big hoax. And if his little girl was really gone, why was he sitting in a bar drinking and not out looking for her every minute of every day? Tommy was flaming mad. Broke the other guy's nose, laid him out. I was putting Tommy in the back of the cruiser when the call came in that Olivia had been returned and she was with Agent James."

"So you drove back across town."

He nods.

"I walked in. James had Olivia in the interview room in the station. There were pictures of all the suspects all over the floor, like they'd been flung off the desk. Agent James was standing there seething. Olivia was crouched on the floor, screaming. Screaming like she was trapped in a nightmare. Like nothing you've ever heard. She was terrified."

"Of her kidnapper?"

"I'm sure. But that's not all. There was a fresh red mark across her face. Apparently, James got so frustrated by Olivia's noncooperation that she slapped her."

"Oh."

"Slapping the dickens out of a little girl? A little girl who's been through that much? Can you imagine?"

"No," I say. "It's inexcusable."

"Yeah," he says, finally looking at me. "I've never come so close to hitting a woman. I picked Olivia up. She was fighting me. Punching me with her fists. Screaming. We took her to the hospital. They sedated her. Kathleen didn't leave her side. She brought Nicole into the room, and they sat there with Olivia night and day. Every time Olivia came to, she screamed like someone was gonna kill her. It was horrible."

"I'm sorry," I say.

"You know, I spanked both my sons," Jacobs says. "Till their butts were bright red, sometimes. Little hellions they were. But they were regular little boys. Getting into trouble half the time just to get a rise out of me. But Olivia? How could she understand something like that? Being taken, who knows where, by . . . who? And then she's brought back and she doesn't get half an hour in her mama's arms before she's pulled away and questioned like she's a *suspect?*"

He bites his lips together until the skin around his mouth goes white. And then he says, "In the hospital, they found bruises all over her. Scrapes, too. She'd been hurt by whoever it was that took her. A social worker came that night. Too late to keep Agent James off of her, but she did a good job afterward. Helped Olivia transition back to regular life. After that, I never managed to question her. I tried, Kathleen tried. Every time, she fell into screaming. Or she would draw these spirals."

"I've seen them."

He gives me a look of surprise, like he wants to ask me how I saw the drawings, then decides he doesn't want to know, shakes his head.

I say, "This is why you didn't want me around, why you didn't want me talking to Olivia."

He nods.

"What happened after that? With Agent James?"

"I called the FBI field office, reported her. She was gone the next day. Replaced by someone else. Agent Sanchez. Seemed keen but young. Very young. For a couple weeks, it seemed like everything was just frozen. Jessica Hoyle was still missing but there were no new leads. No new evidence."

"And then Molly was taken," I say.

"Yes."

I sigh. My chest rasps. My side aches. My leg throbs. I look down at my hands. My palms are still shiny with sweat.

"Olivia came here," I tell him. "Just last night."

I watch as surprise and anger mix on his face.

"Nicole brought her. I didn't ask her to. But she wanted to help. They both did."

His mouth drops open.

"It's because of Lucy," I say. "Olivia was willing to try to work with me because Lucy's been taken, and I think enough time has passed that she felt like she could handle it."

"Could she?"

"For a little while. Sheriff, do you know the story of the Quartz Creek Witch?"

"Of course."

"Well, so does Olivia. And when I asked her about it, she absolutely lost it. She was terrified."

"It's just an old story," he says.

"Maybe not," I say. "Maybe not to Olivia."

"What do you mean?"

"Olivia *believes* it. She's terrified of it. So who, in this town—because it *must* be someone in this town—could be the witch she's remembering?"

He shakes his head.

"Susan McKinney," I say, pushing into deep waters, "was taken in for questioning at the time. Someone must have thought there was something behind the witch story."

"It was the applehead dolls."

"So? My own granny made applehead dolls," I say. "It must have been the same around here? So, what else was it? She told me there'd been an anonymous tip."

He looks away from me and then back and says, "There was. It was from a burner phone so we never knew who the call came from.

It happened right after Molly was taken. They said Susan was doing some kind of old-timey ritual with the girls. Taking them and sacrificing them in the woods. They said Sheriff Kerridge had been covering up for her."

"Why would you believe that?"

"Well, I'm not saying I did. But I had to look into it. At that point? We couldn't ignore anything. We couldn't afford to. And Susan and Donald Kerridge *had* always been close. They grew up together. Their mamas were best friends, and the two of them were thick as thieves. Everyone knew it."

"But you don't know who made the call?"

"No," he says. "It came into the dispatch. It sounded like a man's voice, but it was raspy. We couldn't be sure."

"But you investigated Susan."

"Yes."

"And found nothing?"

He nods.

"What about Rebecca Ziegler? Deena Drake?"

"I have a hard time picturing Rebecca stealing little girls."

"She was present at every single kidnapping," I say.

"True but—"

"I think you're blind to this community, Sheriff. Blind to what's happening under your nose."

Red blotches form on his cheeks, but he doesn't deny it.

"What about Deena Drake?" I ask. "She was there too. Every single time. The church, the picnic, the Andrewses' house."

But even as I say it, I struggle to believe it. I'd been in her house. Gone through her things. I'd found nothing.

"Sheriff Kerridge checked her car the day Jessica was taken," Jacobs says. "Same as he checked everyone else. And she had an alibi for the day Molly was taken. Dwight Hoyle—"

"Died in a meth lab fire three days ago," I say.

"And whose fault is that?" he throws back.

"But with Lucy gone. If Deena—"

He grimaces and says, "It couldn't be her."

"Why not?"

"Because the night of the Fall Festival, the night Lucy was taken? She was with me."

"Where were you?"

"At my house."

"Your—"

"My house. My wife and I are separated. It's not public knowledge but . . . she's gone to stay with her mom in Florida for a few weeks and—"

I realize I'm staring at him, and I force myself to blink. An affair? With Deena Drake? I try to picture them together and realize it's not so improbable after all. Deena is the kind of woman who makes loneliness look elegant without being needy. Tragic without seeming desperate. And him? I guess I can see the rugged sadness that would have attracted her to him.

"You and Deena are seeing each other," I say out loud. Just to confirm it. He nods.

"And you were together that night. The whole night?"

"Until I got the call about Lucy being taken. So, you have to understand, it wasn't her. It couldn't be."

"Great."

I put my now-empty coffee mug on the table in front of me and massage my temples. I realize I've developed the same tunnel vision as everyone else in this town. Hyper-focusing on a story about a witch and, consequently, the women most likely to play the part. My frustration is almost equivalent to my pain, and I find myself wishing the FBI would hurry up and get here. Not that they did much good before.

"You feel like you're chasing your own tail," Jacobs says with a softness I've not heard from him before, and I can understand even better what Deena must see in him.

I groan and make myself stand. He gets to his feet too, obviously receiving the message that I want to be alone.

"Whoever took those girls is almost certainly still in town," I say.

"They're almost certainly the person who shot me this morning. And, yes, I may have gotten myself too involved in this thing and I may be mostly chasing my own tail. But I have promises to keep."

"And miles to go before you sleep," he says, so softly I almost don't hear him.

I notice again the dark circles under his eyes, the hollowness of his cheeks. And I remember that I share them. What had begun as a way for me to make enough money to get my watch out of hock, a way for me to put a nice mountain kid's mind to rest with the knowledge that he'd done the best he could, a way for me to visit Appalachia without actually going home, had turned into something more. Something deeper.

"Stay out of trouble," he says, and leaves.

I take my mug to the sink and rinse it out before heading to the bathroom and standing in the shower, breathing the steam until the water starts to go cold. I get out and wrap a towel around my head, then slap some gauze on my side and my shin. I dress and slide my gun into the holster and pour myself a tall glass of tepid water and drink it all down. I find the bottle of whiskey that Greg Andrews brought over and I drink some of that too. I dress and then go back to bathroom and use the tiny hair dryer Max has provided to take the rest of the damp out of my hair.

I check my gun one more time, pull on my jacket and my bag with a wince, and open my door to find Mandy Hoyle standing on the porch. She's sporting a newish black eye, and the purple makes the ice blue of her iris almost glow. It's a hard reminder that even though it seems like eons have passed since the last time I saw her, it's only been a couple of days. Plenty of time for Tommy to give her a new shiner before borrowing her car on the day the factory exploded.

"Mandy . . ."

She sniffs and says, "I wanted to give this back to you . . ."

She opens a big tote bag that's hanging at her hip, wrestles something out of it, and holds it toward me. It's Max's casebook.

# THIRTY-EIGHT

I STAND ASIDE AND LET her in and, once again, I'm stunned by how slight she is. How fragile-seeming and otherworldly. And I'm reminded of the opposite when she turns again to face me. How resilient she is, how strong.

"It was Tommy," I guess. "He's the one who broke in."

She nods. "I found it this morning."

I take the book from her, open the door, invite her inside. She follows reluctantly, and I go about making coffee. When the pot's sputtering, I open the book on the countertop.

"The book and this box," she says, taking my gun case out and putting it on the counter.

I smile at the case, run my fingers over it, over the place where I know Leo's words are carved on the inside.

"Is it worth a lot?" Mandy asks.

"Yeah," I say. "More than I'd realized."

I put out a basket of Shiloh's cookies. They're a little stale now but still delicious. She doesn't take one.

"The truck's been acting up," she says. "So Tommy took my car to the factory the other day. The sheriff's station has taken it for evidence and I needed wheels, so I asked a friend to come take a look at it this morning. When he did, he found this stuff under the seat. I'd guess Tommy took the box to sell but just hadn't found a buyer yet. With the scrapbook, I don't know why he took it. I went to the hospital and asked him today. He said he was going to give it to me. He said maybe I'd see something in there that would help find Jessica. Who knows with Tommy. He can be thoughtful sometimes. Kind, even."

"I know," I say. No woman stays with a man who is bad every moment of every day. They always stay for the good moments that happen in between. They bask in the shimmer of dappled sunshine that appears between the storms. They weather everything else.

I think of the Happy Paws Veterinary Clinic, the many black eyes my own mom tried to hide over the years, the smell of iodine as I swabbed it onto her swollen lips. I wonder what my mom is doing now, if she's okay, and dismiss the thought as soon as I have it.

I can't save someone who refuses to be saved while Mandy Hoyle is sitting here in my kitchen asking for help finding her only daughter.

The coffee finishes dripping, and I pour two cups and slide one across the counter to Mandy, who finally settles on a barstool. She adds plenty of milk and sugar and takes a cookie too.

"Did you see anything?" I ask. "In the casebook?"

"I don't think so," she says. "It was hard to look through, at first."

She sighs and turns the pages, one after another, her slender fairy fingers traveling over the photographs and newspaper clippings and the little-kid version of Max's handwriting that gradually turns into the grown version.

She shakes her head.

"I want to find Jessica," she says. "I keep thinking that I should *know* something. I should have a mother's intuition or a dream or a gift from the Lord. Anything. Odette—Tommy's sister—she used to believe in all that. Prophetic dreams. Guardian angels and guiding lights. All that kind of thing. But I never . . . I've always had faith, but, you know, it's hard sometimes. Especially when all I can think about is that morning. The morning Jessica was taken. How tired I was. How guilty I felt and still feel for—"

She sniffs and dabs at her good eye with the pad of her thumb. The tear in the black eye makes its way past the swollen flesh and eventually falls and slaps the countertop. It doesn't make a sound.

"I was so tired and I needed to go to work but they hated it when I brought my kids. It shouldn't have been a problem, really, Jessica was so good—"

"Was this at Ellerd's Diner?"

She shakes her head, says, "No, I couldn't. I couldn't work there when my kids were little because they wouldn't let me bring them and I couldn't afford day care. Jessica was old enough to be in Head Start but the program shut down a couple years before. So, usually, if I could swing it, I'd take them over to Mommy's Day Out."

"Mommy's Day Out?"

"Yeah," she says. "At the churches." She takes a nibble of the cookie and stops. Her teeth are hurting. I've seen it before.

"Like a day care?" I ask.

"Well, sort of. Different churches, on different days, would have a time—usually like ten to twelve—where you could drop your kids off. There was one at Valley Methodist every Tuesday. Another one at First Baptist that was two days a week. And another one at Good Hope. Programs like that are supposed to be for housewives. So they can do shopping or whatever, but . . ."

"But you used the time to work."

"Yes. Whatever I could pick up. Cleaning houses mostly. Though Tommy didn't like that. He never liked me cleaning, but what else was I supposed to do? And he was taking building work whenever someone offered. You'd never think it to look at him, but he can build anything. He can just picture it and get ahold of some wood and next thing you know . . . there it is. When we were in high school, he would build these haunted houses."

"Whole houses?"

"Well, no," she says, a faint blush in her cheeks. "There's a lot of old, abandoned homesteads around here. He would use those as the skeleton, put a maze inside, and fill it up with all kinds of things. Ghosts and creepy noises and whatever. Every year a different one. It cost five dollars to get in but it was worth it. I reckon he made a killing every year. That's how I really met him. He was two years ahead of me in school and in a totally different crowd. I was the same year as his sister, Odette, and I wanted to go one year and asked if she would take me. She didn't want to, at first. I think it was sort of embarrassing for her, and she was the sensitive type. Didn't like being startled, you know. Actually—"

She opens the casebook and flips through the pages until she gets to a newspaper clipping about Jessica—the anniversary of the day she was taken. Within the clipping is a photo of Jessica, standing in a park in a white dress and, beside her, a beautiful young woman.

"That's Odette," Mandy says, putting her fingertip beside the young woman's face. The caption under the photo says that the picture was snapped at an Easter-egg hunt hosted by the newspaper the year before Jessica was taken. I remember that Odette probably died not long after this and my gaze shifts between her and Jessica, a sense of revelation sliding through my nerves.

I'd let myself think that Jessica only looked like Mandy, and the resemblance *was* uncanny. But Odette was Tommy's sister, and now I could see his features in her. In both of them. That sharp bone structure. That sly smile. If you'd told me that Jessica was Odette's daughter or little sister, I'd have believed you.

"But it was amazing," Mandy says, still on the topic of the haunted house.

"I was terrified! Honestly, I just about peed my pants and tried to run back out and instead I ran straight into Tommy. Dressed up as the grim reaper. I didn't even recognize him under all those layers of fabric. I found out later he'd dyed a bunch of old grain sacks black and stapled them together into a cloak. You'd think it would've looked terrible but . . ."

She seems to realize she's been rambling and looks up at me again, an apologetic smile on her mouth.

She says, "I hate how much I love him."

I don't know what to say. Don't know how to explain to her that I watched my own mother wrestle with the very same feeling. But she doesn't need me to help carry this conversation. It's one she probably has by herself every day.

She says, "I wish I could go back. Tell myself not to go that night, not to agree to a date with him, not to get in the back of his truck that night. But, honestly, I wouldn't listen to anyone. Everyone tried to tell me. Even Odette, his own sister. But I wouldn't have any of it. And still . . . I can't even say I fully regret it. I have my boys, don't I? And they're the best boys a mama could ask for, despite his blood in their veins. And I hope . . . I *hope* that my girl will come back to me. I heard the FBI is on their way."

"Yes," I say. "They should be here today."

She nods.

"Hopefully they'll do better this time," she says.

"Yes," I say. "Hopefully so."

"Oh—" Mandy says with a start, and I follow her gaze to the kitchen clock.

"I have to go! I'll be late for work. Please tell Max I'm sorry about Tommy taking his book."

I nod and watch her drain the last of her coffee, get her purse, and march toward the door.

"Thanks for the coffee," she says. "And, thank you for listening."

She heads out the door, and I go onto the porch and watch as she climbs into Tommy's truck and eases it around and back down the driveway. I think about Tommy Hoyle. His bad attitude and the bruises he left on Mandy. I think about that photo, hanging in the Hoyle house, of his family before Jessica was taken and I think about the donation money Tommy took to hire a PI that never materialized.

I think about his pitiful pleas for help in the factory and the fact that now he was resting in a hospital bed thanks only to my decent nature. I think about the way he'd brushed right past me the day I visited his house. Muttering about me as if I weren't even there and spitting gravel behind his truck, almost hitting Honey.

"Well," I say, grabbing my keys and my bag. "He can't brush me off now."

# THIRTY-NINE

THE QUARTZ CREEK HOSPITAL is a squat, redbrick, single-story building in the middle of a parking lot riddled with cracked asphalt. I stand aside on my way in to let an ambulance pull into the ER unloading zone and then I head through the front doors. I have avoided hospitals most of my life and even now I think I'd rather be out combing the woods with the sheriff's department than padding down the pale green tile to Tommy Hoyle's room.

"What are you doing here?" a voice asks, and I turn to find Kathleen Jacobs coming around the desk of the nurses' station to greet me.

"I could ask you the same question," I say. "Don't you work nights?"

"Ordinarily, yes. But lately I feel like all I ever do is come here. Barely know my nights from my days now."

"I'm here to talk to Tommy Hoyle," I say.

"Well, we're not supposed to let anyone in," she says. "Outside of family. He's in pretty bad shape."

"Is he conscious?"

"He should be. He's heavily medicated and he's been in and out, but he's been awake today asking for this and that. But really, I can't let you in there. Police orders, and not just Cole. The DEA is coming to interview him and investigate the lab."

"Come on, Kathleen," I say. "I need to talk to him."

She looks toward the door of what I can only assume is Tommy's room and purses her lips, thinking.

I catch her gaze when she looks back and say, "Whoever took Olivia and Jessica, whoever killed Molly, is still out there. And now they have Lucy Evers. He might know something. I have to talk to him."

She sighs through her nose and then gives a tiny nod and ushers me into the room. I'm surprised to find that it's private but, then again, I wouldn't want to put anyone in with Tommy Hoyle either.

"Ten minutes," she says. "And then Teresa's going to be coming around to check vitals. Please don't get me fired."

I nod and check my phone for the time. She edges out of the room and I walk to the foot of Tommy's bed. He's lying with one hand cuffed to the bed rail and his eyes shut. There are bandages on his left arm, disappearing into his hospital gown. Bandages on his left temple and over the left side of his freshly shaved head. There's an oxygen tube stuck in his nose and an IV bag hanging over his bed and all I can think, as I stare at him, is how much this is going to cost Mandy.

"Tommy," I say, nudging him and not bothering to be gentle.

His eyelids flutter.

"Tommy," I say again. "Wake up."

"Huh—" he says as he opens his eyes and squints at me. "Who are you?"

I move around to the side of the bed and pull the chair up next to him, check my phone again for the time.

"I'm the person who pulled your sorry ass out of that meth lab."

"Oh my God," he says. His syllables are mushy, his voice distant. "Oh my God, you're that PI. I told Mandy not to talk to you. I always said a PI was a waste of fucking money. I told Dwight about you. Told him you were going around. Asking questions."

"You talked to Dwight?"

"Yeah . . ." he whines.

"Tommy, did Dwight ever tell you something about seeing a scarecrow at the Andrews house?"

"What?"

"A scarecrow? Did he see a scarecrow at the Andrews house?"

He squints at me like I'm the one who should be doped up and chained to a bed.

"What the hell are you talking about?"

I take a deep breath. Change tack.

"Tommy, they used to say that you took Jessica. Do you remember that?"

He squints at me again, his head coming off the pillow. Then he grimaces and his head falls back. His eyes close tight, but he says, "Nothing but a bunch of fucking rumors. That's all it ever was. Ugly talk. I'd never hurt my baby girl. I'd never hurt her. I told them. I told them then. It was that witch."

"What witch?" I ask. "Who is the witch?"

"What?" he asks. "Witch what?"

The last word turns into a moan and then a high whine.

"The witch," I say. "The Witch of Quartz Creek."

He squints his eyes shut, and tears squeeze out of them and drip down his cheeks.

"She took my pretty baby. My pretty Odette."

"No," I say. "Jessica. She took Jessica. Your daughter."

He shakes his head, eyes still closed, and whispers, "Odette."

I remember the story Mandy told me. How Odette died young. Drank herself to death. How she had tried to warn Mandy away from Tommy. How she hadn't wanted to go to Tommy's haunted house. I imagine Tommy in the maze of rooms he'd built, covered in tattered black fabric, hands grabbing at the girls who paid to walk through and scream at the make-believe horror.

"Tell me about Odette," I go along with him. "Who took her?"

"That witch," he says. "Like I said. She would go see that old witch in the woods. Tell her all kinds of things. Ugly stories. Ugly. Saying I hurt her. Saying I . . . No, I loved Odette. I would never hurt her. I loved her. I loved her more than the world."

"And what happened?"

"Odette told the witch. I know she did. And the witch told the sheriff."

"Jacobs?" I ask. My heart is thumping.

He shakes his head, violently, then seems to regret the movement, and grimaces. He screws up his face some more, and a fresh batch of tears slide down his cheeks.

"Kerridge?" I ask. "Was it Sheriff Kerridge?"

"Yes," he blubbers. "He told me not to touch her. Told me he was sick of men like me. Men . . . like me . . . I *loved* her. I was *scared* of how much I loved her."

He grimaces again, the tears streaming.

"Kerridge asked her questions, but she was a good girl. Wouldn't say nothing bad about me. A good girl. Always went to church, did Odette. Always said her prayers. Every night. Never said a word. Only to the witch. That . . . witch."

"Are you the one who made the anonymous call? The one who pointed at Susan?"

"What? Anony—what?"

"Did you call the sheriff's office from a burner phone, after Molly Andrews was taken, and tell them that the kidnapper was Susan McKinney?"

I look at my phone. Time is running out.

"What? No. No, I told them it was that witch the whole time. Right from the start. I always said that witch took my girl from me. Just like she took Odette. Just like my pretty baby. But that sheriff wouldn't do shit. He hated us Hoyles. He thought we were trash. He saw Odette in her trailer. The day she died, he saw her. And he said it was my fault she drank like she did. He said he would kill me. I'm glad he's dead. I'm glad. Him and that witch. They took my girl. My pretty baby."

He starts to drift off again, talking in circles. I look at the phone one more time and make a break for it, waving to Kathleen as I head back down the hall. I try to tell myself it's the sickly fluorescent lights or the pale green walls or the orange tile floor that's making my stomach roil.

But as I break into the cold October air, I still have an overwhelming urge to be sick.

Because if I understand it right, Odette Hoyle told Susan McKinney that her brother had been abusing her. Susan tried to help her. And maybe, if that's the case, Sheriff Kerridge helped Susan cover up at least one kidnapping.

# FORTY

ON THE WAY BACK to the cabin, I call AJ.

"I think you need to try and get a warrant for Susan McKinney's property."

"That little cabin?" he asks. His voice is muddied, and he cuts out, so I only hear pieces of the next bit. "Jacobs said—FB—so I'm—road and—"

I try to tell him what I've learned from Tommy, but the phone cuts off. Instead, I text the most abbreviated possible message along with a question about whether Susan owns any other buildings on the mountain. I think about how the combined force of the FBI and the local sheriff's station would be better equipped than me to go combing through the woods around Susan's house, but I also wonder what they might have missed ten years ago.

I drive back to Max's farm. I know Susan said there are several paths to her cabin through the woods, but I only know the one. Through Max's field, down the gorge, through the stone circle, and up the hill. On the way, I think about the moments I've spent in Susan's cabin. The way I've grown to like her. The way she reminds me, subconsciously, of my own granny. The way she handed me warm tea for comfort and read my fortune and always pointed me in any direction but her own. The way she appeared as if from nowhere, startling me, looking right through me. The way her wrist was scratched. The way she hadn't been in her cabin this morning when I was getting shot at.

By the time I pull onto the Andrews property my hands are shaking with anger and frustration, but it all turns to cold, sweating panic when I see Shiloh sitting on my front porch, crying.

I park and jump out of the car and I'm standing next to her before I've even registered my movement.

"What happened?" I ask. "Did they find her?"

She wipes her nose and eyes on the sleeve of her shirt and looks up at me.

"They found a shoe," she says.

My heart takes a big swan dive into my belly.

"Is it—"

She shakes her head.

"No," she says, a bitter smile twisting her mouth. "It was a little pink shoe with lights in the heels. They found it out on one of the trails behind the church and they brought it to me and all I could think was why hadn't I ever bought Lucy shoes like that?"

Like the rest of her, Shiloh's tears are big and full. They roll down her cheeks, and she puts her hands up to her face.

"I made her a cake," she says. "This morning I made her a cake. Lemon raspberry. For when she comes back. But then . . . I saw the shoe and . . . I just . . ."

"Oh . . . Oh, I'm so sorry, Shiloh."

She shudders with crying and then scrapes at her face with her thumbs and looks at me.

"I didn't know where else to go," she says. "There are reporters at the bakery, my home, even my parents' house! I had to get away and I . . . I came here."

"Come on," I say. "Come on, let's get you inside."

She follows me in and I lead her to the couch where I'd been sitting, listening to Sheriff Jacobs, only that morning. I pull a blanket from the other end of the couch and put it over her, go to the coffee maker, and flick it on. I look at my phone and see a text from AJ.

*Meeting with FBI now. Working on the warrant.*

I glance at Shiloh, shivering on the couch even under the blanket. I crank up the thermostat and look again at my phone. Wonder how long it will take the FBI to get a warrant to search Susan's place. Wonder where Lucy and Jessica are now. Wonder if I'm wrong about everything. If I'm just chasing my tail again, like Jacobs had said.

"Max texted me this morning," Shiloh says, looking at the cookies. "He said that someone shot at you. Are you okay?"

"Yes," I say. It's more or less true.

"Do you think someone shot at you because you're trying to find the girls?"

"Yes," I say.

"Are you going to stop looking?"

"No," I say.

"Even though you got shot at?"

"Yes."

"Why?"

"It's what I do," I say.

I go back to the kitchen cupboards and take down two mugs, fill them with coffee, add plenty of milk and sugar. I get the plate of cookies I'd set out for Mandy earlier and put the coffee and the sweets down in front of Shiloh.

"Baking is what I do," she says, looking at the cookies. "It's what I've always done when I was upset or depressed or angry. I'm all of those things now. And more."

"I know."

"I never asked," Shiloh says. "You don't have kids, do you?"

"No," I say.

"Do you think you will?"

"I don't know," I say.

She nods and takes a drink of her coffee. Then, I watch as she absently opens the notebook I left lying on the coffee table, pulls out the folded piece of paper with Olivia's spirals all over it. I watch as she traces a long finger along one spiral and then another. Her hands are shaking.

I look down at my own hands. They are the hands I've always had, and they are also my mother's hands, my granny's hands. They have peeled apples and fired guns and held children and thrown punches and turned the pages of book after book after book.

My hands. My mother's hands. My granny's hands.

Will they become a mother's hands once more? Will I pass them down the line?

I don't tell Shiloh that I was pregnant once. That it was still early. That I was still in the Air Force and that the pregnancy had been an accident. That I wasn't sure what I was going to do. That I'd never really wanted kids. That, even so, I couldn't help picturing the child, the way it would look, a cross between myself and the father. That I cried one night, curled around my belly, trying to know what to do. That one day soon after I saw that positive test, I was escorting a prisoner from one base to another. Routine. That we came under fire. That the driver was hit. That the vehicle tumbled off the road, flipping over and over. That I woke up in the hospital and my choice had been taken from me with a single bullet.

That Leo had been there, had taken my hand, and had held me while I cried and told him about the pregnancy. How we felt the loss together. A choice we never got to make. A discussion we never got to have. Would we ever have it again?

"Do you think you'll have children?" she'd asked.

"I don't know," I repeat.

I look back at Shiloh, and she holds my gaze for a long, long moment before giving me a gentle nod.

"Where did this come from?" she asks, holding up the paper full of spirals.

"Olivia Jacobs," I say. "She's drawn them ever since her kidnapping."

"Do you know what they are?" she asks.

"No. Nicole brought her around . . . Oh my God, was it only last night? Anyway, Nicole brought her and I asked her a few questions. She drew those—she's been drawing them for years—and held the paper up to her face. But . . . no, I don't know what it means."

I'm trying to decide whether to tell her how Olivia reacted to my question about the witch story when my phone buzzes. It's AJ.

"What's up?" I ask, stepping outside and onto the porch.

After the warmth of the cabin, the cold air hits hard, and I cough and sputter into the phone.

"You okay?" he asks. "You sound terrible."

My mind swirls. My chest aches. A cough tries to fight its way up my throat, but I suppress it.

"Yeah."

"We got toxicology back," he says. "On Molly Andrews."

"Okay?"

"You know Doc Jenkins said there was evidence of damage to her internal organs? It looks like something called grayanotoxin."

"Grana—what?"

"It's a plant toxin. It's found in Mediterranean rhododendrons, but around here it's found in higher quantities in mountain laurel. Looks like it was either in honey or tea."

"Is it a lethal poison?"

"In high enough quantities it can be," he says. "But it's used recreationally for its hallucinogenic properties, apparently. The side effects can be pretty severe, though. Nausea, vomiting, sweating, even seizures."

"Shit," I say. Thinking about the tea I drank in Susan's house only this morning. The warm feeling that swam through my body. The sleepiness I'd felt as she told me the story.

"You've got to get them out here," I say. "You've got to get the cops on the mountain. I don't know where they are but—"

"I'm working on it," he says. "We should be there soon."

"How soon is soon?"

"Well—" And then I hear another voice. A woman with a DC accent telling everyone it's time for a briefing. There's a dog barking. A rush of other voices.

"I gotta go," AJ says. "But we're on the way. Just stay where you are."

"Sure," I say.

He hangs up, and I look through the window back at the cabin. Shiloh is still sitting there, wrapped up in her blanket, holding her coffee in one hand and the page of spirals in the other. I take a deep inhalation of breath and force myself not to cough as I breathe out.

If anyone has the ability to use this mountain's plants for harm, it's Susan McKinney. But why drug Molly? And why take Molly at all? Why Olivia *or* Molly? And why Lucy now? If the whole scheme was to take Jessica away from an abusive father, then why take the other two girls? Was it really part of some ritual?

"Okay," I whisper to myself. "They're on their way. It's okay."

I remind myself that the real cops have more means of getting these answers than I do. More means of finding Jessica and Lucy than I do. They're on their way. And they'll handle it, I tell myself.

And then I see the silhouette of a man coming up over the ridge and toward the cabin. I realize, as he shambles toward me with his hands in his pockets, that it's Max Andrews.

I walk off the porch and into the field, meeting him halfway.

"You okay?" I ask.

"Yeah," he says. His eyes are red-rimmed, though. He looks even paler and thinner than he did at the start of the week.

"I went down to see Susan," he says.

"You . . . what? What did she say?"

"I wanted to talk to her about Molly. I just . . . I didn't know who else to talk to. Sometimes, Susan is good like that. She listens."

"Yeah," I say. "So . . . was she helpful?"

He shakes his head.

"She didn't have time," he said. "She was leaving."

"Leaving?"

"Yeah, she was saying something about getting them out of there before it was too late."

"Getting who out?"

"I don't know," he says. "I kind of walked up on her and she was muttering to herself."

"Do you know where she was going?"

"No."

"Was she still in the cabin when you left?"

"No, she was leaving when I got there. She was carrying this big heavy basket, and her hair was all wrapped up in a scarf. She followed me off the porch and then waved me goodbye."

"Shit," I hiss, already sprinting back to Honey, wrangling my keys out of my pocket.

I slide behind the wheel and rev the engine. Of all the cars Susan has access to, mine and Max's are probably closest. But given Susan's talent for town gossip, she must know there's always the chance that AJ will be here. So, the next closest would be Deena's. Would it even seem out of the ordinary for her to suddenly appear on Deena's property, to ask for a ride to the nearest town or the nearest bus station or the nearest airport?

On the road to Deena Drake's house, I call AJ.

"Annie?" he says, though his voice is garbled and cutting out. "Ann— we're—the warrant—as soon as—"

"AJ, you're cutting out. If you can hear me—"

But the call dies. I phone him back and get his voicemail and leave him a message. I tell him where I'm going, what I'm doing.

Honey's tires squeal as I pull from the highway onto Lilac Overlook Lane. The scent of the mountains pours in. The cold air burns my lungs.

Leo had called me a crow.

Susan had called me a knight.

In the end, I'm just a girl from the hills with a stubborn streak and a bleeding heart I wear on my sleeve. I am not big or strong. I'm not a crack shot or a genius. But I will do everything I can for Shiloh, and Max, and Mandy, and Olivia, and Quartz Creek itself.

And I will fight like a dog for the truth. Even if it kills me.

# FORTY-ONE

I PULL TO THE TOP of the hill and stop. There are two cars in the driveway. The one farther back, a newer-model gray Buick, I recognize as the Zieglers' car. It sits empty. I press my hand to the hood and find it still warm.

"What are the Zieglers doing here?" I mutter.

Deena's Range Rover is parked in front of it. I approach, my hand around the back of my jeans on the grip of my gun. There's no one behind the wheel, no one in the passenger seat. I look in the backseat and find a couple of decent-sized travel bags ready to go.

The mountaintop is nearly silent. Not even a breeze.

I leave Honey and walk toward the front of the house. My footsteps on the gravel path crunch in a way that feels too loud.

The front door is ajar, and I remember how Deena had left it unlocked the day I visited. I nudge it open, and my teeth bang together as I suppress a gasp at the sight of Bob Ziegler, lying on the floor in a pool of blood. He wheezes and stares at the ceiling, clasping one of his big palms to his side.

"Shit," I whisper, getting to my knees at his side.

"Bob? Bob? Can you hear me?"

He turns his head toward me, eyes wide, and stares.

"G-Gore? Am I hit?"

"Yes," I breathe. "Yes. You're hit."

I move his hand just enough to inspect the wound, but as soon as I take off the pressure, blood gushes out.

"She got me," he gurgles. "She got me. I didn't even see . . . all these years."

The pink in his cheeks is gone, replaced by a sweaty buttermilk color.

"You're gonna make it," I say to him. "But you have to keep holding it. Can you keep holding it?"

"Yes sir," he whispers, but he's drifting off.

"Goddamnit," I breathe. I yank at his belt buckle and thank heaven for slick wool and well-oiled leather as I jostle his belt out of his suit pants and back around his middle. I whip off my sweatshirt and wad it up tight, then secure it over the wound with the belt.

"Help is coming," I tell him as his eyelids flutter. "Hold on, Bob. Help is coming."

I pull my phone out. No service. I try 911, just in case, and get nothing. I type a text to AJ and send it anyway. I stand and look around for a landline. Try to remember if there was one in the kitchen.

"She's a devil," he says. "She's a devil."

"Bob, listen, I—"

But there's a scream. Long and high and shrill as only little girls make.

*Lucy.*

I wipe Bob's blood on my jeans and pull my gun. Rushing up the stairs, trying to find some balance between speed and silence and achieving neither, I sweep the second-story rooms, glad I've already been in here once and know the general layout. Guest bedroom. Empty. Second guest bedroom. Empty. Bathroom. Empty.

Which leaves only Deena's room.

I pause outside it. Take a breath. Listen.

A woman's voice is talking, but low enough that I can't make out the words. A little girl cries. Not screaming this time but weeping. The other voice snaps, and the weeping gets louder. Louder.

"I want my mommy . . ." the little girl wails.

I spin around the doorway and find . . . nothing. An empty room. An empty bed. The door to the closet hanging open. The door to the bathroom also open. Empty. There is no one here.

I wait. Listen.

"Just sit still," Deena's voice says. "Sit still and it'll be okay."

My breath catches in my throat. The sound is coming from behind the tapestry to the left of the bed. I pause. Look at the window and remember how I'd felt so sure that there was something off. Something that didn't fit.

Now I understood. Deena's room was longer in reality than it appeared from within. Standing down in the yard, looking up at the house, the window had been in the middle of the wall, but here, from within, the window was nearly at the edge.

A second room. A panic room. Hidden.

"It'll be okay," Deena says again. "If you just listen and mind. Sit still now."

And I realize I had been wrong. Deena had hidden those girls in this house the whole time. Right under the nose of everyone who visited, everyone who attended her Christmas parties and sang beside her piano, everyone who admired her roses and complimented her décor. Right under the nose of everyone. Including me.

I BREATHE IN A long, silent breath and feel a tickle in my chest that I can't afford. I can't afford the noise, the distraction. I swallow, desperately, in an effort to shut the cough down, and, finally, get it under control.

Again, I ready my gun and nudge the tapestry aside with my foot. Behind it is a thick steel door, the front of it dressed to look exactly like the wattle and daub in the rest of the room. It is hanging open.

I tiptoe inside. This is a panic room, as I thought. But it's been kitted out like a nursery. Two twin beds against the wall, each under a skylight, each adorned with its own handwoven wool blanket. One red, one blue. There are two desks and two chests and two baskets of antique wooden toys and a tray with a carafe of water and a plastic cup and, on the far-thest side of the long room, Deena Drake, sitting, with Lucy Evers at her feet. Deena is sitting very awkwardly. And then the penny drops.

Deena Drake is tied to a chair.

I move toward her.

"Deena," I say. "What—"

And then there is pain. Nothing but pain. It spreads through my skull, a sickening heat. I spin around but I'm already falling.

My gun goes off, but I feel sure I hit nothing. I see a glint of silver. A candlestick. Plaster from the ceiling falls like snow into the pale blond hair of a young woman. Her delicate feylike features and ice blue eyes are unmistakable.

"Jessica?" I say.

She smiles at me.

It's the last thing I see.

# FORTY-TWO

I'M SITTING ON THE porch. I cannot see the driveway or the forest or the holler. I can only see fog. A silver mist as thick as stew. It swirls only feet from my vision.

My granny is sitting behind me, and I can hear the creak of her rocker. I remember the way her ankles were so thick. The way her hands were so warm. The way she chuckled deep in her chest, her bosom bouncing, when she laughed. I don't see any of it now. I only hear her rocker. I can't turn my head. I am stuck, trapped in a body I cannot control.

"Did you find her?" she asks. "The little girl?"

"Yes," I say. "But, by the time I did, she had turned into a monster."

My granny goes on rocking, and now I can hear the knife in her hand. She is peeling an apple. I hear the gritty rip of skin from flesh. The undoing of a thing.

"Every apple has a little poison inside it," she says.

"I know," I say.

I wish I could turn to her. I wish I could move.

I can't.

Pain blooms in my skull and wraps around my face like icy fingers. It wraps around my eyes and tugs at my mouth. My teeth are exploding and my tongue is burning.

I want to bury my face in my hands but I can't. I want to shut my eyes against the pain but I can't.

The fog swirls and swirls again and there is a little girl standing in the road. She's wearing dirty jeans and a T-shirt. She is me.

She is holding a gun. She raises it. Aims.

*BANG!*

"Miss Gore—" a voice says.

I open my eyes. I'm coughing.

"Miss Gore?"

The voice is Deena Drake. I blink, focus. Lucy is sitting beside me. She has a cup in her hands. My face and hair are wet. My head is throbbing. I sit up and roll over and vomit onto the thick pile carpet. The room spins. I feel for my gun. It's gone.

"She took it," Deena says.

"Jessica," I breathe.

"Yes," Deena says. She sighs. Her hands are still tied to the chair. They are tied with a blue velvet sash. Her ankles are tied with a thin cord. It looks like a curtain cord, small, braided silk. I reach into my back pocket, feel for my phone. It, too, is gone.

"She took that as well," Deena says. There's a pause and then she says, "You have blood all over your shirt."

I look down.

"It's Bob's," I say. "He was downstairs. What was he doing here?"

She shakes her head.

"He was coming to collect some cookies I'd made for the search party. Jessica killed him?"

"Probably."

I lean against the chest of drawers and look up at her.

"You," I say, my voice gravel and acid. "You took the girls."

"Jessica, Olivia, Molly," she says. "Yes."

Then she asks, "Do you think you could untie me? Lucy tried but . . ."

"No offense," I say. "But—well, some offense, actually—you're a kidnapper who's been holding two children in captivity for the last ten years. I don't trust you."

I get to my feet and stumble around the room. There are no windows here. Only the skylights. The door is shut and locked. It's made of heavy steel. I run my fingers over the seams, uselessly.

I look back at Lucy. She's huddled on the blue bed, her knees tucked under her chin, watching me with big brown eyes.

"But you didn't take Lucy?" I ask Deena.

She shakes her head.

"That was Jessica," she says.

"Why . . . Jesus Christ, Deena, what the hell did you do?"

She lets out a breath so heavy-sounding it seems like she's been holding it the better part of a decade.

"I wanted children," she says.

"Lots of people want children," I say.

But it's as if she doesn't hear me. Or doesn't want to. As if she's been waiting all these years to unburden herself, she simply starts talking.

"I wanted them desperately. And the whole time that Hoyle woman was bringing her children in this house."

"Mandy?" I say, feeling my way around the edges of the room for any-place that might have some give. The place where the door had been feels like a solid wall. Completely sealed.

"What was Mandy doing here?" I ask, probing for cracks and finding nothing.

"She cleaned for me," Deena says. "She used to come twice a week, and she'd bring Jessica and that little toddler boy with her. Then I saw she had another one on the way. Why? Why does God give babies to people who don't even *want them*? And she certainly couldn't take *care* of them. You should've seen the state of Jessica. Half the time, her hair was a tangled mess. Rats nest."

I sigh and rub my palms over my face, then realize they are still sticky with Bob's blood.

"Finally, I got pregnant," she says. "Finally. After so many years of trying. So many tears and so many tests in the trash. I was in my twelfth week when Harvey died. I hadn't even really started to show. The night he died, I cried so hard I thought it would kill me. I thought my heart would shatter from the pain. And then . . . it got so much worse."

I stop my searching and turn to look at her. Her eyes are glazed over, a million miles away.

"I delivered twins that night. On the bathroom floor. They were so tiny. Like two little perfect plums. Purple and shiny."

Her breath catches, and I watch her struggle. On the bed, Lucy is staring at me.

"Deena—" I say.

"I buried them in the rose garden. And, three days later, I buried Harvey. And every day after that for two weeks, I would go into the library and sit in his chair and take out his gun and look at it."

She stops herself, shakes her head.

"But I couldn't . . . I wasn't strong enough. Brave enough. Instead, one morning, I went for a walk in the forest and found myself standing on the porch of Susan McKinney's cabin. I'd heard about her from Mandy. I thought, perhaps, she could help me somehow. Give me something that would let me sleep for good."

I could picture the scene as Deena spoke. The beautiful grieving widow standing, hopeless, on the doorstep of a witch. No better than a beggar woman in the worst winter of her life. Willing to do anything, give anything, to make the pain stop.

"She gave me tea. Told me it would take time. That's what she said. The same stupid, worthless platitudes as everyone else. She gave me a book. Told me that perhaps something in it would help me find peace in the thing I could not have."

She frowns. The memory looks so bitter that, for a moment, I think Deena Drake might spit on the floor. Instead, she sniffs and keeps going.

"Did it?" I ask. "Did it help?"

"It was a book of folklore," Deena says. "Old superstitions. But it told of an old ritual. Making poppets to represent the ones you have lost, carrying them with you until the loss is less painful."

"And the poppets—"

"Were applehead dolls, yes. And so I made two of them. One for each of my baby girls."

I go back to searching the room. There's a small closet full of blue and red dresses, some velvet, some cotton, some silk, some fine linen, all trimmed in lace. They hang above a rack of little satin slippers. Doll clothes, but woman-sized. I shiver and close the door.

I am exhausted. My whole body hurts. And now I am trapped in a room with one psychopath while another waits outside the door getting ready to do who knows what. I breathe through my nose, look around.

There is a little bathroom through a doorway. It features a toilet and pedestal sink and small shower. I wash my hands, then wash my mouth out, splash water on my face, come back into the main room.

To the left of the door, there's an oil painting of a white rabbit. I try to take it off the wall and find that it is attached by hinges and that it hides a prize. There's a keypad set into the wall.

"She's changed it," Deena says, still distant but less dreamy. "I already got Lucy to try."

"Let's try again," I say.

Deena tells me the numbers. I punch them in. Nothing happens.

"Christ," I breathe. And when I breathe, I cough. And when I cough my head throbs. I put my fingers to my skull and feel a gooey wetness. I decide to focus on literally anything else. "So you . . . what? You've got the poppets and . . . now what?"

"I had them with me one day when I went to the church. I finished my practice and stood and looked out the window. There was Jessica. She was sitting on the swing set, swinging. All by herself. Her mother was asleep in the car. Honestly. It was disgraceful."

She laughs a little at the memory, and then tears come to her eyes.

"I felt a presence in me," she says. "It told me that the girl should be mine. Was meant to be mine, all along. I walked outside and I asked her if she would like to come with me. She said yes."

I think I might vomit again but I fight the urge and work my way around the room, looking for some other way out, some other weapon, anything I can use. I open the chests and look around. There are wooden tops and the disembodied head of a Lovely Lady Lavender doll. Her eyes shine, bright and violet, at me.

Deena goes on. "She said yes. And so I took her and I left the doll behind. I had made a trade. The magic had worked."

"What about Sheriff Kerridge?" I ask. "Didn't he search your car?"

She nods, gives a little smile at the memory.

"I was so sure he would take her away from me. Instead, he looked straight at her and shut the door. That's when I knew the magic had truly worked. That's when I knew. Later, he came to the house. He told me that Tommy Hoyle had abused his sister and that he'd seen Tommy out with Jessica and the way he'd had his hands on her . . . he knew. He knew he had to protect her. He knew that I should be her rightful mother. He told me that I should wait a few months, then take Jessica and leave town and never come back."

"And you agreed?"

"Yes."

"But that wasn't enough, was it? You made two dolls to replace your twins."

"Yes."

"So, you took Olivia."

"Yes. She was so beautiful but . . . she was defective, wasn't she? All wrong. I'd had no idea. Not until I brought her back here and discovered that she was broken."

I dig through the chest. I find nothing that could be used as a weapon. Why didn't people give girls wooden swords? Baseball bats? Golf clubs?

"I had a vision," Deena continues. "Of sitting at my piano and playing while my little girls sang along." She laughs. "It's all I wanted."

"And Olivia doesn't sing along," I say.

"No," she says. "I thought, perhaps, she was merely highly strung. I learned from the book how to make tea that drops your inhibition. Lets you see and feel things that you normally cannot see or feel."

"The mountain laurel plant," I say.

"Yes. But it didn't do any good. Olivia only cried and screamed. She never spoke or sang. No matter what we tried. Jessica was . . . especially violent."

I think about the bruises they'd found on Olivia's arms and legs when she was returned. I feel sick again, but I get to my feet and continue working through the room. I find gauzy nightgowns and frilly dresses and silky underthings in the drawers; nothing else. There's a silver tray holding a wooden hairbrush with boar bristles and scented oils of various kinds, all in useless plastic bottles. There's not even a nail file.

"Sheriff Kerridge came to see me. He knew, of course, that I'd taken her. He said he'd made a terrible mistake. That we both had. That we'd have to tell the truth and face the consequences. I couldn't have that. Even if Olivia was broken, I would simply have to replace her. And I couldn't do that if Kerridge told everyone the truth."

I think about Susan McKinney's relationship with Kerridge. How she found him dead on his kitchen floor, apparently from a heart attack.

"I went to his house," Deena says. "I brought cake and said that we should talk about it. I knew he had heart problems. It didn't take much. He ate. I didn't. I watched him die and then I left and took the cake with me."

"And Olivia?"

"I took her back," Deena says, defensively. As if that made up for everything. "I didn't think she would ever be able to tell anyone what had happened to her, but . . . just in case."

"You drugged her."

"Yes. And I told her that if she ever said who took her that the Witch of Quartz Creek would come to her house and kill every single person inside it."

"She was only five years old," I say.

She shrugs, lets out a tired breath. She's coming to the end of her story, and she seems tired in the telling. Ready to go wherever it is that she is going next.

"And Molly?" I say, moving into the bathroom.

"Molly was so beautiful," Deena says. "Such a good little girl, so eager to please."

I listen as I unscrew the shower head from its pipe. I lay the shower head down on the toilet tank, then start unscrewing the shower head's riser pipe from the wall. The pipe makes a grating sound as I turn it and, unsure of what Jessica may be able to hear from wherever she is, I go slowly. Very slowly.

"I brought a cookie for Molly the day I took her," Deena says. "And she went right to sleep. I put her in the car and then I started back toward the house to tell Janice goodbye and I saw that man."

"Dwight Hoyle," I say.

"Yes. The plumber. We exchanged pleasantries and he said he was moving his truck and I left, feeling relieved that he hadn't looked in the backseat of my car. But, later that night, he called me. He said he knew what I'd done. He wanted money."

I think about all the stuff in the Hoyle household. The new TV, laptop. The new truck. The fact that they'd not worked real jobs the last ten years and lived, better than they should have been able to, on Dwight's disability.

"I agreed, of course. On the condition that he make a phone call for me."

"Susan McKinney," I say.

"Yes," she says. "He made the anonymous phone call. The police spent time investigating Susan instead of me. And then I started paying him. What choice did I have? At first, it was five hundred a month. Then a thousand. It was all I could afford. I tried to explain to him that most of the money was gone. That my family cut me off when I married Harvey instead of the man they'd picked for me. That Harvey's factory had been dying and that he'd put everything he had into it. Harvey's pension left me with a thousand a month. I went through what was left of the savings, sold my jewelry, my furs. I tried to sell the house, but it was tied up in a land trust. Harvey had been such a conservationist. He'd wanted the home and land to be preserved as hunting grounds, turned into a park of some kind once both of us were gone."

Her voice is wistful, with a tinge of annoyance. I think about the house, the car, the furniture, and the appliances. None of it less than ten years old. I'd seen this kind of thing before in old-money houses where no new money is coming in. The walls crumbling around them as they await the inevitable.

"What about the scarecrow?" I ask Deena.

"The what?"

"The scarecrow that you saw, on the day you took Molly. Why did you make that up?"

"I didn't," Deena says. "That was true. I really was startled by a figure in the distance. A scarecrow in a black cloak."

"Ooof," I say as the pipe finally comes free in my hand.

Lucy wanders into the bathroom and sits on the toilet seat and watches me.

"You're Max's friend," she says.

"That's right," I say. "I'm here to help you."

She nods.

"When the blond lady comes back," I whisper to Lucy, "I want you to go into that linen closet right there, understand? Squeeze really small and hide. Can you do that?"

I point to the tiny cupboard that holds perfect white towels and washcloths on cedar shelves. Lucy nods.

"I'm hungry," she says.

"I know," I say. "We'll get you something good to eat soon. I saw your mama today."

Lucy's eyes light up at the mention of her mother. It breaks my heart. I have to get us out of this.

"She said she made you a cake," I say. "Lemon raspberry."

Lucy grins and claps her hands.

"Remember," I say. "The closet."

She nods again.

In the main room, Deena continues, "He tried to get more out of me but, eventually, I managed to convince him that I was already paying as much as I could. That he would either have to keep taking the thousand a month or turn me in and get nothing. Thankfully, he accepted. He and his wife moved out of town, and each month I withdrew one thousand dollars from the bank and sent it to a post office box in Charlotte."

"But then they moved back," I say, opening the linen closet door so it's ready for Lucy.

"Yes," she says. "And I had the feeling that the longer that man was around his cousin again, the more he might decide to tell the truth. I couldn't have that. I was trying to figure out how I could get close enough to them to . . . Well, I didn't have to, in the end. You took care of that. I had no idea they'd turned the old factory into a drug lab."

There's a little laugh, and I breathe out a long sigh. I've just about had it with Deena's trip down memory lane. I've been on high alert for too long. I'm exhausted, my adrenaline running thin. My head throbs. My vision is hazy. The room spins. I close my eyes, and when I open them, I realize Deena is talking again.

". . . happy, but I worried the girls would become homesick. What could I do? Someday they would be big enough to question their life with me. Maybe even overpower me, run away. So, I gave them the tea and I told them they were sick. That if they went home, they would make their families sick, and that I was the only one who could take care of them. They belonged with me. I simply had to make them see that. And, of course, it worked. They were only four. I knew that, eventually, they would forget all about the family they had before."

I think about Jessica Hoyle. Think about the fact that she wasn't four. Like me, she was undersized, underestimated. She was weeks away from her sixth birthday when she was taken, about to begin school, already reading.

I test the weight of the pipe in my hand. It's awkward and S-shaped, not optimal for whacking. Still, I bang it against my palm a few times. At least the Drakes didn't skimp on fixtures. The pipe is heavy. It'll do.

"But I didn't take Lucy," she says. "She was a gift."

"From Jessica," I say.

"Yes," Deena says. "I think she missed her sister, Molly."

"What happened to Molly?" I ask.

"I don't know," she says. "One day she was here and then . . . you came. And she was gone. Like a bird, she flew away."

Her voice still has that airy, dreamy quality, and I think Deena Drake probably broke in half the day her twins came silent into the world. With her husband already dead, all alone in this house, no one to talk to, she buried one half of herself with her family and lived on like a ghost. Half a person, no sense of right or wrong.

I hear clicking in the room and gesture for Lucy to get into the linen closet. She goes, squatting down deep against the inside corner.

"It's gonna be okay," I whisper. She looks up at me and nods, but there are tears in her eyes. I take a deep breath and close the closet door.

I give my palm another whack with the pipe, then shove it down the back of my jeans, go into the main room, stand behind Deena.

The door opens. Jessica comes back inside. She has my gun.

She is pointing it at Deena and me, erratic, unfocused. She is wearing one of Deena's dresses now instead of the long velvet doll dress with the lace frills. Her hair is pulled away from her face and braided into a plait that hangs most of the way down her back. She looks beautiful. And terrifying.

"Okay," she says. She looks at me. "I wasn't expecting you. I thought for sure once I'd shot you, you'd go to the hospital, leave, die . . . At least you'd stop this foolishness. But, no. You told Deena. You said you wouldn't stop searching. I heard you. And I knew it was true."

"Jessica—" I start.

She points the gun at me and smiles.

"Don't talk to me," she says softly. "It's your fault Molly died."

I must make a face, because Jessica smiles even bigger and waves the gun around like I'm being silly. Like she's talking to a child. I realize this is probably the only way she's been spoken to her entire life.

"Don't you know?" she says, clicking her teeth. *Tsk. Tsk. Tsk.* "I thought you must have figured it out. Molly and I used to sneak out *all the time.* Poor Deena. No clue. Molly, though, she loved Deena. She *believed* Deena. She thought our families had sent us to Deena because we were sick. Deena would let us write letters to our families—which she never sent—and our families would send us letters—which Deena wrote—back. Deena kept all of it in a drawer in her bureau. I found them years ago. But, no matter how many times I tried to tell her, Molly always believed Deena. She was like that. So trusting. She loved Deena. More than she loved me. But then, one day, we were in the kitchen, eating strawberries. We knew Deena would be in the garden the whole afternoon—she always is when she's planting. That's when you came and stood right out there on the front porch and ruined everything. Talking about how sad poor Max was. Oh, poor Max. Whatever happened to poor Molly?"

She laughs.

"Silly," she says. "Silly Molly. She ran away. I had to catch her. Stop her. I couldn't let her ruin what we have, could I? Not when I'm so close . . ."

"Close to what?" I ask.

"Close," she says. "Deena was bored with us."

Deena starts to say something, but Jessica points the gun at her, eyebrows raised like she's daring Deena to say something else. Deena shuts up.

Behind Jessica, a shaft of light widens. The door is opening. Is it a breeze? Is someone there? Does Jessica have an accomplice? My mind races.

She is beautiful, young, intelligent. She's obviously had the run of this place well enough to figure out how to shoot a gun, how to drive a car. For how else could she have kidnapped Lucy? She must have been on the internet, gotten into Deena's computer. Could she have connected with someone? And would someone help her with . . . whatever this plan is? Whatever she's about to do?

"Deena didn't want us anymore," she says, eyes wide with mocking anger. "She'd been drugging us for years. I didn't care. I liked the tea. I liked the dreams. But sometimes I didn't drink mine. I poured it down the drain or gave it to Molly. Then, Deena would take her Ambien and go to sleep and I'd sneak out. Sometimes, I could get Molly to skip her tea and go with me."

"Jessica—" Deena starts again.

Jessica closes the distance between herself and Deena, puts the gun to Deena's forehead.

"I had a plan," she growls. "I had a *plan.* I was going to take Molly and leave. I have your passport. It's not expired yet and I look enough like you to pass, if I cut my hair, dress older. I was going to take her and leave. We could start over somewhere. Somewhere *nice.* I'd been taking cash out of your purse for years. Ten dollars here. Twenty there. A hundred sometimes. All hidden in a little box under the porch."

Jessica looks at me. Her eyes are glassy with tears, but she is seething, her cheeks red.

"Molly left and ruined everything! She betrayed me. She was going to give up *everything.* You know we could see her old house through the telescope in the guest bedroom? We used to watch the lights of her parents' house twinkling. She used to ask me if they would ever find a cure for our sickness. I told her yes, someday, and I meant it. I was going to give her some actual vitamins and tell her they were a new medicine and that now we had to go away together to get more of it. But then she ran away. I had to stop her. And Deena . . . she didn't care about us anymore."

She sneers at Deena. Hisses, "She was screwing that man. Right downstairs on the sofa. He was talking about leaving his wife."

Her face changes, and she seems to transform, doing a fair impression of Cole Jacobs. "Oh Deena, your hands are so soft. I love the way they feel."

And then she adjusts her posture and goes into Deena's voice, "Oh Cole . . . I love the way you touch me. Oh . . . oh . . ."

She looks long at Deena, smirking. Then back to me.

"They were talking about going away, just the two of them. And then what would happen to us?"

"You could've left," I say. "You could've gone back to your family."

She laughs.

"Why would I want that? I *chose* to go with Deena. I got to live in a castle. Like Rapunzel. I didn't have to go to school. I got fancy food and a new mother who didn't cry all the time and no father who . . . No father at all."

"Jessica—"

"Deena was *devoted.*" She looks again at Deena, and her pretty Cupid's bow lips turn into a snarl. "At least she *used to be.* Until that man came along. Until me and Molly didn't look like little girls anymore."

She sighs.

"Everyone gets *old,*" she snarls at Deena. "Even you."

"My darling girl—" Deena starts, and then stops when the barrel of the gun swings toward her face, inches from her temple.

Behind her, the door opens all the way. My heart thuds. While Jessica has her attention focused solely on Deena, I watch.

Silently, Shiloh steps into the room in socked feet. She's holding a .45 Colt at her hip. She takes in the scene. I put my hand on the pipe stuffed in the back of my jeans.

"It's time now," Jessica says. "This is the end."

Jessica points the gun at me, cocks it.

Shiloh levels her gun, trains it on the back of Jessica's head.

I shout, "Shoulder!"

Jessica whips around. Shiloh shoots. I pull the pipe from my jeans.

*BANG!*

I feel the warmth of Jessica's blood splatter my face. Jessica falls to her knees. A bloom of red spreads from her right shoulder. It saturates the pale pink of her borrowed grown-up dress and her white-blond braid.

Angry, eyes wide, grimacing, Jessica switches my gun to her other hand, aims toward Shiloh.

"Mommy!" Lucy cries, running from the bathroom.

Jessica swings the gun around toward Lucy.

I smack Jessica with the pipe, right across the cheek. She goes down, hits the floor with a thud.

I look at Shiloh. Shiloh looks at me.

I pick my gun up from the floor.

Shiloh slides her Colt into the back of her jeans, picks up her daughter, hugs her close to her chest.

"You found her," Shiloh says.

She cries into her little girl's hair.

# FORTY-THREE

H OW ARE YOU?" SHILOH asks.

I shrug. Shrugging hurts.

We're sitting in a hospital room. I have spent the night here. I want to leave as soon as possible. I've already pulled off all the wires that lead to the beeping machines, the liquid delivery machines, the machines that call the nice people in scrubs.

Shiloh has brought me a clean change of clothes and has promised to take me back to the cabin, where Honey is waiting for me. I slip a fresh pair of underwear and a new-washed pair of jeans on under my thin hospital gown.

"I can't tell you how grateful I am," she says as she holds out the T-shirt she brought. It's black and soft and smells like the detergent in Crow Caw Cabin.

"I'm the one who's grateful," I say. "That's a hell of a piece you were packing."

She laughs.

"I can't believe it," I say. "The whole time. If anyone had just shown you Olivia's drawings—"

"I still might not have realized it," she says. "I was so desperate with worry."

I'd left her sitting on the couch in the cabin, looking at Olivia's spirals, while I went tearing off to search for Susan.

"My mom taught me to draw roses the same way," she says. "And I pipe them on cakes just like that."

That was why she'd come to Deena's. She knew Deena was the only one in town with roses that could leave an impression like that.

"The last thing I expected, though," she says, "was to see Jessica Hoyle holding a gun."

"I know," I say.

I grimace as I pull the shirt on over my various wounds and sore places. When my head emerges, AJ is there. He's standing in the doorway in his deputy uniform.

"Hey," he says. "She wants to talk to you."

"Me?"

"If you're up for it."

"Yeah, but . . . why?"

"I think she needs to lay it all at someone's feet and, for whatever reason, yours are the feet she's picked."

I sigh. I think about fate and Max Andrews coming into Roxanne's that morning. About him going to Susan and getting his cards read. About her telling him to find a warrior from another mountain, one who will understand. I think about Mandy and Tommy and that too-familiar muddy holler.

"Okay," I say.

I pull my hair up and look around for an elastic to hold it. They've taken mine. I grunt. Shiloh pulls one from her wrist, holds it out to me. I really would marry this woman. If I ever felt so inclined to marry anyone. If I ever became a whole other person. There are good people in this town, I think. They deserve so much happiness after so much tragedy.

I take the elastic and finish my ponytail.

"Thanks," I say.

"I'll wait for you out front."

"Okay."

I follow AJ out of the room and through the hall.

"I'm surprised Jacobs is letting me talk to her," I say.

"Sheriff Jacobs has put himself on suspension," AJ says as we walk. "So, I'm kind of in charge at the moment."

"Couldn't think of a better man," I say.

AJ snorts. Then he stops short, turns back toward me.

"I'm sorry," he says.

"About what?"

"I wasn't there in time. I'm sorry."

He'd been the first to the scene, after Shiloh. He'd got my call, but it had been so garbled that he couldn't understand any of it. Instead, it was Susan McKinney who'd finally reached him. She'd called from her satellite phone when she came to the top of the mountain to pick rose hips and saw Bob Ziegler lying motionless just beyond the open doorway in a pool of blood. She'd turned and run back into the forest to hide and wait for the cops.

"I'm sorry," he says again.

"Please don't be," I say. "You're not my keeper."

"I know."

"And this is just my job."

"I know."

"Okay."

"Can I make it up to you?" he asks.

"I feel like you already know the answer to that."

I wink at him, or try to. With my injuries and my aching body, I probably just look like I have something in my eye.

Still, he grins and brings a big hand up to squeeze my shoulder. Then, he turns back and leads me to another room and opens the door.

We pass the room where Bob Ziegler rests. I pause just outside it and see Rebecca Ziegler at his bedside, reading her Bible while he sleeps. Rebecca looks up and sees me and raises her hand in a little wave. I wave back.

I'd not believed it when I told him he would make it, but, thankfully, there are better doctors in this town than me.

"Where's Tommy?" I ask, realizing that this is the room he'd been in the day before when I'd questioned him about his sister.

"They moved him to another wing," he says. "In light of his history. With Odette. With Jessica. They didn't want the two of them anywhere near each other."

"This is a knot that's going to take a long time to untangle, I think."

"Yes," he says. "The FBI have started going through everything. Dwight and Elaine's property. Any evidence they can find on Tommy Hoyle's past crimes. Everything that links anyone to Deena Drake. The way she was involved with Jacobs, the way Kerridge helped her ten years ago. I think there's going to be a lot of report writing in my future."

"So much of crime fighting is what happens after the action," I say. "In the end, we spend most of our time just doing paperwork. I suspect that's the real reason Batman wears a mask. Filing reports and logging evidence and giving testimony in court is way less sexy than punching a bunch of guys and disappearing into the shadows. But it's just as heroic."

"You think so?"

"Well, no," I say. "If I could, I'd be Batman. But real-life law enforcement officials tend to take a dim view of masked vigilantism."

He laughs softly, and pauses in the hall and looks at me.

"You did a good job, Annie," he says. "You found the truth."

"Yes," I say. "Not in time for Molly, though."

"But in time for Lucy. In time for Shiloh. In time for Jessica and Mandy. And Max will heal. It'll take time. But at least he won't be stuck in limbo anymore."

I nod. AJ had already found the letters Molly had written to Max over the years. Already made copies of all of them and given them to him. And already Max had read them, with his father at his side, and then put them into the box he kept in his closet.

"He'll heal," AJ says, again. "Thanks to you."

He gives my shoulder a squeeze and we walk a little farther in relative silence, the hospital noises buzzing around us. He stops at another door and says, "You ready?"

"Yes."

Inside, Jessica Hoyle is sitting in a hospital bed. She's wearing a pale blue hospital gown, and the tape from her wound dressing peeks out from above and below the sleeve. She is handcuffed to the bed.

Mandy Hoyle sits beside her. Mandy looks at me when I enter, and her eyes instantly brim with tears. She stands and comes to me and wraps her arms around me and gives me a hug far stronger and tighter than I'd ever have imagined she could manage. It was a mistake, I know, to have ever thought of Mandy as frail or weak. An easy mistake. She has the hands, the arms, the strength, the embrace of a mother.

"You found her," she says. "You said you would."

I look over her shoulder to the young woman sitting on the bed, glaring at us. I know this isn't the reunion Mandy wanted. But it *is* a reunion. It is something. Her daughter is alive. She's here.

"Mandy—" I start, as she pulls out of the embrace. But she shakes her head, a soft sad smile on her mouth. There's not really anything else to say.

"I'm going to go get some coffee while the two of you talk," she says.

She pats my arm and straightens her purse on her shoulder and leaves.

The door shuts behind us. AJ stands against it. I go and sit in the chair beside Jessica. She stares at me the whole time. I rest my hands in my lap and look at her. She looks at me. Her eyes are rimmed in red. She glances at AJ and then back at me.

"You ruined it," she says, finally.

"I know," I say.

"I was a princess," she says. "I was a princess in a castle and soon I was going to leave and have my own life."

"I know."

She sniffs. Her hair is still braided. It coils in a long, white-gold rope over her good shoulder and into her lap.

"I didn't want to kill Molly. I—" She pauses when her voice cracks, then goes on in a whisper. "I loved her. She was my sister. I . . . I was going to take us far away. But . . . as soon as you came, and she heard about Max . . ."

She bows her head, and tears fall into the braid in her lap.

"If she'd gone to Max, she would've told him everything. And Deena would've been arrested and they'd have taken all her beautiful things and her beautiful castle and I'd have had *nothing*. Just like before. She ran away before I could stop her. She got all the way down the mountain. I tried to talk to her. I tried to take her home. She fought me. I never . . . I didn't know she could fight me. She never had before."

Jessica looks back at me, and even though her face is red and swollen from crying, she is still beautiful. Her features are cool and sharp like a diamond.

"I loved her," she says, her voice steady. "I loved Molly."

I nod.

"I tried . . ." She stops and falters, her voice strangled with feeling. "I tried to give her a pretty death. She looked just like a doll. A beautiful dead doll."

"I know," I say.

We sit for a long moment, Jessica staring at her hands.

"Jessica," I say. "Tell me why you took Lucy."

She looks at me again, bites her lips together, and then says, "I . . . I took Lucy because, well, at first, I took her for Deena. I thought a new little dolly would make her interested again. And, I knew if I took Lucy while Deena was with someone else that no one could say it was her who did it. Everyone would have to stop looking at our house."

"You took her car?"

"Yes."

"How did you learn to drive?"

"The internet," she says. "Deena's computer. Easy."

"Okay."

"I dressed in some of Deena's old clothes, a nice coat and hat. I went to the Fall Festival and went around the edge of the woods and there was a little girl just sitting there. I said I was a princess and asked her if she wanted to see a real castle and she said yes and followed me. It was nothing. She got into the car and we drove back to the house. By the time Deena came home in that man's car, I'd given her some of Deena's tea and she was asleep."

Jessica sighs, looks away again.

"I thought Deena would be happy. But she didn't even seem to care that Molly was dead. She . . . she was just interested in that man. Like we were never even her daughters to begin with."

Her voice breaks again, and she hiccups into a burbling cry.

"I . . . I missed Molly."

She bites her lips together, and they are two bright, bruised petals when she releases them.

"So, I was just going to take Lucy for myself. A new sister. We would take the money I'd saved and we'd go away. Disappear. I was taking the bags out to the car when that man came. He saw me. So, I had to hurt him. And then you came. I tried to think what I could do. I thought if I shot both the man and you and then made Deena drink all her Ambien mixed in her tea, then maybe it would look like suicide. Like she had shot both of you and then killed herself. I even wrote a note on her computer. Put her name on it. Everything. That's what I was going to do. But then . . . that woman shot me."

"Yes," I say. "Mothers can be like that. Protective."

"Not my mother," she says.

"Do you mean Deena?"

She shakes her head and looks toward the door where Mandy had just exited.

"Did your father hurt you?" I ask. "Did you tell your mother about it?"
She shakes her head.

"I don't . . . I don't know," she says. She closes her eyes tight in frustration. "I don't *think* so. But I was so little. I remember being in the house with them. I remember my big brother, Tam. I loved Tam. I remember him always being with me. Always watching over me. But then he went to school. And then I . . . Everything got so messy. I still don't . . . Everything is like being lost in the woods. I don't know what is dreams and what is memories. I can't figure it out."

"You will," I say. "In time. It will take time. But you have people who love you. People who will want to help you."

She shakes her head. I get up and AJ opens the door for me, and I take a deep breath when I get into the hall. A few FBI agents in black jackets mill around anonymously, here to finish unraveling the tapestry that Deena and Jessica have spent the last ten years weaving.

They break apart as Mandy pushes through them, coming toward me.

"Mandy," I say, stopping her. She smiles at me, hands me a coffee.

"Y'all done already?"

"I think so," I say. "I think she's told me all she needed to say."

"Mandy, do you know the story of the Witch of Quartz Creek?"

"Sure," she says.

"Can you tell it to me?"

"Here?"

"If you don't mind."

"Well, there was a woman," she says. "A woman who was beautiful but poor. She had two beautiful daughters who were her pride and joy. She loved them above everything else and so, when the hardest winter of a hundred years came, and her daughters were like to die of hunger, she took them up the mountain to where a witch lived. The witch had an apple orchard that no snow could touch, and the woman knew that if her daughters lived with the witch, they would never starve. She gave her daughters to the witch on that day. The witch agreed to feed them dainties and clothe them in finery and raise them like princesses. She took the girls into her house.

"But the woman was powerful sad about it. She loved her daughters, like I said. Loved them more than the world. She cried and cried at the witch's doorstep. And the witch told her that she would curse the daughters if the woman did not leave. The woman said she would leave. The witch gave her a sack of apples, apples that would never rot but would stay fresh until eaten. And the woman ate all of the apples and, after every one, she planted the seeds.

"That's why there's so many apple trees in Quartz Creek. And it's why none of them produce apples. Not a single one. They never have. Because they were planted in grief, bathed in a mother's tears. Stories say that when the woman's daughters return to her, the apples will finally grow."

I find myself smiling at her.

"Mandy, do you know why there are so many versions of this story?"

She shrugs and takes a sip of her coffee and then says, "Gosh, you know, I think it's like anything else. It changes in the telling. And that story's been told over and over. You know, my sister didn't know Rapunzel was named after the greens her mama stole when she was pregnant?"

"Was she?" I ask.

Mandy laughs and then nods back toward the room where her daughter lies. Damaged but alive and found at last.

"I'd better get back," she says.

"We've got a social worker on the way," AJ tells me when she's gone. "I think they're going to have their hands full with Jessica."

"I think you're right," I say. "Where's Deena?"

"She's in custody."

"What's going to happen to her?"

"Her family sent an attorney up from Savannah. Sounds like they haven't forsaken her after all. Deena hasn't said a word since the woman got here. She's pushing for an insanity plea, probably end up in a private psychiatric place down in Georgia."

"Probably," I agree.

I sigh and lean back against the cold hospital wall, press my fingertips to my face, rub my eyes. Sometimes, it's the calm that comes after the storm that's the hardest. When there's nobody left to fight, nothing left to find, no one left to save.

All that's left is you and your thoughts, your memories, as your mind starts shifting everything around, finding new contexts for old hurts.

"I'm going back to the cabin," I say when I see Shiloh approaching, carrying a pile of my things.

"Okay," he says. "See you later?

I nod.

"You ready?" Shiloh asks.

"Yeah," I say. "Time to go."

I let her lead me out of the hospital, away from the beeping and the medicine smell and the beautiful doll I finally found.

# EPILOGUE

I'M AT A GAS station in Tennessee giving Honey a nice big gulp.

"Almost done," I say, patting her rear.

My phone buzzes in my pocket.

"Can't leave you alone for five goddamn minutes," Leo says. "Heard you got into an unholy shoot-out in some hillbilly castle."

He's been off-grid for three days.

I laugh. Laughing still hurts. But I say, "You could say that."

I put the pump back in the slot. Open Honey's door. Get back behind the wheel with a wince.

"You okay?" he asks.

"Yeah."

"You find out what you need to find out?" he asks.

"Yeah. I think I did."

I look in the rearview at the woodblock print of the crows flying up from the field. This is what I finally accepted when Max tried to pay me for my work on the case and I told him to keep his money, take the internship offer, and become the artist he is meant to be. I would have to leave my watch in hock for another week. At least.

Max had given me a strong hug and, in it, I had felt some change in him. His story had not ended happily. But, also, it had not ended at all. Merely changed direction.

When I left Quartz Creek, they were preparing for Molly's funeral. Molly would be buried next to her mother. As far as I knew, Shiloh and AJ and the Jacobs family and Tam Hoyle would all be in attendance. But I'd been to enough funerals in my life. It was past time for me to leave town.

On my way out, I'd visited Mandy, and she told me that she had moved her boys out of the Hoyle property and into a little house in town. One Bob and Rebecca had helped her find. She had taken her sock drawer money and hired two attorneys. One to file her divorce and one to figure out Jessica's defense.

I paid one last visit to Shiloh's bakery, bought two loaves of pumpkin bread and a box of cinnamon rolls to take on the road with me. She hugged me. Told me to keep in touch. I said I would, and meant it.

I spent one last night with AJ. He brought me the kind of greasy, cheese-covered, deep-fried Mexican food you can only find in the South. I kissed him. Made love to him. No one jokingly offered to marry the other. The time for that was over.

I took one last walk to Susan McKinney's cabin.

"I'm sorry I thought it was you," I said.

"I'm sorrier that I didn't see what was going on," she said. "I should have seen it. She was eaten up with grief."

"We all have a blind spot," I told her. She offered to read my cards one more time and I accepted.

"There will always be another battle," she said. "Another journey."

"I know," I said.

She handed me a jug of elderberry wine and kissed both of my cheeks, hard, like she was pressing magic into my skin.

"Take care of yourself," she said.

I said okay.

Now, I turn the key. I start up Honey and she rumbles to life. I strap in and pull away from the gas station and farther into the mountains.

"I'm back stateside now," Leo says. His voice wraps around me, unfurls a secret warmth inside me. It is constant, endless. Leo has always been the one, from the time he sat down across from me and asked me to join him. Since that day, Leo meant *home.* However far apart we were, whatever else we did, whoever else we were with, it was and always would be us.

"I'm glad you're back," I say.

"You still up for that drink?" he asks. "I can come to you."

"Let's make it dinner," I say. "I'll meet you at Roxanne's."

# ACKNOWLEDGMENTS

First and foremost, thank you to Scott. In addition to all the encouraging and loving and supporting that comes with husbanding, I have never met someone with a more brilliant mind for stories or a more generous spirit when it comes to discussing them. No one has helped me become the writer I am more than him.

Thank you to Kristin, who has read greater than one million (I counted) of my words over these many years. I am immeasurably grateful for her patience, humor, and intelligence, but, most of all, her friendship.

I owe special thanks to Rachel, my first reader, trusted friend, and the recipient of many, many eleventh-hour realizations and brainstorming sessions. I'm so glad we both took that class.

Thanks also to Andrew, who generously stepped in last minute and gave me both a break and some much-needed feedback. And thanks to Shawn, who taught me to throw a punch, take a kick, and the value of a good elbow.

The Naslund-Mann Graduate School of Writing at Spalding University was invaluable to me as a young writer, and the mentors, workshop leaders, and fellow writers I met there provided me with an outstanding education and set me on the right path. Similarly, I cannot imagine where I would be without the mentorship of Steve Cleberg and Sherry Crabtree, who changed the course of my life.

I am exceedingly grateful to my agent, Alice Spielburg, who has taken it upon herself to shepherd this socially awkward, introverted, anxious writer through the highs and lows of publishing. My work is how I communicate with the world and Alice is the steadfast champion of my voice.

At Minotaur, I owe a debt of gratitude to Madeline Houpt, not only for believing in this book but also for her kind and thoughtful suggestions in improving it. Thanks also to my copy editor, Thomas Cherwin, for his many saves and for teaching me the difference between blond/blonde and proofreaders Ken Diamond and Erin Barker. Likewise, I am exceedingly appreciative of Hector DeJean, Stephen Erickson, Ally Demeter, Maria Snelling, Drew Kilman, David Baldeosingh Rotstein, Lena Shekhter, Gabriel Guma, Alisa Trager, and Kiffin Steurer from the Minotaur team.

Thank you to my mother, Cynthia Rand, for filling my life with words, for never limiting my access to them, for always encouraging my habit for them. From Little Bear to Lear, her voice is the echo in my mind, late at night, that says, "Just one more page. One more page."

I could never have written this book—or any other—without the lessons in resilience, faith, and determination I learned at the knee of the many women who populated my youth. Strong, smart, and stubborn, every one; mountain women don't quit.

Lastly, thanks to Bunny, who has been there since the beginning.

# ABOUT THE AUTHOR

Matt Kallish

**Archer Sullivan** is a ninth-generation Appalachian. She's moved thirty-seven times and has lived everywhere from Monticello, Kentucky, to Manhattan, New York, and from Black Mountain, North Carolina, to Beverly Hills, California. Her work has appeared in *Ellery Queen Mystery Magazine, Tough, Shotgun Honey, Reckon Review, Rock and a Hard Place* magazine, and *The Best Mystery Stories of the Year 2024.*